T0064227

GHOSTMEN:
the Journey of Your Dreams!

GHOSTMEN:
the Journey of Your Dreams!

Dr P. C. Sharma

PARTRIDGE

To order additional copies of this book, contact
Partridge India
000 800 10062 62
orders.india@partridgepublishing.com

www.partridgepublishing.com/india

DISCLAIMER

This book is completely a work of fiction. However, actual names of certain places and geographical features have been used for the purpose of ease of relating to the settings for the reader. Besides the names of places, any resemblances to a person or real events will merely be a coincidence. Likewise, social or religious customs and performances described in the book may also not be taken as actualities. There is no criticism or satire on any place, person, religion, region, or society. The author respects all religions and social groups and their traditions. Readers are requested to savour the story as a work of literature meant for light and leisurely reading and not to search for all these things in ground realities as existing today.

———❖———

To dear Nitin, my youngest son who made it all possible, and the grandchildren, who kept me agile and working fit by their cuteness and naughty actions.

Children—the *hope*.

PREFACE

Childhood and young student life, by far, are the most loved and cherished periods of one's life—which are perhaps the most missed and remembered later in life during struggles or leisure times, like that of the retired people. This fiction work, *Ghostmen*, is the fulfilment of that very urge as a tribute to that very past, student life of college and university days. The author wrote this novel with that very mindset, of college life around the catchment area surrounding his Balrampur College and Gorakhpur University, where he had lived for five years and had been on several outings in the jungles. Reminiscing with all those friends from the days of yore (though not naming some) with fondness and tremendous regard—all the teachers and staff, as well as everyone else who had breathed the same air, felt the warmth of the area where he had passed through many unforgettable events and incidents that have come to be lifelong memories, which were further enriched by subsequent life experiences and maturity. It is my cherished dream that the old-timers, in their good health and happiness, with the same freshness and energy, enjoy this dramatised memoir with their children and grandchildren and can still feel that connection with the old times and, of course, with me.

This is the story of a perennial stream. The water (students) keeps on flowing forward, but the stream—the institutional life—remains the same. Thus, this is the story of every student, of every youth aspiring for high goals in life. Most of the events are from my own life and those of my erstwhile class fellows, albeit attributed in the story to its characters.

The story is based on social supernatural beliefs, practices, myths, and sayings, without naming any particular social group. Some may doubt the very existence of supernatural things like ghostmen and the role they play. I would like to invite the attention of all such people to the fact that even in this twenty-first century, these beliefs are prevalent as legends among the local folk and find acceptance even in the most advanced places, like the capital city, Delhi, and Noida or Greater Noida. Those interested to explore the depth to which these extend may hire a taxi for traveling from Noida to Greater Noida late in the night on the expressway and hear a common tale of a ghost figure, a pony, from the driver. Years ago, I heard a story from IT and software professionals serving in South Delhi of a procession of ghostmen close to Sarita Vihar on the *mazar* of the Peer, on the median of the Delhi-Mathura road. They even said that they had savoured some delicious sweets therein. And those who took the sweets but did not consume them right away found these turned into earthen pieces the next morning.

If such things are still being discussed and believed even in the modern societies of scientists with reverence, the description of tribal folk culture and people living pastoral life, without such lore, would be incomplete. However, without going into discussion about the existence of a paranormal world, the story may be enjoyed as a means of getting closer to a way of life. Moreover, it is a work of fiction, having no limit to mind and imagination, a travail into the land of fantasies.

Life is a composite of complex things. It cannot be predicted by set norms or formulae, like that of mathematical sciences. No psychological or medical science can provide guidelines for a trouble-free life for certain. All around us, there are numerous instances of people getting unexpected and disproportionate results for their efforts. Miracles do happen—maybe—for those who believe in them. Reasons for and against may be given up to any extent, but the fact remains that every living being, being an element of nature, is controlled by all universal forces or elements—visible and invisible, natural and supernatural. We always remain surrounded by these powers, not knowing what may be in store the next moment. In facing new challenging situations, we get scared and apprehensive, fearing every moment the unknown and the unexpected.

In a similar situation was Agastya when, in the spirit of doing something unique to prove himself to his favourite professor, he took up a mandatory project for his master's course in the dense Tarai jungles. Scared, and more so after the advice of the forest officers, he ventured into the jungle. What unknown from the green canopy of dense forests unfurls for him? Join and travel to the fantasy land of surprises with him and experience for yourself as you flip through the pages ahead. Wish you journey of joys.

Dr P. C. Sharma

ACKNOWLEDGEMENT

Gratefully I convey my sincere thanks to all those, known and unknown to me, who in their own ways have helped me bring out this book. The first known one is my wife, who kept a congenial working atmosphere in the house and, without being much demanding on my time, had been helping me carry out my work. The other one who desired me to write something like this book is my youngest son, Nitin Atreya. After I scripted it, he, his friend Shikha, who has now become his soul mate, and their friends joined together to give it the shape of this book and brought out a single beautiful copy of it. I sincerely appreciate the efforts of all of them, especially that of Shikha, who would come over a long distance, discuss, and take away the text for typing. Their friend, who keyed it in, was a big encouragement to me because she showed keen interest in the story and was constantly asking for more and more matter. Other people who deserve credit are those who designed the cover page, interior, look, etc., and gave me a pleasant surprise and the honour of releasing it during the marriage of Nitin and Shikha. My God, what a wonderful surprise it was! I thank and bless them all from the core of my heart. Technically, thereafter, it became so convenient for me. I made all my observations and corrections on that book, only preserving it with me as my life's most precious treasure, the mother of this issue. Later, Shikha and Nitin discussed and edited it several times.

My sincere good wishes also flow out to my son Gaurav, who despite being a very busy senior government officer spared the time to edit it and encouraged me with his opinions and suggestions about it. His wife, Ruchi, also provided him all the moral support in the process, as did his children, Agastya and Gauri. My other sons Amit and Gagan, their wives Ritu and Kalapna, and granddaughters Aadya and Anika helped me in day-to-day computing work, while the youngest one, Asmi, helped me in carrying out my work cheerfully and lightheartedly. May God bless them all!

I also wish to thank M/S Partridge Publishing and their whole team who made this book see the dawn of the day and have undertaken its marketing.

Last but not the least, my gratitude is for you, my dear readers, whose interest and likings have been my guiding light at all times while I wrote this story. In a way, you had been helping me in my work, and you are the real judge of my efforts. Trust you will find it interesting and useful. If there is anything not up to your liking, it is for limitations on my part and my incapability! I do hope that with your broadmindedness you will excuse me.

Rest is all up to him, the Almighty, and his creations, of which I'm but a tiny part!

Dr P. C. Sharma.

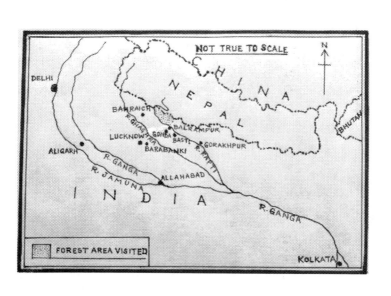

AT THE COLLEGE

Circa 1960: Balrampur (UP)

PG College, Department of Sociology

At the end of the lecture, Professor Soram asked his students, 'Well, students, how many of you've started working on your project?' No response. 'You know, this project is a prerequisite, mandatory requirement for the completion of this master's degree programme, and this is the high time. You should finish comprehensively at least fieldwork during the ensuing Dushahra and autumn break. You won't have time after the break. Then you would be under tremendous pressure of preparing for the theory papers. Why're you not planning according to this timeline?' He took a long, measured look at the students and continued, 'What's preventing you from starting work on the project? Look, it's the only time you have. Always take the pressure head on so that you have enough time for exigencies. There is so much to do and so little a time. Hurry up now, decide upon an area of study, and submit your synopsis.'

After all these instructions, the professor looked at the class for their reactions. There was absolute silence in the class, not even a whisper. Just as the professor was about to leave the class, a hand hesitatingly rose up.

'Yes, Agastya! What's it for you to say?'

'Sir, would you mind suggesting some project titles?'

Agastya had a question. He was amongst the most earnest and upbeat students in the class. He wanted to know if Professor Soram would suggest some project titles. He wasn't looking for an easy job or a shortcut but just some direction.

A teacher knows his students very well, and so did Professor Soram. So he said, 'It won't be fair on my part to suggest any such thing. Your thorough study of the subject will give you an insight into innumerable such topics. However, in larger interest of you all, I will suggest that you take up a need-based topic of your choice which could also serve as the basis for your higher studies. Analytical findings and the outcome of your project must meet some necessity and must satisfy curiosity of your minds. Such findings must present a viable solution to some problems. You must keep in mind that it's useful and interesting enough to attract and inspire others as well. For coming several years, students would keep on referring to your work. A good work would also give you confidence and advantage in your personal interview and viva for your final percentage and grading. Hope this satisfies you.' Throwing the matter open to the class, he added, 'Any more doubts?' Professor stood quietly, looking at the class, waiting for some time, and sensing nothing coming up, left the class.

Agastya was in deep thought. Professor Soram was his favourite, a friend, philosopher, and guide in the true sense and, above all, a great human being. This was probably the last time they were pulled up by the professor, who was known for his sincerity and penchant for perfection. Agastya was sincerely keen on maintaining his image high in his idol's eyes, so he made up his mind to do something unique and appreciable, and that too within the specific time frame.

As soon as the professor left, Agastya also left for his favourite place on the college campus. He took a cup of tea from the canteen on his way to the Maharajah Dig Vijay Singh's Statue Hall stairs. Reaching there, he sat down on the front stairs of the hall with a serious face, sipping tea and gazing upon the distant dark-green sheet of thick Tarai forest and sharply rising Himalayas in front. He was having absolutely no clue on how to proceed further. All that he knew was that he had to be quick now on his project. In the meantime, his class fellows Balendu, Nidhi, and Bali also reached there to join him.

'Oh god, why am I so confused? Nothing seems to be working out,' he mumbled to himself. Seeing him, they also started staring towards the woods as though the woods had some answer to their disposition. He exclaimed, 'Nature! Nature, including man, is ultimate in creation. It has its own guiding principles, man may find solutions to his all problems in nature.'

3

'What man? Any luck so far? You've been looking into the woods for quite some time. Is that what you want to study?' asked Bali.

Agastya looked at Bali and his two other friends, gave a blank gaze straight into their eyes, and then giving a look towards the northern forests, got up and said, 'See you tomorrow, friends. Going home now.' He then left the place.

Balendu and Nidhi felt a little awkward at his sudden leaving but thought maybe it was best not to disturb him at this point in time. Next day, Agastya walked in confidently in the class; he seemed to have decided on his work.

'Looks like you got the idea of what you would be doing in field study,' remarked Balendu.

'Yeah, I want to study the jungles.'

'Jungles, what about the jungles? Dear, you seemed to be obsessed with the woods since yesterday.'

'I don't know for sure, but I have always been amazed by what lies inside the jungle. It is so dense, it's like a puzzle. We know that people live in the interiors of the Tarai region. But we don't know how do they live. What do they do? What is their livelihood? How do they think? It's not merely a green coverage but has been having a whole different life therein. I'm planning to knock on the threshold of the Tarai jungles, to study the life of Tarai tribal people, Tharu tribe.' And the more he thought about it and discussed with his friends, the more convinced he was to take up this subject.

'Wow, you made it sound pretty romantic!' remarked Nidhi.

'You may say so, romantic! But it would be a difficult and challenging study and may be interesting too. I'm yet to figure out the details, but pretty sure, I would study the Tarai jungles. Very soon I would be collecting required details and submit my synopsis.'

Agastya wasn't sure if his plan would be okayed, but he was fascinated by the thick jungles of the foot region of the Himalayas. Agastya had to start work on the idea soon. In the next few days he gathered relevant information about the Tarai region and prepared a synopsis of the project under the title 'Impact of Modernisation on the Life of Tribal People—A Case Study of Tharu Tribe of the Tarai Region of District Gonda (UP)'.*

'Discuss the title again,' directed the professor. Agastya again discussed the synopsis with his favourite teacher and then submitted it for approval in the department. A few days later, Agastya was called by the HOD for a personal interview and discussion on the project. After some modifications and suggestions, the synopsis was approved. 'Make sure you don't get lost there, and also don't lose track of the work in the jungle. The jungles are quite overwhelming, but difficult and challenging too. Would be needing lot of information and preparations in advance before entering in the area. I'm glad you took up this study. I

---

* Balrampur, now a distrct was a Tahsil of district Gonda then.

can only wish you good luck. All the best,' advised Professor Soram.

Agastya wasn't sure if this was just a good wish or there was some underlying meaning to it. More often than not, experience is the best teacher. This time Agastya would experience what his teacher meant.

In the next days he gathered necessary information and data about the area and made necessary preparations, including obtaining reservations and permission passes from the Forest Department and police, because being adjacent to the international boundary with Nepal, that was a sensitive and restricted area. He contacted forest officers for their advice for going and staying in the forest area. They suggested for him to contact Mr Ram Nayak Mishra in the Northern Forest Range office. He had served in the area. But for the last two days he hadn't been seen there. This day, as he walked out of the office with the permission papers, he bumped into an officer, felt sorry, and with due respect asked him, 'Sir, where can I find Ram Nanak Mishra, sir?'

'What business you have with him?'

'Something really important, sir. Can you please guide me to him? I wanted to meet him for quite some time. I am told that he is the only one who can help me in my research work, as he is well aware with area allotted to me.'

'Well, I'm Ram Nayak Mishra, and I will be glad to help you in your work.' He led Agastya into his room and, occupying a chair, said, 'The forest is a calm, quiet, yet dangerous place to be in. It appears as if there is a divine design there, yet danger could knock you from anywhere. I would suggest that for the first couple of days you should keep yourself confined to your accommodation and not move out much. It would help you get comfortable and familiar with the area. And as you watch the life from your guest house, you will get some idea of the locality, life of the people, their movement and daily routine. The birds and animals in the forest also have a very peculiar language. If you want to stay there, it is as important to study the totality of nature—wildlife and people alike—as your project study. But never try to disturb the natural movement of wildlife. Also never try to get in the way of people before you know them well. Just listen to them and obey, especially if you want to take their snaps or visit religious places. A slight displeasure of theirs may be a risk to your life. And mind it, in that case no one will be able to help you. The tribal people are submissive, very respectful, and decent but can be really dangerous if offended in the name of their rituals and customs. In that case, they don't spare anyone. Any rule is meaningless. It would be better if you engage a local person with you so long as you are there. Else I don't see that you will be able to do your work. Don't hold negative thought, start with a positive thoughts.' After advising him, Mishra sent for Bahadur, who was from that area, telling him to go with Agastya to guide him further and give him some more information about the area as desired by him.

Phew! Was he trying to scare me? Maybe not, he is just trying to be nice and telling me all that I need to know before I get to the work. But it is scary, whatever said and done. I don't understand this kind of life—one doesn't have any freedom, you can't do anything by your own choice. The wildlife restricts our movement majorly. Agastya was pretty dazzled by all the information Mishra gave him. Thanking Mishra and taking Bahadur along with him, he reached to a shady area in front of the tea stall. Agastya had a long chat with Bahadur to know details of the area. Bahadur shared that village life was pretty simple yet hectic. People depended on cattle heads, fields, and forests for their livelihood. These were part of their life-supporting economy. They grew food grains, pulses, and vegetables in their fields. And collected various things, like *rudraksha*, herbs, and honey from forests, prepared *kattha* (catechu), and also went for fishing. And some people worked for the contractors who collect building materials like stone pebbles and sand, which were further used for construction in plains. Mostly people lived in mud and thatched houses in the village. Agastya was quite amazed at this view of life; he had always read/heard that people lived like this but had never seen it himself. This would be the first time he would actually be in such a habitat.

Gathering all this information, Agastya started making all possible preliminary preparations for the field survey of the northern part of Gonda District touching the international boundary with Nepal. He thought autumn break would be just fine to go there in the forthcoming Durga Puja and Dushahra holidays starting 6 October for ten days, as the rains would have rejuvenated the whole forest area as though natural beauty had just taken a shower, and there would be greenery all around. At the same time, the rains would be over, and the pleasing cold of early October would have set in by then. That would be the most suitable time for fieldwork.

After gathering all the necessary information and study material, Agastya met his friends. Once he explained the project and working plan, Balendu expressed his inability to accompany him during the Dushahra break due to his father's illness. But Nidhi said that she would discuss with her parents and told him not to consider her as his responsibility. She wanted to join Agastya and work on the research. But Agastya didn't want anyone to join him in this preliminary trip, especially a girl. He wasn't sure what he might get there. If Nidhi joined him, he would have that extra responsibility, which he didn't want at this stage. Agastya convinced her not to come along with him to an unknown area and risk the uncertainties of the jungle. He thought it would be better to face the risks and dangers of the dense wildlife-infested forests, antisocial elements, local tribal taboos, and conservative practices. Nidhi had no option but to stay back there, convinced with Agastya's plan to join him in the next trip.

———————•◦•———————

JOURNEY TO FANTASY LAND OF THARUS

Having convinced his friends, Agastya went back to his place and started preparing for his trip. He spent the night tossing and turning in bed, thinking about the exciting adventure that was before him. He felt scared, apprehensive, and overwhelmed of how he would handle the project in hand. When he got up the next morning, he felt charged and excited but not sure if he had really slept the night. He quickly picked up his stuff and left for the bus stop to board the first bus to Bahraich at about 4.00 a.m. Curious to see the land of his dreams, he reached the bus stand, boarded the bus already set to move. In another few minutes, it started moving out of the stand, and after coming out of the city on the clear main road in the dark, it reached its scary high speed. Only the driver could see the road ahead. Agastya had hardly settled down in the bus that the conductor called the passengers of the fifteenth milestone going to Kishanpur to come to the front door to get down. Agastya exclaimed, 'So soon?'

'Liking the bus so much. If you don't want to get down, get a ticket for Bahraich and come with us for a long journey. This is not a bullock cart, this is a bus, saab. Fifteenth mile point has come.' The conductor blew his whistle and the bus halted. Agastya and some fellow passengers got down. As he got down, he found himself in the first so-called jungle situation; he was all alone on a cold October morning, and it was still very dark.

Before he could realise his situation, his fellow passengers were fast moving away. He rushed towards one of them and asked for advice as to how to go to Kishanpur Rapti Ghat and further to Dera Chowk. The man directed Agastya to follow the mud road and suggested, 'You have to travel a long distance. It would be better if you wait here for some time and hire a mule from this side village after the day breaks. Early morning you will find some people with mules here.' And before Agastya could expect anything more, the man had moved on. A minute's company in the middle of the jungle was a big relief for him, but he was all alone now. He was finding it difficult to even stand there alone amidst the dark and fear of the unknown. He was scared some animal might pounce on him anytime from any side. Animals are always very close to the village in such regions and always smell for poultry, kitchens, and cattle heads, etc. But the only choice Agastya had was to just face it straight in the eye and deal with it. Every passing vehicle was a respite as it reminded him of life around, yet the silence after the vehicles moved past him was almost killing him. He set his eyes keenly on the eastern sky, hoping for the sun to emerge sooner than other days.

As the first sign of daylight emerged, he realised what it meant to witness light after a stretch of darkness. With the high-pitched crowing of the cock, he could hear the movement of villagers moving from one place to another, beginning their daily chores. He walked closer to the village side and asked a man coming from the village on his way to the jungle with water bottle in hand, 'Where to hire a pony to reach the other side of the river?'

'Saab, you wait here. On my coming back soon, I will send someone with the pony.'

'Thank you, how much will he charge?'

'That you have to ask him. I will send him.'

So far the journey was full of new experiences. Challenging, but things were working out for him one by one. Though he didn't know what the next step would be. The man with the pony came soon. It was calm and quiet, a cool autumn morning of a peaceful rural area. There was something so lively yet peaceful. So far Agastya's mind was preoccupied with the loneliness and fear of uncertainties ahead. But now it was daytime at least he had the company of the pony man, and his luggage was on the back of a pony. He was now free to see and appreciate the nostalgic arrival of the day. The sweet chill of the cool breeze, the changing colour of the sky, the wet dew on the grass, chirping birds— all these were unfolding nature's bounty in front of Agastya. He was talking and responding to the pony man while enjoying the natural surroundings. Though he didn't come from a big metro himself, but still, being in such wilderness was turning out to be a completely different experience altogether. He followed the advice of the pony man to ride the pony so that they could reach their destination faster. The pony man was actively making different sounds to make the pony move faster. They kept chatting about different topics and didn't realise when the sun had gone so high and it was getting hot. The pony man put a small cloth sheet on his head while Agastya put on a jungle cap. By 9, 9.30 they reached the ferry point at the bank of River Rapti. Agastya paid the pony man and thanked him for the service. He saw the boat coming from the other side. As soon as it reached the bank, the passengers got down. Agastya got on to get a seat and enjoyed the river's flow and the view. The pony man got on to return with other customers. In a few minutes all got down and were dispersed; only some people on the boat were sitting with covered heads, and a boat man was standing on high, looking in possible directions people may come from for a boat. They waited for about another half an hour. Here they didn't count time in minutes and seconds but in slots of hours. They didn't go by watches but by their instinct and needs. It took them about an hour to cross a broad 200-foot river. As he got down on the other bank, he felt like having a cup of tea and walked to the nearby tea stall. He settled down, had his packed lunch, and placed the order. As he sipped his tea, the charm and calmness of the area started settling within him. He felt as if the anxiety and apprehension of the day's travel and what lay ahead of him was not bothering him anymore. The greenery around, the simplicity of the rustic life, the gushing sound of the river flowing by his side were gradually growing on him. Agastya asked the tea stall owner for his onward journey towards Dera Chowk. The owner advised Agastya to wait there for some time, which is when some more people would be going that side with their ponies. 'Ponies went in early hours, say, by 8.00 a.m., so that they may come back in time. Surely some people will go, you may go with them.' In another round of the boat came a group of four, five people with some ration items and other goods. They hired two ponies for Kalyan-Bhai contractor's base place. The tea stall owner talked to them and asked Agastya to join them. He also introduced Agastya and asked them to take care of him. This was their everyday business. Passing through thick jungle stretches, walking on jungle trails, going through dry riverbeds, and crossing small water flows and going through open spaces and fields. They reached the destination base by 4.00 p.m. There were three big mud rooms with a wide, big thatched shade in front. On one side in a covered veranda was a big hearth made of mud and stones, fired and fuelled with thick tree wood for twenty-four hours. At mealtimes, one pushed the wood in to activate the fire to prepare tea or meals. For the rest of the time, the fire was kept at low for them to activate the hearth as and when required. As soon as they reached there, the people welcomed them, asked about things outside in the plains. And they were served hot tea with some sweet and salty snacks. After tea and some rest, Agastya felt active and fresh, and thanking them, he asked for his onward journey to Dera.

The owner told him that it was late to start the journey for Dera Chowk so advised him to rest there for the night and then start the journey next morning. He slept well and was woken up by the chores people were trying to finish in the morning. As he moved out he saw a thick piece of wood being burnt in the big clay oven as breakfast was being prepared. Agastya had a longish chat with the contractor. He collected all the relevant information and decided to move on. 'Thank you for the help and information that you gave me. It's of great help.'

'Oh no! This is nothing. This is our life. Did you take your breakfast?' Looking for one of his workers, he called, 'Oh, Surajwa, bring a glass of tea and some parathas.' Suraj served Agastya breakfast and the contractor further continued, 'You carry on, but I must move on. I have to go to the site. After you finish your breakfast, get ready to move with your luggage. But wait here only till you find someone going upward. Suraj will guide you on that. Actually the forest is a wonderful place to be in, but then you got to be careful, aware of its nature and patterns. The forest is infested with wildlife and sometimes also serves as an abode for antisocial elements. You will always be their best target—an outsider who looks educated, they will see you as a threat. I'm not trying to scare you, just got to be careful. You need to travel about six miles further for the guest house at Dera Chowk Village. There the caretaker would help cook and do all the stuff to make your daily life comfortable. He will also guide you how to traverse through the jungles, what precautions to take, and so on. While you are there, you must engage in someone who knows the place well and can work as your security man.'

It seemed the list of instructions would never come to an end. Everyone he had met so far, their notions about the forest were actually making Agastya more and more curious about the place—and somewhat scared too.

The contractor left riding a horse and instructed his men to take care of Agastya. Agastya asked Suraj to keep an eye out if someone passed by going up to Dera Chowk, and relaxed under a tree on a hand-woven cot. Life was some kind of a romance for him right now—something exciting, scary, and unknown. He was treading a path with an objective; something in his heart told him it would probably be the best trip taken by him so far. But he was scared also, scared of the unknown. There was a shine in his eyes; some say that the eyes speak out all we have in our mind and body. About an hour later or so, Agastya heard someone calling him from a distance. He saw Suraj running towards him. 'Saab-ji, come, I will take you to a nearby sand-lifting base of another contractor. Two folks from there are going to Dera. I have told them to wait till we reach there. It's about half a mile from here. We will have to be fast though. I have told them to wait for us, but still.'

Agastya got up hurriedly and started following Suraj. Reaching there, Suraj told them, 'Here's our saab from the city, going to Dera, guide and help him on the way.' On the way the two fellows had been helping Agastya carry his haversack. Walking through a narrow footpath through dense forests, heart-throbbing calmness, and beautiful landscape for about two hours, they reached Dera. It was an exciting journey for Agastya.

AT DERA CHOWK

Seeing some people arrive near the guest house, the caretaker went there and asked them as to who they were. Agastya came forward and told him, 'I'm Agastya, from Balrampur, have come here with due permission to stay for about ten days for a study project work.'

Hearing this, the caretaker exclaimed, 'Balrampur!' and got thoughtful. Soon coming to normalcy, he introduced himself. 'I'm Kālu Ram Joshi, caretaker here. Come, please come. I'm happy.' And he picked up the load of Agastya to take in.

'But why you got serious on my coming?' Agastya expressed his doubt to Joshi.

'Nothing, saab-ji, just like that. Who comes here? You would have nice time here. And me a good company.' Going in, he asked Agastya to follow. Agastya turned to the fellows, thanked them, and asked them to come and have some water and rest. They both could take water outside only and, expressing their pleasure, moved on for their destination. And Joshi helped Agastya settle into the guest house. Soon with a cup of tea, he came to the door and saw a small village in front. It was Dera Chowk, a small village settlement amidst agricultural fields in a closed clearing of land, having green walls of forest all around. In the forest on the eastern edge of these fields was the guest house, about 200 yards away from the cluster of houses. Agastya could see that the guest house was on a slightly higher land, having forest on three sides and facing the open clearing in front. Agastya walked into the guest house; the glazed veranda led him into the common room. He saw the bathroom and found there was no light and water. The bathroom had a semi-dry flush system. He walked out a little amazed, wondering how he would be going to manage; these were basic things, and he had never done without them. He felt quite flustered in the absence of these basic amenities. He came into the living room, asking for some water. He wasn't sure what was going on in his mind—scared to be in such a place, or was he worried about the work? Would he be able to complete the work? Would he encounter any danger? So many thoughts were running through his mind. His feelings were divided. Something within him was telling him to just go back and take up another project, but still something stronger prompted him to stay and carry on. It wasn't that he would be ashamed if he returned; it wasn't that he would be called a coward if he returned. But something else, some voice inside him or maybe around him, was coaxing him to stay. His thought process was interrupted by someone calling him from outside.

Kālu Joshi had returned with a bucket full of water and offered some to Agastya. 'This well is all-seasons well. In fact, in the monsoons the water reaches up to the brim.' Joshi also arranged for water in the bathroom and then asked for some money to go buy kerosene and ration items. Kerosene would serve for lighting lamps as well as for the stove. 'On my way, I will ask someone to get some wood here. You may pay that person directly.' Joshi dusted the rooms and set the bed and study table for Agastya and left for the village. Just as he was beginning to settle in, he remembered Mishra's advice to check for any unwanted things, like snakes, scorpions, rats, spiders, or any other dangerous things. Danger doesn't come knocking at one's door; it always comes unnoticed from the direction not thought of. Agastya was carefully following everything that was being told to him about life in the forest. But now he was there, and there was time for him to start feeling comfortable. He bolted all doors, windows, the veranda grills for safety against any intruder—men or wild animals. He took a deep sigh of relief that there was nothing unwanted. Just a set of documents someone might have forgotten. Feeling safe, he rested in the rocking chair in the veranda overlooking the jungle, stretched his legs on the table in front, and let himself totally loose. He sat there thinking about the stark difference in the life here in the village with the fast and busy life of the cities. The mundane objects, like newspapers, time (the clock, maybe), news, have no value here. The only piece of technology he had seen so far was a small radio and transistor; Joshi told him that people usually used it to get weather and farming-related information and some folk or filmy songs.

'Arey, saab-ji, where are you lost?'

'Oh no, nothing much. Just relaxing.'

'Looks like you are missing your people!'

Agastya wondered if that was true. He was sure feeling at a loss with things, maybe the newness of the atmosphere or the lack of his own space. But yeah, he felt Nidhi and Balendu could have served a great purpose, though getting Nidhi to a place like this could be problematic in the first place. At the same time Agastya knew that it didn't matter, now that he was here. He should just finish up his work and do a good job at it.

In the meantime, Agastya saw some lady walking towards the guest house with a load of wood on her head. She put the load on one side of the guest house, closer to the kitchen, sat on the stairs, and said, 'Babu, I have brought very heavy load, dry wood, it is of very good quality. I will take two rupees for this.' He took out two rupees and paid her. She stood up facing him, constantly gazing at him; she extended her right arm and murmured something inaudible.

In the meantime, Joshi arrived with some purchased items. Joshi could sense something wrong, so he came running and said, 'What are you doing? Got money? Now go.' She looked at Joshi in annoyance and walked off. Joshi stood there for a moment until she was gone. Then he turned to Agastya and alerted him. 'Saab! Keep away from such ladies here! Do not give them chance to be face to face and look into your eyes. And if some happens to face you and murmur something, get away immediately or try to interrupt her or bring something, maybe a leaf, a stem of a thin plant, or even a piece of paper, in between. There are some ladies who have been in the village for a long time and have practiced the art of witchcraft. I know this lady, that's why I came running as soon as I saw her coming this way and interrupted the mantra. The mantra could have got you into a deep trouble otherwise. That's why she got annoyed with me and went away.'

What kind of a place's this? You have to be scared of people too. Agastya didn't believe all this but then was curious to know how these people thought. 'What about men?' asked Agastya.

'Men do not practice such things. They remain busy in their work and you can depend on them. Among men, there are some who treat common troubles, locally referred to as ojhas—witchcraft doctors. They mainly operate from their houses or places of worships, burial or cremation-grounds, etc. Among ladies, not all ladies practise this. But some are very tricky, young children and outsiders like you can easily fall prey to them. Even local people stay alert of them. Better you put on a red thread or a yellow cloth with *ram* written on it, or put tilak on your forehead. You could also approach an ojha to make sure you are not affected by any of these mantras.' Joshi paused for a while but then thought it would be in the best interest of Agastya to give him some more information. 'Here you will find that many ladies have pets—like goat, male sheep, rabbit, or some bird, like parrot—in their homes. Actually, these are not their pets but men or women turned into pets by their magic. So keep yourself careful and safe,' advised Joshi.

'Oh no, you believe in all such things in this age too. I don't! How do you keep yourself safe from these people?'

'You are always safe with working-class people. Some local people practise such things in all areas. But however educated a person may be, if in trouble—maybe of physical, family, monetary, courts, or of any other type—approaches these people. It's more here, but even outside, beyond Rapti, in plains, people believe in these things. I can tell about a renowned university professor from Banaras who, on disappearing of his grandson, instead of approaching police, approached ojhas. About police he felt that that would be more problematic than problem-solving. News all around. People will start flooding in. Bringing no solution but to oblige us, saying, "See as soon as we came to know, we rushed to enquire well-being." Keeping aside our problem, we will be managing them.

'Over and above this, he preferred ojhas for finding out answers to doubts such as, is the boy aged about fifteen alive? Which place has he gone to? By when would he arrive home? And by doings what all could his coming home be fast and sure? Ojhas gave several answers with multiple possibilities. And also suggested several religious and witchcraft performances. After some time, the boy reached home himself.' After a pause, he continued in a low voice, 'Well, it was my responsibility, duty to guide you through all these things. Now it's up to you to follow it or not. I obviously can't force you. But I want you safe, at least for so long as you are here.'

Telling all this to Agastya, Joshi moved to the kitchen. Agastya didn't bother much; he just relaxed and started planning as to where and how to start the fieldwork. Joshi came to his room and said, 'Saab-ji, I have prepared only rice and dal, as it was getting late.'

'No problem, I'm more interested in work. Have done with my planning for the day,' said Agastya. Joshi laid a simple lunch on the centre table with a glass of water and got busy in winding up the kitchen for dinner. Joshi informed Agastya and went to the village for some time. Agastya also went to his room. He planned for his fieldwork for a while and then took a short nap. About five in the evening, he came out to the lawn in the front side. He walked in front from one end to the other for some time, observing the village to get an overall view of what all activities were going on. Cattle were coming to the village from the fields; some men and women were going to the well to fetch water. Some were coming from the forest with their catches, like fish, or small bundle of grass and wood on their head or back. He wanted to explore the rearward–forest side of the guest house, but that was infested with wild growth, and it wasn't needed also.

He then moved inside to get ready for work and started loading his bag with essential items, like writing material, proforma to collect data, questionnaire, the camera, some eatables, and accessories, like a first-aid box, soap, folding knife, file, and papers. As he packed his stuff for the next day, he felt a rush of excitement in his mind to take a round of the village; he just wanted to see the village of the deep forest: How does it look like? What were the people like? What exactly did they do? Excited but with a little hesitation, because Joshi wasn't around. He moved out with a notepad and a pen. Agastya thought that the village head would be a good place to begin with, just for acquaintance. Alone he started for the village. Reaching there, he asked for the village head; people directed him to the house of Birang Bahadur Singh. He recalled that Joshi had told him that the village head had about four acres of land and some ten cattle heads. Reaching his house with due regard, apprehensively, he told Birang Bahadur about his project; Birang Bahadur expressed happiness that a person from the city would study his village and went on to show his house. Agastya took some photographs of Birang and his family, assuring that he would send these to him from Balrampur. He thanked Birang Bahadur and, informing of his coming again, begged for his permission to leave. After leaving his place, he went around the whole village. It was a cluster of some sixty huts and mud houses. Most of the houses were mud houses roofed with tiles or weeds. Only two houses were big enough and good looking. One was that of Village Head Birang Bahadur and the other one that of the village businessman, Lala-ji. Otherwise, all houses looked alike, with low mud walls and, in structure, a big room serving as a common-room-cum-main-sitting-area. In the common room, they usually had a big cylindrical structure mainly built for storing food grains and their valuables, including valuable clothes. Doors and windows were decorated with mirrors, mirror pieces, and local decorative patterns in red and white—natural colours. After this short village visit, he felt encouraged and confident and wanted to know more, but scared as he was, thinking that in excitement he might invite some trouble, he decided to return to the guest house before the fall of darkness to keep safe.

Reaching the guest house, he asked Joshi to get milk from the village, as he was feeling like having tea. But Joshi plainly said, 'Saab-ji, can't go out to village this time. It's not safe going to village in the evening twilight and fall of darkness. It's the most favourable time for ladies to try their witchcraft and black magic on mainly outsiders."

'Okay, don't go. But do you have lemon? Let us have black lemon tea.'

'Lemon tea? I haven't tried ever. You'll have to help me prepare it.'

Agastya joined Joshi in preparing lemon tea. And both enjoyed it. In the meantime, a boy also arrived with some milk. After taking milk, Joshi told him, 'Here, there's no storing facility of milk. So supply half, half kilograms at both morning, evening times.'

---

*   This had been experienced by the author himself in real life. The help flatly refused to bring milk in the evening from the village of the area. Tired of the walking and running of the day, we two were sitting and waiting for a lift at a sand supply base close to the village and had to have black tea—tea without milk.

The boy was about to go when, enjoying the refreshing tea, Agastya asked him, 'So simple a life, you all must be saving a lot of money here.'

'Oh no, sir, we get things in exchange of things, or we borrow for some time. We have very little money. We have very little to sell for money, like this milk today and our petty seasonal labour.'

After he left, relaxing, Agastya asked Joshi, 'Which place you come from, Joshi?'

'I'm from Basti, saab-ji.'*

'How long have you been here, and how you happened to come?'

'I'm a Forest Department employee, serving here for last four years.'

'You developed liking for the place?'

---

* About the city of Basti, there was a popular humorous saying in those days by some Hindi poet (most probably by Dinkar): '"Basti" ko "basti" kahun, kako kahun "ujar"?'

First, *Basti* is a proper noun, a township. Another word *basti* means 'a settlement, inhabited place', and *ujar/ujad* means 'a deserted place'. Meaning thereby is 'If I say (address) "Basti" a "basti" (an inhabited place), to what sort of place would I call a "deserted place"?'

'Well, I have started enjoying the place now, as if I was always here. By now, I know all the people of the area. And they also know me, that I'm from Forest Department. They are good to me because they know I can restrict their movement for the reasons best known only to me.'

'You must be having another guest house here. Where's that?'

'Not in this district.'

'I'm here for a week. What all places can you take me to?'

'Tomorrow you can visit this village and a kattha [catechu] factory nearby. After that, you can take one direction side per day and cover the entire area.'

While talking, Agastya was relaxing in an armchair and Joshi was making preparations for dinner. Agastya again asked, 'Joshi, you seem to be educated, coming from city life, even then you believe in things like black magic and persons being changed or transformed into sheep, goat, and birds.'

'Saab-ji, you stay here for some time, you will also see yourself and would start believing in all these. Earlier even I didn't believe. But after seeing and experiencing, I had to.'

Thinking no use in talking more to convince Joshi, Agastya preferred to change the topic and asked him, 'Joshi-ji, now let's come to dinner part. Keep in mind I'm pure vegetarian. What's there in dinner?'

'Nothing of that sort. Here would be only simple veg dinner.'

'There's no light here. And outside's scary pitch dark. I can't do anything but to wait for dinner.'

Joshi advised him not to go out in the dark, which could be dangerous. Nature's beautiful, but friend or foe to none. It had its law, sparing none. Like a burning lamp, attractive for flies, but these are killed on it. Joshi asked to wait a little; dinner was ready.

After some time, they had their dinner. And after dinner, Joshi asked at what time he would take tea in the morning. Agastya told him that he would get up early to enjoy the morning freshness of the jungle and that he didn't take bed tea. So Joshi told him that he would come at seven in the morning to prepare breakfast and packed lunch. Saying so, he assured all was done for the day and wished good night, to see him in the morning. And Agastya securely locked himself in for the night. It was the first time Agastya had moved outside of his home and stayed alone, all by himself, and that, too, in the solitude of a thick jungle, totally unaware of what all was happening all around him. But he had made up his mind, as there was no choice. Whatever would be the situation, he would brave it.

Life here in the village was pretty relaxed. Day started with dawn, and with the setting of sun, it ends. There was no light, absolutely nothing to do after fall of darkness. People remained confined in their houses in the night, sleeping in the perfect silence of the forest. But in this silence too,

Agastya wasn't getting sleep. This silence was becoming oppressive to him. Still, when the day's tiredness proved heavier, not knowing, Agastya quietly slipped into sleep. But it didn't take long that he felt disturbed and got up. He felt as if someone was pulling away his coverlet from over his body. He had come to his full senses, still feeling the coverlet being pulled. He couldn't understand it at all. He got into a sitting position, frantically searching for the torch. He lit the lamp and took some water. After visiting the restroom, thinking this might have been due to his own physical or new-place reasons, he tried to relax and sleep. But sleep is such a thing that the more you try to get it, the farther it goes away. After vain efforts for sleep, he got up and checked all the latches and bolts. Finding them all intact, he again returned to his bed and simply lay effortlessly. He passed into semi-sleep condition. Suddenly he felt finger-tips moving on the soles of his feet. Coming to his senses, he moved his feet here and there, pulled up, and pushed down. But no use. He was continuously feeling fingers moving and titillating him to tickled uneasiness. Again he got up and looked around. It was still dark. He checked his wristwatch—only 2.00. He pulled up some socks and put the sheet aside. He lit his lamp and placed it on the table for the rest of the night and got into bed to let the rest of the night pass. Let whatsoever happen; that was his time. He kept lying on the bed with closed eyes. It was still dark or it was light of the dawn—he didn't know. He opened his eyes at the knock on the door and the call of 'Saab-ji!' by Joshi. He looked around and uttered, 'Arey, night's over. Joshi 'as come.' He got up and opened the door. Getting Joshi in, he narrated the whole incident of the night to him.

Without any reaction, Joshi simply said, 'Saab-ji. This's undisturbed their jungle area. Some passing-by gentle spirit had played fun with you. These don't harm anybody. You just relax.' Joshi was preparing breakfast and packed lunch, and Agastya sat outside on a chair, with his back to the forest, facing the village. Joshi, seeing him sitting like this, at once came and alerted him, 'Saab-ji, never give your back to forest, the unseen. Always face the unforeseen or you would be in great trouble. In seconds, trouble may come. If alert and facing it, one can get so much from the nature. But if not facing and not alert, in no time one becomes past element here.'

Both got in. Finishing breakfast, they soon set out to go to the village for a survey. As they were about to move, there reached the village boy, with his milk pot hanging in one hand. Agastya was happy and asked Joshi, 'See, Joshi-ji, milk has come. Let's be late by few minutes, at least we'll have tea. Didn't get even yester-eve.' Joshi took the milk and asked the boy to bring some during the evening also and returned to the kitchen to make tea. In the meantime Agastya caught hold of the boy and asked him, 'How old are you?'

The boy didn't know. When he started getting it, he said, 'Uncle says eight years back was big jungle fire. And I was seven then. That's it'

'How long you're here in this village?'

'Don't know. From all the time. We all. Only Lala Jagannath here for some years. Businessman. He 'as made fortune so soon. His family lives in big city.'

'What about your health and education here?'

'Nature God take our care. Now there's a doctor and a small school also in nearby village, some five miles in Village Bangdu. Sometimes a nurse also there. There's one ojha also here, and almost every aged person suggest some traditional cure to problems.'

'Good, at least something is there.' In the meantime, Joshi came with two cups of tea. They made it three. They finished with it, and within the next fifteen minutes, they both were in the village and started the work.

They started the survey with the first house as they entered the village. Joshi called the house owner. A lady came out and said, 'He is not here, gone for the work.'

'See, saab is here from city, wants to ask you something about you and your family,' told Joshi.

'What for, what can I tell?' asked the woman.

In the meantime, several ladies and children gathered around but were supportive because of Joshi. 'Saab will write a book, the name of our village will appear in a book. The entire country will come to know about us!' said Joshi

'Okay. So what do you want to know?'

'Name of your husband, I guess he is the owner of the house?'

She remained quiet, and someone else answered on her behalf.

'Kalu Ram.' Agastya confirmed from the woman, and she noded in affirmation. 'How many persons living in this house in your family?'

'We two and our children,' said the lady.

'How many children?' Agastya asked.

She turned her back. And that was the end to the conversation with her. 'How on earth could he ask for counting my children? The guy has got bad omen for us.'

Joshi explained to Agastya that these people do not consider it good that anybody should count their children. There was no particular reason behind this sort of thinking, but they think 'children and cattle heads are God's gift, and these should not come in counting. If come in counting or in other's eyes, might start decreasing'.

Joshi asked another one around the corner, who told him that they had three children, one son aged four years and two daughters of six and two. Somehow at the persuasion of Joshi, she could be convinced to answer further.

'What does your man do for earning a living?'

'Casual labour,' replied the woman.

'How much he earns in a day or month?'

The lady did not tell anything again. Another lady helped. 'Around three to four rupees on working days, coming to about fifty to sixty rupees a month, and then gets things from the forest.'

On his tour around the village, he also went inside a few houses and saw them from inside. But he could gather only some limited information from the family members themselves; the remaining information was picked up through neighbours and the other male members of the family. Thanks to Joshi, everything turned out well during the survey; without him, it could have been pretty difficult in the village—not because Agastya wasn't up to the job but because Agastya was an outsider and might be harmed. He could be considered a potential threat.

While the survey was on, Joshi noticed something suspicious in the house of one of the ladies. He found a goat of a little abnormal nature. But he thought it better to keep quite lest it disturb Agastya's work. Also, the lady might figure out Joshi's intention and might harm them. Ever since Joshi had seen this goat, he had been thinking about it; there was surely something strange about it. Was the goat a goat or some person transformed into one? All the children of the village and some men present in the village followed the two throughout the survey. It seemed to be a rare, strange activity in the village. Agastya had been taking snaps of the houses, places of worship, village gods, water point, residence-cum-shop of Jagannath-Seth, men and women in their work, and also overall view of the village fields and forest. This would make it easier to give credibility to his project work.

AGASTYA MEETS PRIYA

Once done with the households in the village, Agastya asked Joshi, 'Let us go to Seth Jagannath's house and get some information about his life and experiences here.' Joshi was okay with the idea, and both walked slowly to Lala's residence and, on reaching there, knocked on the closed door.

A young girl of about Agastya's age opened the door and asked, 'Yes?'

'I'm a student from Balrampur, wanted some information for a project, if Seth-ji is there?'

'Well, he is not around as of now. Can I help in any way?'

'Oh . . . thanks. We will come again later in the evening. Will that be fine?'

'Sure.'

'Cool. Thanks once again.'

'No issues. Bye,' Priya said.

'Issues? I'm still unmarried. These children aren't mine. These are your . . . I mean . . .' Agastya said.

'Neither mine.'

All burst into laughter. Laughing with her hand on her mouth and lowering her face, she turned in.

They planned to get back in the evening and planned that they could go to a catechu juice–treating plant, a catechu factory, right then. The plant was about two miles from there. It was just about noon; they could easily go there and get back in time. They started walking down a narrow trail to the catechu-plant. Agastya was very quiet and not asking any questions to Joshi. Joshi was a seasoned man and knew that some encounters lasted for seconds but left a long-lasting impact. Agastya was walking faster, as if he had a goal. Of course, he had one. He had to get back to Seth-ji's house before the end of the day. In about forty minutes they reached a small clearing on the side of a dry bed called Thor-Tibba. There, under a high, big asbestos sheet covering, was a big, long narrow furnace. On this were two rows of earthen pitchers, fixed at four on each side. In these pitchers *khair* wood chips were being boiled in water. First, they were being boiled in the first pitcher for a while. Once they discharged colour sufficiently, these chips then were removed into the next. And the water in the first one, and likewise in the second and so on, was left to boil to turn into a thick substance by getting water evaporated. Finally, after these chips discharged the complete substance, they were thrown out to use for fuel or pulp for paper. And the water of the pitchers was boiled to leave behind the dry paste of the *khair* substance. This's then given the shape of small solid bricks. This was *kattha* (catechu), used in Indian medicines, as a red substance on betel leaves, and for many other purposes. There were ten workers performing their different works of keeping constant fire for sufficient heat under the pitchers and changing chips from one pitcher to another, stirring, treating the paste, and packing the *khair* tree substance into bricks, etc.

It was a good time spent at the plant. It seemed as if the time had come to a standstill for as long as he was studying the process. This whole thing was so overwhelming. Agastya hadn't seen anything like this before. But as soon as he was done with it, he felt a lot of time had passed and there wouldn't be enough time to get to Lala-ji's house again. But his watch told him otherwise. He again walked at a fast pace, only to find that Seth-ji got back from work. Reaching the guest house, he did not wait for long and started on for Lala-ji's, Seth Jagannath's house. Reaching there, he knocked at the door. Luckily, this time, Lala-ji was there, and he came to open the door. Seeing Joshi and some official-type young man, he took them in. Joshi introduced Agastya and explained their purpose. Agastya collected all relevant information and family details. At its completion, Lala-ji was saying, 'It's a happy surprise, Joshi-ji and Agastya. It's rare you are here, Joshi.' They were asked to stay for some more time. Agastya took it as a wish-come-true opportunity. And they settled on a lavish tea. At tea, they all became informal and had light chit-chat. Now was the time for their moving to the guest house. Scared of the night, Agastya wanted more time to pass with someone. And now he had a beautiful reason also—the girl Priya. So he invited Seth-ji and his whole family to the guest house for the evening. This being a rare opportunity in a place like Dera, and for good change, Seth-ji accepted it heartily. Surely expecting this to be a memorable evening right up to late in the night, they were all excited. And the preparations for the same were started on both sides.

Joshi started arranging and preparing tea, snacks, and dinner items for the evening. Thinking of the coming of Priya with her parents, relaxing in his chair, Agastya gave a whole set of instructions to Joshi on how to prepare for the evening. Joshi knew what best he could do in this place and would always be well prepared for any situation. Though Agastya was doubtful, Joshi knew that Lala-ji would come. He had twice been to his place. There was quite a chance he would come to kind of enquire about the new guest in the forest. Joshi moved out to get some stuff for the evening. Agastya was lying on the back of the easy-chair, his face covered under a hand towel. Various thoughts of today's work kept cropping up in his mind: about the area visited, the survey, but above all the lady whom he met. Though he hardly talked or spent time with her, there was something about her that struck him. He wanted to talk to her again and again, to spend more time in company of someone. He kept dreaming about the evening to come. But just then he got up with a jolt. He screamed, 'Huh? Who's there?' There wasn't anyone. But he found that the small hand-towel on his face got onto the other chair. It had probably blown away by the wind. He looked around, got up, and took a glass of water. He strolled around in the veranda and then sat down on his chair, thinking as to what had happened. He had heard a voice again, but very soon he brushed it off. He thought of information he had collected for his project, the main work he was there for, before it lost connectivity and relevance in his mind. He started analysing the information to give it a meaningful shape and also prepared a brief note for each activity before it got confusing and all mixed up. Very soon, he was ready with a brief report. Finishing his report, he came to the door and stood there, gazing towards the village. He strolled in the front yard and sincerely hoped for Priya's coming. He had nothing to do except hope for their coming. No wonder in his loneliness the time had come to a standstill. Nobody to talk to, no one who could understand his mind. Seeing the forest, he thought, *These are so dense, there must definitely be so many secrets and so many worlds hidden in these. God alone knows, how do the sages stay here in complete loneliness? It is in complete contradiction to the maddening crowds of the cities—the apex of civilisation and kaleidoscope of development.* He was lost in the wilderness of the thick forest and mountains standing behind the green wall. Then blue and white curtains, one above the other, piercing the endless space of sky. Like the endless space of sky above were the wild thoughts of Agastya in the wilderness of nature.

'Saab-ji, I have got spinach, brinjal, onion, and potatoes. I will prepare bhajia, pakoras of these'

'Oh wow, pakoras! Would be really good in this weather. Do you also have green chillies and sauces? Come, I will also help you. How long will you work alone?'

'Saab-ji, this isn't a big thing. You rest. After all, you 'ad a hectic day. You must be tired.'

Just then they saw Priya and her parents on the door.

'Hello, namaste, please come! Would you like to sit here in the lawn or in the inside?'

'Well . . .' Jagannath began to say.

'It's quite nice out here,' but Priya completed the sentence.

'Yeah, even we would prefer the lawn. It's nice and pleasant here,' Agastya said.

Priya expressed thanks for calling them over.

'My pleasure. It would be wonderful company here in loneliness. And you are such a wonderful people.'

They all preferred to sit outside, which was so pleasing in the cool evening time, with a view of the whole surrounding, with birds returning to their nests, flying over in the sky.

'I'm sorry you came twice, but I was out for some work. Actually, I got stuck with something and got late. I have a small shop in our residence and also have some wholesale trading of some products. I and my wife live here. Priya, my daughter whom you have already met, lives in Lucknow for her studies. Her brother and sister live in Gonda for their education.'

'Do you find this place good prospect for business?' Agastya asked.

'Yes, the place's good. It's not far off also. On two, three occasions, in the rainy seasons, water rises so high in Rapti that at that time you can't cross it, even by boat. But rest of the time it's quite good. In winters and summers, at times, on some ghats, people cross it even without boat. And now heard there is also a proposal for a seasonal bridge here and permanent bridge at Bijlipur,' Lala said.

'What got you interested in this place, in such interior?' Agastya continued.

'I used to visit this area with the contractors and business people coming to this area. Gradually, thought of developing my own business here and to have a permanent base, to give it stability. My residence here has helped my business grow. The people with whom I deal with feel confident that they are not doing business with a stranger but with a man having a permanent base,' Jagannath responded.

'How do the children take your living here?' Agastya asked.

'They are grown up now and busy in their studies. They understand it is a part of business and life, and then I'm not at far-off place. I keep on visiting them there, and in the holidays they also come here, it is a good change for them to experience this type of life too,' responded Jagannath.

Jagannath could see the enormous questions in Agastya's eyes, but he was feeling hesitant to ask. How many questions can one ask? Many things are to be understood by experiencing them, not by queries. But still Jagannath thought of catering to the curiosity of this young mind lest he feel completely overwhelmed with this place.

'The lifestyle here is quite different from that of the city life. There is no point in comparing the two. These are two distinct realms. And comparing the two won't get you anywhere. These may be taken as complementary to each other rather than competitors. These are supportive to each other. Even Indian monsoons are because of this region. All hydroelectric power projects of North India are all along in Lower Himalayas—Kashmir in the west to Assam in the east. Because it's easy to tame big rivers in their upper course in mountains, needing only one dam across the river in a gorge. Rest done itself by relief. And sooner or later, you get used to the life you select for yourself and start living. Let's say, for the medical system here. People have learnt a way to deal with that too.'

'But why should you compromise with things like medical facilities? Shouldn't it be provided to the people by the government?' argued Agastya.

'You are right, it should be provided by the government. But then a lot of things fall into that "should be" category. What would you do if these aren't there? People find a way. After all, only the fittest survive. Moreover, governments are now for past some thousand years, whereas these people are living in their habitat, with the nature right from the inception of human race and from the time these jungles are here. We are demanding facilities, and things are improving also. But people can't give up living. Even people don't accept new changes so easily. There are some modern doctors in the area, but people, instead of going to them, prefer to go to witchcraft practitioners and for traditional local practices. You may find it hard to believe, even many modern doctors go to ojhas for such practices for their troubles here.'

Agastya was widening his understanding about the villages and life at large. Priya and her mother had been silent listeners, but then for how long? There was a limit for everything, and Priya was getting impatient now. She had felt absolutely neglected so far, as if she were some instrument. If this were the case, she should rather have not come. She interrupted and gave her point of view, but no one seemed to have taken the hint so far. Finally, she got to talking about the futility of projects like this, saying forcefully, 'Projects like these aren't scientific. They are based on people's perception. Projects and researches are done only in labs under the microscope.'

Agastya rebutted it. 'That's just one aspect of knowledge. But social changes, reforms, and improvements come through social interactions and field studies, not from labs.'

Well, that was surely some hint to someone. And instead of hot discussion, they preferred hot tea and snacks. The atmosphere got a little light, and everyone started enjoying in the cool early twilight period of the evening. To top it all, Joshi arrived with a plate of hot bhajia or pakoras—roasted mixed-gram flour and vegetables, like spinach, fresh chips of brinjal, potatoes, etc. Everyone salivated looking at the pakoras or bhajias; indeed, the pakoras made the gathering more enjoyable and lively.

'Please have, I would be bringing more,' said Joshi, going back to kitchen.

Agastya offered it to everyone, and they got to talking about life in general in the village, Priya's interests, her studies, and her experience with city life, so on and so forth. There was no dearth of topics; Agastya had become a familiar person now to them, as if they had known each other for a long time. Finally Agastya had found some company in the solitude of this jungle. He was no longer alone, and the jungle wasn't an unknown place to him. They went on chatting about light topics and jokes, enjoying the pakoras. Joshi came with another service. They all had praise for Joshi.

'Good, Joshi, you prepared these so well, very nice, and delicious,' said Mrs Jagannath.

'He does things with perfection. And so helping for everyone, doesn't look an outsider,' said Jagannath. Besides this, the natural peaceful location added so much to their enjoyment. It was like a real picnic.

The new guest was a welcome change to the village also. This was a good change from the routine and mundane life for everyone. Jagannath wanted Joshi to show them the guest house, in and around. Agastya suggested for Priya to have a long stay here after exams in the summer. But she had lived there for quite a long time, and based on her past experience, she explained, 'It surely isn't as hot as Lucknow, Balrampur, or Gonda, but this place isn't as comfortable as I thought it to be either. There is a problem of water scarcity, and then the biggest fear there in summer is that of forest fire, which becomes so common in summer. For days, together people here don't take rest, only run and run here and there. To avoid and control the forest fire. They clear a long narrow passage with dry leaves, grass, and woods and bushes in the forest for their movement through this, and also ground fire doesn't cross the clear passage. And put on a fire on the opposite side of the village so that the fire doesn't spread to the village side but goes from village to jungle, and the meeting wildfire dies. Fire mostly dies reaching the edge of such passage because of no dry leaves or bushes ahead there in the passage. And many wildlife get burnt alive in the fire, giving foul smell. Rest run to villages and safe places. Such places are fair-weather places, good only for a holiday, not for permanent living. One must live in the place or area where seeking future. Dad had a reason to be here, and probably you, Sociologist, also. But it isn't my calling. I have my very clear life plan—to take up a career in paramedicine or education. You too, I feel, if so liked this place, could be here and do some social service.'

But Agastya too had his mind very clear; he wanted to take up administrative services or politics. That wasn't too far off from social service as well, as she suggested. Priya and Agastya had debate-type discussions on several topics, but ultimately they both realised that they had a nice conversation and were getting comfortable with each other. Agastya was more than happy that he had some company in this forest. But was that all? Day was to pass on the baton to the motherly comforting night with dark wings. So leaving everything as it was, Joshi took Seth-ji and his family, with Agastya following them, to the interior and around the guest house and brought them back to the front area, which was so lively a little before by their get-together.

Darkness had started spreading its wings, and it was time to be home for Jagannath and family. Everyone was very happy! Agastya expressed sincere thanks to everyone to have taken out time and come to him. When you are all alone in a secluded place where you don't know anyone, you realise what belongingness means. People ask this question every now and then about our belongingness. And the answer typically lies in some territory or some region. But in more ways than one, one belongs to a place on earth where one's soul is complete. And that's something which can only be felt but not explained. In the wilderness of any space, a companion can at least get you closer to feeling one with your soul, if not complete. Agastya kept looking at Priya, and she too knew there was a connection. Their eyes met and something had clicked; something had worked. They sure would like to meet again. Jagannath invited Agastya for dinner. Agastya was probably the happiest person on earth.

His project was going fine, but this journey was taking another meaning too and a beautiful one. They discussed the time for the dinner. But Agastya knew somewhere that he didn't want it to be very soon. It probably wouldn't send the right signal, and he still didn't want to share his heart with anyone, not even with the lady. A thought needs to germinate into an idea before it can be explained. Agastya wanted the right timing. He left it to a point that he would confirm before coming and he would try to come in the next couple of days.

They bid adieu. Agastya saw Priya and her parents moving to the village. He stood there like a statue, looking towards them until they disappeared somewhere in the smoke and darkness nearing the village, and was drowned in loneliness again. His silence and loneliness was broken by Joshi, who spoke loudly, 'Saab-ji, now come in, it is dark outside, come in with one chair, rest I will do. Let me finish this small work and I am coming.' Agastya got in with one chair. Joshi was busy finishing his work and then came to Agastya for dinner. It had been a long busy day for Joshi, so he wanted to finish it before it got too late for next day's preparations. They both had dinner together, and then Joshi left for his place. Agastya closed all doors and windows and bolted them all from inside. A lamp was lit and kept on the shelf in the veranda, and Agastya strolled there for some time before retiring to his bed in an attempt to get sleep.

PRIYA GOES TO SEE DEVIKA

Agastya's newly found companion was with him but only in mind and in thoughts; physically he was lonely, and the darkness around only seemed to surmount it. He thought about the day and how it seemed to have changed his life. It was one thing in the morning and quite another in the evening. Some wise men have rightly said that it's all in the journey; one doesn't know what the journey may unfold for him. But there were more reasons than one to figure out. He was deep asleep when he heard another sound as if knocking on the door. Agastya knew he couldn't and wouldn't open the door, but then who was it in this darkness in this jungle? He sat in his bed, thinking what to do, but then just decided to stay, out of fear. It might have been some wildlife trying to get in, having smelt a human being. Thankfully, the doors were strong enough, or at least that's what he thought. Tired as he was, he kept lying and went into sleep once again. Suddenly he got up with a jolt, as if someone pulled his sheet, asking him, 'How could you be sleeping?' Agastya had felt this before too so felt all the more restless, the same incident again. He knew it was some human's action. But there was no one to be seen. He woke up early but stayed in bed for some time. He took a glass of water from the bedside and kept sipping it while he thought about the night. He was getting restless to share it with Joshi, but there was still time for him to come. He had a long tough time the previous day and wanted to rest for more. But he started getting ready while he somewhere waited for Joshi. On his coming in the morning, he said to him, 'I felt the same voice again tonight.'

Joshi wasn't amused or surprised. 'This is a forest, saab-ji, a place on earth not open to the developments of the civilisation. This is the world in its truest form, you will find here everything in its true form.'

Not satisfied, but what else could he do? So he asked, 'Where are we going today?'

'May go to Khairi, about three miles in the east.' Agastya agreed, and they both went through the jungle, talking aloud and hitting the ground here and there. Agastya had learnt that no one goes through the forest quietly. As they talked and moved, they did notice some birds, wild hens, and rabbits run away fast through the vegetation. Colourful sunrays were passing through the branches as if some light beams were being thrown by projectors in a cinema hall. The light on the dewdrops shone on the grass blades like radiating diamond particles. Birds were chirping, and the animals were enjoying in their natural surrounding; they could see some monkeys in far-off tress. Joshi was walking completely alert with a sharp sight all around, but Agastya was scared. Sometimes both were scared of the silence too, of what it may unfold. Joshi used to be scared for Agastya lest he got in some trouble for his negligence. Though there were some harmless animals, he hadn't been in such close proximity to them ever. It was the unknown which bothered him; he didn't know what all he would encounter on this path. Thankfully, this fearful journey came to an end soon and they reached an open area, a dry bed of a small seasonal flow. Agastya had a sigh of relief and said, 'Thank God, we are in open and safer place now.'

'Safer place? Saab-ji, this is more dangerous, you are not able to see big animals ready to attack in their hunting positions, but it is possible that they are watching us. We are in open, open to all dangers. Most of the times, big cats keep hiding close to such open places, waiting for and watching their prey come in such open for water and play, or for sun in winters.[*]

Agastya was all the more frightened. The sigh of relief just lasted a moment, but it was appropriate for Joshi to have warned him so that he can take care of himself and things around him. They tried to cross the dry bed as quickly as possible and reach Khairi. In another fifteen minutes or so, they reached the village and asked for the village head. They were directed to the house of Dilawar Singh, who

---

[*] The author had the real experience of this danger in this bear-infested jungle, running through a dry bed to reach a safe place in the sharp falling darkness with one fellow, Ranjit Singh. We were strictly warned by locals not to use guns. Our fastest possible running was looking much less to us.

seemed quite prosperous. His house was big enough, made of baked bricks with tiled roof. He offered them water and locally prepared snacks of boiled thrashed rice called there *chiwra*. Agastya sought help to conduct the survey, and he came around, more than keen to help. He helped Agastya be able to easily survey the village, about fifty houses and huts in about one-and-a-half hours. Thanks to the village head for the work done pretty fast, now they were free for the day. By noon they had finished work and were free to get back to the guest house. But Agastya wanted to rest in the cool shade of a big shady tree just close to the village. They had lunch there, and Agastya took a short nap under the tree. Joshi also rested but didn't sleep, just to be watchful, to protect themselves from any risk. In a place like this, animals could smell men from a long distance, depending on the direction of the wind. After a short rest there, they started on their return journey and reached the guest house safely and timely.

There would be Dushahra after three days, recollected Agastya, and though he was away from family and friends, he should be doing something. He thought of going to Jagannath's place; he could also check about some celebrations in the village. He was a welcome guest at Jagannath's house, and his other children had also come home for the vacations. He thought there could be fun for sure, now that his entire family would be together. They would be doing something. Priya's younger brother and sister also got on talking terms with Agastya very soon, and they started enjoying the company of one another. Priya and Agastya would also exchange their ideas here and there and catch eye to eye every now and then. They knew they had a friend in each other. During their talks, in one such meeting, Priya told him about her dearest friend, Devika, in nearby Village Haati. They were classmates and had spent most of their time together. Agastya was curious to know more about her so-close friend. Priya told that the last time she had met Devika was about two years back; she hadn't been well for a long time now, and Priya hadn't been able to go and meet her during this period. Life had been quite busy and hectic for her too, and then whatever little time she got off, she wished to spend it with her parents. Devika was very active, friendly, and socially active before she fell ill. She was under some kind of trauma, and whatever people suggested had been tried; she just hadn't been able to come out of it.

'What happened? Why in trauma?' asked Agastya.

'She had developed close friendship with a young guy named Rohan, who used to visit this area often for some project work, something like what brought you here. The relationship between Devika and that guy blossomed with every visit, and it was going stronger. Sometimes you just know internally that this person is meant for you. You don't need a special kind of understanding to know that. It was all going fine for them. But he suddenly went missing. Devika fell ill trying to meet him, but in vain. Her parents tried to contact Rohan's parents, but even they didn't have any clue of their son. His family was also shaken up as to where could he just get lost in thin air. Devika has a very strong feeling that he is somewhere in this forest, probably he has reached a place where he can't find his way back from.

Sometimes life takes you on some paths which seems like path of no return. But she is hopeful of his return, and since then she has been waiting. She hasn't pursued her studies further. Devika's parents tried to find another match for her, but then she refused as has already found her soul mate and wanted to wait for.' She started feeling heavy and sentimental and paused for some time and continued further. 'I feel sometimes the air around you also has an influence on what you think and how you understand things. This land has been the abode of Sita and Draupadi, who devoted their lives completely to the men in their life. It may seem strange, but I think the soil where you live does influence your state of being.'

Agastya was spellbound by this story and just didn't know how to react and what to say. But somewhere, he did want to find a way he could help. He wasn't very sure if it was for Priya that he wanted to help or there was something else pushing him to find Rohan. Agastya checked with Joshi if Haati was on their list. He would like to meet Devika. Priya also wanted to join in the trip but needed her parents' permission to join in.

On getting the appropriate time, Agastya spoke, 'Uncle, tomorrow I would go to Bangdu and, day after tomorrow, to Haati. In Haati, Priya said, she has a friend, Devika, who is not well for quite some time. Priya seems keen to go to Haati and see Devika. It will be good for Devika too, maybe it will help her recover her health. If you allow Priya to go, it would be nice tour for all of us.'

'How will she go through these thick forests?' asked Priya's mom.

'Let me check out some options. I will let you know tomorrow about how it could be planned out,' explained Jagannath.

'That should be great. I will make a move right now and then check with you tomorrow.'

Agastya was looking forward for the Haati trip, but right now he should worry about Bangdu and the information that he can possibly get from there. As he reached the guest house, he asked Joshi for some tea. Something struck his mind that the papers lying there might give some clue about the person who worked on these. So he decided to go through the papers he had seen in the other room. As these papers appeared to be related to that area, he asked Joshi to carefully clean the papers. After Joshi cleaned and arranged these and Agastya finished his tea, they both went through these and found these were surely related to some project work. There they also got an ID of some Rohan Kumar.

'We got it! This could probably be Devika's friend.'

From the project papers, he couldn't clearly read what the project dealt with, else it could have given him some clue. However, on some papers he could see date marks of three years back. *Three years past? If these belonged to him, he must be here only in this area. But where could he be here for years?* Agastya questioned himself.

'Saab-ji, now there can be only two possibilities. The first one, he's caught up by some man-eater. And he's no more. Or the second one, that some black magician's keeping him transformed into some pet,' suggested Joshi. He further added, 'There are least chances of first one because no traces of any person being killed in this area came to our notice. Any such unfortunate incident doesn't go unnoticed by us, and mostly people come to know of it. Even we come to know of wildlife, when any big one's killed. Many people every day go to forests for their livelihood. They bring information out to public and to us. And forest people also remain watchful. We even know of every lion, bear, or elephant of the forest. We maintain their population record. So there's greater possibility of second one. He must be here in the area as captive of someone, and I'm working on this.'

'That's good. Your second possibility has given us a purpose, and it'll keep us active,' said Agastya. He wanted to check with Priya if she could recognise him through the picture on the ID card, though it was pretty tattered by now. Agastya was excited and baffled too—Mishra was right there, in a lot hidden in this forest. He had to now find Rohan, as if finding Rohan were his new-found mission in life. Tomorrow morning they would be out to Bangdu and would be back by afternoon. On his way back he should check with Priya. He kept the ID card and the papers in the backpack. That night, Agastya couldn't sleep; he was thinking about the ID card, Rohan, and what could have possibly happened to him. First thing in the morning, he tried to pick bits from Joshi about that guy. Joshi could recognise the face, but all he knew was that Rohan was a very daring guy and he had ventured into the forest alone a lot number of times. He had gone back from the guest house some two-and-a-half years back but never came back after that. Joshi didn't know if the project was over or was something else. Agastya told Joshi about Devika and her plight and confided in him that if he were the same person, then he needed Joshi's help to find Rohan. They got busy preparing for the day, and by 7.30, they left for Bangdu, passing through the village. Walking about twelve hundred meters of small agricultural field, they entered the deep forest. Now they would have to cross three different stretches of forest and two riverbeds to reach Bangdu. Reaching there, Agastya went to the house of the village head, Janak Singh. People here in the villages were extremely hospitable. Janak Singh treated them with great warmth and offered water and local snacks. Agastya interviewed him, collected information, and requested him for help in the village-survey. He was more or less getting some similar kind of information from these villages. He collected information, sketched some features, took some snaps, including that of Janak Singh and a family photograph of his family. He also met schoolteachers and a doctor-cum-nursing-person. In the school itself, there was a letter box. The teachers used to handle this also. The postal staff went there weekly except for some urgent communication. It took a little longer for Agastya to go around this village, and then Janak Singh invited them to his home. They sat there for some time and relaxed and had lunch too. After a sumptuous lunch, the hot noon sun was making it difficult for them to walk. But Agastya wanted to check about Rohan as soon as possible; in spite of this being hot noon, they started on their return.

Cool shades and water points on the way compelled them to rest awhile in some places. Agastya lay on the ground with closed eyes and took a short nap. All his tiredness was gone as he touched the soil. After all, everything begins from here and come to rest here only in the lap of Mother Earth. The jungle experience of these couple of days had made Agastya a bit more confident and bold. Except for small animals, like rabbits, deer, and jacks, etc., he did not see even a single big cat or bear, elephant, python, bison, or boars, etc. They must have been deep in the jungle, away from the places of movement of people and the habitations. Though they took rest on the way, they reached Dera by 3.00 and went straight to Priya's house. He showed Rohan's snap to Priya, and she could recognise him, though she wasn't completely sure, as the photograph wasn't in a very good condition. Now Agastya was all the more keen to look for Rohan. He just wanted to do something for a student who had come for study and the families affected. He got back to the guest house and started working on the reports for his trips so far. It was important for him to collect information and furnish reports for the data collected so far so that his mind was free from this side. In the night also he made all preparations needed for the next day and retired to bed.

Next morning, he was ready to leave for Haati and got thinking about Jagannath. He was a very gentle, experienced, and successful man. In so little a time, he had done well in his business. He was very compassionate at the same time. He strongly felt that Priya's visit to Devika would help her recover, and maybe she would get back get her normal life soon enough. The two, Agastya and Joshi, left for the village with their necessary items, and in about fifteen minutes, they were at Lala-ji's house. Priya was already ready, and they all finished their breakfast soon. While they were taking breakfast, Jagannath kept on passing instructions and advised, 'The village head, Jagat Bahadur, is very well known to me. Priya, you must try and meet him also and convey my regards. They are known to us for a very long time and are very nice and gentle people.' Priya was happy at how her dad had managed all relationships. He had been doing the right thing at the right time in the right way. And he was always available for everyone. For reasons only known to him, he had been quite friendly with Agastya too and had taken good care of him, to ensure that nothing went wrong for him. He further advised, 'Be careful on the way, don't throw a stick, stone, or anything on the trees or bushes to avoid honeybee from attacking you. Monkeys can be very risky on this stretch.' Jagannath had been brave to send off her daughter through the difficult trails, but somewhere deep inside him was the worry that time and situation should not prove his decision wrong. Jumman, the escort, was ready with sufficient packed lunch, a water jar, a bag with some eatables, and some first-aid material. Priya's mom also gave a small folding umbrella as a gift for Devika. She had packed it nicely.

'Right, Mama, Papa, we make a move now.'

'Okay, dear, take care and all the best. I would be happy to hear from you that Devika's doing well and's fit and fine now.'

Thus they left the house on way to Haati. Jagannath went to see them off. The group walked on and on and looked back. Jagannath was still standing near the village and waving to them till they entered downward into a dry riverbed, crossed a small rill of water, and reached the other side of the dry bed into a dense forest area. The vegetation was beautiful and all fresh. Jumman was much ahead of everyone; being a regular trekker of this place, he could walk fast. Also, he would be able to sense danger well in advance. Joshi walked close to them and was being watchful on all sides. With both Jumman and Joshi taking care of everything, Agastya was quite relaxed and happy in the forest in the very special company he had on the journey. They were going on hand in hand, talking, sharing experiences and instances, that there was a sudden thunderous roar, not far off in the jungle and the noise of the fast running of some big animals, with the churning of bushes, twigs and all. The heartbeat of these two turned fast. Agastya put both his hands on his ears. Joshi and Jumman, running, got close to both of these and put their ears to the direction of the running of animals. Then came the sharp helpless shriek from the choking throat of some animal becoming slow and slow. And then all was quiet, as if there happened nothing. Though for one life the world was finished. And then started the explanation of the happening by Jumman.

'Surely it was lion. Went from very close of us. Must have been going with us side by side and poor deer fell in the way. That saved us. Thank God. We didn't expect it, such a clever animal. Had been going on with patience.'

For a moment Agastya was frightened, but the two Js boosted their morale. Agastya was happy on this new and unique experience, though he would be more careful now on. And again coming to their normal life, he was confident that with Priya, he would be able to do something for Devika besides his project. It would be nice even if they could cheer her up for a while. In the meantime, Priya expressed, 'I'm happy the way my dad arranged for everything. He's very caring, sometimes even a little care at the right time can do wonders to someone's life. It's all about timing in life. If you don't do right thing at the right time, it's as good as not done. Maybe our meeting with Devika'll make convincing difference.'

'Amen.'

They were guiding each other on the way. They knew that it was because of each other that they had decided to take on this journey. The project was surely to be done, but now there was a mission. The mission of Devika and Rohan too. And with good hopes for Devika in their heart, they were going to her place. Priya was really excited to meet her. It would be really great to see her after years. She would be giving her a good surprise, as she didn't know that Priya was visiting her. At the same time, Priya was a little wary also about her health, not sure in what condition they might find her. But then this was one way Priya could make a difference. They had travelled a long distance without realising the heat and the long walk. Jumman was waiting ahead under a big shady tree, and slowly everyone joined him.

'Take a little break and have something to eat. We still have to go long distance.' If only Jumman knew that it hadn't been any trouble for the young hearts, for love always shelters you from hardship.

Joshi asked, looking towards Agastya, 'How 'as your journey been today?'

Agastya paused before answering, thinking if this question meant something else, if he had heard them or saw them so close together. But he gathered to say, 'It's bright and nice today, and we are so many people, so it 'as become still well a day.' Maybe he, heart to heart, must have been wishing none of the other two had been there with them. Though mindfully, both the Js, Joshi and Jumman, were walking either long ahead or back. To change the topic, being somewhat uncomfortable with Joshi's questioning, Agastya asked Jumman, 'Jumman, you must be frequent visitor to all these places.'

'Yes, saab, we have to come into these forests every day. Our everyday needs are met from the forests.'

'You aren't scared of animals or what?' Agastya asked.

'Well, actually speaking, there's nothing to be scared of. Every living being on this earth wishes to happily coexist, but it's we humans which keep destroying their homeland and trouble them. And when disturbed, they attack us.' Jumman had been in the woods for all his life and now he felt very at home in the jungle. He further said, 'Actually, here more than animals, it is the witchcraft that people remain scared of. They may do anything to anyone for their pleasure.'

Agastya had heard about this earlier from Joshi also and now Joshi was in a dominating position because his view was supported by someone who was from these places only.

'Are there any here?' asked Agastya.

'There are lots of them in this area. They are mostly women in almost every village, amongst men they are witchcraft doctors, ojhas. Men aren't so troublesome in this respect. They work only when somebody approaches them or against their enemies. But the witchcraft women go on practising this for all kinds of petty reasons—like to please souls of their deceased's, to offer them some sacrifice, to cure some disease, or for fun, transforming some innocent into their some pet or to prove or reprove their magic mantras on full moon, new-moon nights, or during eclipses. In the absence of a person, also they may send their magical power on him or her. But that's rare. Generally they try on person in their direct eyesight at any time. But preferable days are as said right before, and mostly at twilight, noon, and midnight times. Sometimes they just do it in competition with some other such one or to prove their strength over others or in the society, for recognition. Sometimes some of these also claim that they also know of the previous life of the people. And that they can tell it about.'

To change the topic, Agastya said, 'Maybe for scaring simple innocent locals.'

'Saab-ji, not for scaring locals. Of course, locals recognise and have regard for this knowledge and for people practising this. But many times they have killed also such ladies doubting them harming village people. It's this that they fear, locals. After all, they have to live in this very society. And for this they find their easy target in outsiders. And on learning and testing their magic, they try on their easy targets.'

'It's getting too scary. Let's change the topic.'

'Saab-ji, by closing our eyes, the trouble doesn't go away. Have to keep alert and ready to face for any eventuality.'

'That's right. But you are with us. I'm feeling quite safe under your guidance and care. And this is the most wonderful time I have ever had, never had such a nice trekking experience. But the clock is ticking fast, and I just hope that the time may come to a halt,' expressed Agastya

Priya was happy that they felt alike but thought it best not to say anything. The two had created a microcosm in this macrocosm, lost in each other in this wilderness. After about two hours' trekking, they came out of the last stretch of the forest and saw Village Haati amidst forests surrounded by small agricultural fields. At the outset, Haati looked like a comparatively bigger village. Jumman knew this place inside out. From the eastern side, a fair-weather road was also connecting; they could see some trucks and jeeps driving past that road. Very soon they were near the village and got on to the road towards the village. The village was fenced with thorny bushes and trees. In the night, after taking all cattle heads, goats, sheep, and people inside the village, they blocked the entry points also with wood and bamboo gates. This helped them keep their domestic animals and people safe from unexpected dangers at night.

Priya was happy that she would be meeting her friend. Agastya was happy for Priya. We are always happier in the happiness of our dear ones. In fact, that's where real happiness lies. Priya had been to Devika's house earlier also, so she did not find it difficult to lead the group to her house. It was a well-built house, made of mud, baked bricks, tiles, wood, and tin shades. On one side of the main entrance was the sitting room. The sitting-room door was open, and she could see someone lying there who looked like Devika but someone very skinny and had no charm on the face. She got closer to the room; it was surely Devika. Priya knew she was Devika but didn't want to believe it so.

Devika gave a blank look to Priya and asked, 'Who comes here?' Without responding, Priya got closer and, sitting on the bed close to her, hugged her. She was so excited to see Devika, had never felt such immense joy and sorrow at the same time. On the very instant moment of the hug, without Priya telling her, Devika could know who it was. 'I was sure you would came 'ere to give me a surprise. Isn't it?' Devika was so right. Even though they tried very hard, both of them couldn't help the tears rolling down their cheeks. Priya was there only to meet her. Both hugged each other tightly, and everyone from the family gathered around to meet Priya and the other fellows.

After meeting her friend, Priya came to Aunt, Devika's mom, paid her regards, and conveyed her parents' regards' feelings. She too was overwhelmed by this unexpected happy surprise. Devika's mother was a complete institution of hospitality. She made sure everyone was sitting comfortably and then offered them water.

Suddenly everyone witnessed a spurt of energy in Devika; she got up and sat on the couch near her bed. 'Priya, I can't believe it is you sitting so close to me. I'm so happy, can't tell you. You know what I mean? It's like I haven't felt so much at comfort in such a long time.'

Devika's mother left the room to allow the friends to talk while she would be preparing lunch.

'So how did you get here?' asked Devika.

'Actually Agastya has recently come to our village to do some research project. He shared his planning of coming here. I told him that I would also like to come along, as I wanted to meet you. He was so nice that he spoke to my dad and convinced him that everything's going to be just fine. So I'm here,' Priya responded.

That's when Devika's younger sister came in with tea and snacks. Priya introduced Agastya, Joshi, and Jumman. 'After tea, these two would go for the village survey, and we'll have all the time to ourselves. I guess they would get free by lunchtime.'

Priya reached for her bag and took out the packet and handed it over to Devika. 'Here, this is for you. Daddy and Mummy sent this for you.'

'I appreciate this gesture, but, sweetheart, it wasn't really needed. They have sent my most valuable gift to me—my sister.' She opened the packet and tears started flowing down her cheeks; something unexplainable crossed her mind.

Just then, Devika's mom walked in. 'So how are your parents and everyone else in the family?'

'Everyone is doing fine, Aunt. How have you all been?'

'We all are fine, just that Devika seems to have gone into some kind of depression. But today with your coming, she is doing just fine, as if she was always like this. Your coming has been more than anything else. You have rejuvenated Devika, given a new life to her and all of us. We have forgotten all those worries when we saw her laughing, sitting, and talking like this. You have given us a new hope for her life. We are hopeful that she will start a new life henceforth.'

'Of course, Aunt, Devika is a brave girl, she will come out just fine. Right, Devika?'

Devika agreed. 'I now feel I need to move on in life. What are you doing nowadays, Priya?'

'I'm in my final year of MSc Botany from Lucknow University, had come Dera in festival holidays, and it just so happened that I could come here too and meet my sister.'

In the meantime, Devika's father also came in. Devika's mom turned towards him and said, 'See, Priya Beti from Dera has come to meet us and has given us the most precious gift of our life. Just seeing her, in no time, Devika is totally changed and full of energy today.'

'So nice of you, Priya Beti, to have taken out time to meet us. We are so pleased,' said Surya Dev, father of Devika.

Agastya and the two Js, after the introduction with the family members and having had their refreshment and rest, left the place—Agastya and Joshi for the village survey and Jumman for visiting some relation in that very village.

There in the village, Agastya and Joshi first of all went to the village head, Jagat Bahadur. Agastya, with due regard, introduced himself and Joshi and briefed him about his purpose of going there and conveyed the regards of Seth Jagannath. It was so important for him to get his support. He also told him, 'Priya is also here and should visit you sometime later in the day. She is right now busy with her friend Devika.'

Jagat Bahadur assured Agastya of all possible help in conducting the village survey. Agastya tried to get information about the village from Jagat Bahadur so that he could begin with the survey. This village was a cluster of about eighty households, amongst which 50 per cent of the residents came from outside and settled down here, making this place their temporary base. Most of the people here were engaged in trade across the border. Some dealt in pastoral products; some acted as service providers.

Agastya moved on to the village to conduct the survey. He met the village people and got all the required information about them. This village was also quite along the same lines as Dera; people were sceptical about sharing information. In fact, they didn't know the details with such finality. It's okay not to know exact things. Life here ran on approximation; it might not be too bad. Agastya completed the work and got back to Devika's house. By then Devika and Priya had moved to Devika's room inside; Devika was a little tired and wanted to take it easy. Her room was quite a personal space for Devika, but still she was okay with having Agastya with them in the room. Priya understood that there was something magical there, as Devika was very particular about allowing people whom she had met only for the first time inside her room. And this was the first time Devika had seen or heard about Agastya. Agastya glanced around the room and was feeling that it was done in quite good taste. Just then his eyes fell on a picture, a photo same as the one they had seen in the guest house. Agastya and Priya looked at each other as if they just knew what they were thinking and what to do next. They didn't know how, but at least the 'what' part of the question was solved. But this wasn't the right time to focus on it.

DEVIKA GETS WELL

Seeing the photograph, Agastya looked towards Devika and just passed a remark in humour. 'Hmm . . . so this is the guy you have been thinking about?'

Devika nodded and looked down. Agastya immediately said, 'I don't know how you would react to it, but this morning as I got up, I had this feeling that someone talked to me. Now it does make sense. I don't remember exactly, but the voice said, "See, you are going to see Devika, pat her with love, and assure her I have not betrayed her faith and love," and here I perform my duty.'

Everyone was spellbound for a while—Priya felt it wasn't something like Agastya speaking, and Devika felt it was Rohan speaking; it was more like his style. Or maybe it was her imagination; as much as she would have wanted it otherwise, Agastya was simply sharing a dream. Though a dream, Devika's faith and love in Rohan was renewed. Till now she was fighting an internal battle; it looked as if she was betrayed, but she didn't want to believe it. She felt a spurt of energy and confidence in her, as if someone had returned her spirits. 'I guess I will start life all over again. I will be a different Devika now.'

Everyone said in chorus, 'Good, Devika. All the best.'

'We are with you. We'll do everything possible for you and try to find out Rohan too. We'll remain in constant touch with you,' said Agastya.

'Thanks, you have given me a new life.' Devika burst out crying; for once she wanted to cry her heart out.

All she knew was, she hadn't been so happy for some time now. She had been brooding for what wasn't around, but it was only today she realised what she had, and she would rather be happy about it. What's gone is gone, not that she wouldn't feel the pain anymore. But like they said, the show must go on.

Agastya had always felt this project was something more than just a project; some of that type was beginning to take shape. 'This is so strange. As soon as I got into this land, I knew it wasn't like a routine project for my course. I knew there would be something more to it but didn't know what. There is a new purpose and direction.'

'Maybe we can find Rohan one day,' Joshi said.

'May your words come true. Hope he is hale and hearty wherever he is,' said Devika.

'This day has given us all a new meaning, let's celebrate. Happiness begets happiness,' replied Agastya.

'Yeah, that's very true,' said Devika.

'But now it's time for us to go. You should come over to Dera sometime next week. I would leave by the end of next week. So we have about a week or so to celebrate,' said Agastya.

At first Devika felt that she might not be able to walk to Dera, but then she questioned herself, *Why not? This is for Rohan.* She must go there and celebrate the beginning of this endeavour. Devika was full of life and purpose. 'How about thirteenth of October? I will come to Priya, and from there we all'll come to guest house. Should this be an overnight thing?'

'Quite so,' added Priya.

'Fine. I wouldn't like to return same day in the dark,' said Devika.

'Of course, there's no question about that. I'm surprised such a thought even crossed your mind. Done, we are going to have a big evening on the thirteenth,' said Agastya.

'Her energy is also scaring me. I hope she'll be able to walk all that way to Dera. Else we can plan it when you come next for your project. Would you finish your project just with this visit?' Priya asked Agastya.

'No, no. This is just the initial visit. I'll have to come again with my teammates to extend the study. You are right, Priya. I think we should do it later, when Devika is completely fit,' said Agastya.

'Oh! Come on. Don't be a spoilsport. It's decided we are doing it on the thirteenth. Nothing seems a hurdle when you have a purpose in mind, and coupled with fun, there is no better way,' said Devika.

BACK TO DERA

It was time for them to get back to their guest house. In the meantime, before leaving, Priya made it a point to see Uncle Jagat Bahadur, who was also so happy to see her. And then on her return from Jagat Bahadur's place, they bid good-bye to one another and started walking towards their village. Devika's younger brother and sister also joined to say bye. Priya and Agastya thanked their hosts for everything and asked all of them to come to Dera. Jumman picked up all their packs, refilled the water pot, and started on their return journey. They especially thanked Devika's mom for her hospitality and asked her to convey their regards to Uncle, who had gone again. Devika's brother and sister came up to the village entry gate to see them off. Waving finally there, they took off on their journey back home. Agastya and Priya were pretty happy with this visit.

'So how did it feel to meet Devika after such a long time?'

'Oh, it was simply great and I'm glad it did well to her. Somewhere I was pretty scared that I didn't know what shape I'll meet her. Thank God it all went fine. I'm so happy. But, Agastya, I couldn't understand one thing . . .'

'What's that bothering you? Don't know if would be able to solve your problem. But surely it must be some worth-sharing genuine thing which's bothering a head like yours. You can share it with me.'

'Devika 'ad been seriously sick and bedridden for last almost two years—a so sociable, healthy, beautiful girl was turned into skeleton and 'as suffered so much. All costly treatments and medicines have gone ineffective. How could it be that she miraculously got perfectly all right within no time? Became absolutely normal in a sudden stroke of time? Touch wood, her healthy state goes on life long.'

'Surely your inquisitiveness's very genuine. But be sure it wasn't a miracle. It's as scientific as a mathematical calculation. I'm not a medico doc nor any expert but, being a psycho graduate, can certainly give rational, acceptable explanation to it.

'What's that? Would you tell me?'

'Dear, she wasn't physically sick. Her physical sickness was due to her mental stress and botheration. And as regards mind, there are mainly two types of mental disorders. One's physical, and the other one psyche. Physical disorders like accidental or other injuries, less or more blood circulation to mind, ruptures, tumours, less oxygen reaching to mind, causing unconsciousness or coma, and likewise several more. Prolonged diseases, improper diet, malnutrition, impure water, hormones in the body may be other reasons. These can only be treated and cured by medico docs with medicines, surgery, or by their other devices.

'Also in this category are problems caused by nervous system and decaying of brain cells, mainly causing problems like Parkinson's—muscular rigidity, trembling—and Alzheimer's, gradual mental deterioration, memory loss. These may be due to reasons related to heredity, aging, or other physical conditions. But by dietary control, physical, mental exercises, deep breathing—deep breathing improves capacity of lungs and provide more oxygen to mind and other body parts, making them healthier—and willpower. These problems, if not cured completely, the process of these can certainly be much slowed and delayed.*

'The other type of mental problems are psychological, caused by mainly physical or lifestyle reasons but affecting only thinking and behaviour of a person. These further may cause physical, body-related problems also and are at times more dangerous than the first one because the patient may cause harm to self as well as to others due to abnormal behaviour and no control on mind and body. In these psyche problems, till such time the person affected has control over mind and body, can listen, and understand, he or she, by coming to logical understanding, in a fraction of a second

---

* These are proven realities. Keeping fit without medication by keeping busy, balanced diet, simple exercises, deep breathing, and set routine. But not discarding proper medical care and treatment. That is the biggest contribution of scientific progress to mankind.

may come to normalcy. Likewise, within no time, on very first of emotional shock may pass into abnormality also. Once the person loses control over mind, psychiatrists and mental homes are required. Otherwise, the person himself can cure these completely by logical thinking and willpower within no time. Because realisation of right or wrong's not a time-taking process. Improvement in body conditions may be gradual, which is seen over a period of time. But mind becomes okay right at the same time of realisation.

'Your friend Devika was the victim of emotional shock and isolation in this remote place. The moment she got the logical reason and purpose to live a normal active life like she has lived before, she got fine. And this she got from your love and affection. Her mind got fully occupied by you, your love, and her past association with you. No place was left in her mind for all else. Once the problem got out of mind, it got out. Can't enter in again without reason. Passing into mental shocks, or recovery from these, are mostly abrupt.'

'Good scientific knowledge. Thanks. But how many would know all this?'

'Must know about ourselves. Our mind has tremendous power. Except accidents and viral, most of our physical, body-related and mental problems are due to our thinking so and can be delayed, if not cured. Doctors must be consulted. But even doctors can't treat us without using our willpower. However big doctor there may be, first wins our confidence and faith and then treats. Even in doctor's treatment, our willpower works and make us recover. Our negative thoughts produce toxins in our body, making us sick, whereas positive thinking's the cure for all problems—may be physical, mental, or social adjustments. I think this is enough for now. For more, may go for detailed study. For now enjoy jungle tracking. God knows when we can be here again.'

'Quite useful information given. And you said you aren't expert. So sound knowledge you have. You are psycho or sociologist?'

'Maybe none of the two. It's too early to say. I'm only preparing for master's in socio. Even yours must be the same case.'

'Maybe you are right. I'll see after final result. For the present, how was your survey work today? Did you get the desired information?'

'Yeah, it was quite good. In fact, with the help of the village head, it got done pretty fast. That's how I could come and spend some time with you all.'

'Yeah, yeah, I could see that, how happy you were to meet Devika.'

'Oh! Feeling jealous. Great. I was just getting friendly because she's your friend. But jokes apart, I'm really surprised to know about Rohan. I have a feeling he's somewhere in this jungle, God knows in what shape. It's been quite some time, and you can't win over time. Time is usually the deciding factors in our lives.'

And now they had decided to find out more about Rohan. Maybe Joshi could help them in this endeavour; he'd have more information and understanding of this area. In their journey from here, everything was uncertain. Right now they were only speculating and imagining things but hoped they would be doing something good and useful. Both Priya and Agastya felt somewhere deep inside them that this day would have a deep impact on their lives; how, why, and where were still unknown. At the same time, Priya was more concerned about the actions of Devika.

Devika and her family were overjoyed with the sudden change in Devika, her getting back into spirit. Over the years, what so costly treatment couldn't do, a simple loving and caring visit had done. They assured her of their full support in arranging a happy get-together treat in Dera Chowk, in the guest house on 13 October; they all started planning and making necessary arrangements. They decided to send some workers and a cook for assessing requirements and to make the arrangements beforehand so that they wouldn't waste time that day. Surya Dev went to Dera to invite Jagannath, Birang Bahadur Singh, and other friends with their families. Surya Dev shared the miraculous recovery of Devika on the visit of Priya. In a joyous mood, Surya thanked Jagan family for thinking of them and sending Priya to see Devika and expressed, 'Dear, we had no idea your meeting her could be so effective for her. Else we would have invited you much earlier.'

'Uncle, things occurs at their pre-destined time. Waqt se pahle, aur bhagya se zyada, kabhi kisi ko kuch nahin milta.

I think this is just apt for everything, good and bad, in life. We just have to carry on with our work—the situations, time, and our luck make our efforts creditable or otherwise.'

'You are right, daughter. But in my long life, I have also seen that God chooses his choicest of people to fulfil his motives. For us, you were God's messenger. May God bless you! See you, and now I would like to make a move, have to go to some other places and also to see arrangements for tomorrow. You are all invited, please keep the day free. It will be great to spend some relaxed time with you all. We will begin with the worship of goddess during these Navratris, followed by lunch, and then just chat through the night,' said Surya Dev.

'We will surely join you, but why don't you tell us some work? You just cater to the guests, you can leave the rest to us. Don't bother, it'll be done. We'll have good time.'

'Surely this's your work, all being done by you only. Right now, I will make a move.'

Finishing his work in the village, he went to the guest house. People were working in the lawn and kitchen and cleaning up the rooms. Someone was setting up the dais for the puja and for people to sit around it. It looked like a preparation for a big wedding, and why not? After all, it was as auspicious as a big occasion. In all these arrangements, Agastya picked up Rohan's papers and kept it in his bag lest they were seen by anyone else. Up till now, there was no evidence that this man and Devika's man were the same, so why get some fizzy emotions in the air? He wanted to work on this information all by himself and on some success would talk about it. As the day was turning into dusk, workers retired for the day and Agastya got busy interpreting the data and information gathered from Village Haati and giving it a useful form to be able to write a brief report. Joshi also left for his place to take some work.

Next morning, Priya told her mother that she had some work with Agastya so she was going to the guest house. Her mom was a little suspicious of her body language; she knew there was a motive in her going there. But she didn't find it right to question her at this point in time. After informing her mom, she almost ran to the guest house. And both of them examined the papers, hunting for some more links into Rohan's mystery. Maybe Joshi could find something more important in these papers. They started looking for more relevant papers in other rooms. Agastya had instructed all the workers to just pile up in one corner the papers they saw in any room. At least this much was clear: that he came to this guest house about two years back or so. Both of them sat in the veranda, thinking how to proceed further.

'Do you think we should take help of police to find out something about Rohan and also to know what action his college or family have taken?' Priya asked.

'Priya, we'll talk about all this tomorrow. Right now, I'm in a very good mood and want to enjoy your company. Let's not think of any other thing,' Agastya responded. 'So what do you want to talk about?'

'Hmmm . . .'

'What about us?' Agastya continued.

'You see, we came from different paths, and we'll move on to our different journeys in a few days. But I have a feeling that this is not it. I don't know if you have ever met some people, had been good friends with them, and suddenly lost touch with them?' Priya said.

'Hmm. Yeah, it 'as happened. Several such cases. But it's okay.'

'But were you like good friends with them?'

'Yeah, I spent some good time with them. But everyone has different journeys to take. So they moved on to their jobs, and I to mine.'

'Do you feel bad about it, that they aren't around with you, or do you feel they cheated you?'

'Nah, nah, nothing of that sort. I don't think anyone ever decided to move away without a reason. It just so happened. It'll be great to meet them again.'

'And you must have met some people whose loss you haven't been able to come to terms with yet,' Priya went on.

'Yeah. Surely. Sometimes I feel there is still so much to talk about with them, but then, you know, what the point is if not possible? So I'm just letting it go,' Agastya responded.

'But have you ever wondered why for some people we struggle so hard to meet and for some we just don't bother as much?'

'Hmm . . . Do you have an answer?'

'I don't know if it's an answer. But I have figured out a reason why we encounter such feelings. I feel we all have a purpose in each other's life. When that purpose is over, people move away. But when they still have some purpose in our lives or we have a purpose in their lives, it keeps bothering us. And we live together till we've common purposes. Every relationship has a closure. Destiny controls these.'

'Hmm . . . I guess that makes a lot of sense, but I haven't looked at it like that ever.'

'Yeah, and I have a very strong feeling that our purpose isn't over yet,' Priya remarked.

'What's our purpose?' Agastya asked.

'I don't know. Time will tell, if you allow and are ready to read the signs.'

'What signs?'

'I don't know too, but if you are connected with the nature, nature also connects with you. And we both are elements of nature. Aren't we connected to each other?'

Priya didn't say much after. She was just gazing into the sky.

'Come on, lady–turned-philosopher, let's prepare for the event,' Agastya said.

'Besides the event, also there are things. In the fine weather, just relax, us two,' Priya countered.

'Ma'am! Nothing's fine, only misunderstanding of thine. Come to senses, and see what's to be done,' said Agastya.

'What sort of man you are? Spoiled the mood,' she said. Reluctantly she got up to follow him.

They moved around the guest house to check what was to be done. As they checked every room, Devika and everyone else arrived at the guest house.

'Hey, everyone is here. It already looks so festive,' said Priya.

'Oh! Priya, I'm so happy to be out of the house after such a long time.'

'We all too are so happy that you are feeling so good.'

'So I am, dear. But right now, I want to rest awhile. I have been walking for quite some time, didn't like pony ride.'

'Sure, sure,' said Priya. 'Move to any of the rooms and have rest. In fact, I would suggest that let's have breakfast, and then everyone can take rest for a while.'

Everyone had a quick breakfast and moved to the other rooms for a short rest to regain energy for the rest of the activities. Rooms were set for use of both the families. Mattresses were spread on the floor, with bed sheets properly laid out. Just then the priest also came in. Agastya offered to take care of the priest while everyone else rested awhile. Devika wanted to settle in a different room so that they could discuss Rohan's papers. Agastya, thinking it could be risky for her, tried to avoid it and told her to see these after the event. But she insisted and told him that now she was a different girl, strong enough to come across any type of information. With no choice left, Priya took her to the other room and called for Agastya to join them. Devika had a glance at those papers, and tears rolled down her cheek. Everyone at once knew that these belonged to Devika's Rohan. They tried to console her.

'No need to worry. Now we are all together. We will surely do something about it.'

PUJA AND DOUBTFUL SADHUS

They all returned to the common room. Soon everything was ready. The priest called everybody to join so that the puja could be started. Surya Dev, Jagannath, Birang Bahadur Singh, with their wives, occupied their seats in the front row, close to the priest. Devika was called to perform the starting rituals. The ceremony went on for a couple of hours; there was silence everywhere. After puja, Devika was asked to give away offerings of eatables (prasad) to all present there. As she was distributing prasad, a team of saintly-looking persons, sadhus, passed by the front of the guest house. They stopped as they saw that some worship was going on and there was good offering of eatables. They moved closer to the entrance of the guest house and bowed to the holy seat of the deity, and Devika distributed prasad to each one of them. Joshi was witnessing every single movement; being a man of the jungles, he was extra careful about any abnormal action and gesture. All these sadhus except one blessed her. One of them simply took the prasad and passed on without looking up at the giver or uttering any word of good wish; he looked weak and tired, somewhat the sick type. Joshi got suspicious at his action. As the puja and lunch got over, most people went back to their houses except the close family members of Devika and Priya, who had planned to spend the night together at the guest house, as it had got late in the day. The priests were also requested to stay back for some more time so that appropriate offerings could be made to them. As Devika's and Priya's moms got together to make arrangements for the priests, Surya Dev asked the high priest to predict something regarding her future.

The priest took Devika's right hand in his hands and examined her palm, observed her face closely, and said, 'The worst in her life is already over. I think today she would have met a long-lost dear one, someone who would turn to be an important part of her life. Now onward he'll very well be in her life.'

Devika thought to herself that the priest could be referring to Rohan's papers.

To Priya he said, 'You have gone through some experience which'll change your years to come. It could be a person or just a discussion with someone. You'll go far ahead in life, but always be careful to identify what's important in life and what's not.'

Priya was quite dazzled, especially with the last words of the priest. She didn't know what it meant or even where it was directed. But she was determined to move on as of now and not waste time trying to figure out what it could mean. Time would tell; after all, it was about the future.

Que sera sera—whatever will be will be. The future was not ours to see.

The girls joined their moms in the arrangements. Agastya moved on to check if everything was in place for dinner. Everyone was tired, so they decided to have tea together first. Devika, Priya, Agastya, and Joshi were sitting separately in the open. Joshi pointed out to Agastya that amongst the saintly-looking men that came by, when Devika was distributing prasad, one of them was looking weak and tired. The girls looked at each other; they hadn't noticed anything like that, but why was Joshi pointing it out?

'You are right, Joshi. Even I saw that. But how is it relevant?' said Agastya.

'If you noticed, they were talking as they approached our guest house. The group leader said, "I think we have taken the wrong way. Since it has got late now, let's take a shortcut. How's our goat?" And the goat bleated. As they left from this place, I saw them almost running into the dense forest, and, saab-ji, that's a rarely used trail. It's a very dangerous one, and from there, you can simply get into the jungles of Nepal in less than an hour.'

'So?'

'I think that male called a goat was brainwashed Rohan.' said Joshi.

'What? What are you talking about? How can that be possible?' asked Agastya.

'Devika, did you feel anything different when you were giving away the prasad to the saints?' asked Joshi.

Devika was a little puzzled. She didn't know if she felt anything different, and if at all she did, was that of some significance?

'Explain to me the whole thing. What are you trying to say?' asked Agastya.

'Saab-ji, I told you about the black-magic thing. You may not believe me, but for Rohan and Devika's sake, let's try and explore on the lines I'm thinking.'

They decided to go Joshi's way; after all, he was the man of the jungles. Agastya proposed that while Joshi got information from the jungle, he would go to Rohan's house and try and get some information from them as to what they did after he was known to be missing.

'Devika, you needn't worry, you live your way. We would jointly put effort in this. Its success would definitely be our biggest gain. But the failure shouldn't be taken to heart. It would be just our bad luck.'

'Surely I wish he comes back hale and hearty. It's a matter of faith. It's not about getting together with him. It's more about my sincerity for him—in love and in belief itself. I'm thinking of pursuing something different in life now rather than just being here in the village.'

In the other room, the families were discussing the same problem. It was quite some time that they were all sitting away. Surya Dev and Jagannath asked them to join so that further activities could be started. Agastya came forward and discussed Joshi's observation and their plan as of now with Surya Dev. He mainly wanted to take an opinion from someone educated and worldly wise. Surya Dev did not completely deny Joshi's story. 'I have never witnessed anything of this sort, but I have certainly heard many such stories. But the point is, even if it's not true, we can give it a try. We may find some other information which could prove to be relevant for Rohan's search. I'm not sure if we can find Rohan after such a long time. What I'm looking at is that at least Devika'll have a purpose, and maybe it'll get her closure with respect to this episode in her life. But what you and I'll tell Priya, that she shouldn't divert herself from her studies and look into this. However, if needed, she can help us. Everything has a time and place in life. This's the time for studies for her. Now here is this get-together, a rare time. Come and join us to make this time a real memorable and enjoyable one.'

Jagannath and Agastya joined the group. Dinner was laid out, and everyone enjoyed a relaxed meal after a long day's work and fun. After dinner, Jagannath invited Surya Dev's family to his place for a night's stay. But Surya Dev begged to be excused, saying, 'Thanks for inviting. Don't bother about our stay. This's wonderful place, we will be all very comfortable here. It's a matter of just a few hours, we would like to start from here back to our place early morning.'

Devika requested for Priya to stay back so that they could have some more time together. Leaving Priya behind, Jagannath's family also left for home. Surya Dev and his wife went into one room, and the children decided to chat for some more there. Priya asked Devika, 'So how are you feeling now? You must be tired. Let's go and sleep.'

'Of course. I didn't ask you to stay back just for sleeping. We would spend some more time together. So now, tell me, when are we meeting again? You and Agastya would be out for your studies. You two may still be meeting, but I would be left alone in this remoteness of the forest, thinking of impossibilities, with no realities coming my way. Hope this does not become my last meeting with you,' said Devika.

'Why are you thinking so? In fact, I don't know when and how we'll be able to meet. But this's my place. I'll be often coming here to meet my parents. I would definitely meet you. I don't know about Agastya. But don't lose heart, don't think like that even before they take shape in your mind. Keep your morale high as it was on the day of our first meeting. I'll also try and write to you,' Priya said.

Everyone got a little sombre. Breaking the silence, Agastya pointed to Devika and said, 'Devika, why don't you also plan to rejoin your studies? Any course of your choice, at a convenient place. You are already a graduate, you can go for studies in management or law or any other such course or master's degree in some subject of your choice. I'm sure this would help you in materialising your dreams, and you would find it easy to contact us also.'

'I'm also thinking on the same lines for last two days. I had a talk with my father also. I'm going to try to pursue study of law in Gonda,' Devika said.

Priya was posing thoughtfully and remained sitting quietly. As Devika hadn't yet fully recovered and had been busy the whole day, they all decided to take some rest, as she would have to leave also early in the morning.

Agastya, turning towards Priya, said, 'Village survey I've done and still have three days at my disposal. I'm thinking we go to Kuhar Lake day after tomorrow. Tomorrow is Dushahra, you may also like to spend time with your family, and I'm also interested in the festival of this place. Would be a rare thing for me, a student of sociology. What do you say?'

'As it suits you.'

Agastya wondered why he got such a cold reaction from Priya, but probably this wasn't the right time to have a one-to-one with Priya to identify. Agastya bid good night to everyone and came to his mattress and slipped in quietly, as everyone else in the room was asleep. He could still hear the two friends talking, but he soon passed into his world of dreams. It seemed like he had hardly slept when he heard Surya Dev involved in early chores. He hurriedly got up and said, 'Good morning, Uncle. I'll ask Joshi to prepare tea for all.'

'Thank you, it's not needed. Otherwise, these workers could have done this. We in the villages are mostly not in the habit of taking bed tea. In any case, in about two hours we would be at home. It's going to be enjoyable walk in wee hours of the day.'

Devika's mother thanked Agastya for the good time they had with him and said, 'Do come to our place before you leave for your home, and stay overnight with us there.' She pointed to a big packet and said, 'I'm leaving some snacks for you, hope you will like it.'

'Aunt, I would have loved to be there but won't be able to make it this time. Would be leaving in two days and have to visit a few places more. But surely next time. My study of this area isn't over yet. I'll come again.'

She spoke to Priya and thanked her for everything good that happened to them because of her. She gave her a warm hug and invited her to visit them again. By now, Devika had also come out of the guest house and bid good-bye to everyone. Both Priya and Agastya remained standing at the entrance of the guest house, seeing them off. There was still time for dawn to fully break. Agastya went back to his mattress and lay there for some more rest. He was tired, hadn't really slept through the night.

Priya got a little worried. 'What happened to you? Why are you sleeping now?'

'Oh, nothing really. I just wanted to lie down for a while. Or rather, I will drop you to your place and then come back and rest.'

'Nah, it's okay. You may take rest. I'll just get fresh and then we can go home.'

Agastya was way too tired to respond to Priya. As she moved out in the lawn, he slept off. Priya went into the kitchen, made tea for herself, and sat down in her chair in the lawn, gazing towards the forest. Only she knew what she was thinking about.

'Wah, you are sitting here! I am sorry. I don't know when I slept off again. I will just change and come, will escort you to your home.'

He changed his outfit and came out, and they started walking towards her place. They were both quiet, not talking much to each other. Priya was waiting to spend some more time with Agastya, but now when she got that time, it was like she didn't know what to say. It seemed as if they were in a blissful conversation; they were in perfect communion without having said anything to each other. Sometimes words aren't enough to say, and sometimes you don't need them at all. Priya looked at Agastya and thanked him.

'Thanking for what? I think you have made a difference in my life. There's much change.'

'What are you going to do about Rohan?'

'I don't have a very clear idea. Let's talk tomorrow when we go to the lake. It's festival time today, you also spend some time with your family. I want to concentrate on my survey a bit and see how far I have reached.'

SEARCH FOR ROHAN

Leaving Priya at her place, on coming back, Agastya asked Joshi, 'Yesterday you were talking about the male goat that accompanied the sadhus. I don't believe in this belief system completely. But for Rohan's sake, I want to go with you on this. Please help me understand how we can proceed.'

'Thank you, saab-ji. I appreciate your openness. I understand that you won't believe in anything like this, you may not have encountered any such story in the cities. Here, in this region along the Himalayas up to north-east, changing people into animals is a common practice of witchcraft. Basically, it is believed that they change people into animals so that others don't get to know. Most often, people who visit such places from outside fall prey. Natives of this area are well aware, so they are careful of such movements of the witchcraft people. Sometimes they kidnap distant males for sacrificing, but mostly children. There have been some lucky fellows who have been able to escape or could be rescued from the clutches of these cruel persons with the help of some of their kind-hearted neighbours. I'm not sure, but this time two cases have come to my knowledge.

It's believed that these people possess some magical powers and tricks. And not only these witchcraft people but also some gangs of criminals kidnap people to use them for their work. We can explore them further to get more information. Sometimes they totally change the person into pet animal. And sometimes brainwash the person in such a way that the victim consider himself or herself as that animal who obeying them behaves like that. One case, I identified a male goat in this village Dera in the house of a lady. I doubt that one because of its some abnormal behaviour, it was kind of weird. I didn't point it out to you at that time because your survey could get interrupted. I'm sure the lady got suspicious, that was all the more reason, and I kept quiet at that time. This was on the day you conducted your survey in this village. As I told you, the second case was when Devika was distributing the prasad. To my mind those weren't sadhus but some gang people disguised as sadhus, might have gone towards the Himalayas. I'm told they have their bases there. Though that area is close to this guest house, but it actually lies in the Nepal territory and we can't go there. Most often it is believed that one would be able to ward off such troubles if wearing something red or maybe a red tilak, spot on forehead, and fast on Tuesdays. Tuesday is a day for Lord Hanuman. He is considered to be the god who keeps troubles away from one's life. It is not funny, you know there's such power in our Indian system of putting a red tilak on someone who is going for some important work. People here believe if you start any work with a good omen and sacred ritual, it is likely to turn out all odds into fine. And a tilak, a red robe, all of these things are just a way to make sure you start with a positive mind.'

'Hmm . . . that's nice. I think to begin with, I would carry the ID card with me to get about ten copies of his photograph and would leave all his papers here only. You please ensure that these papers left here aren't lost or destroyed by any visitor to the guest house.'

'You don't have to bother about all that. I'll take full care. This I'll do. But assure nothing like involving police would be done from there by you or any other one. If anything would be done, it would be from here only, from within this jungle,' said Joshi firmly.

DUSHAHRA CELEBRATION

'Right, Joshi, getting late, have to go to Lala-ji's house to join Dushahra puja. Go and get ready soon.' Within minutes both were ready and started off for Lala-ji's house. There, things were already set for puja. He found things were not different as from his own house. The same way with cow dung symbolic of Rama was made on the cleaned and washed floor. Puja was performed as per Hindu rituals, and sweets offered to the Lord were distributed among all. Then all had lunch and parted to meet again after a short while at the grounds near the village god for community Dushahra celebration.

This surely must be a colourful cultural event, as it is the local tribal way of celebration. Whereas in the house of Lala-ji, it was performed the way the people celebrated in their houses in the outer plains. Lala-ji himself had migrated from the area of Agastya—Gonda. Here, Agastya felt worth visiting the event for personal experience as well as for the project. In the afternoon, singing religious songs, people were gathering in their colourful costumes, with produce from their fields or from their handicrafts as offerings. A sacred fire was prepared, where worship was performed and offerings were placed around. There was some unpleasant part also for Agastya, and that was that people brought a healthy male buffalo for sacrifice, and several others also brought their goats and chicks for offering. But he could not speak a word. That could be risky. He kept himself a mum onlooker. He took some photographs and simply sat and watched. Placing their offerings near the sacred fire, they were singing and dancing around it. After some rounds around the fire, they brought the *bhainsa* (male buffalo) close to the fire, and with this there came a man especially prepared for the purpose of sacrificing the *bhainsa*, for over a month giving him VIP treatment. He was to behead the animal in one blow of his very special big dagger. If he couldn't do so, he would be meted out a very bad treatment and dishonour, nor would that half-neck-cut animal be sacrificed. The next year would be a year of god's curse for the community. And if successfully sacrificed in one blow, a turban would be tied on his head, and he would be given hero-like treatment. *Bhainsa* was brought; the sacrificer was also standing close to the animal's neck with dagger in his hand and anger on his face. Worship was started. After worship a little water was sprinkled on the animal. No vibration on the skin of the animal. All turned sad. The goddess hadn't accepted the animal. Again worship. Again sprinkling of water. This time it shivered,-vibrated a little. All rejoiced at the shivering of the poor creature. More water was sprinkled on the animal and also on the sacrificer. Vermilion was put on the forehead of the animal. A flower garland was put around its horns. And then came the final moment. The priest signalled to the man to be ready with his dagger. People started yelling, 'Jai Bhawani, Jai Bhawani!' The man also shouted, 'Jai Bhawani!', and going high up on his toes, he charged with his dagger with his full might. He separated the head of the creature from its body in one blow. This cheered everyone but for some, like Priya and Agastya. The sacrificer was picked up by the people. A new turban was tied on his head, and gifts were given to him. And with this started the sacrifices of others brought there—animals and birds. Similarly goats and chicks were chopped off from neck in one blow only. A few drops of blood were put in the fire, and the rest was kept for the family as god's blessing. During this part, Agastya and Priya were sitting, covering their eyes with their hands. (Here it may be mentioned that as of now, in community celebrations, the animals' and birds' sacrifices are replaced by symbolic figures made from vegetables and fruits, like pumpkins, mangoes, guavas, pears, bananas, oranges, etc. These are given the animals' shapes by inserting small twigs and wooden sticks in these and sacrificed by cutting and offering these in the fire.) After these, some cultural items and some competitions of the young ones, like wrestling, sword fighting, and bamboo (*lathee*) skill shows were put up. At the end came the interesting part of it. And it was for matchmaking of the prospective, eligible young boys and girls for marriages. In one place puffed rice and sweets mix were kept. Girls used to come, take some mix of puffed rice and sweets, and give it to the boy of her choice. The boy willing to marry that girl used to happily accept and eat it up. And the unwilling one used to see around and, bowing to her, used to offer this in the sacred fire. It went on for quite some time. At times, Priya teased Agastya, saying,

'See, she'll be all right for you. Go and sit down among those boys, good opportunity or may remain alone for life.' Agastya also passed humorous remarks. This way they both enjoyed the event. The programme ended with the prayer by all with the priest and blessings of the priest.

After the celebration, they dispersed. Jagannath left for his house, and Agastya with Joshi for the guest house and had a rest after almost two days' continuous running about. By evening, Agastya got up and asked Joshi, 'It's going to be evening, come, we would sit out in the open. It looks gorgeous, very soothing and beautiful, especially at the dusk and dawn times.'

'Provided you aren't caught by some trouble here and you have power on your back. Dushahra, Diwali—new and full-moon-nights—are dangerous too. Considering these powerful zodiac times, witchcraft people try their tricks on people,' said Joshi abruptly, and he moved out with one chair. Agastya also picked up one chair, following behind him. Joshi said, 'One is enough, I would sit on the ground, truly in the lap of nature.' And Agastya left his. They got out and sat—Agastya in a chair and Joshi in front of him on the grassy ground.

Joshi asked, 'Tomorrow morning going to Kuhar Lake?'

'Yes, after this visit, I want to have at least one complete day at my disposal, to have full rest. I will 'ave to wind up my all work done here and plan for return journey,' Agastya answered.

'That's right, it should be,' said Joshi. He further asked, 'Would be leaving at what time?'

'Say by six thirty or seven in the morning so that we come back by two thirty or three,' said Agastya.

'That should be fine, going would be comfortable and easily would be back by three,' Joshi said.

'Can we take bath and do swimming there?'

'Shouldn't take chance. Soon after monsoons the water, its swampy soil with lot of weeds and other rainy-season growth harbouring lot of snakes, and insects all around on banks and in shallow water, may be risky.'

'Thanks, what all we would be needing to carry?'

'You would know better. I think the same as for your village survey, some snacks, packed lunch, your pen, paper, camera, water bottle, jungle cap, stick, etc.'

'Then come early tomorrow and prepare breakfast and packed lunch,' said Agastya.

They were talking on all these topics when their attention was distracted by the arrival of Jagannath, his wife, and his daughter Priya.

Joshi went inside to get chairs. Agastya stood up, leaving his chair for Mrs Jagannath, saying, 'Come on, Aunt, have your seat.' She took her seat. Joshi brought out two more chairs in one round and offered these to Jagannath and Priya. By then Agastya had also brought one out for himself and got seated.

'As yet we haven't taken tea, now we would. Joshi-ji, please get us good hot tea,' said Agastya, and Joshi left for the kitchen.

'So have seen Dushahra celebrations of this place. This is in very simple way. Earlier there used to be many sacrifices etc., lot many buffalos, goats, sheep, birds used to be virtually cut by throat and sacrificed. In the past, there have been instances of even human-sacrifices in remote by witchcrafters. But now don't hear such things. Though some people still do sacrifices of even human beings, but much more silently in far remote places. That's punishable, serious crime,' said Jagannath. He further asked, 'What else was going on?'

'Nothing, we were just planning for going to Kuhar Lake tomorrow morning,' said Agastya.

'That's fine, would be good change,' said Jagannath. He further said, 'Tomorrow, Priya may not be able to go. However, if you want any help or someone to go with you, I can arrange. In the morning Priya has some prearranged engagement, and evening would be inconvenient due to hot sultry afternoon of October.'

'Thanks, Uncle, it is all right, Joshi's company would be enough. There's not much of work,' said Agastya. By now Joshi had come with a table, placed it centrally close to them, and went back to get tea. He came with tea and snacks left behind by Mrs Surya Dev. Priya helped in serving.

All four were talking about yesterday's celebration and enjoying tea. Agastya asked Priya, 'As to when would you be going to Lucknow?'

'There's still one week, would be going on 23 October by afternoon 2.30 train from Balrampur,' said Priya.

'Don't feel like leaving her away, but can't help. After all, she 'as to go for her studies. Same is the case with other children. I and Lala-ji miss them very much. But I can't leave him also alone here,' said Mrs Jagannath.

'All this, we are doing for children only,' said Jagannath. 'When are you going?' asked Jagannath, looking at Agastya.

'I would be leaving in the morning of 16 October, day after tomorrow,' replied Agastya.

'Sixteenth's final?' asked Jagannath. He further said, 'I'll see if some people would be going on the day. You can reach Balrampur same day.'

'Would one person be enough as escort-cum-guide, or more persons required for safety reasons?' asked Agastya.

'One would be enough. Better you hire a pony up to Kishan Nagar Ghat. Go riding pony. It will take you faster without tiredness. Start by six. Easily you would reach Balrampur by afternoon,' said Jagannath.

'Please help me in making this arrangement. I know nothing about this place. At the most, can ask Joshi to find out pony and escort,' said Agastya.

'Surely. Don't worry, no need bothering Joshi for this thing. We keep on going, sometime we are required to go in emergencies all of a sudden. We do such arrangements. We will discuss this on sixteenth,' said Jagannath. He further said, 'You do your work, make your other preparations, leaving journey part to me.'

'Talking about your going's appearing disturbing and unpleasant to us. We know this's not your place, you came here for your short-time work. Even then we would miss you, whenever would be coming this side and on all important occasions,' said Mrs Jagannath with a heavy heart.

'This happy time's turning into serious atmosphere. This parting is becoming difficult for me also. Let us change the topic and turn it into happy evening with a song by Priya,' said Agastya.

'Song and me, forget it,' Priya responded.

'Right, I'll sing, you dance on it,' Agastya said.

'I'm feeling like laughing, without sing song, what a situation you created, love song and dancing. Two lovers now would be running around in the fields and forest. Would be good film shoot, Producer Saab,' joked Priya.

'Okay, now other thing, I kept on fearing during whole Dushahra celebration, thinking lest the puffed rice and sweet mix come in front of me anytime,' Agastya said.

'So you were mentally ready. I'm sorry. I stopped her. She was coming to you with the offer. She was suitable for you. Rich, having two sheep, so healthy, and you know, you yourself have seen all that! I thought you two were made for each other. Don't feel sorry, chances are still there,' Priya said.

'But you didn't come.'

'You hadn't even had your face washed.'

'If you say yes, I would go for even taking bath.'

'Now keep on taking bath for whole year, and come here on next Dushahra.'

'If after a year, why not today? It is Dushahra Day today.'

'Now I would have to go and search for her, maybe she must have gone with someone else.'

'You made my fiancée go away from me, now as a punishment, you should make that offer to me.'

'Go and keep on seeing sweet dreams of your choice. And again topic change.'

'Okay, as you wish and order. Now you float a topic,' Agastya said.

'Now the topic is, you and Joshi both get ready. Come with us to our place for dinner. And you would be there for happy pastime till late in the night.'

'We are sitting here, why we don't continue here only? Joshi-ji'll prepare simple dinner,' Agastya offered.

'This I leave to Papa. His decision will be final,' Priya said.

'It's a festival day, someone may drop at our place. Today lunch was just a hurried affair, we couldn't sit together due to village festival. At noon Joshi could not come to us. And you are here only for two days. For breakfast and lunch, we won't insist, but dinner, you both would be taking with us for rest of all the days,' Jagannath said.

'You made me speechless, what can I say now? And Priya has already said your words would be final. No choice but to accept the good offer. But no formality, it should be very simple and normal, everyday type,' Agastya said.

'Yeah. We take simple vegetarian food only. We aren't going to do anything special. This's just to sit together. Who knows when we meet again?' Jagannath replied.

'We would meet very often, Uncle, here and also at Balrampur,' said Agastya

'Lala-ji, now let's move. It is now quite some time past, have to prepare dinner also,' said Mrs Jagannath to her husband.

'Yeah, we make a move. Why don't you also come along?' asked Jagannath.

'We would shortly be following you,' replied Agastya.

'Come to your convenience. We are going, come, Priya,' said Jagannath.

She got up to go. The three walked on, with Jagannath saying, 'Would be waiting for you, right, Joshi-ji?'

'Right, sir,' repeated Joshi.

After they left, Joshi murmured, 'Would sit there till late night.'

'No, tomorrow early morning we would have to go. In fact, they invited so forcefully, couldn't say no,' said Agastya.

'Here also don't have much to do, would get confined in right from so early evening till morning, unlike cities, where life hardly stops even in late night,' Joshi said. 'Perhaps this makes difference between people of villages and cities, they become so rich and advanced because they work more for longer hours, even in night. Whereas here, in village, people do set work of their cattle, fields, and forests. Nights are long dead period here. Even days in off-agricultural seasons, during heavy rains and also in dry. They measure time only

in four—morning, before noon, after noon, and evening—
or only in two, day and night. In cities, people read time up
to minutes and seconds also and even beyond up to fraction
of a second.'

'That's true, man has become machine there. They
work and work, without time for themselves,' said Agastya.

'Why do they work so much? Taxing their body and
mind. All the time they remain under stress and strain,
losing charm of life,' asked Joshi, citing the lifestyle of rural
life. 'They see the charm in earning and spending. They
keep on trying to earn more and more. Their needs, desires,
and requirements are so many. Here in villages, they can
live even if they don't have anything. They don't have to pay
for their stay, electricity, water, for going from their place of
stay to place of their work. Their clothing and food are also
very simple, mostly produced here from naturally produced
local items. Even for medical needs, depending either on
witchcraft doctors (ojha) or they use the roots, barks, leaves,
fruits, and flowers of plants and trees etc. They don't feel
sorry even if the life of someone goes away for such practices.
Then they simply take it as the wish of God. Whereas in
the cities, even for breathing pure air, people have to travel
long distance for parks and open spaces by spending money.'

'Here also, people whose requirements are more
like that of Seth-ji or Surya Dev, etc., they got even their
children educated outside, and they are spending money,
they are having good earning here,' replied Agastya.

'But one thing's there, saab, these people here in forests aren't lesser happy. I think happiness and peace aren't related to income and expenditure, big, big houses, social status, plenty of haves, but these are related to the state of mind and feeling of contentment,' said Joshi.

'Yeah, you are right, happiness and peace of mind can't be attained by running after the worldly affairs. For these, one has to sit and look within him- or herself instead of joining the race for worldly passions, which detract from the path of peace and sublime knowledge,' said Agastya. He further said, 'Joshi, you look to be knowledgeable, have become philosopher.'

'No, saab-ji. I'm a poor man, don't know philosophy and philosophers. But in a way everyone has his or her philosophy to his or her levels of thoughts. These are everyone's topics and concerns,' said Joshi. He added further, 'One thing more, saab-ji. You'll have to accept, the tribal way of life, closeness to nature's the best way to health and's the requirement of this time. It is a different thing that people in big cities and metros can't go for it.'

'Yes, it is true. God has made human beings, not the sick. Sickness's the creation of human beings by wrongdoings and unnatural ways of life. Here, people live in direct contact of nature. They breathe pure air, drink pure water, work and live in the sun, in pure earth and mud, eat chemicals-free food grains, vegetables, and fruits and also fresh meat or fish. There is no pollution and use of chemicals, not even in the forms of allopathic medicines and drugs, which people don't take here. Whereas in cities people don't know for what they have paid for and what are they getting and eating. Even mothers feeding their babies on health-hazardous chemically prepared milk, thinking it as pure milk. Milk, butter, vegetables, food grains, fruits, salad items are all chemically prepared and washed in chemicals. People are unknowingly and in the state of their helplessness taking in poisons in the form of adulterated eatables, drinking polluted arsenic water unfit even for watering plants, and taking bath. Breathing air highly polluted, expelled through exhaust from factories and automobiles. Even earth is polluted by dumps of factory wastes. Urban centres have been coming up as tumours on the earthly body. These forest habitats of the tribes are the lungs of the habitat earth. And see the pantheists, the man is deforesting and thinning out their very forests, inviting danger to his own existence by creating ecological imbalances,' said Agastya. After a pause he further said, 'I think this is enough for now. It is going to be dark. What time would like to go, there also we would be talking only.'

'Right, saab-ji, let's take chairs in,' Joshi said.

They took the chairs and other things inside the guest house, and both started getting ready to go. In fifteen minutes, both joined to go, and in the next ten minutes, they were at Jagannath's residence. Jagannath welcomed them. All got seated in the sitting room. Off and on Priya had been coming there, serving water, tea, snacks, and also joining them in gossip. All had dinner together. And after dinner, Agastya and Joshi reached back the guest house.

VISIT TO KUHAR LAKE

Next day, on 14 October early morning, they both got ready and started for Kuhar Lake in the north-east of the Dera guest house, some ten to twelve miles. On the way, Agastya was feeling quite lonely though Joshi was walking on his side. But today, he was also not much talkative and active like other days. Joshi has noticed some behavioural change in him so tried to keep him active and alert.

After about two-and-a-half hours, they reached village Kuhar. Outside the village there was a big banyan tree and a water point close by. They had rest there for some time and then took a round of the village. Since this village was not in his survey schedule, he decided to take some photographs and collected some data and then reached the lake, which was about 200 yards from the village. It was a beautiful artificial multipurpose lake. A high arc-shaped, strong earthen dam had been constructed across a wide dry bed of a rainy-season-flowing rivulet flowing downward between two distant spurs of the Shivalik Range. The length of the dam was about two miles. The top of it was about two yards wide of levelled mud road.

The structure had its maximum height of about twenty-five feet. In the rivulet bed, the lowest surface base level across the section, rising on both sides gradually and finally merging with its zero heights on the two spurs. It had two well-constructed outlets, with water-releasing levers and gates to release lake water into two canals from these headwaters of the two canals for irrigation in dry season in the adjacent agricultural fields, downward the dam. Besides irrigation, the dam had controlled soil erosion, the increased level of ground sub-surface water giving life to trees and plants all around. The lake had become a fish culture centre for the local people here. Tourists also came to the place for picnics, sightseeing, and change. As it was a permanent source of water, even in dry season, a lot of many wildlife could also be seen in the adjoining forests. When they reached in hot-sun time, at a far-off distance some elephants were enjoying their bath and water games in the lake. These animals didn't come to the village side of the dam because there were no forests but open agricultural fields, there was human population in the village, and the deepest water in the lake was on this side. In the same way, tourists and visitors didn't go to the other forest and spur sides of the lake, which were risky places.

Agastya was happy to see the beautiful blended spot, a mixture of human efforts and nature, where man had converted natural resources into such a useful thing which had changed the geography, economy, and life of the people in the area. He was astonished to see the beauty of the place and thought why a place like this was not popular. There could have been a great influx of visitors to this place. This might have been due to the remoteness of the place and the lack of transportation link. Though there is fair weather all season, a twenty-mile mud cartroad from this place to the railway-station on the narrow-gauge Gonda-Gorakhpur loop railway line.

This was some of the information Agastya could gather about the dam to quench his curiosity. But there was much more going through his mind. They both reached the closest village-side canal headwater point, a cement, concrete, and brickwork construction, with steps descending into the lake water on the two sides of the water-releasing control lever up to five yards each side. They, Agastya and Joshi, were the only two there trying to enjoy in every possible way. The village population was very little. They rarely came to the lake. They mainly remained busy in their fields or forests. Since there was no marketing of fish, they caught fish for their home consumption only. In the lake, on the water line were lying some half-floating long cylindrical dugout-boat-type tree trunks. About half the length of these were out of the water on dry land, keeping these from floating away. These were skilfully used by local villagers for fishing. The lake was full of water to its capacity, as it was soon after rains and the water was not used for irrigation also by then.

Both Agastya and Joshi settled down on the flat top road of dyke close to the headwaters under the shade of a tree. Agastya was lost in the beauty of the lake, with reflections of marginal weeds, trees, and distant mountains in the background on the water. White and red lilies mixed with weeds all around in the shallow marginal water, with fat ducklings actively busy in eating aquatic insects and small fish. High in the clean, fast after-monsoon blue sky were floating away patches of light-grey and contrasting white clouds and birds. Rolling waves on the surface of the lake were fast approaching and breaking on the water line bank. Water was still not crystal clear. Complete silt of this rainwater was not yet settled down. But it was in no way less in beauty, looking gorgeous, heart throbbing, and full-moon-like beautiful. He could well imagine its different looks in different seasons and in different times—two months from now, the water would turn into a clear greenish blue, but then it would go its low bottom with marshes, thick weeds, and aquatic vegetation all around. It had its own beauty and significance in every season and time of the year.

He was missing Priya or Nidhi at this time in his heart. But he had hardly thought of them when his attention was diverted by the call of Joshi for breakfast and tea. He turned a little to his left-towards Joshi when he was surprised to see some female with umbrella on with her escort, coming towards them on the left-side dyke. Agastya said to Joshi, 'Joshi, see, some lady is coming. Here also some sophisticated people like her?'

Surprisingly Joshi saw that side and murmured, 'Saab-ji, to me she appears not coming to our side but to us only. She appears to be Devika.'

'Devika! Here?' In the meantime she got still closer.

'Yes, saab-ji. Very sure now. She's Devika.'

Now Priya or Nidhi got out of the mind of Agastya, and he started thinking of Devika and asked Joshi, 'Now wait, let her come close, then only open breakfast items.'

Soon the female figure was distinct and in recognisable distance. And both were surprised to see she was Devika. In exclamation Agastya, standing and walking slowly some steps towards her, smilingly, said aloud, 'Devika, here! What a big surprise, difficult to believe.' Taking Devika's hand in his, Agastya came back to his place with Devika. And the two took their seats on the grassy land. Her escort kept his load near her and sat down a little way.

Joshi offered her a glass of water. She took it and sat quietly for some time. Then she said, 'There is nothing surprising. This is only about six, six-and-a-half miles from my village. The way is shady, and coming here isn't much exertive. In your yesterday's programme you had said that you would be coming here. So I thought, let me also come here, would meet you for one more time. Can't say when we meet again. I asked Mom and Dad. Dad arranged it.'

'You didn't get tired?' asked Agastya.

'No, no. I'm not so weak now. This is not so much,' replied Devika.

'Even then you took up this adventure. Great,' said Joshi.

She was cheerful. Her face had turned red and sweaty.

'Now relax and have breakfast. We too haven't taken as yet,' said Agastya. Then turning to Joshi, he said, 'Bring whatever you have.'

'Mom has also given something. Let me see it.' She pulled her bag closer, took out water bottle and eatables, and passed these on to Joshi, saying, 'Joshi, please take this also and serve mixing the two, mine one is totally veg preparations, we knew you are vegies.' She said again, 'Joshi Brother, please give just five minutes. I want a short rest.' And she went close to the tree. Keeping her bag under her head, she lay down straight with closed eyes.

Joshi also repacked the items put aside. 'It's all fine, we will take a bit later'.

Agastya was happy and looked more active. He also lay down, his body stretched on the ground, saying, 'What else we've to do here, except to relax and enjoy?'

After a short time she got up, feeling relaxed; she reached the water on steps, washed her feet, hand, and face, got blotted with towel, and coming to Joshi, said, 'I would join you in serving breakfast.' The others too washed hands and got ready. Joshi and Devika prepared plates and served Agastya, her escort, and herself; two, three services were done.

'It had become good picnic, food preparations are very good and fresh, and Devika has made it lively,' said Agastya.

'It suddenly came to my mind to come and be in your company at least for one more day. Almost for pretty two years I remained lifeless, in distress. You and Priya came that day to us. That has given me new life. Now want to live it to full zest,' said Devika. After taking their breakfast, they enjoyed the sips of hot and refreshing tea prepared by Joshi there.

Now they were feeling fresh and energetic. The escort who had come with Devika asked for permission to go to the side village, where he had some known ones. Devika permitted him two or three hours. Now they three were left there. Agastya had taken out his camera. Joshi remained sitting on the headwater under the shade. Agastya snapped him with the lake in the background. He snapped Devika also in several poses and locations. They sang several songs turn by turn and duets, ran short distances, catching each other on the dykes, walked through side forests, went to the other headwaters too hand in hand, and sat there, putting their legs in the water. She also sat close to Agastya, keeping her legs in the water and body close to him, resting her head in the lap of Agastya for several minutes. Agastya soothed her head, shoulders, and upper back; she got totally relaxed and refreshed thoroughly. For Agastya it was unbelievable that an extrovert girl like her could have remained confined to her house for so long. They both spent several hours together and returned to their place under the tree, where Joshi was sitting. They had chit-chat and finally settled for lunch and enjoyed it. For the helper, they left some food in the packet. It was still enough for three, four persons.

After lunch they relaxed in the shade for some time, as it was now hot in the sun. 'It is enough of rest, let us get up now and 'ave some fun near water. And then time to move back home,' said Devika.

All three got up. While walking to the headwater steps, slowly Devika said, 'Agastya, to me it appears as if God 'as sent you here for me.'

'No, nothing like that, don't flatter me. I came here for my work. It is my good luck, unbelievably, I got good friends like you and Priya, with their open-hearted, broadminded parents who didn't hesitate in sending their young daughters with an unknown young boy. Who would believe all this in our conservative, old-traditional society?' said Agastya.

'Their daughter's life is gifted to them by you,' said Devika.

Talking thus, they reached the steps. There they sat on the lowest step, with their feet in water. Devika had brought with her small-sized pieces of sweet cakes in sufficient quantity. And here she started throwing, one, one, two, two pieces in the water, for which big, big fish gathered there, grabbing these pieces. It was a treat to the eyes and big fun seeing these fish quarrelling among themselves and jumping even out of the water and made the water full of life. Some tortoises also gathered there. These animals became so familiar and friendly that these started coming so close to Devika and even tried to snatch the eatable from her hands. All enjoyed this so much that they forgot even to notice the fast passing of time. Seeing this fun for quite some time,

Devika decided to put an end to it and threw all the pieces in one go and waved her empty hands to them. Shortly all the animals disappeared and the water became quite still as before.

Then suddenly another fun had struck in the mind of Agastya. He said to Joshi, 'Joshi, let us try rowing one of these so-called dugout boat.'

'Do you know how to swim?' asked Devika.

'Somewhat, to fight out in emergency,' replied Agastya. 'But we would not take you on the dugout in the water.'

'Saab, may not be possible to row these. Unlike boats, these are not flat-bottomed but completely round, roller-type straight trunks of trees. We won't be able to keep balance on these. Would suddenly roll, and we would be drowning in this deep water with our slightest misbalance. Sitting in it is also not possible, you can only stand or sit with legs in water. With much practice these people use these,' said Joshi.

'Doesn't matter, let's try.' said Agastya

And at a short distance from their place of sitting, Agastya, pushing a dugout down in the water, called Joshi to join. Both got on in the hollow part of it. Joshi couldn't stand, and bent forward on his hands, resting on the dugout. In the meantime, the dugout had gone to a distance due to the push. Agastya tried to manage at his end with a bamboo he got from there inside the dugout and pushed the dugout further into deep water. But on the very first push with the bamboo, both of them got misbalanced and the dugout rolled, with water filling it, and sank, and the two, Agastya and Joshi, were in deep water, fighting for breath, beating the water with their hands and legs with shoes and all their clothes on. Due to the sudden fall and water entering their nose and ears, they got nervous also. However, they managed to come swimming towards land. But nearing land they found another dangerous belt of thick monsoon and aquatic growth of long weeds and forest bushes, floating vegetation, mosses, etc., full of snakes, crabs, and frogs. With mud and swamp below, this was the shallow water flooding the low-forest growth due to the high rise of monsoon water in the lake. Here, swimming or walking were both difficult. But fighting for life—with shoes, clothes, and body full of mud, leeches, and other small-sized aquatic insects—they managed to come ashore.

Devika, running on the dyke, was shouting for help, and her escort also reached there by then and ran to the spot and with his stick beat out the way to scare away the snakes etc. Both of them felt completely nervous, tired, and exhausted in this hardly five-minute hive drama. They coughed and sneezed for another two, three minutes. They had no extra clothes and remained in the same wet dress and lay down on the flat top of the dyke for some time, got up, and seeing Devika equally nervous, burst into laughter. Devika showed a little anger and expressed, 'Now feeling like laughing? Making my breathing stopped. I was thinking, "Why have I come?" But good I'm here, could see it, and could do my bit, I could."*

'Sorry. You got so upset because of me. I took this risky step in spite of your warning. But, dear, should do some adventurous on outing. It 'as become memorable for whole life. Could also see how caring and bold you are, in so short a time how fast you arranged help,' said Agastya.

In the meantime two or three men from side-by fields also reached the spot and helped console them. Also, they, getting into deep water, could bring the sunk dugout out to the bank, as it was a valuable thing for the villagers. Agastya offered them some rupees, but they did not accept, saying, 'The water god saved your lives, that's more than any money to us. We're happy. But be careful for future.' They further said, 'Babu, this's not your work. Only they whose work it is can use these. For others, it's self-invited trouble.'

'All's well that ends well,' said Agastya and took out the thermos with hot tea, which refreshed them. Now they were as happy as before. It was now parting time; each one had been casting an eye sometimes on the lake and sometimes on the parting friends. Heart and head had become heavy.

---

* In real life, this has happened with the author and his room-mate, Ranjit Singh (one year junior, master's course). It was a cold February afternoon. Scared of the boatmen and Professor I/c Camp, we both in fully drenched heavy clothing ran into the deep forest till fall of dark and our clothes got some dried up.

Joshi and Devika's help packed up their loads. Agastya and Joshi had become a little dry.

'It has become an ever-remembering eventful day of my life,' said Devika. She further said, addressing Agastya, 'Why don't you stay for some more days? There must be time for college to reopen.'

'It won't be possible. I've some important work which has to be finished before holidays're over. In fact, who knew I'll get friends like you here? And this place would become so attractive for whole life,' said Agastya.

'But now that it had become, stay here,' she said.

'Wish I could. I would've been very happy.'

'What would you be doing tomorrow?'

'Preparation for closing up and going the next-day morning.'

'Why don't you come to us?'

'I would've surely come but on last day can't make it. On my earliest opportunity, I would surely make it to meet you.' He wrote and passed an address chit to Devika. 'You keep my address and communicate to tie up such programmes of visit.' And he took her address too.

'We can't stay here today for any more time. Have to go through dense dark forest. So take on your way. See you,' said Devika. Turning to her escort, she said, 'Come on, pick up your all things to move.'

'Ladies first. You move on your happy return, bye,' said Agastya.

'Bye.' She started going on with her escort, looking back again and again. She had walked some distance, but Agastya and Joshi remained standing. Devika saw them back, still standing. She spoke aloud, 'You too go. Your way is much longer. Reach your place before darkness. Please go on or I'll have to go much faster to disappear fast from your sight.'

'Go by your ease or comfortable speed. We are going,' said Agastya and started moving by giving her high hand wave.

Now both were going on their ways, recalling the moments of the whole day passed together. Devika was satisfied, thinking what a good change and god-given opportunity she had created and availed and enjoyed to the full, which Priya had missed. Agastya took it a successful visit which would give better shape and perfection to his project. It could have been simply a visit to a beautiful place to him without Priya, but Devika had made up the deficiency of the absence of Priya in an equally enjoyable way. This would further add to the betterment of Devika, he thought.

Devika had been covering her distance, just thinking about her new and revived friendship. There was none to share ideas with her. From time to time she asked her escort to stop for rest to take some eatables or to control speed. Contrary to her, Agastya and Joshi could go faster. At times, Joshi had been advising to Agastya to stay for rest; for comforting him, he would offer snacks to eat. He had been doing all possible to make the journey timely and comfortable. At the same time, he had been sharing thoughts with him, such as saying, 'Saab-ji, Devika has made our programme of today very lively and joyful. We two would have been just sitting dull and mum, passing the day. But then she appeared at the scene, making the day lively with grace and decency.'

'Yes, you are very right, she had made it a memorable day. Here, I have least hesitation in saying the success of my whole programme and this friendship with Priya and Devika is but for one single person, and that is you, Joshi-ji. Without you I couldn't have even stayed in the guest house, what to say of the rest of the work,' said Agastya.

'Leave it, saab-ji, what else I had to do? I got your good company and had these enjoyable days. Who comes here except some of our departmental officers or some businessmen etc.? With them, life remains formal routine type, not active, lively, and thoughtful as in being with you. All these days, I had been feeling as part of your programmes. I had been feeling as if my work is being done. Or I'm meeting my friends, doing something for my own people. In fact, I would miss you in the time to come. Alone, I would be sitting in the campus or in my hutment, waiting for someone to come my side,' said Joshi. He further said, 'Saab, may I ask something, if you don't mind?'

'Yah, yah, why hesitating? Ask,' said Agastya.

'These two are very nice, beautiful girls. I don't know with what mind they have come so close to you. You met them two, three times, and so much friendship is developed. In your college and place, you had been living for so long, there you must have developed friendship and love with several other boys and girls. You would be having your family commitments also, in cases like marriages etc. How far these two girls may depend on you for a love of that type?' asked Joshi.

'Joshi, I have developed friendship with them without consideration of whether she is a girl or boy. A friend is a friend, like a leader is a leader, an officer is an officer, a teacher is a teacher. I have made this thing very clear to Priya. And for Devika, I think she won't try that type of love for anyone. She is trying to forget her past, and in the form of friendship, she is in the process of developing her social circle for a new beginning. I'm helping her on these lines. She is intelligent and bold, a girl of good character and now of high ambitions also. May God help her.'

In between Joshi interrupted, 'God has helped her. He can take a person to light and great heights from any darkness and depths.'

'That's true. Priya is also beautiful, bold, intelligent, and sociable, mod girl. I have made everything clear to her. And she has accepted that. Marriage shouldn't be a condition in friendship of opposite sexes, unless it comes through by sheer good luck. This much of understanding and distance should always be kept in mind. A friendship with a selfish motive of anyone is not a friendship. It can't go a long way,' said Agastya.

'That's good. I was thinking, the innocent girls may not find them astray on the path of love,' said Joshi.

'Love of friendship is different from love for lovemaking or attraction for some personality traits of opposite sex. In love of friendship, there is pure love of doing all best possible for well-being and safety of a friend, be same or opposite sex. There is always a sense of humanity and duty as towards a family member, understanding the need of the friend. It starts in the soil of humanity. Whereas in love for lovemaking or sex attraction, it originates in the garden of Adam and Eve. Here, there is hesitation at every step, in every mind, due to physical and social bindings, restriction, taboos, and other such things. This, if not tackled intelligently and timely, may result into many social, physical, and mental-health problems and complexes in the personality of an individual. And if tackled intelligently, it can produce geniuses of all times, like Kalidas, Surdas, Tulsidas, Meera, Shakespeare, Farhaad, etc., are some to be named,' said Agastya

'Good saab-ji, you have explained a deep thoughtful aspect of human life. I am sure these girls must be going on for humanistic friendly love. Without any shock in their life.'

'Joshi, you are a real good friend. Even in their absence, you are thinking about their well-being and good future.

This is the foremost best quality of a human being. Those who always keep others' well-being in their foresight and work for the sufferings of others are the true human beings and true worshipers of him.'

'You are right, saab-ji, your words are true, but you are speaking too high about me, what good I can do to others,' said Joshi.

'Your simple and timely help to a needy may save one's life or can make a big difference for good. Like it had been a little before. Hadn't you been there, I alone might be resting underwater forever. Your company gave me confidence, and I could struggle to safety. Devika did her bit, however small it was, just away outside. But very relevant, some people could come and helped us in their way. One must not hesitate in doing a good deed, thinking it an insignificant in the eyes of people in terms of money and its magnitude. But must do it to our capacity and forget about it. Shouldn't talk about what we have done for anyone. Every good deed is reward in itself, a services to God.'

'You are ethically very sound for your age, have been talking saintly. In these good talks we have covered our distance without knowing how long we travelled. See, our place has come. And clothes've also gone dry.'

'Nothing wisely, these are the talks of common men. People, especially young, fall prey ignorantly by very small beginnings, like jokes, humour, and sometimes ego satisfaction, to big complications, even life-taking problems. If one becomes a little aware, cautious, and self-controlled at the very start or later at any stage, can save herself or himself of big mental and physical tortures. A self-controlled one always remains mentally sound. And mentally sound a self-controlled one.'

'True, saab-ji, wish people especially of sensitive age remain safe of such their future-affecting problems.'

BACK TO PAVILION

They reached the guest house, and reaching there, Joshi said, 'Saab, stay out, I am getting a chair. Relax and take tea, then do any other thing'. Joshi opened the guest house, got in, unloaded his load, and brought two chairs out. Agastya got seated in one. Joshi went back to get tea.

Agastya was sitting alone, with his back to the village, and facing the forests. Joshi was inside, brewing tea. Agastya could hear the feeble sound of distant footsteps. He turned back and saw Jagannath and Priya coming towards him. He got up and, from the main door only, called Joshi and informed him of their coming, to bring two more cups of tea and walked towards them to receive them. Joshi also had come out with two more chairs and joined to receive them. After they all settled down, Joshi went in to fetch tea.

'It appears you have just arrived' Jagannath said.

'Yah, I didn't even have in, was sitting out to rest and relax,' Agastya responded.

'Hope we haven't disturbed you?' Priya said.

128

'No, no, not at all, we'll feel more relaxed in your company and light gossips,' said Agastya.

'Visited Kuhar Lake?' Jagannath asked.

'Yah, it is beautiful place, a good picnic spot for change with family and friends,' Agastya answered.

'How was the journey?' asked Jagannath.

'Had no problem, it's not much of distance, must be about ten miles. It was good on narrow path through thick jungle, shady forests. We had enough snacks, went on eating and chatting. In this short time, I have become used to this sort of tracking.' Addressing Priya, he said, 'You have missed it. And we missed you throughout the day.'

In the meantime, Joshi had come with tea and served it to all. Taking a cup for himself, he got seated on the grassy surface close to them. Taking a sip in jolly mood, Joshi spoke, 'Oh, it was so nice a day today, though Saab could have got us drowned in the lake. God saved us.'

'Is it? Lake is to its full depth, in its width and wilderness at this time. How it happened?' asked Jagannath.

'Saab insisted on rowing a local-type dugout boat. We both got on it, and he pushed it, to row in the deep water. But being it roller-type round and not flat, it rolled, we falling in deep water with our shoes and all clothes on. We are still in wet clothes, these are not fully dried up. Saab got water in his ears and nose. But we were hardly twelve, fifteen feet away from shore and managed to come out of deep water and marginal weeds full of snakes and other aquatic life and mud. Lying there, he kept on coughing and sneezing for quite some time. Then got normal and took it in a sporting manner. It was good we both knew somewhat of swimming.'

'And you say it good, enjoyable tour? Thank God it couldn't be tragic. Otherwise, like Rohan's, in some other corner of this guest house your project papers could be lying.' Priya said, stopping her tea.

'It couldn't have been a tragic one. We knew a little of how to swim. We are resident of eastern UP, the land of rivers and floods in monsoon, not from desert or high Himalayas. And now have come back safe. It 'as become an adventure, memorable for life. So no need to be panicky. Enjoy the tea and the evening. Don't remain afraid of a thing which has not happened and is not likely to reoccur,' said Agastya.

'It takes sacrifice of at least one life every year. There said to be some lake goddess who takes it from the people taking bath, swimming, or boating in the lake. Sometime even from the steps people slip in deep water, and mostly swimmers get drowned, non-swimmers keep away safe. Local people would wait any such occurrence, and only after that they would enter in water for fishing. If there is no such incident with some person and fishing time's passing, they would have some puja [worship] and animal sacrifice, or from wheat flour they make human idol and sacrifice it. I am a fool, haven't told you all this before. I must have precautioned you. My fault,' said Priya.

'Don't feel guilty, sitting out here, that too when nothing has happened. And you haven't done anything. Tenderness of heart, ladies' characteristic,' Agastya said.

'That's what's troubling me, that I didn't do anything. And kept you ignorant. Ignorant fall prey easily and mostly. Thank God you are safe,' Priya said.

'Now stop thinking all this. I wouldn't have even talked about. Do you think I would tell all this in my family on my return?' said Agastya. He further said, 'Tomorrow I would get up leisurely and wouldn't have any outing programme. Would prepare for going back and would remain in holiday mood.'

'Now what is your programme for today? Would you be able to come for dinner? Or we send it here through someone, for your convenience?' Jagannath asked.

'Don't take all that trouble. We would take it here,' Agastya replied.

'No, Joshi must also be tired, dinner would not be prepared here. It would be from our place. It is your choice, you would take it at our place or in the guest house,' Jagannath said.

'If it is so, we would come to your place. We aren't so tired,' Agastya said.

'That's good, would be waiting for you there, now we must make a move,' Jagannath said.

'Why in so much hurry? Feel easy and comfortable, go after some time. Let us have good pastime here in this open cool evening,' Agastya offered.

'Would be going and telling Priya's mom to cook dinner a bit early,' Jagannath said.

'Then surely I won't let you go, let her do her normal usual cooking. We will take that simple one only. We all will go together,' Agastya said.

'It will all be simple only. Now you also get fresh, take bath, and get ready for coming there. You had a whole day outing. Take some rest before coming and sitting there,' Jagannath said. 'Now let us move. Come on, Priya, let's go.'

Jagannath and Priya got up and started going. Agastya and Joshi also walked with them, Joshi holding the torchlight in his hand. Slowly, leisurely they walked to the village. A little short of the village, they stopped, and Agastya and Joshi sought to turn back. Jagannath and Priya were saying, 'Right then, see you.' They walked on to their home, and Agastya and Joshi returned to the guest house. Reaching the guest house, Agastya went in to get fresh and rest. And Joshi went to his place to get ready.

After about an hour, Agastya and Joshi met again to go to Jagannath's place, and they reached there and joined the family at dinner. After dinner, Priya's mom remained busy in the kitchen to wind up after dinner. And Jagannath, Priya, Agastya, and Joshi remained occupied in after-dinner leisure games, chit-chat, and sweet dishes. Mrs Jagannath also joined them for some time, and then Agastya asked for departure. Priya also asked her dad if she could go with them.

He said, 'If you so want. Okay, no problem.'

Agastya said immediately, 'It's okay, Uncle, why bother her?'

'It's all right if you don't want my company,' said Priya.

'Don't say like this. You are welcome.'

And Priya also joined them. All three left and reached the guest house.

After Priya left the house with Agastya, her mom asked Lala-jI, 'You just allowed young grown-up girl to go in the night?'

'She is intelligent grown-up. We must trust her. What difference it makes whether it's a day or a night? All the times she remains away from us. Why create doubt in her mind, putting restrictions?'

Reaching the guest house, Joshi left for his place, and these two got in the guest house, changed to their nightdresses, and got together in the same bed for the night. Before falling into sleep, they chatted for quite a long while.

'How was your day?' asked Agastya.

'It was all fine. In the afternoon, there was a function and puja in my friend's family. She has invited me days in advance. Otherwise, I would have surely accompanied you to the lake,' said Priya.

'Had you been there, it would have been really enjoyable. Devika had come there. We all would have enjoyed it. We enjoyed it otherwise also. But I and Devika too have been missing you all the time. She several times remembered you.'

'Really! She came there? This is a news to me. She has become so much strong and active.'

'Yah, she had come with an escort. She said she wanted to come out for a change and that she had taken a chance to come today with the hope that I would reach there, as we were talking the other day,' said Agastya.

Priya looked cheerfully excited on hearing about Devika's coming to the lake. But at the same time, she had become a bit thoughtful too. And for some time she remained lost in herself. She didn't even respond to Agastya's calling her. Agastya patted her right shoulder to bring her in active senses. Agastya asked, 'Hey, what happened? Where lost? Lost in Devika's coming there?'

'No, nothing, just in thoughts how enjoyable it could have been. Why didn't you postpone for one more day?'

'I had no time left with me. And I didn't know about programme. I planned thinking you must have already seen. I would just go to see it, since it is in my area of study. It has been good also. Otherwise, Devika's all efforts would have been waste, and whole day she would have been sitting there alone, cursing me after taking long on foot journey,' said Agastya.

'Have become so caring for Devika. What's matter? Hope everything is all right, my number is not cut.'

'How can your number be cut? Don't fear of your self-created, baseless fear.'

'Now would have to put in extra efforts to keep you pleased. And to remain in the front line of your girlfriends.'

'Sure, that's right. You must put in extra efforts, not to please me—I would always remain pleased with you even if you keep on fighting with me—but to keep the time happy and enjoyable.'

'Yes, boss, tell me what I'm required to do.'

'To my mind, nothing. Because your mere presence makes it cheerful for me.' He pulled her close, his arms clinging together.

'You said you would get up late in the morning, so we would remain like this whole night.'

'Not necessary, I can go to mattress.'

'Oh no, is my number cut if we have to remain in limits? We can remain by sleeping together also.'

'That's true. As you please. We can sleep together, here or on mattress.'

'It's okay here. We would be closer.'

In all such talks they slipped into sleep. Agastya got up early, finished daily chores, and started walking out in the open. Priya also got ready and had come out. Agastya asked, 'Now would like to go home or here only? Breakfast would be ready after Joshi comes. Tea I'll get you.'

'I'll prepare tea myself. You needn't worry,' said Priya, and she got in and, after few minutes, came out with a cup of tea in her hand. 'You, you won't take it?'

'No, thanks, you carry on.'

After tea, both were sitting out. Agastya had been thinking what all he had to do for the day and where he should start from. Hell of a business. So much to do. Had to prepare report for submission. This was what he came for. How would this friendship of this group continue? How and where would they be meeting? What would be its shape and activities? Would he be able to come again in the area, and what for? These were some of the questions coming to his mind. Whereas perhaps Priya was not bothering her head for any such thinking. She knew on her way to Lucknow or Gonda she would manage to meet Agastya, and to this area, she could come easily, as this was her own area.

The major turning point of her life, which may come now, would be her marriage, like for most of Indian girls. She might have left it to God and her parents. Maybe with this thing in mind, she had become so open, so close to him, and even her parents could give a loose rope, taking Agastya as a suitable prospective boy. Besides freedom to females with social restrictions and taboos on movements of girls, here, so much liberty was given to Priya and Devika. But due to good education, moral values, family impressions, there had not been any misuse of freedom by these youths. They had been maintaining their social dignity.

Agastya told her, 'Today you be my guest till evening. In the evening, we would go to your place, would ask Uncle what arrangement he has planned for me. Would confirm it. Would have dinner and would come back, making Uncle as custodian of my beloved thing I would be leaving behind here. As I would be going early morning tomorrow, you would be disturbed and left behind alone here. So tonight you stay at your place.'

'Wow, I'm happy. I'm your beloved thing. And you are leaving me here for some time. Keep on feeling happy and have your face wash. Dear, I'm not a thing to be left behind with someone. Moreover, I'm not going to stay here. A matter of a few days more, I would be away among my friends—boy friends—in big place, Lucknow. I would see if you come with marriage party with band and take away me with you, or you come as a guest to bless the couple—Priya and . . . someone, someone.'

'Speak good, good, and only good. Let someone else may not become true,' said Agastya

'What else, my going with someone else? Think deeply. I would not wait for long. Let my final-year studies be over. I would go for marriage soon with a boyfriend. I won't wait for long, I won't feel like living alone now. Don't ask your custodian for your thing if you are slow thinker.'

'Is your MSc your goal of life? Think of some bigger thing which would give you your identity. What's hurry for marriage?'

'Things don't think. You want your thing to remain booked for you. And then choose from amongst several things. I won't be going to worship and wait for my love with big projects. Soon prepare yourself as capable to win, or I would be going to select the best from the aspirants of me.'

'I know you would select the best one. "My best wishes." But I also know your selected best wouldn't be better than this rejected poor fellow.'

'Not rejected fellow at present. At this time, selection power is with you to select this poor thing for yourself. You have full marks in your hands. But if you don't exercise your power and don't select in time, things will change. And this poor creature would select, making you an object of selection—a thing.'

'I have already given full marks to you. Selected and reserved. What else you want me to do? You tell.'

'Confirmation of the parents and acceptance in their presence, ring, etc.'

'This will also be done. Let the time come. Let you and your parents think on these lines. Living without you would be difficult for me too. But can't help it. Other more important things are before us, like preparation for life has to be done, like education and settling down in life have to be first to be worthy enough and ask for your hand. Otherwise, you will cut my marks. What we have been doing is the children's game. But the life ahead is altogether a different thing. One must be capable of facing it and live it purposefully.'

'Right, dear, will wait and watch. It has gone quite long. Should get ready. By the way, what is the limit of your leisure? Can this day's work be stretched on another day to come?'

'No, all leisure for today only, tomorrow will be a fast-running day.'

'Okay. And now I think I must go home.'

'To your convenience. I get ready soon to escort you to your place. I would wait there for your getting ready,' said Agastya. Priya okayed it. Soon they were ready to move. Joshi also reached there.

'Joshi, you prepare your breakfast and have it. I am going with her.'

PRIYA DISCLOSES HER LOVE TO HER PARENTS

Both reached the village, the residence of Priya. Agastya sat down in the sitting room, and Priya got busy in her daily morning schedule and got ready. Jagannath also joined Agastya in the sitting room and spoke to Agastya, 'So visited your project area, now ready for return journey?'

'Yes, Uncle. Uncle, could you find out someone for going with me tomorrow?' Agastya asked. By then Priya also reached there.

'Yeah, two persons might go ferry Ghat Kishanpur. Will go or not can't be said right now, as these are not sure till last. Some drop their activity. Some others may go. By evening today I'll set the things and let you know. We would come to you in the evening,' Jagannath responded.

'You keep his one precious thing with you for some time, Papa,' said Priya and laughed. Agastya also couldn't control himself and laughed with her.

'That's for sure. But what is there in this to laugh about?' said Jagannath, looking towards both of them.

'There is not something but big thing for you,' said Priya.

'For me! And I don't know, at least tell me,' Jagannath remarked.

In the meantime, the mom of Priya also came in with breakfast items and started serving them. Taking a plate of breakfast, Priya, addressing Agastya, asked, 'Should I tell?'

'What do you want to say? Don't keep us in suspense. Now do tell,' Jagannath ordered.

'Okay, I tell. A little before, we were sitting in the open outside guest house, discussing his going back. He said he would be going back, making you as a custodian of his one thing. At appropriate time he would come and would take his thing back from you,' said Priya.

'I would be happy to be custodian. But what is that thing so dear to him which can't take along with?' asked Jagannath.

'Priya, don't tell any more till such time I leave the place. Or else I may be caught badly,' Agastya said.

'You would be caught badly, not by ear only but completely,' Priya said.

Hearing all this, Priya's mom also stayed after serving breakfast, waiting to hear what she had to say.

'Don't pull and stretch this suspense any longer, daughter. What is that valuable thing he got from this area during his tour and wants to keep it here with us?' Jagannath urged.

'Papa, his that valuable thing which he has quietly stolen from you is your beloved daughter—me. He would like to leave me with you till such time he comes with marriage party,' said Priya.

Agastya, looking down, stopped even chewing what he had in his mouth. He got still. Even the hand with the spoon stopped where it was, to wait for any further reactions of Uncle and Aunty. The atmosphere of the room had become somewhat tense for a moment. Agastya felt embarrassed for a moment. But soon, with the loud laughter of Jagannath, the tenseness changed into something light and joyful. Laughing, he said, 'Oh, things have gone up to that level. What can we say if you have chosen and liked each other? You've solved our big problem. All the time we had been mentally occupied as to who can be dependable and boy of faith where our daughter would be able to live happily. It was pressing hard in our mind. Well, we are happy with you. May God bless you with happiness. Surely, my son, we would be your happy and proud custodian.' Looking to Priya, he continued, 'By telling this, you've given us a very happy surprise. This Dushahra has come to us as a lucky and happy Dushahra. Sitting at home, God has sent us a good son.' Addressing his wife, he said, 'Oh, fortunate one, go and share this good news with some sweets, and call other children also.'

Mrs Jagannath went back happily and came back there with sweets; she was also happy whole family joined in happy and gay mood and enjoyed the sweets.

'Uncle, may I say something' asked Agastya

'Yes, yes. Why not? Speak without hesitation, my son.'

'Uncle, whatever Priya has said is true. I honour you and whatever you said. Be sure none of us has betrayed your faith and the liberty you have given us,' said Agastya. He continued further, 'Of course, Priya had been with me day and night all alone, but we had been as friends only, not even loose talking.'

'Sure, dear son, we trust our children—you both. There's no need to say anything.'

After breakfast, they both got ready for going to the guest house. Priya took some sweets for Joshi and left for the guest house with Agastya, telling that now they would be coming with Joshi after lunch and would be taking early dinner. For Agastya would be going early to the guest house.

At the guest house, they called Joshi and broke the news to him, giving him sweets. Priya said, 'Wish I could give this good news to Devika also, she would be angry on me.'

'I will do this good job, not today but soon, before you leave for your college,' said Joshi.

'Thank you, brother,' said Priya.

Joshi, after doing some light work here and there, started his kitchen work for lunch.

'After helping Agastya in his packing and report work, etc., I would be helping you in kitchen work,' said Priya.

Both Agastya and Priya started setting papers of the report in systematic order that no link was missing. Reports were set and packed. Then came his personal luggage items; leaving aside his items of daily use, they finished this also soon, leaving the final packing for the final departure time only. After lunch, they set the kitchen right. Agastya called Joshi and said, 'Joshi Brother, you extended your full help and care to me. It's for your help and support that I could complete my work. I got a brother here in jungle. This tour has changed my life. Now you rest, and join us for going to Priya's place for dinner. Tomorrow morning I would leave very early, so you can finally calculate and tell me by evening what all you have spent on purchases, the value of the things you used from your stores, and guest house charges. I mean, total what all I need to pay. There is sufficient time. Take your own time. Tell me by evening, when we meet to go to the village.'

'Right, I will tell you. Saab, today I'm very happy. What I wished has come true. May God keep you both always happy.'

'Yeah, yesterday only, you were expressing your worries about Priya and Devika and wished them best of their future. Who can say of future? But I have done whatever I could. And Priya got it confirmed by telling about our love to her parents, who have accepted it.'

'Joshi Brother, what were you telling Agastya yesterday about me?' Priya said.

'Nothing, only this much, that saab please see that the feelings of Priya are not hurt, her heart is not broken. And that Devika also moves on in safe and proper lines,' said Joshi.

'Oh, dear brother, you are so much concerned, you are my true well-wisher. You will be my dear brother for whole of my life,' Priya said.

'Now wish Devika also gets her fiancé—project surveyor whose half-done work's lying here in the guest house. Joshi, I think that credit will also go to you. You only will do that big job of giving new life to Devika, Rohan, and their family members and to we all people. Do whatever you can. We would be with you even for monetary help,' Agastya said.

'Surely, saab-ji, I'll do my best, and I'm very hopeful,' said Joshi. He further said, 'Right, saab, now I go, would be back at tea time.' And he moved out of the guest house. After a minute or two, she got up and closed the main door, and both moved to the bedroom for post-lunch rest; as no packing etc. work was left, both were totally relaxed. Now after telling her parents of their love and nuptial decision and her parents' acceptance of this, she looked more confident, active, and cheerful.

Both now felt different. Priya was expecting such change anytime. Because she knew 'most of the parents, once their daughter get grown up, without any consideration of education or stage of education, as soon as they get suitable boy, fix up her marriage'. Here, for Priya it had happened suddenly to her own choice. And she had liberty to complete her studies and even to pursue it further. Agastya was also happy he got a sociable, educated girl of his choice.

'Priya, for a moment I felt you have put me in a very embarrassing situation at your home, that too when taking breakfast, leaving no chance of running out.'

'That—running out—you could not do otherwise also.'

'Why, you mean I can't run? Run to safety?'

'Surely you can run. Run as much as you want. But where could have you gone from these jungles? And do you think we would have let you run away? I'm a jungle girl, could have got you transformed into male goat. Man at night and at other safe times. And goat when others seeing or going out. But could have been good for you. Without you doing anything, could be feeding you so well with soft green grass. May see, try. Chances are still there. What'll you get from this hard work—projects, PG studies, degree, competitions, and all? Here, you only need to just say no to this beautiful, faithful loving girl—daughter of Seth-ji, the big resourceful man of jungles—and need to try a little running away. Then all lines would be clear for green pasture and soft green grass, doing nothing, no burning of midnight oil for studies etc. See, what a good offer.'

'Oh my god, where have you sent me? Had studied so much but failed to study true quality of a so-called simple, cute faithful girl. Save me from her faithfulness and good offer. Oh goddess, with my both folded hands, beg your pardon, allow me to go to my home, parents must be waiting.'

'No need to trouble God. Darling, you are very much going your home with all your body parts intact. Didn't like the good offer? It's all right. I'm happy with your this acceptance of mine.'

'Thank God, such a complicated thing turned so simple. But how could you gather courage to convey such a thing to Father, a girl conveying of her love affair's marriage to father? Quite untraditional, a rare, unheard thing. The matter which could have lingered on for years insignificantly and unnoticed, could be your father trying searching a suitable boy at several places, you got finalised in just minutes,' said Agastya.

'Coming to her own, a lady can do anything. I just gathered my courage and at an appropriate time informed my parents. They have already been liking you, my work has been made easy by you, by impressing them so much that they had been allowing their grown-up daughter to stay with you day and night,' said Priya.

'How are you feeling today?' Agastya asked.

'Great and excited, having no control on my emotions. But sorry, I would have this happy time only for short duration. We are together for an hour or so. Tonight you would be leaving, don't know when and where we meet again. How long we would live like this separately.'

'Time passes away very fast, you won't even come to know when this would have passed away. This would become our sweet memorable past. Now pray to God everything goes well with us. And we get settled well in our life with good education and good career. And good things require good preparations, hard work, good control on self, and sacrifice.'

'We have a very little time with us, would we spend this too in just knowledgeable talks and sleeping only?'

'These are useful, good talks. And we need to take well-thought-out decisions. What else we can do?'

'Darling, we have decided to marry. My parents have consented for this. What about your family members and your parents? Would they accept our decision?'

'Why not? Who wouldn't be happy to get a nice family member like you?'

'Hope you would talk to them, that you have finalised your life partner, and would try your best to convince them.

And do inform me of their reactions and how have they accepted it.'

'Sure, I would inform you each and every thing. If they select some other girl for me, I'll inform that also. Her details, like how much more beautiful, charming, to how much better place she belongs to, etc., etc.'

'Agastya, you are going tomorrow?'

'Yes!'

'Then why don't you run away today only? Right now. Or you want to rest in some witchcraft doc's home here. You haven't experienced them. They beat more than an enemy can. Not only beatings but putting bitter smoke in nostrils and eyes. Administer many torturous things on their patients to get evil spirits off them. And then bitter juice of so many plants. Maybe they transform you into some pet. So if your destiny's becoming a pet, why don't you become my pet? Giving you VIP treatment,' spoke Priya, shouting, standing up.

'Why right now?'

'Because then I'll be completing the project you came here for. Neither the project would ever be complete nor would you ever go out of this area. After Rohan, now there'll be your search for some time.'

'Arey wah! Maybe unknowingly, but you have enacted a possibility of disappearing of Rohan, and line of action we may take. This's the line Joshi's working on.'

'Not you, I'll search for Rohan. I'll search him out for Devika for her love. But you don't look to be going safe on your legs.'

'I, I would go safely and comfortably. My father-in-law would be arranging escort and a pony for me.'

'Father-in-law? My foot! Go and find out some donkey from the outside village fields, go away with it, and there marry with that, they would love to have that.' Saying that, Priya had come out and sat down in the chair in the veranda in false anger. Agastya came out, caught her from behind, and took her, lifting her into the room.

'I didn't know you look so charming in anger, I would have said it much earlier,' Agastya teased.

'Much earlier. When? When we even didn't know each other?'

'No, a little later, when started knowing each other.'

'Then I wouldn't have been here. You must have been alone sitting here, killing flies and mosquitoes.'

'Flies and mosquitoes?'

'Or else what? Could you have been killing lions? Doubt can kill mosquito even. They would be laughing on the brave killer, Agastya.'

'Don't tell this, I would go right now to jungle and would come back with some good kill.'

'Go soon. If come back, tell us that it is you. I would be here for a week only. Rest the good people of the place would do, and that fatty, hefty Dushahra Day girl would take good care of you. Your family may also accept her, caring girl.'

'Now, enough's enough. You have spoken too much. I'll show you and prove the saying "Behind every successful man, there's a woman" true,' Agastya said.

'What would you do of such type?'

'I have thought of a big plan.'

'What have you planned? I have my doubts you can at all.'

'I'll make you mom.'

'Me! Mom? A little earlier you were making me wife, I conveyed the same to Papa. Now mom?'

'Oh, not mine but of our child.'

'You won't be doing that also. At the time of doing such, you would be teaching a lesson on self-control. Anyway, go ahead with your wise plan of bravery, oh brave papa of my loving child.'

'I'll make you mummy . . .

'How many times you would make me mummy? Take it, as if I have become mummy, then go ahead. What's next?'

'I would take you and the child to my parents and request them, saying, "Papa, here is your brave daughter-in-law [*bahu*], she saved my life from lions and bears in jungle. Now, no choice left, accept her with child and give your blessings." And they would accept you.'

'And where was that battlefield? Where were you dying fighting lions and bears and I saved you, my brave heart? What would you say about it? Hardly, it 'asn't been a week that you have been away from caring cover of your dear mummy. In these seven days, you have made a girl mummy also. Surely you deserve praises.'

'Here on the edge of the jungle, I'll say. I was going to enter the forest full of lions, bears, pythons, and whatnot, suddenly you came and stopped me entering the forest, and I was saved. Anything wrong in it?'

'No, no, it's perfect, foolproof. In your first go, you'll succeed. You would have your full family—your mom, dad, brothers, sisters, and over and above this, wife and child without marriage. But when will you start making me mummy?'

'Don't worry about that. I have a plan for that also.'

'What's that plan?'

'Oh, why are you in so hurry? You know this is second project. One project is already in my hand. Let me complete the first project first.'

'Agastya!'

'Yes.'

'Dear, it looks to me . . .'

'What?'

'You would complete your first project only.'

'And my second project? That's also my project, I'll complete that also.'

'Your second project will be completed by someone else,' Priya said. 'Wasn't I telling you? At the right time of action, you would be delivering a talk on some very useful topic. Agastya . . . What should I do of you?' She further said, 'Why didn't you push your boat with full strength yesterday to let it go to very, very deep distant water?'

'I did it with full strength, but it could go only some feet away.'

'It should have gone hundreds of feet without Joshi. Hard luck.'

'Tomorrow, I would be crossing Rapti.'

'Don't try there. There in the boat would be many more, whereas a fool should go alone.'

'I'll come again.'

'"Again" means? You think now you will go? Would complete your master's course, then some other course, then searching some appropriate job, and then settling down, a matter of six to eight years at least. Then will come here "again". By then I will be making my two, three children play, not as part of your project but of someone else's. Got it, my learned friend of wisdom? From here, go to some temple and go on ringing worship bells. Yet another good project may strike to your mind.' She further said, 'There are people who believe in proper planning. It is good. But they plan too much, go on planning and discussing, again planning and planning. There are another type of people who devote less on planning but believe in action and do the things. They learn by doing things, experience make them perfect. There are yet another who neither plan nor take action, they discuss persons their failures and achievements. Saw me, on seventh we met. On twelfth I was with you in night. And on fifteenth got approval of my parents on our decision. Whereas for a simple decision which you have decided finally, you are taking an eight-years-long project. In which above category of people you fall, put yourself?'

'You will see very soon.'

'All these were the pastime talks. I know we would be together as self-controlled, self-made friends who have done very successfully without any mental pressure on any of us. I will see and wait for your happy communication at an early date,' said Priya.

'Sure, ours is a big joint family. I have a younger brother, a sister, and two cousins. Mom, Dad, Uncle—elder papa, and Aunt—elder mom,' said Agastya. He further continued, 'In Balrampur, I am living in a rented room for past several years. This is my final year, and future depends on God's wish.'

'Time has gone fast, we met per chance so suddenly, had least inclination towards love etc., haven't thought of friendship with boys or even girls, nothing except studies. By God's grace had been coming first in all classes, which further made me cautious to maintain my position. Papa has been in search of some suitable boy for my marriage, but I had been discouraging such things. So he was worried about my marriage. How would I agree to it and all? But you have come in my life so suddenly. I don't know how have I advanced so much, and now how would be of my position in exams? This has given good relief to my parents but don't know of my own, how I would live now on. Will see and would keep informing you,' said Priya.

'What is your journey plan for going to Lucknow?' asked Agastya.

'I would leave on twenty-third. Would reach Balrampur Railway Station by 2.00 p.m. with my whole family, Mom, Dad, brother, sister. From there would be catching 2.30 train for Gonda. Would be there for a day, then would go to Lucknow. Brother, sister would stay at Gonda, Mom, Dad would come back here after my brother and sister are set for their studies, after two three days. That's all about my return journey.'

'How do you come to Balrampur from here?' asked Agastya.

'From here we go on ponies up to Kishanpur Ghat. By four thirty or five we would leave with packed eatables for breakfast and lunch. From Kishanpur other side, we hire a cart up to road, from there by bus. And then by train up to Gonda,' said Priya.

'We have got late, evening's approaching fast. Get ready fast. I have also to get my journey arrangements confirmed.'

They got ready, came out of the guest house, and found Joshi sitting there.

'Joshi, why sitting out, didn't knock?' said Agastya.

'I thought you have very little time today to be with each other. Don't know when you meet again. So didn't disturb you.'

'Oh, this applies on you also, cannot say when would be meeting you. We were just busy in talks and got late.'

They all moved to Priya's house, where Jagannath confirmed the hiring of a pony. The pony man would reach him by 4.00 a.m. at the guest house. Two more labourers for their work would be going. All three, with the pony, would be going with Agastya. After dinner, Agastya and Joshi left for the guest house, asking Priya to stay back at her home.

The next day by 4.00 a.m., the two labourers and the pony man, with the pony, were at Jagannath's house. There, Priya's mom gave packed eatables for breakfast and lunch and some other gifts—some showpieces made in China, clothes, etc. They gave a separate packet of eatables to the pony man for him. Jagannath and Priya accompanied them to the guest house. There Agastya was ready. Joshi had prepared tea and offered a cup to all with some snacks. In a few minutes after tea, they were ready to move. They met with heavy hearts to part.

Jagannath said, 'Son, now come soon and would be staying with us.'

'Lala-ji, he will come to his place, my residence also. Saab-ji, don't forget this poor fellow. Keep on writing. So many people came here and I served them. But Rohan and Agastya would ever be in my heart and mind,' said Joshi.

'How can I forget you? Do meet when happen to come that side.' Agastya, further attending to Priya, said, 'Right then, we make a move. We would meet on twenty-third at Balrampur Bus Stop. See you all.' And he started on his journey.

PRIYA MEETS PARENTS OF AGASTYA

Twenty-third of October. Balrampur Bus Stop. Time, about 1.30 p.m. Agastya was waiting for the arrival of the bus. He had been waiting for about fifteen minutes. By 1.45, approaching fast, a bus arrived. Coolies, rickshaw pullers, and Tonga men rushed towards it. Agastya also went to the bus and saw its signboard; it was from the desired Bahraich side. Then he watched the passengers getting down. After several passengers, he saw Priya showing her hand on the window. Her eyes were also searching someone. Both saw each other and smiled. Following her came her other family members. Agastya reached the bus door to help them take their luggage down. Getting down, they put their luggage close to the bus and checked their things. Priya's mom called Jagannath and said, 'Now get a horse cart for station hurriedly.'

'Aunt, let's move to this nearby hotel and restaurant,' said Agastya.

'Oh, sonny, we would miss train,' said Mrs Jagannath.

'Doesn't matter, Aunt, Gonda is not far off. May go by another train at 5.00 p.m.,' said Agastya.

He took them to the nearby Hotel Safari. Agastya had booked a double room in that. They occupied it; the ladies got fresh, followed by the gents. Then they shifted to the restaurant room and occupied seats on one side of it. At the same time reached Agastya with four girls and two boys. Agastya introduced them by name. 'This is Nidhi, my classmate, Balendu, also my classmate, both boy and girl friends—mangetars [prospective couple]. Nidhi's and mine was the same project. She was also to come with me, but I suggested her to come on second visit, as it was a new and difficult area for us. She may come there in December.'

'She would be welcomed there, and she will stay with us,' said Jagannath.

Agastya further introduced Madhuri, Kanika, Rashmi, and Sumit. In the meantime, Devika also arrived there. She met Priya with both open, extended arms and clinging, congratulating her and Agastya. She was also introduced to each one. Devika paid her regards to Uncle and Aunt and congratulated them.

Priya asked her, 'How come you could come here? Good, given happy surprise.'

'Now I'll keep on meeting. I had come yesterday. I knew your programme. You told me, then Agastya confirmed rest. Bro Joshi has given me the good news.'

They all occupied their seats and were served cold drinks. Agastya asked Priya to come out to main entrance and asked, 'You haven't become mama yet, didn't bring the main character of my project, our child?'

'How could have I? That day I insisted on you so much to make me mom, but you didn't do anything except giving lecture. Lectures don't make a girl mom. I'm a bio stud,' laughingly said Priya. She further said, 'Still there is time. Do something for your project to bore me a child. Or should I go for someone else's child?'

In the meantime, a young boy of about ten or eleven came closer to them. Agastya expressed his happiness on his arrival. The boy came still closer and touched their feet. They blessed him. Agastya, naming him Rupesh, introduced him to Priya and said, 'He's from nearby village, just like my younger brother to me. I take care of his studies.'

Rupesh said, 'I'm so happy to know of your today's programme. Had come to join and help for suitable work I can do.'

Agastya asked him to join them and not to bother about the work part. The boy Rupesh moved to the programme site.

On Rupesh's moving on, Agastya, pointing to him, asked Priya, 'He's like my son to me. Will he do?'

'Will surely do. But won't he be somewhat bigger, darling? But what else can we do now? He'll do. Rest you tackle it all.' Priya laughed aloud.

Agastya tried to laugh but could only give false smile with Priya and said, 'There's no time, Priya, save me, they have come.'

Priya asked, 'Who?'

'Those very persons I'm scared of,' said Agastya.

'Of whom you are scared?'

Agastya told Priya, 'There is no time to talk, come and touch their feet, my parents.' Both walked few steps forward, reached a middle-aged couple coming towards the main entrance, and bowed down to touch their feet, saying, 'Namaskar ["I bow to thee"].'

Agastya's mom picked Priya up and took her in her arms—close to bosom—and, looking at her face, said, 'Be happy, daughter. May God save you from malignant look of others. Wonderful, you are much more beautiful than we could think of. You saw Agastya's dad, we were unnecessarily getting worried. Thinking and thinking, "What type of girl could it be liked by Agastya?" But seeing you, our worries are over, we are happy.' There only, she offered a gift to her.

Agastya's father also said, 'Really she is very good, with intelligent look.' Looking at Agastya, he said, 'Oe, how come you could get such a nice girl so suddenly?' He also came to her and took her in his arms and blessed her by putting his hand on her head. They kept standing there and talking. Agastya asked them to come in. But his dad said, 'Oh, what's there inside? We are with our daughter here, for whom we came all the way. Our coming has become successful, seeing and meeting her. May God keep you both happy.'

In the meantime, seeing the time passing, Jagannath said, 'Oh, where have these children gone? Time is passing away, we have to catch train also.' He got up to see them outside and came to the main entrance. Here he saw them all standing. He also reached them and paid his regards to the parents of Agastya. Agastya introduced him to his parents and vice versa. Agastya's parents expressed their happiness and big satisfaction on seeing Priya and meeting him. And the three walked to the refreshment room. Agastya and Priya followed them hand in hand.

'Got fatty on hearing so much about your beauty,' Agastya teased.

'Why getting jealous?' Priya pressed Agastya's hand.

'I'm pass without doing project. Out of fear I have done everything so quick. Which category of people now you will put me in?'

'Top action men. So much is arranged in so short of time, none of us ever thought of it. I am so happy. Oh, Agastya, you are so nice,' said Priya.

They all reached the place. Agastya introduced each one of his family: Madhuri, Mom, and Dad and Rashmi and Kanika as elder and younger sisters. Priya saw them and smiled and gave a happy look to Agastya, feeling how secretly he had done and kept everything to him and so soon got approval of their love and future relations. He made work of her parents so easy. What a warm acceptance she got. She felt deeply impressed and obliged. And the same way felt the mom and dad of Priya. They met, embracing each other. Priya now felt differently for Agastya and his parents and sisters. Priya and parents had never thought that on the way they would be getting such a big happy surprise. It had become a big event and a memorable day of their life, for which they were least prepared. Now they enjoyed lunch together. Jagannath and Mrs Jagannath welcomed and loved Devika. Priya and Agastya also met her open-heartedly. All enjoyed the occasion, and now was the parting time. The parents of Agastya gave some more gifts and boxes of sweets to Priya and her friend Devika. The parents of Priya offered to pay the hotel bill, but Agastya didn't let them. However, they also gave Rs100 each to the parents and sisters of Agastya and boxes of sweets and fruits.

Jagannath desired to move to the railway station for the train to Gonda. But Radhey Shyam, father of Agastya, offered to him that they had come by their own vehicle, a ten-seater Sumo, and now in another hour would be going back via Gonda. They could easily come along with them. Jagannath accepted this offer, saying, 'We would be happy to be with you for some more time, provided you break your journey at our place at least for some time.'

Radhey Shyam agreed to it. Radhey Shyam said to Jagannath, 'So now you relax here for some time. We will come soon and pick you up. We have some work and would go Agastya's place.' They all were excited. Radhey Shyam picked up all the local guests, to drop them at their local places. Devika stayed with Priya in her room, where they chatted joyfully.

By 3.30 p.m., Radhey Shyam reached the hotel, and they all boarded the vehicle, and together all started on their way to Gonda. By 4.30 p.m., they were there at the place of Jagannath. He made the guests comfortable, and the whole family made a hurried effort to arrange high tea and some gifts for the parents and sisters of Agastya. Agastya did not accompany them. He stayed at Balrampur for his studies and project.

Radhey Shyam started on his further journey to his place in Barabanki with his wife and children. Throughout their journey, they were happily talking of Priya, her impressive appearance and beauty. They were considering them and Agastya lucky to get a nice prospective bride like Priya so suddenly. Reaching home, they spoke highly to all others of the family.

At the place of Jagannath, all the family members were so surprised to know this development. The uncle and aunt and cousins of Priya were happy, though they expressed sadness for missing the occasion and desired to see Agastya.

At Balrampur, it were Agastya, Devika, and the classmates of Agastya—Nidhi and Balendu etc. Devika was staying with her relations there. But she was a frequent visitor to Agastya's place. This day from the hotel both moved to Agastya's place. There she asked Agastya, 'It is good development. How it happened so suddenly. On fourteenth we were together at the lake. That day, you didn't mention any such thing'.

'There wasn't anything. It was on fifteenth morning, suddenly in just humorous talk at the place of Priya at breakfast, I just spoke to Priya to come in my life. She questioned me if I would accept her. I had no choice but to yes, which Uncle, Aunty accepted happily. Coming here at my place, I talked to my parents, and they said they won't have any objection if the girl is okay. For that they came here and approved her. This part of story you've seen yourself. Your friend is accepted by all.'

BACK TO COLLEGES

'Undoubtedly, she is very good. And it's good that you are engaged. You both are my friends. Our group would be together, marriages would not bifurcate or break our group. Any other person could never have understood us or Priya so well and help us achieve our mission. Though if she might haven't changed, you'll see Priya now would be different type till her exams. Nothing can distract her from her main goal. In her free time, in friend circle she is different, which luckily you got. And got impressed and got my sisterly friend. But for another eight to nine months you forget her,' Devika said.

'That would be good, at least I would be able to complete my exams too. And myself and you would be doing many important other things during this time,' Agastya replied.

'That's right, you too wouldn't be distracted.'

Then reached Nidhi and Balendu there. 'Well done, dear friend. Today we could understand why you had been running around for last some days. You are great. Didn't let us know what the matter is. Today in the hotel too, after the arrival of Priya and your parents, we could know your real game. Anyway, thank you very much. You made us part of your personal programme. And we could share the joyful event and could see and meet Priya,' said Balendu.

Nidhi said, 'I do agree with Balendu, express my sincere thanks and happiness.' Nidhi further said, 'Now help me in completion of my project too. I am totally dependent on you. You didn't take me on tour, though I had convinced my family members and Balendu too, and I was ready. Now what would I do?'

'You need not worry about it. I have full data in detail. Your project would be complete with mine. Photographs are in plenty, you can take as many as you need. I surveyed and worked keeping your project too in mind. Our going first time was difficult. Now it would be easy. If at all you want first-hand knowledge, we can plan a short trip. I or Devika can take you to the area. And you can stay at the guest house of Dera or with the family of Priya or Devika. So no worry, you start your work and complete your project first. Tour, you can take up any time,' said Agastya.

Two days later, on the twenty-fifth, Priya left for Lucknow. There on the Barabanki station, Radhey Shyam and the family members of Agastya took her down from the train to a hotel, where they had arranged a get-together. She was presented some gifts and packed eatables. She was told not to worry for going to Lucknow. It was a matter of about twenty miles, and she would be dropped to her place by car. It was a jolly good family get-together, where all family members could see and meet Priya. In the evening, some two to three family members, including a lady, dropped her to her destination in Lucknow. And now Priya was in Lucknow.

In Balrampur, Agastya, Nidhi, Balendu, and Devika, all formed a small group. Devika had developed an interest in politics. Studied the political climate in the district in respect to the national scenario. To remain in touch with the youth force, she joined a law course in a PG college at Gonda; here she could get a seat with late fee and managed to get a room in a ladies' hostel. In the college, law classes were in the evening. She had become a busy social worker, a student, and a politician. She had made Gonda her base, but she had been working from another base at Balrampur, where successfully Agastya, Nidhi, and Balendu too became inclined to politics. She had become a youth leader and had been touring and working in various parts of the district and town and had been working for the welfare of ladies, senior citizens, children, and the downtrodden in the less privileged areas of the cities and especially in the villages and tribal forest in the northern parts of the district.

Agastya, Nidhi, and Balendu were active with Devika, but at present they were busy in their studies too. In Gonda also, Devika had widened her friends' and supporters' circle. And at times she had been having informal meetings at tea at some convenient places, some in Gonda and Balrampur, at their own expenses, as a part of their future preparations.

In Lucknow, Priya had been busy in her studies, away from her surroundings and what was going on in her home or with Agastya are any other one. However, she had a common friend, Asmi, in her class, who was very friendly with Devika. She was from Balrampur and had been meeting her and Agastya. She had been keeping Priya well informed about that front. But only as information update with least effect on her routine work. Several times Agastya wrote her emotional, long, long love letters, inviting her mind to several things of those few days of their lives. In return he got, 'Received your letter dated . . . I am fine here. See you. Yours loving, Priya.' Sometimes her response was missing, and sometimes he got this type of text on a leaf off her notebook. Folded and posted *barang* (without ticket, addressee to be charged double the cost of the ticket). Gradually he lost interest in writing to her, thinking she might not be finding time to write or maybe due to restrictions and inconvenience she might be facing. He thought it better to forget her up to the coming April, the time for ending exams. And he dropped perhaps his last official type for the time, reading, 'Dear P. I am fine and busy, trust the same for u. Loving, A.'

This bore quick fruit. Priya felt so amused going through Agustya's letter that she sent a quick reply, writing, 'Dearest A, I am happy and could read your this letter with bursting laughter, which I got after months. This is greatly satisfying that you have learnt the art of "tit for tat" and has applied back on me. Besides this, hope you still need me to bear a child to convince your parents. Don't worry, I will try from here. Hoping for the best to you. Yours loving, P.'

This had infused a new hope of humour in Agastya. He wrote a big love letter to her, with an underlined 'N. B. Dear, as you have seen, my parents are over convinced. No child is needed now. And you at least don't try for a good thing at wrong time, wrong place, and with wrong way. Your loving fearful designate hubby, A'. For which he did not get any reply, and he settled down quietly in his work.

BIRTH OF A NEW POLITICAL PARTY

Devika was hardly busy in her studies but busy in her social and political works, expanding the list of her supporters and fellow workers. She had studied various parties, success stories of the parties and their persons, origin of parties, their rises and falls, break-ups, unions, etc., and their prospects and chances. In which party she could have recognition and say and all that. Ultimately, she decided to have a party of her own, a new party in which she would be on top and could accommodate her favourite persons. People worked for their own growth and the growth of their party. She had started working on these lines, and she was in search of an experienced person for expert guidance. As her stars had taken a favourable turn for her, an old leader, Dina Nath Attri, of the prominent national-level Bahujan Hitaya Dal, seeing the domination of young new-generation leaders advocating for power and position in the hands of young leadership, resigned his position and party and active politics on health grounds, to have a peaceful retired life.

After his resignation was accepted, Devika visited him with Agastya, Nidhi, Balendu, and two more at his residence in Allahabad with a bouquet of flowers, seeking time from him. She told him her purpose of coming to him all the way from Gonda to Allahabad. She apprised him of her age (about twenty-four), educational qualification (science graduate and student of law), her hold on the youth in particular and in the public in general, what all social works she and her fellow workers had been doing. And that ultimately they wanted to enter active politics with their own party, which would soon be a state- and national-level party, as they would be having their party workers from every section of society throughout the country.

Hearing all this, with his past experience of working with the young lot of politicians, he flatly said, 'No, I am sorry, my age isn't permitting to work in active politics. I have left a well-established, prominent national-level party in which I was in top executive position. It's no longer possible for me to work as party worker. I appreciate your efforts and way of working. My sincere blessings and good wishes to you and all your party workers. But excuse me. I'm sorry. I'm disappointing future leaders of the country like you who are full of enthusiasm and zeal.'

Agastya came forward, caught his feet, and said, 'Your Honour, we haven't come to pull you in politics, nor we would like you to work anymore. We would not work with you. We'll work under your guidance. You would be our supremo. We all would be caring and serving you. Under your guidance, we want to try a clean politics to serve for the cause of humanity. Kindly don't say no and let our mission meet its end before its start.'

And all fell on his feet. For some time, Dina Nath remained silent with closed eyes. Then gradually opening his eyes, he stretched his hands to the heads of these bowing on his feet. Picking them up, he said, 'Okay, tell me what you want me to do.'

'You give your blessings to the party workers. For record and registration of the party. On your letterhead pad, kindly just write few lines that you hereby give your consent to be the party supremo—founder chairman of the new party Rashtriya Manavtawadi Dal. We leave here the Dal agenda, its by-laws, and some press notes. Kindly go through these at your convenience. We go now, to come tomorrow. We will discuss these and would go for party registration and press conference.'

'Right, will see you, and since you are my children, why don't you stay here with me for the time you are in Allahabad? Already you must be short of funds at this stage. Moreover, soon I will be able to understand the text and discuss it. By tomorrow morning we will be able to go for its registration. Can't I look after my enthusiastic children?'

All of them were looking at one another and had no words to express their happiness. However, collecting his courage, Agastya said, 'Da-Da-ji, we don't want any inconvenience to you.'

'What inconvenience? The moment you enter good politics, you becomes public man. Your property becomes public property. Won't you help a needy or will recommend for government grant which you will hardly get in time? Now since I have done a joyous folly of saying yes to you, then you milk this yes-man cow to its full. Why hesitate? We will stay together, eat together, work together, and fight the odds together. The two girls may go to this side room, and you all young men to this side room. I'm alone for a week. A help would come. I couldn't offer you tea. Girls, you go to kitchen and prepare tea for all. After tea, one of you can go down there on the right, there is a vegetable shop, get vegetables and fruits of your choice. I'm going to my working room for about two hours and would rest. You get fresh, settle down, and with the help of the domestic help, can get busy in preparations for lunch. So feel comfortable,' said Dina Nath, and after tea, he went to his room with all the Dal documents. Whereas the group was still in the sitting room.

'Unbelievably nice leader we got. Not only for politics but also to shape our life and character. How lucky we are, living under his guidance. I would consider better than being in high position,' said Devika. Others too joined in her feelings and sentiments. They all occupied their places in their respective rooms, got fresh, had a short rest, and Balendu went down to the roadside vegetable shop and brought vegetables and fruits for salad. In the meantime, the domestic help had come, and they, mainly girls, got busy in the preparation of lunch.

After about two hours, Dina Nath came out of the main sitting room. They talked about the Dal text; he suggested some points. On common consent they approved it, and he handed it over to Agastya to show to Devika and all the others and get the final copies of the text ready.

In the afternoon, post lunch, they called an advocate for the registration work of the Dal, with the final list of office bearers. With the name of Dina Nath Attri on the top as Founding Member—Chairman, Devika as Vice Chairperson, and so on up to number 15. The very next day, it was registered, and the first press conference was held on the sacred land of the sangam (confluence) of Ganga Yamuna and Saraswati (Invisible River), giving this the name Triveni.

It was a successful conference, conducted under the chairmanship of Dina Nath Attri. Spokesman Balendu also answered several queries of the press people and public. Press notes were handed to media persons; a good tea party was arranged. And thus a new political party, Rashtriya Manavtawadi Dal, had come into existence in a big way at the sacred land, Prayag, the land of scholars and politicians.

After this big achievement, the group sought permission from the supremo to go back to Gonda. Now for the next four months, Devika would work actively in close association of the supremo with other party workers except Agastya, Nidhi, Balendu, and other students who would take up their exams in the coming April. During this time from January to April, Devika, with non-student workers, would work in strengthening the party by appointing macro-level, district-, state-, and national-level committees and office bearers in consultation with the supremo to identify the resources and plans for party fundraising, to prepare action plans for the coming one year and framing review committees. Though Devika was also a student, she was not keen to take exams. She had decided to work in strengthening the party and making recognition in the public. And she was doing it very successfully.

On one of Devika's tours to her area, Nidhi also joined her, and both visited the main places, like Dera Village, the guest house, Haati, and other places on the way. She also had been to the house of Priya and Devika and also met prominent persons, including Kālu Ram Joshi.

When Devika was seriously busy in her political pursuits, the student workers, Agastya, Nidhi, Balendu, and others, were busy in their studies and appeared in their exams, which were over by mid April. Priya had also finished her exams and also the practical. But she hadn't come home and was still in Lucknow. Now all workers were again together. There was no pressure of exams. Devika, Agastya, Nidhi and Balendu put the development of the northern district area on their priority in their agenda. And for this, they prepared a request letter with signature of the public of the area, demanding the construction of a seasonal bridge on Rapti at Kishanpur Ghat, a permanent bridge at Bijlipur, and a surfaced mettled road from the fifteen-mile point on the Balrampur-Bahraich road to Haati via Kishanpur Ghat and Dera Chowk. The group workers were fully prepared to press their demand with the government in Lucknow, with agitations and press conferences.

They reached Lucknow, met Priya and asked her to join them. Though, she was not keen in the beginning, but realising the importance of the bridge and road for her area, she joined them.

The group met the chief minister, handed over their request letter to know why the area had been so neglected, and why the two things so important for the area had not been done so far. The CM contacted the Rural Development Ministry, who informed the CM that next day by 11.00 a.m. they would be able to submit the list of such works with the latest positions. The CM assured the group of his full support and directed them to go to the concerned ministry. The group stayed at Lucknow for the night. Agastya contacted Priya and asked about her future plan, but she said that she would stay in Lucknow only and that she would not join politics. In the evening also, she did not go and stay with the group or Agastya but remained at her place. She was preparing for competitive exams.

The next day, the group had a meeting. Priya also joined them. And at the scheduled time, they all met the secretary of the Rural Development Ministry, giving reference to the chief minister's talk of the previous day. The secretary informed them that they had already taken up the seasonal Rapti Bridge at Kishanpur Ghat and a twenty-mile-length all-season surfaced road from Balrampur Road to the contractor's base point, four miles short of Dera Chowk, and a fifty-mile all-season jeepable, semi-surfaced road across Haati, along the Nepal border about one to three miles away from the border, connecting it with a railhead in the east. The sealed tenders of these works had been invited. Satisfied and left with no more queries, thanking the secretary, the group left for Balrampur.

Since the group had obtained signatures and thumb impressions of the people of the area on the demand letter for Rapti Bridge and the roads, the public all got the impression that these young boys and girls, Devika and the others, were getting these things done for them, which were otherwise also already in the pipeline. But these workers got the credit of these. One afternoon the group, including Priya, organised its meeting in Lucknow to discuss as to how to get the political advantage or credit of this work and publicity of their efforts and party. And they decided to hold a press conference for a wide coverage in the papers. But Priya resisted to it. She told them boldly, 'If you will hold press-conference and would give coverage in the papers, neither you in person nor your party would get any credit, but you both would get big discredit and bad name. Because after seeing in the paper, the ruling party and the government would never like any other political party or organisation to get political benefit and publicity for any reasons. Government would stop these works for indefinite time, and you would not be able to face the people, you obtained their signatures and thumb impression. You would be at great loss, and the public will suffer for your overactiveness. So without letting government and minister know that you are politician, let the work come up in your area. If the works are done, at least in the area you would become their sincere, they would take as if you got these done. The people there in that area would not see these papers but the work. So I would advise to sit quietly on this issue, pursue this matter, and see progress, keep on visiting the area and meeting people as frequently as possible.'

Pondering their heads on the issue, everyone praised the idea of Priya and decided neither to call for press conference nor to give publicity to this matter in the papers. Devika exclaimed to Priya, 'Good, good idea, you are good thinker and think thoroughly. Here, for the betterment of the area, these works must come up fast for our benefit.'

Priya simply said, 'Nothing like that. This was just my opinion, it worked, I'm happy. You will get many opportunities and hundreds of ways for the party publicity and your popularity.'

After the meeting, Priya left for her place, and the rest of the group members, including Agastya, left for Gonda and further to Balrampur. Again, Priya got busy in her studies. The group members got busy in party activities, following the guidance of Dina Nath. They also opened bank accounts in the name of the party in Gonda, Lucknow and New Delhi. Established offices in Lucknow and New Delhi in small rented buildings, and started fundraising and membership drive. Supremo, i.e., Dina Nath, National Secretary Agastya, and Treasurer Balendu Prasad were controlling the income and expenditures of the party.

Thus, gradually, the line of action of the party workers was streamlined, and the work was geared up in its automation. Devika and Agastya had been working and moving mostly at all times together. Now their sphere was much widened, up to New Delhi, Lucknow, Allahabad, Gonda, Balrampur, and many other places of importance in the state and the country. Balendu, Nidhi, and the others remained mostly confined to the district level or, at the most, up to Lucknow.

By mid June, the tenders of the work were finalised and the work orders were issued to two separate companies— the bridge to Bridge Construction Corporation and the two roads with minor bridges in their length to M/S Tarai Road and Bridges Builders Co., with the time clause to finish the work within one-and-a-half year, i.e., 31 December 1963. The two companies established their site offices on the highest point near the bank of Rapti and in the deep interior in Village Haati to complete the basic preliminary work before the onset of the monsoon and then to see the monsoon and study the quantum of discharge of water and the river's flow and span, etc., so that by the end of September, the work could be started in full swing. On this much only, news spread in the whole area, and the two girls, Devika and Priya, had become popular figures, the voice of the people of area. By the end of June, Devika and Agastya visited the area, and both were surprised to see how they were accepted and treated by the public in the area. Even those whom they never saw before remained with them and served them as guides and helpers, and they expressed their gratitude for the good work on the Rapti bridges and roads being done for the area and its people. On this tour, both realised the worth of the frank advice and words of Priya, discouraging them to try to take political advantage of these works and publicity campaigns, which now they were automatically getting. They both accepted her as their worthy and sincere adviser and counsellor.

On their visit to Dera, they met Joshi also, who was also very happy, saying, 'Devika-ji and saab-ji, for you both, I'm no longer in isolation. This has become a central place. My home, which was two days apart in fair weather, is now at only four hours' journey in all seasons. Now this area will be no longer primitive and conservative, it will progress. People of this area will worship you. Priya did not come with you?'

'No, she couldn't come, she is busy in her work in Lucknow. Would come later,' said Agastya.

Both relaxed there for some time.

After this, the people followed them to Village Haati, where they stayed for the night. Next day, in the morning, both left for Balrampur; by evening they were there.

This was the second fortnight of June; the results of different exams were being declared. Priya, maintaining her earlier record, passed her MSc in botany in first class, first position, the gold medallist of her college. Agastya, Nidhi, and Balendu passed with first division and others with good marks.

One day, Agastya, sitting with Devika, spoke to her, 'Devika, you left your exam. You should have taken it. We would have taken up more work in rest of time.'

'It's all right, that wasn't my aim, and I joined college only to come closer to students, the youth masses. I have my clear goal in my vision. Graduation is enough for me. If I'll ever do, I'll do privately MA political science. I would prefer to channelise my all efforts only in one direction to achieve my goal. I'm moving with my "only one point" programme, and that is politics now. You see our three months' achievements. These are quite satisfying'.

'That's true, your one-point programme is our strength,' said Agastya

'Wish Priya could have joined us, but she'll never join politics. She's scholar type. Ours will be fluctuating uncertain career. Sometimes on the sky, sometimes down on earth. Uncertain for years. But with satisfaction of the working for the people by living with them, we are happy. Whereas she wants to lead set life away from everyday uncertainties. That's good—individual's liking—and then she has worked so hard for whole of her life so far. She would be living among equally qualified scholars. Here, even uneducated or much less educated may be enjoying better place and position. Here, education or scholastics is no criteria, so let her feel happy the way she wants,' said Devika

'That's right. In fact, I thought she would be free after her MSc and would be with us. But she has her different plans. Can't help it.'

'Actually, obtaining educational degrees can't be an aim, it can only be means to achieve some other goals, and that must be achieved.'

'Yeah, why should she scarify her ambitions, her interests for our plans? She must pursue her interests and goals. We shouldn't impose our wishes, desires, and likings on others. However close to us she or he may be. Let everyone excel in his or her own field of interests and capabilities,' Agastya added.

'Let her see different fields, compare, and choose the most appropriate befitting to her, where she can get working and job satisfaction. In fact, we two 'ad been together for years. You've seen how much fast friends we are. Whatever I could understand of her, I told you the very first day at Balrampur, she lives in her present. When she was with you, she was completely devoted to you, enjoyed your company. But once she 'as gone for studies and career, she left every other thing away. And the result's before you,' Devika remarked.

'We are friends, we can't interfere in one another's personal works and interests. Let everyone grow in his or her own field of interest in his or her own way. We should be helpful, sharing difficulties, problems, and happiness. We expect that we are kept well informed by each one of us and that we work together in the areas of common interest. That's all.'

'She is good friend, sisterly to me. I have all respect for her, I would follow her instructions and desires. She can dictate her likings on me. But I would never ask her to do a particular work against her liking. But one thing about her, everyone would have to accept is that she is very capable, logical, and systematic in her work.'

'Yeah, she knows when the iron is hot to strike on it. She can get her works done very efficiently in no time. We'll see what she chooses for herself and in what way she can be helpful to us in our mission.'

'Yeah, entirely her choice and sweet will. Whenever we would go to her side, we would meet her. Would keep her well informed about our works and achievements. Rest up to her. In the construction works of Rapti Bridge and roads, she 'as helped us a lot. In a way, these works are coming up because of her. For our ignorance, we could have become the cause of stoppage of these otherwise coming-up works.'

The monsoons had started; touring to the northern part and villages had become difficult and unadvisable unless there were some emergency. Their activities got confined to urban areas. The workers concentrated on fundraising and enrolling new members. They enrolled students in colleges, including senior students at the opening of colleges. Here, Dina Nath's experience, recognition, and public image had helped them, especially for fundraising: the balances in the party accounts in banks in New Delhi, Lucknow,

Gonda, and Balrampur had gone up, and with this went up high their confidence and sphere of activities. The heavy torrential rains caused the Rapti and Ghaghra Rivers to create havoc due to high flood in their lower reaches in the district of Gonda, Basti, Faizabad, and Gorakhpur. The party workers, forgetting their political gains, reached to the rescue of the people, collecting help and donations from the public and joining with government machinery in disaster management work. They did not have any party or politics in mind, but they had only service to the needy in their mind, and for this they had become very popular in their large area, with the recognition of selfless workers in the government departments also. In their flood relief drive, Priya also remained actively involved with her base at Gonda. She formed a group of girls and boys of her neighbourhood; they collected help in cash and kind from the public in large quantities and transmitted them further to the fieldworkers for distributions to the flood-affected people. For about fifteen days, she remained busy with the party workers.

———————————— •◆• ————————————

PRIYA SETTLES DOWN
IN LUCKNOW

After the flood situation coming under control, Priya joined her family and was planning on going back to Lucknow, thinking as to what to do next after her MSc besides her preparations for competitive exams. In the forenoon of the day, she was about to leave when the postman rang the doorbell and delivered an envelope to her. She opened it, in curiosity and excitement to go through its text. She could hardly read it whole when she shouted to her mother with joy. 'Mom, with your blessings, I got college lectureship in Lucknow in the reputed Girls' P.G. College!' The whole family gathered around her. Elders took the letter from her. Reading again and again, they congratulated her. It had become a joyous moment for the family. She was the first from the family to go for service—that, too, at a reputable post. Mother immediately took her to the temples and offered flowers and sweets there. On their return, they purchased packets of sweets for the family members and friends. She wrote a letter to her father, conveying the good news, and went to the party office. There she came to know that Devika and Agastya were in Balrampur, so she left a message for both of them about her selection and went back home. Coming home, she postponed her departure until the next day.

Next day, Priya left for Lucknow. Reaching there, she joined her duties. Thus, her life was set on a smooth track, and Lucknow had become her place of work. For some months, she remained confined to her teaching, learning related college works and serious subject studies. But soon she made contact with the senior staff and professors in various local colleges and the university. She selected a topic of studies and got it registered for a research project for a PhD degree and started spreading the wings of her recognition and social services. She organised a group of fellow workers and students. She shifted to a close-by working-women's hostel, got a telephone connection, and became a regular subscriber to a standard-chartered daily and some periodicals of high literary taste. At the same time, she had started a free counselling corner for needy students of any class of any school or college for both boys and girls. Soon, Priya was a well-known figure in the academic sphere in a big city like Lucknow, and she had become too busy to find time for family members and friends.

One day, Agastya and Devika came to meet her and for her opinion on some party work. She helped them in their work for the party and common causes simply by phone calls. But for personal meetings and talks, she could hardly meet them except for 'Hi, hellos'. They saw her minute-to-minute busy; even her lunch she would take working on several tasks side by side and standing or running around.

They couldn't say anything and preferred to go back by next train.

Priya could not go even to her home at Gonda nor to see her father at Dera Chowk. After waiting for about seven to eight months, her parents came to see her at Lucknow. There she made arrangements for their food and stay. She asked about their well-being and about her brother, sister, and other family members as a hurried affair, but she could hardly sit and talk to them. In the night, she came when they were asleep and left early in the morning when they were still in their cosy beds in chilly winter. However, they came out and told her that they too were busy and would be going back by next train. They asked her to find time to come to them and wished her all the best. They got ready and left for Gonda.

On their way back, Jagannath and his wife met Agastya and Devika at Balrampur. They talked about Priya and said, 'We hadn't seen her for past several months. So went to see her. But she could hardly meet. Hurriedly came to us for few minutes. Don't know when she took her meals, when did she came to rest and sleep, and in the morning also we had to make efforts to see her when she was about to leave, and then we had come in her absence. Had never thought of this type of life for her.'

'Don't worry, Uncle, she herself has chosen this life for her. And then this is the beginning of careers. Everyone has to put in extra efforts in the beginning, things will change for good,' Agastya said.

'Can we plan for her marriage this way?' enquired Jagannath.

Agastya replied, 'Why're you worried about her marriage? Leave this to her. What's the hurry for it?'

'Look who's talking!' came the prompt rebuttal from Jagannath. 'We've proposed her marriage with you. We, your parents, and you, all were so keen for the marriage. And now, you appear totally indifferent. Have the things changed?'

'Uncle, nothing has changed. We are friends and we are all together. Agastya hasn't changed a little. We also had gone to her only about two weeks back. In fact, she had done a very important work for us out there. But she couldn't meet even us, her best friends. That is how the life is in cities. And then she has herself developed this style of working, doing so many things together—research for her doctorate, helping the poor, needy children and girls in their personal problems, other social service, in addition to the responsibilities of the college. She is no longer only yours, now she belongs to the whole society. You must feel proud!' Devika advocated the case for her dearest friend.

Agastya also added, 'That's right! Even though I'm not married to her, for any reason best known to her. If she doesn't marry me, I will always feel happy and proud of our friendship. Merely because of our proposals she doesn't become bound to marry me. We can't snatch her out of such a purposeful, honourable life simply because she is not able to give us time.'

'In fact, it's an honour for us that from amongst us, a close friend of ours has come out with such a status,' Devika affirmed.

'We are unable to understand how you see it. But make her realise and convince her to spare time to come to Dera,' said Jagannath painfully. Devika and Agastya had assured them of doing their best and that they would surely come to Dera together with Priya.

After Jagannath and his wife left Balrampur, several things were coming to their minds. Mrs Jagan asked her husband, 'Priya's dad, how has Priya changed so much that she has given up her personal life totally? Is it because of the nearness of Devika and Agastya? She has come so close to him that Priya decided to keep away and remain lost in other works? Now neither she has time to think about herself nor for things like marriage.'

'Maybe, and may not be. She has accepted the post of lecturer for herself, not because of them. Now since she was there in the field of education, where everyone comes to think high. Everyone remains busy to learn more and more. And to know what new has come from whom. She has developed new vista and different ways to help the needy. She is doing more saintly jobs than the saints. I don't think she has gone to her own sphere due to this petty thing that Devika and Agastya are working together. Moreover, there is behavioural change in these two. Nor I could see any attractive behaviour in these two for each other. They are leading a simple life of work persons and not as lovers.'

'Would they show you their love life? Who knows when the things take turn, and which way? When was the life of a boy and a girl living together safe?'

'It has been always safe with the reasonable good people of higher taste and high ambitions. They become helpful to each other to achieve their goals.'

'Otherwise also, what can we do with the grown-up children? No choice but to leave everything to the god,' Mrs Jagannath said.

In all these talks they did not realise when the distance was covered. Life at the ghat had become lively; bridge and roadworks were going on in full swing. A good number of workers had made their temporary huts and tents and construction of stores etc. Easily, with a jeep only, they could cross the river, going over the temporary seasonal bridge now, which was to facilitate labours in their quick movement across the river with loads of construction material. Thus, easily they reached Dera.

Devika and Agastya had been as busy as Priya. But they were not duty bound like office goers or people, children sitting and waiting for them as for Priya in her free-counselling centre. Their whole time was for the party and the public. They were spreading their area of work to the adjoining districts and then further to other adjacent districts so that the public of their area might favour them in the elections, if it came to that. They must prove heavier over their counterparts of other political parties by their work done.

SEARCH OF FOREST AREA

Kālu Ram Joshi was working on his mission with all sincerity. On several Tuesdays he had kept a fast and had been to the village, to the side of the house in which he saw some suspicious male goat. He had tried several times but always found the lady there. However, on one Tuesday, he found the lady had to go out in some emergency, and Joshi could try all his remedies—i.e., in his fast, he went there in a ruddle-coloured robe (garment), put the sandal paste and the vermilion on the forehead of the male goat, and made the male goat see his face in the mirror. But with no results. The male goat remained a male goat and did not change into any other form and remained the same male goat as it was.

Joshi was not satisfied with his getting no result for so much of his sincere efforts. Rather, he got discouraged. However, he tried to find the reasons for the abnormality in this male goat. He tried to find out the history of this. He talked to some aged persons of the village. As he was a Forest Department employee, villagers respected him and had been listening and obeying him. He had been here only for the last four, five years, so he tried to find out its history from elderly people. One day he met Mangloo, aged about forty-five and neighbour of the lady. Joshi asked him, 'Mangloo, how long this male goat is with your neighbour lady?'

'Saab-ji, this is for last eight to ten years,' replied Mangloo.

'Sure?'

'Ji, very sure.'

'Where and how did she get it?'

'Her mother had gifted this goat, some half bag full of rice, two big, big pumpkins, and one ripened jackfruit.' While expressing big, big size of pumpkins, jackfruit, Mangloo too, with open, widened hands, was fattening. 'She gave this so much that we had gathered at her place to see these rich gifts. At that time, this was small male goat of about six months,' said Mangloo.

'Why this male goat and the lady behave in abnormal way for each other and individually?' asked Joshi.

'After giving these big gifts in Dushahra days, her mother passed away of some disease. This lady being the only daughter of her parents was very much attached to her. And this is the last gift of a mother to her daughter. This lady has been taking special care of this male goat as a token of her remembrance. Moreover, her husband and son, about fifteen years, are living out as labour with a forest contractor.

They are lucky, earning a good living. They get two times meal to their full appetite and good earning too. After full one year, both came three years back. They had come with fifty rupees (about one USD). Thus, she is a well-off lady. She is emotionally attached to the male goat. Feed it heavily. She hasn't ever thought of it to scarify on any occasion, all these years or to sell it away,' said Mangloo.

'I heard some ladies and gents change some human beings to animal or bird and keep them as captives for their use in suitable hours. Have you too heard any such thing?' asked Joshi.

'Yeah, there said to be many such persons. But have heard only. Never seen so far. Heard such changed persons are kept in the secret part of their houses, away from onlookers' eyes.'

'I had same impression about this goat. What do you think about it? Could it be some changed person? See, here I directly come to the issue without knowing your closeness to the lady. You may or may not like it. Would you say anything about it?'

'Our relations are of a good neighbours. I'm scared of witchcraft practices. And I hate these things, keeping any person as captive without realising his or her and family fate and conditions. God punishes such people,' said Mangloo

'That's good you don't like all this. Would you help such captives? God will reward you for the good work.'

'Surely, but what can I do?' asked Mangloo.

'You just inform me if you come to know any such case. We both will find out the reality or will change the animal or bird into the real one, men or women, as the case would be.'

'But the witchcraft man or woman may play his or her tries on me. I'll no longer be man or able to do anything,' said Mangloo.

'Nothing will happen to you. You just have to come to me as soon as you see something abnormal. You can further develop your resources or links with the persons in the area. You would get plenty of such cases. You would be happy to help them join their families. I'll pay you cash. Rupees ten per such case. And rupees ten per month to be with me. I'll also recommend you and help you get daily-wages job or temporary job on monthly basis, which would be more than rupees fifty per month. You will earn thousands in a year,' said Joshi.

'Thousands . . . aa-ai . . .'

'Yeah, thousands, you'll get thousands, that too of honesty, pleasing God, and I'll allow you enter and roam about in the forest,' said Joshi to Mangloo. 'The job of forest will take time, I'll try when saab would come. For the other one, rupees ten a month and rupees ten per case, you can come to me even from today right from now on. You will be coming and meeting me. People may doubt you, so tell them I have employed you on some government's petty job. No worry.

'Now onward your job is to be watchful in the villages, Dera and others. Whenever you happen to go to any side, identify such lady or man who play on witchcraft practices, locate if there is any changed animal or bird. And also note the movements of saints or sadhus in the forest, their routes, actions, places of stay, and if they are carrying some doubtful load or any such thing,' said Joshi.

'Right, saab-ji, now onward I'll be with you at your service. I'll follow your instructions,' said Mangloo.

Joshi needed a helper from among such persons. He would be taking his help, but what he would be doing, he told no one. In the case of this male goat, he did not find any truth. But he wanted to find out how far there was substance in all such fears and tales of the people. Mainly he was doing all this to find Rohan Kumar. In fact, he wanted to keep an eye on the movement of sadhus and other such people passing though the forests with doubtful activities.

Joshi had become more resourceful with the help of Mangloo. And Mangloo too, who so far had nothing to do in the village except to keep a few goats and two, three cows. Besides these he had been bringing wild grass and dry wood, some leaves, barks, honey, etc., from the forests, which he could still bring. Moreover, now he can get such things more, as he would be moving in the forests more freely. At the same time, he had been helping Joshi in his guest house work also. Even he had been attending to some visitors to the guest house. Helping Joshi get vegetables, ration items, etc., from the village shops for the visitors, and in the cooking work.

Thus, he had become a good help to Joshi. At times, Mangloo had been taking meals with Joshi in the guest house or even sometimes Joshi would send him to some place and had been giving him packed meals and, at the end of the month, some twenty-five to thirty rupees, so Mangloo was happy. Joshi was also waiting for some of his big saab or some contractors who could give Mangloo some temporary work so that he could see some hundreds of rupees at a time in his hands.

As luck would have it, one day, some businessman came to the guest house; a contractor showed licence to Joshi and also showed some four or five types of plants and told him he was a contractor for the supply of herbal medicinal plants, barks, roots, etc. If someone could collect these for him from the forest, he would get a good commission. Joshi presented Mangloo, and if need be, he would get some more persons. Joshi obtained the requirement and assured him of sufficient collection. He took him to Jagannath, got their terms finalised, and the agreement was done. And that Mangloo would be one for this work. Jagannath was happy to get a good business, sitting at home, doing not much of it. He accepted Mangloo as one of his persons. From the next day both Mangloo and Joshi had started going deep into the forests in different directions, going and crossing to the neighbouring villages and small forest settlements. Joshi and the others were gathering the herbs and collecting with Jagannath, who had been supplying these in bulk to the contractor and getting commission amount for further distribution of the money among themselves. It had been coming to about 300 rupees to Mangloo, 200 rupees to one other helper, and about 500 rupees to Joshi. Mangloo was so happy to see so much money for the first time. He was not able to count. He counted in twenties in five places, making a hundred. He was not understanding what to do with so much money. He was crazy for Rs50/- in a year for his neighbour; here at his home he got Rs300 plus in a month.* Now Mangloo felt too much obliged to Joshi. Besides Mangloo, Joshi had obliged several people from the village and others known to him. The central figure, the wholesaler for the centre, Jagannath, had been getting about Rs5,000 per month after meeting out all his other expenses of giving to the gathering team, sending the gathered herbs to the contractor in the city, etc. He too felt much obliged to Joshi for this good added income and a new business avenue, sitting at home in this place. Now he was even thinking to expand this and make it a good business.

Joshi had his eyes on something else. He had trained Mangloo as messenger and helper who could work secretly in the forest and villages as an informer for him. He could now observe and analyse things to establish causes and effects. By now, he had developed the skill of a secret forest worker.

————————————●————————————

* In the 1960s, a college lecturer's monthly pay packet was about Rs200 plus 40 DA. In 1963, the author, as geography teacher in a government higher secondary school (HP), was getting Rs208 total, including five advance increments of Rs8 each for good division in master's course and was living in a good two-bedroom house on rent at Rs20 per month. His monthly hotel charges for lunch and dinner were Rs40 per month.

So this was all the more substantial reason for Mangloo to be so happy.

MANGLOO GOES
FOR THE FIRE

One day he had gone for gathering herbs deep in the forest away from Bangdu Village. He saw some smoke rising above the thick forest canopy. He went in the direction of the smoke and saw from a distance that a group of seven, eight persons were cooking, as nomads do in the jungle. He introduced himself as a helper of a big forest officer, and without disturbing them, he simply asked the commonly expected question, 'Who you all are?'

'We are saints on our way from religious places to sacred Himalayas in India and Nepal. Forest and mountains are areas of our stay. Sorry if we have caused any inconvenience,' said one of the saints.

Knowingly he didn't go into detail and simply instructed them to be careful about fire, to put it out with water after their work was done, and to bury the fire under some earth. Instructing thus, he left the place in the direction he had come from without casting an eye on them.

He got back to the guest house and told Joshi, 'Saab-ji, there's a group of people conducting some doubtful activities. They said they are saints on pilgrimage. It was about four miles north of Bangdu in the deep jungle. I'm sure they are not saints but activists and smugglers involved in nefarious activities. Since Nepal is very vigilant and has tightened security on the border, they must be having their hideout base in the Indian territory somewhere nearby.'

'Mangloo, very good, you have become a very good informer. Now I'll do the needful. Don't worry, you have done your job very well and big service to the nation. I'm sure your information's correct,' said Joshi.

Joshi quickly went and met his immediate senior officer and informed him of the presence of these gangsters in the forest and requested him for further action. Joshi also conveyed that this was the work of the police or border security force. 'We should rather contact them.'

Joshi approached the BSF camp nearest to him and contacted the camp in-charge in privacy and requested him to send two persons in plain clothes but well equipped with wireless system and weapons. He also requested that there should be sufficient forces close to the site where these gangsters were found. This would help Joshi to call for help at the right time, and they would also be able to reach Joshi within no time.

The BSF commanding officer understood Joshi's idea. He prepared the action plan and asked two persons to go with Joshi. Joshi arranged the forest officers' appearance for them. As per the plan, they were to present themselves as senior forest officers. Joshi and Mangloo followed them as their attendants but guided them to the site where Mangloo had seen the so-called saints. The four combed through the forest and advanced with telescopes and other sensitive aids. A large force followed them closely. From a safe distance they could locate an armed vigilant man sitting up on a tree with some powerful weapon to guard his fellows. They reached close to him under the tree, aimed at him, and asked him to quietly come down and surrender. Seeing his life in danger, he obeyed. They brought him back to a safe distance from where even loud voices would not reach his men to alert them. Through their questioning techniques, they started getting information about the base, its strength, locations, positions of their guards, and the activities of the group. Because of the absence of their guard and any communication from his point, nobody could alert them. The commandant decided to surround the group and their hideout without wasting any more time. They took this man and advanced forcefully to the place. This was a completely unexpected attack; the gangsters could not do anything and were captured by the force. Some BSF guards were also sent on other forest path trails so that no one could escape from their positions. The commandant was right in his approach; two such persons with arms and ammunition were caught running for escape. It was a huge success for the BSF; they caught twenty-six persons from the criminal hideout base. Among these, there were some eight most-wanted criminals of international and interstate gangs, notorious criminals involved in murders, dacoities, kidnappings, robberies, and smuggling of arms, ammunitions, and drugs. In this process, four victims were rescued; they were kept as captives and were living miserably, being threatened daily for their resistance in joining their criminal world. Besides these, the BSF also got an unimaginable and unexpected huge haul of smuggled goods, including SLRs, anti-aircraft guns, MGs, LMGs, Sten guns, AK-47 rifles, pistols, various types of cartridges, grenades, mines, time bomb sets, drugs, hashish, ganja, marijuana, huge amounts of foreign currencies of several countries, and foreign goods, gold biscuits, silver, copper wire, things of daily use, toys, etc., made in mainly China, Japan, Thailand. Radio transistors, transmitters, binoculars, telescopes, etc., were also recovered. It looked as if it was a big base for the entry of foreign goods and arms and ammunitions of all types for terrorists in the country through Nepal.

The captives, especially the educated young men, were caught and brought here to meet their manpower need, after making them drug addicts and their brainwashing.

This successful prompt action of the BSF and the big haul was certainly a big service to the nation and was going to award the commandant in a big way. He was very happy on this windfall success and creditable opportunity given to him by Joshi. He was in a way thanking his stars for carefully listening to Joshi.

Among the captives rescued from the criminals, Joshi saw a person very much resembling Rohan. He asked the commandant to send a message to Agastya and Devika at Balrampur to identify, which the commandant sent by wireless through the police. The cost of this capture's haul was estimated over rupees 120 crores. It was so much that the commandant had to call for extra forces and mules to transport it to the BSF camp and then to the nearest safe place at Balrampur and, from there, further to Lucknow Cantt at the earliest. Radio signals were sent to BSF headquarters, who further informed the government agencies, police headquarters, and media. The next two days were very busy for the BSF camp commandant.

There was a big rush of BSF forces, police officials and force, media persons from TV, radio, newspapers, journalists, forest officials, and local leaders. The achievement of the BSF camp commandant was highly lauded. But the camp commandant with him brought Kālu Ram Joshi and Mangloo to the forefront. This became first-page news on all the newspapers of North India on the fifth of April 1961 and main news on all TV and radio channels, with photographs of Commandant, Kālu Ram Joshi, and Mangloo. The government declared an award of rupees fifty lakh to the whole BSF team, including rupees one lakh to K. R. Joshi and 20,000 to Mangloo, with letters of appreciation to all. And now Mangloo too had become a regular employee of the Forest Department, attached to the guest house with Joshi. Through Joshi the Forest Department also had got the credit of this anti-drug, anti-terrorism, and anti-national and social activities drive's success.

By now Agastya and Devika had also got the messages, and Priya saw this news and photograph of Joshi on the first page of the newspaper at her place and in the college library. They couldn't resist the temptation to meet Joshi, Mangloo, and the BSF camp commandant and staff. They all reached there at their earliest, and at the same day, by evening they were there. Since the guest house was fully occupied by high departmental officials of police, administration, and forest, the trio of friends—Priya, Devika, and Agastya— stayed at the house of Jagannath. The three friends, with Joshi, Mangloo, and the family members, had no other work there but to talk and to have fun. Jagannath also told them how Joshi had given him a big source of honest, good earning. Priya was happy and surprised. In her heart she was thinking what Joshi was and how beneficial he had been to her in person and her family. While enjoying their family get-together, the three decided to honour the BSF camp commandant and other officers in the presence of the locals, forest, police, and officials from Balrampur, village heads, and prominent persons in the campus of the guest house shortly, at the convenience of the commandant. The three called for the heads of the neighbouring villages and other prominent persons. They jointly decided to honour the BSF personnel. They also finalised the venue—the guest house—the menu of the lunch, a short folk cultural programme, a few short talks, and some gift presentation to each invitee. Joshi and Mangloo were in the list of invitees. With this detail of the programme, five persons—the three plus the village head of Dera and Jagannath—went to invite the commandant and requested for him to spare some time to be with them and apprised him of their programme. Commandant was happy to receive them and consented to their programme. He agreed to be with them at lunch with his other senior officers of the camp but on the day after tomorrow, i.e., on the ninth, as on the eighth they had their own programme. And the commandant invited them to lunch on the eighth, for which they couldn't say no, and accepted.

The next day, the five reached the camp at about 1.00 p.m. They were welcomed and given the VIP treatment. Joshi and Mangloo were also there. Drinks and soft drinks were served. Joshi and Village Head Birang Bahadur Singh took pegs of scotch, but Jagannath, Agastya, and the two girls took only soft drinks. The BSF jawans (soldiers) had rum to their full quota capacity. Then with the drinks, the officers and the guests met each other and had their free talks and shared light jokes. Drinks were followed by soup service, which continued for some time with chit-chat.

After, they all assembled to a shady ground, where jawans were sitting in their position in a rectangular formation, facing the row of chairs placed in an arc shape at a distance.

All had taken their positions. The commandant extended a warm welcome to all the guests and invited the master of the ceremony to conduct the programme. He invited men from amongst the BSF personnel to sing songs, perform small skits or group dances, play musical instruments, and they gave appreciable performances. Everyone enjoyed the programme. This was followed by a round of brief speeches. First of all, Commandant addressed all and cheered up the high morale of the camp personnel.

He highlighted the contribution of the group of four friends, i.e., Agastya, Priya, Devika, and Joshi, for this whole area.

He said, 'The real credit of our lifetime, this big achievement, goes to this group. In fact, in search of their yet another friend Rohan, they had planned to search this area, as he had disappeared about three years back in this forest. Joshi, who had been living in this area, was entrusted this task, which he accepted and performed so well. For his help, Joshi called and trained Mangloo, who has become an expert. In search of their friend Rohan, they were keeping eye on doubtful persons moving in the forest. There, this activity has brought the big credit to them and for us. A big service has been done to the nation, saved the country and our society of big disaster. And you all will be happy to know that this is the group of friends which has made our lives so easy and has brought our families and society so close to us by getting the Rapti Bridge and the two roads constructed. Now anytime in your family emergencies and in other problems like sickness, injuries, and also for national security in the form of easy and all-time movement of security forces, anytime, you would be able to reach big cities and your places just in one or two hours, which used to take two days in fair weather—otherwise, sometimes like high floods, impossible.'

This was applauded by a bang of cheers and clapping.

'So you can see the example in front of you, how constructive the friendship can be. Not only this, these four members have helped each other to reach to their excellence.

One of them, Priya, has become a professor of botany and a big social worker. Agastya and Devika, prominent leaders of this area and the country, and Joshi is with—you see his name and fame and fortune. He has become a national hero and lakhpati in just a few months of joining this group. And Mangloo too got his share of name, fame, and richness just for being in this good company. We feel proud to have the four with us today. We honour them with these flowers and mementos. And thank them so sincerely.'

A bouquet and a BSF insignia mounted on a beautiful base as mementos to each one was presented and the same way to other guests. Some other VIPs also expressed their feelings. Then was called Priya. She thanked the commandant and the other personnel for the honour given to her and her friends and congratulated all the BSF personnel on their big achievement.

She further said, 'Commandant Sir's par excellence, a thorough gentleman, and a highly successful officer. It is he for whom this big disaster could be averted in no time without any casualty, bloodshed, or any loss of anything, because he has worked as elder brother of each one of you. He gave due importance even to the poorest of poors. See, he worked to the advice of Joshi, who is only a caretaker of a small jungle guest house. He treated Joshi respectably in his office, went to privacy on his saying, and put his force with him. He succeeded because he has not uprooted himself from the ground level. People working under him feel honoured and confident and are ready to do anything for him. And that he could have proper coordination with the local population. I, on my own behalf and on behalf of my friends Agastya, Devika, and Joshi, thank the commandant and his staff for the honour and mementos given to us. We will keep these, the name of BSF, in high esteem. Thanks.'

Then last of all came the deputy commandant, and he proposed a vote of thanks for all.

This programme was followed by a sumptuous lunch, and all parted. At the parting, Devika again requested for the commandant to spare time and to come to their programme the next day. The commandant said, 'We are greatly obliged by your gracious presence, will surely come.'

These five had seen the type of function today, especially the village head and Jagannath, and decided to organise it the same way, minus the drinks. They also collected items of handicrafts from different villages to honour and present to the officers. And the venue area was cleaned and set for function.

The next day—i.e., on the ninth of April—cooks started their work in the kitchen, and the helps were working in the shady area for sitting and open-area lunch. A separate cooking was done by the village people themselves for the general public. By twelve, the invitees and audiences started coming to the venue, and at twelve thirty, the programme started. Outside officers couldn't come, except one Forest Range officer. The commandant and his five immediate subordinate officers and representatives of each group, sections, and platoons arrived at the guest house. The village head and Agastya received them and took them to the guest house lobby. There they sat and waited for the start of the function. The Forest Range officer also joined them. It was here Agastya and Priya took them to the room corner where Rohan's report papers were still kept. They also showed his college ID photograph, and his body identification marks were mentioned to confirm the identity of Rohan from among the rescued captives of the busted gang. The heads of the villages, Surya Dev, all the invitees, and a good number of workers in the area and the villagers also reached the venue of the programme.

Everyone had taken a seat. The function started at twelve thirty sharp. Agastya conducted the programme. He extended a warm welcome to the guests, with garlands of flowers, and a round mark of sandalwood paste on their foreheads (tilak) was put by the younger sister of Priya and the daughter of the village head. Agastya invited Priya to welcome the guests. Priya came and delivered her short speech.

'Honourable guests, village heads, all elders present here, dear brothers and sisters, and my fellow friends. I, on behalf of my own and on behalf of all of you, welcome the commandant, his team of officers of the BSF camp, the Forest Range officer, and other guests. We have gathered here to honour the BSF officers and their team and our friends Joshi and Mangloo for their successful anti-criminal drive operation in this forest, who saved the country of a big disaster. In fact, we the people of this border area are the maximum beneficiaries of their action. These are the BSF personnel and forest officers who remain alert day and night, even in inclement weather, heavy rains, wildfire, break of serious diseases, criminals, whatever type of danger may come their way, including the insurgency or danger from across the border, they protect us. We are living peacefully, taking care of our family and property, earning our living because of their protecting us, this whole area. Their contribution, tough duty, and sacrifice is well recognised all over the country. Our—this effort of honouring and highlighting their importance is just showing a small candle to the sun. I have no words to express our gratitude to them and expect similar good coordination and strong ties between population and BSF and Forest Department. Thank you.'

This was followed by a thunder of clapping. Others also spoke, and then spoke the commandant. 'Dear organisers of this programme, people of this area, and all those who are from other outside areas working here. I, on behalf of myself and all BSF personnel, thank you for the honour given to us. In fact, whatever we have been doing, that is our duty. But our work has been made easy by all of you, which would have otherwise become very difficult, if not impossible, without your cooperation. Hope to get similar help and support from you all in future too. Thanks.'

The range officer on the occasion honoured Joshi and Mangloo. He praised the two for their act of intelligence and bravery. And presented a cheque of rupees25,000 to Joshi and rupees 5,000 to Mangloo, with appreciation letters and a letter of regular appointment to Mangloo with his attachment with Joshi at the guest house.

Devika proposed a vote of thanks, and Village Head Birang Bahadur Singh presented mementos to all the guests—the BSF officers and the Forest Range officer.

This had become a big festive occasion for the village people. They enjoyed the community lunch, listened to the leaders of the area and officers, came to know of big happenings in their area, and got a sort of awareness. They had become more aware now and would keep their eyes on suspicious people around them, especially while moving in the forest.

Thus ended the honouring ceremony. And the BSF officers left for their camp, leaving a good image of being public friendly among the people. The range officer also had made his preparations to reach Balrampur soon. At a distance of four miles was his jeep; up to that point Joshi and Mangloo would help him carry his small luggage, and soon they started. All the village heads together came to Devika, Priya, and Agastya. They expressed their sincere thanks to them for the nice ceremony in which all the people of the area could join. They also expressed their gratitude to them for the services these three were doing for them, and they affirmed their faith in them and their full support to them. Gradually the whole campus was clear; all had gone except the few workers who were busy in winding up the kitchens, cleaning the used dishes, plates, and cutlery, etc. Others were winding up the seating arrangements. Joshi and Mangloo had left with the range officer. Away in the marginal end towards the forests were the heaps of used leaf plates (*pattals*). On this heap had gathered some dogs, donkeys, etc., searching their food, and in a way, they were cleaning this garbage.

Out of the organisers, now only three—Agastya, Priya, and Devika—were left with a sigh of relief. They went to the guest house lobby, pulled their chairs, and sat in. There was an expression of happiness and satisfaction on their faces. They were cheerful with signs of maturity.

In the relaxing mood Devika asked Priya, 'How's my dear sister doing there? Today at least you are sitting with us and we are talking to each other. It is after long time we are sitting this way.'

Priya replied, 'With your good wishes, I'm fine and doing well there. With our responsibilities, we all three have become busy.'

'Not busy, but you have become very busy. We feel your absence on all important occasions and miss you and your valued advice in our day-to-day working,' said Agastya.

'I am not away from you three, you two and Joshi. See, on slightest information, I have come,' replied Priya.

'This is good, you could come. May also see the impact of your being here. Your presence has added grace to the programme,' said Devika.

'No, no, don't speak so high for me. I'm simply a teacher. You people are leaders, this sort of celebrations are your everyday business,' said Priya.

'We are not leaders, we are poor social workers and followers of your instructions and suggestions. You have always given mature, sincere advice. You will always have your high position in our organisation,' said Agastya.

'How are you feeling there, away from home and this small group of ours?' asked Devika.

'Not much change. I was already at Lucknow for past some years. Regarding this group, I feel always with this group. Besides, this hardly have time to think. Various activities keep me busy. This much of sacrifice one would have to do if wants to do something in life,' said Priya.

'You must keep some time for yourself too. You are not a machine. You have a personal life, your family, friends, and relations. These things also help in personal growth. What good can an all-the-time-occupied mind think and contribute?' said Agastya.

'What I'm doing is all for me. It is the beginning of a new life. Gradually things will be set, I think I'll be able to find some more time for myself,' said Priya.

Devika changed the topic, saying, 'Well, Joshi 'as done wonders. A big thing, for which he 'as been rewarded too. We are here for him today.'

'Yeah, never expected he would do such a big thing. Within no time, life of so many people have changed, including his own. And see Mangloo, he will be a rich man, a government servant. He himself couldn't have ever thought of it. This is luck, and this is life. This too is because of Joshi. Mangloo would be worshiping Joshi,' said Priya. Also she asked Devika and Agastya to move to her house for stay. But they preferred to stay at the guest house.

'Why here in the evening? Won't you stay with us in the village?' asked Priya.

'I'll go there. Would meet Uncle, Aunt. But today I would prefer to stay here. I would be thinking and planning something, you both can stay together,' said Agastya.

'Won't allow me in your thinking and planning now, when have become your follower. I would also be with you, staying here,' said Devika.

'Why, you both are segregating me, then I'll also come here,' said Priya.

'No question of segregation, never think of it. Better you stay with parents, came after so long. Ours is different thing. We keep on coming here and also have been meeting you,' said Agastya.

'As you advise, boss. Even then, I may overstay a day with my parents, but I would be with you today and tonight,' said Priya.

'I'm thinking on yet another alternative, there is sufficient time, may go to my house, leaving Agastya with you,' said Devika.

'Aye, dear, keep your ideas to your mind, you won't go anywhere today. Will be with me. You need not leave Agastya. Keep him too with you,' Priya said.

'What? You two friend have made me a ball. Passing one to another. One's leaving me. Another one is not accepting. Don't want to keep me, either of you. But hope you won't make me a ball, playing, kicking me out away,' said Agastya.

'No, no, please don't use these words. You may throw us away. But even then we won't mind and will come to you. We have highest regard for you. We worship you by heart. You are honourable for us,' said Priya, and Devika dittoed.

'Don't mind, just a passing remark. I too have high regards for both of you,' said Agastya. He further said, 'Right now, we three are here. After some time Joshi would also come. Tomorrow we would be going back. We have only this time today to sit together to discuss things, especially about Rohan.'

'About Rohan! Surely I would be keen to discuss. But the matter would be, I think, political matter, and my line, teaching, is different. I don't think I would be able to contribute much, and of any significance,' said Priya.

'At present, our prime interest is Rohan. We would have to prepare an action plan for him,' Agastya said.

'What sort of action plan? And what would be the areas of priority in your plan?' asked Devika.

'To my mind, first of all we should take up all the four rescued captives, to help them come out of trauma. Ensuring their recovery from their weakness, diseases, and mental abnormality due to drugs, etc. Then their proper identification, rehabilitation, and legally getting them proved guilt-free, innocent, and help them join their families. These are the main things we need to do for these four persons. It is up to you if you can do this much for all four or only for Rohan,' said Agastya.

'We would be happy to do this much for all the four. I think by virtue of being human beings we need to do this much. They all are equal to us,' said Priya.

'Yes, we need to contact the police authorities under whom these people are kept,' Devika said.

'All these people and the members of the gang have been sent to Lucknow. All are in tight security. The rescued four persons are under special health care, with a psychologist visiting and having special sessions with them. We will approach authorities to meet them and, following the instructions of authorities, would try to provide them homely atmosphere. This may help them recover fast,' said Agastya.

'In Lucknow, I'll try at my level on the points suggest by Agastya. I'll form a group for this purpose only.' Priya pointed to Agastya. 'You give a copy of his photographs, other particulars, like date of birth, body identification marks, his college ID card number, college address, his permanent address, etc., so that if it is Rohan, he is correctly identified and his identity is established. You just provide these particulars to me and leave the rest to me. I'll give you hale and hearty normal Rohan as he must have been before.'

'I'll provide you all required information. Whatever I have here, you can take today. Only home address I have to get from his college,' said Agastya.

'Good enough. Priya took up this responsibility. We would concentrate on other things,' said Devika.

'Aye, bahini [sister], you can't escape your responsibilities. I'll do everything there. But you both have to remain in direct contact with me, visiting Lucknow frequently,' said Priya.

'Sure, we won't give any chance to point out any slackness on our part,' Devika replied.

The day was now turning to evening time. Joshi and Mangloo had also arrived back and joined them. All were happy to be together. Devika asked him, 'Joshi came quite fast, we were thinking you would come by 7.30.'

'Yeah, we too were thinking the same. But about halfway, our department people met us. They were coming here to take sir. So we were freed to return back, and we reached in time before fall of dark could meet you,' said Joshi. And he sat down on a wooden stool, instructing Mangloo to bring tea for all.

Agastya apprised him of the plan they had prepared for Rohan and said further, 'We were appreciating your efforts to find out Rohan. Your plan had been par excellence, a foolproof plan, involving Mangloo and training him in such a way. Turned an ordinary man into an expert. We have no words to express for your great contribution. We can't say thanks to you, it is not used in friends. You have done your job, the real main work. Rest we will do now to bring him up.'

'When are you going there to meet them? Heard they are in Lucknow,' asked Joshi.

'Tomorrow Priya will go to Lucknow. She'll find out whereabouts of these people there. And necessary formalities to meet them. Then on her calling we would go,' said Devika.

'Why don't you too go along with? Maybe she alone, get fainted there, seeing their conditions,' said Joshi.

'You advise we all should go together on the very first day?' asked Devika.

'See if you can go. Maybe you get some surprise there. Out of the four, you may get some more friend besides Rohan,' said Joshi, casting a sarcastic smile and eye-to-eye contact on each one of the three.

'Let us see if we could. Otherwise, we would rush to the place on the first call of Priya. Moreover, we are not sure also how much it would take to find them and to complete all required formalities,' said Devika.

Mangloo had come with tea and served it to all. He took his cup and also sat close to them. All the three thanked Mangloo and congratulated him.

After tea they decided to go to the village to the house of Priya. The previous night they had stayed there. They all, including Joshi, reached there and met Jagannath. They sat for some time in the sitting room. And then they expressed their desire to go to the guest house, from where they would go to Balrampur in the early morning.

Jagannath said, 'Here your stay arrangements and dinner, everything is ready, why 're you going there? From here arrangements have been made for Priya, so you can also go along with us up to Balrampur.'

They had no choice but to agree and decided to stay there. Jagannath asked Joshi and Mangloo also to join at dinner. They all had dinner together and a memorable evening. After dinner, Joshi met Agastya, Priya, and Devika, embracing each one, and parted with a weeping face, saying, 'Don't know when we meet again in life. Can't say where I go tomorrow. Wish you all happiness and all the best in life. Bye-bye.'

'Here, we too are coming with you to see you off,' said the three friends.

'No, not necessary, don't bother. It's my place. Going all the time,' said Joshi, and he left quietly with Mangloo, looking towards them.

The three stayed back. They prepared for the morning journey. Agastya gave the details of Rohan to Priya and said, 'Reaching Balrampur, we will see if we too can go directly further up to Lucknow.'

Priya said, 'Tomorrow I would go up to Gonda, would stay there for the night, next morning would go to Lucknow.'

The next morning, they started on their journey and reached Balrampur by 1.30 p.m. to the place of stay of Agastya. After having lunch there, Agastya offered to Priya that he would escort her up to Gonda and come back by evening train. But Priya said, 'It's not required. I'll go.'

Agastya went up to the railway station to help her board the 2.30 p.m. train and see her off.

Priya reached her home and stayed for the night there. It was her first homecoming after she joined the service at Lucknow. She was received very warmly. A lot of complaints came from all family members for her not visiting them for so long and having no communication with them. Their major thing of complaint was 'You are now in service and self-dependent, why didn't spare time to come home and didn't remain in touch with the family?'. However, she pacified all. There it had become a festive occasion in the family for the night. Next morning, she left for Lucknow and reached her place by noon. After her lunch and a little rest, she picked up her set daily routine.

PRIYA HELPS THE
CAPTIVES RECOVER

She made several phone calls to her contacts and tried to find out where the four rescued persons were kept in Lucknow and who the authority she could contact for permission to see them was. At last, she could know the right person, his office address, and his contact number. Next morning, in the office hours, with one of her well familiar colleague, she went to the deputy superintendent of police, Central District, Lucknow. The office of the DSP (Security) made a thorough enquiry and got her identity and purpose of visit established as to why they were interested in these four persons. After the full satisfaction of the officers, they were allowed to meet the DSP concerned. He got the whereabouts of the four persons and learnt that these four persons were not in their normal health conditions. They had been physically and mentally tortured. Hence, they had been kept in the isolation ward, away from the public, and no one was allowed to meet them. They were also not in a position to talk. They were in trauma and their condition was pathetic. So the officer expressed inability to help them see the four persons for at least another two months. He also advised her to keep in touch as, when things change, he'd do his best to help her.

Priya returned to her place and informed Devika of the details and advised them not to come for this purpose until she found it possible. The whole day Priya thought about the issue, the pathetic condition of the four poor fellows, and thought if she could do something for them.

The next day, in the office hours, Priya contacted the DSP and expressed her desire to help these fellows. The officer asked Priya to prepare her project and line of action as to how she proposed to help them and to come to his office to discuss it. He also obtained her contact number and address. Two days later, Priya was called by her principal in her office. She went and found the DSP sitting there with the principal. The officer told the principal that Priya had offered a good social service to help the distressed. It would be a good help to humanity if these persons recovered to their normalcy and joined their families, who must have accepted them dead or lost forever. She would be giving them a new life and so much unexpected happiness to so many. He asked Priya her programme in the presence of the principal. Priya said, 'I would be taking them in my confidence by giving them love and simple gifts, flowers, fruits, and some eatables. And then would be involving them in our simple, homely small group games, activities, and counselling.'

The principal also approved of the idea and assured her full support and also promised to provide a lady expert from the psychology department to help Priya in her venture. The DSP requested the principal to call the psychology person also to the meeting. And the principal called her also, who too agreed to the service. The DSP, then thanking the principal and the two lecturers, Priya and the psychologist, said, 'Right then, I'm going. Would prepare a report of today's meeting. This will be submitted to the DIG [deputy inspector general]. With his approval, we'll proceed further and would inform you accordingly. Actually, why I came here is that the department has planned for sending them to Bareilly Mental Asylum, but for your project, I'll try to convince the authorities to retain them here for some more time and see the progress. Because what I feel is, once sent to mental, they'll be put aside as part a process with no future hopes. Even their family members wouldn't know where they are. Who'll take personal special interest in them. Here, under designed for them, especially this project, they'll be under family-type personal care of tender-hearted ladies. Hope very soon they'll join their families. Our thanks to you for joining hands with police.'

'Working with you for a noble cause and success would be our great pleasure,' said the principal.

The officer left the office. The principal appreciated the work Priya had been doing with the students and asked the two lecturers, Priya and the psychologist, to do their best for the success of the ensuing project.

After two days, the DSP contacted the principal and requested this of her: 'The DIG is keen to meet Priya and the psychologist and wants to discuss the project. An inspector in plain clothes and private car is reaching the college, kindly spare the two, and if possible, you too may come. Please also keep all this information as top secret.'

The principal called the two and kept ready to go to the DIG. In another few minutes, the inspector reported to the principal, and the three left with the inspector. In about another twenty-five minutes they were in the office of the DSP, who welcomed them and took them to the DIG.

The DIG welcomed them and said, 'I'm happy, Ma'am Principal, for the initiative and keen interest you and your young professors are taking in big social causes. This would help us in big way and would prove a strong tie and coordination between police and public. A good new experiment and new hope.' He looked to Priya. 'Please take extra care that the eatables and fruits are not handled by any other outsider and that no outsider is mixed with your students, enter this restricted area. Their life is at stake. Great danger to their lives's surrounding from all sides. In the process of doing good to them, hope we don't put them in serious danger.' The three assured the DIG of their best possible efforts and maximum possible care. The DIG pointed to the DSP and said, 'Be extra careful. Your carefulness will help the young people in achieving the goal. Keep in mind, safety first, they are our responsibility.'

The DSP also assured the DIG his all-out safety efforts and that the DIG need not worry. At the close of the meeting, the DSP arranged for their getting back to the college. In the college, the principal too asked Priya to be extra careful. It was a very serious matter, and it should be kept confidential.

After another two days, the DSP, who was appointed as the coordinator of this programme, sent the time schedule to the principal, and from the next day, a private car was arranged by the DSP for the two lecturers' to and fro transportation. On the first day, the principal accompanied her two lecturers. They went to the tight-security area. On one side of this was a cell section in which serious criminals under remand and custody were kept. And on the other side a big guest house type with several rooms, lobbies, and facility of accommodation was there. They reached the cell side first—they could have a look of the criminal gang members caught from the forest kept there—and reached the place where these four rescued persons were kept with all care, well shaved, dressed hair, good food and clothes, etc. All the four were brought and made to sit comfortably in a well-furnished room. These three with the DSP reached the room and saw them. On the very first sight of them, Priya got stunned and fainted. The other lecturer and principal supported her not to let her fall on the floor, and in the state of unconsciousness, she was taken to a close-by three-seater sofa, making her lie straight on her back. The DSP called the doctor from the same campus and requested the DIG to come. In the next few minutes, the doctor and the DIG were there.

The DIG asked, 'What happened?'

The DSP answered, 'Our main person of the team, Priya, got fainted on the very first sight of them. Never thought she would prove so weak. I'm sorry to put this proposal to you and start this.'

The DIG responded, 'No, no, don't worry. I'm sure it's not her weakness or fear to cause her faint. There looks something else of serious nature, which will come out soon. It's good you took up this project. There is some strange, valuable thing for us. Just wait and watch for a short while.'

The principal was sprinkling water on her face and patted her on her cheeks and kept calling her in a loving voice, 'Priya, listen, beti [daughter] . . . Beti Priya . . .' and so on.

After a few minutes Priya opened her eyes a little and got some consciousness, murmuring in a very low voice, 'No, no, it's not possible.' And she got quiet.

The principal asked her, 'Priya, what's not possible?'

The DIG said to the DSP, 'Saw. I told you. You will get some valuable thing. It's not due to fear to her. But there is some big shock to her. She has seen something unbelievable, and that's what we want. Unknowingly you have done a big thing.'

Priya got a little more conscious. Now in a bolder voice, she uttered, 'No, no, it's not possible. How could he be here?'

The principal said, 'Priya, be brave. Who couldn't be here?'

'This . . . this man, Kālu Ram Joshi, can't be here.'

'He is Kālu Ram Joshi? How do you know?' asked the principal.

'He's Joshi, caretaker of my village forest guest house. But how's he here? Day before yesterday, he was at dinner at my place. He got this big haul and gang captured. How 'as he come here? And if he is here and had been captive for some years, then who's there serving at the guest house? Five, six days back two cash awards of rupees one lakh and rupees 25,000 had been given to him. His range officer gave him award of rupees 25,000. This serious matter needs to be probed into.'

The doctor was also surprised but, finding her normal, left the place.

The four poor men were just sitting and gazing with broad, open, unblinking eyes. Priya further said, 'Don't worry. I'll do my best. I'll help them. This is all the more reason to help them. Out of these four, two are my close ones, this Joshi and this one, Rohan. The addresses of these two are here.' She took out a diary from her bag and showed it to the DIG. The DSP took it and noted down the two addresses.

The DIG spoke to the DSP, 'Much of your problem is solved. And another case for investigation has to be started.

You note down what Priya has said. Make the principal and psychologist the two witnesses. And initiate the case. We will send a team with photograph of this man to Dera Chowk, the guest house, with Gonda Police. Also call the Gonda Forest Department with personal dossier of Joshi with his photograph. And the college authorities with given roll number, admission form, photograph, and personal identification marks, etc., of Rohan Kumar. Also call BSF camp commandant with identity and photographs of the persons they captured. Let him too confirm the identity of the persons they arrested and those who are here.'

It was becoming difficult for Priya to become normal. But she tried hard and decided to handle the group. The DIG told DSP to prepare tea for all the seven there with some snacks and fruits available there. The DSP further ordered for an inspector as desired. The DIG took the DSP to his car, talking to him, and said to him, 'Saw how important information you got. Now see what comes out of this investigation.' And the two left the place with instructions to the inspector. 'After tea, whenever they want to leave, ensure safe return of the four to their safe places under strict supervision. And arrange for their drop at the college.' Inspector saluted with 'Sir' and returned to the principal and the staff.

They were sitting there with the four. Priya patted them, tried to talk to them, asked for their names, etc., asked them to do something, like 'Please get me that paper. Put this hankie there. Take this water. Drink it', just to see how reactive and responsive they were.

After some time tea was served. They didn't respond to it. Nor did they take any snack. Priya took the faces of each one of them in her palms, loved them, looking in their eyes. Keeping one hand on their shoulder, by her other hand she asked them to hold the cup and sip it (for them, tea wasn't so hot but extra sweetened). This few minutes' exercise with each one made them enjoy the tea and snack she gave by her hand. Thus, they all took tea together. They didn't speak a word, but they started responding to her instructions. And it appeared that they liked this meeting. Priya then picked up a ball and threw it to them and asked them to send it back, which they attempted. And after several attempts, encouraged with laughter, smiles, and cheers, they started stopping the ball and throwing it back to the person of their choice or from whom they got it. After a play for about twenty minutes, they changed to music; musical tune of thrilling songs were put on. The three ladies started taking dancing steps and actions and made them stand with them. In their simple way, just by moving their bodies, legs, and hands, they tried. Then Priya showed them a small album with some photographs of River Rapti, the ghat, Dera, Haati, and Kuhar Lake and the forest areas. On some photographs they took more time and looked to each other. Then they sat and shared fruits together. In fruits, they preferred bananas; one of them took an apple. They started taking it as it is. But Priya peeled it for them and cut the apple into four pieces, taking the core and seeds out. The principal and psychologist also took a banana and, showing them, peeled it. The next banana they took and, without any instructions, peeled and ate.

After spending about an hour with them, the three ladies expressed their desire to go back to college. The inspector took charge of the four and asked them to move to their rooms. But at parting, they kept watching the three ladies, even turning their neck back, and parted unwillingly. Then the ladies also left for their college by the vehicle arranged for them. Coming to the college, Priya informed Devika and Agastya about Joshi and her first day's experience of being with them.

In late evening, at about 10.00 p.m., the DSP contacted the principal on the phone and informed her of the remarkable changes in their behaviour. He said, 'Today they are living like some sensible persons. They are responding to the calls. They took dinner also with urge of taking it and looking to each other with friendly look. Thanks, ma'am, for your cooperation. Kindly also convey our sincere thanks to Miss Priya and the psychologist, ma'am.'

The principal also exchanged the courtesies and said, 'Sir, it's our duty to help you. You are taking so much pains for these poor fellows. They are lucky they are under your care. We would be happy if we could be of any help in your mission. I'll convey your feeling to both of the staff. Thanks for giving us a chance to serve the needy.'

The DSP said, 'My pleasure, ma'am. Thanks and good night.' In return, he heard 'Good night', putting an end to the conversation.

After some time, there came a call from the DIG, adding, 'Good evening, ma'am, I'll be obliged if you could spare your staff for some more time. All these four have come to the state of saying something about them. It'll be a big favour to us. I request you also to kindly keep on supervising this project. Please convey my feelings to the two nice, my daughterly girls. And don't hesitate for any requirement transport or escort, etc., from our side. Sorry to bother you in the late hour.'

'We the whole college staff and students are with you, sir. We would consider ourselves fortunate if could be of any help for good to the society. Thanks for your encouraging words. Thanks.'

'Thanks, ma'am. I'm grateful. Good night.'

'So nice of you, sir. Good night.'

On the following day in the college, the principal called Priya, the psychologist, and the time schedule coordinator. The principal apprised Priya and the other staff of the encouraging changes just in one day and the encouraging response of the police authorities. She further said, 'Seeing this, I have no choice but to continue this new project. Hence'—pointing to the timetable in-charge—'you adjust their periods and keep them free of college responsibilities after 2.30 p.m. till further instructions from me.' And they dispersed.

At 2.30 the police inspector arrived in plain clothes and a privately hired car. Today the principal didn't accompany them. Only the two teachers went on their mission.

Today as soon as they were freed from their rooms, they straightaway had gone to their common sitting room and looked at the teachers with some familiar look and sat as the teachers had asked them to sit. Priya asked them their names. When she asked (yet to be confirmed) Joshi and Rohan, they gave a look as if saying, 'Why is she asking me my name? Doesn't she know it? Casting an eye of hope?' Today they didn't require much of extra effort to get anything done by them. They looked happy to get a civilised world and the women characters in their real-life drama. They didn't speak anything today also, but they were cooperating in a better way and were more responsive. Priya had brought some books. She gave one book each to them. They took the books, saw their covers, opened them, turned over the pages in a way as if they understood the books. At tea, they took tea and snacks without anyone coming to them. Yesterday the meeting was strenuous for the principal and staff, but today it wasn't so. It was being enjoyed by each one. Priya and the psychologists tried their techniques to enable them to speak and improve their condition by speech therapy. They tried to show them shapes of mouth and tongue and spoke words close to their faces, which they also tried. In their every action and reaction, there was much improvement. About one hour was a happy period of their get-together. At the end, they parted with parting feelings and expressions on their faces. This process continued for a week. They were able to speak some words and were able to recollect some events of their lives.

On the other side, the police was interrogating the gang members also about the particulars of each one of them, about their others fellows, their sphere of activities, their area of action, criminal acts they had committed—with time, dates, places, and magnitude, etc. From them also police asked about these four persons. From where they were kidnapped, how they were kidnapped, how they were used, how they had been treated, and how they had reached this state of their health, etc., etc. From them also useful information was obtained; still there was a lot to come out. These hard-core criminals were very cunning; much of the information they were giving was confusing, misleading, false, and at times contradictory. Hence, it was not made public and was kept confidential.

FAKE KALU RAM
JOSHI DISAPPEARS

After a week's time, the camp commandant, the Forest Range officer, Devika, Agastya, and police officers from Balrampur and Gonda, and authorities from Rohan's college arrived with all available records with them. Agastya was with some photographers. By the time they arrived there, it was afternoon. Priya, with her colleague, was with the group. The DIG and the DSP, with their other staff, were also there. Jagannath had also come to see all this and to meet his daughter.

On the very first sight, Agastya and Devika were in a state of utter confusion. They could only say, 'How is it possible?' The camp commandant and the range officer were also confused. How was this man here? And if he were Joshi, who was that man exactly with the same appearance calling himself Joshi? To whom had they given the cheque of rupees one lakh?

The range officer said, 'Yeah, the same man. I gave him rupees 25,000.'

The DSP from Balrampur said, 'As per instructions from the headquarters, we have made enquiries, traced the two cheques. These have been credit into the bank account of Kālu Ram Joshi at his hometown, Basti. We have enquired and confirmed his wife has been getting monthly family expenses every month. Every month, he has been visiting the family and passing on money. For last few months had been giving rupees 500 more. But for one-and-half years has never stayed there for more than an hour.'

'This is greatly surprising. Even yesterday, I met Joshi in my village. He asked me if I'm going to Balrampur and Lucknow. On my saying yes, he asked me to convey his regards to Devika, Agastya, and Priya. He further asked me to tell these not to forget him and that he'll keep up the commitment of his remaining as a true friend. At me he kept on gazing and said, "Good-bye, Seth-ji. Don't forget me. Who knows which parting may become the last?" And wished me all the best, happy journey. Till I could see, by turning back, saw him looking towards me,' said Jagannath.

The camp commandant said, 'These four are the same whom we rescued from the base of the gang. You may see their photographs, fingerprints, body identification marks, etc. There is no change.'

'As per our records also, the same facts and same persons,' said the DSP from Balrampur.

And this headquarter's DSP also confirmed and said, 'These are the same persons as handed over to us. Now you may see the person who has become Joshi there. Fake man has been in government service, enjoying facilities. But strange he has been serving too faithfully and could get such a big thing happen. Rescued these four people. He had not been rival to Joshi for job.'

'I would be sending a team to Dera Chowk to find facts. Hope these Joshis are not twins. The reality would be established. Case would be initiated against fake one. Even if it is one of the twins,' said the DSP from Balrampur, instructing his inspector accompanying him from Balrampur to initiate the case on the basis of enquiry initiated by headquarters, Lucknow. 'And go there, Dera, with your team.' He further instructed to keep this information confidential. 'And go there at earliest so that he doesn't get alert and disappears before you reach. We are now straightaway going to Balrampur from here. You must go non-stop on horses with weapons. There is no phone service, he won't know to be alert.'

'Though he had been with us and has served us sincerely, but we would like to know the reality,' said Agastya.

'He has done well to everyone. Has saved the family of real Joshi of starvation and getting perished. Had come to know of his disappearance for one-and-a-half year. Who could be this divine soul? Who has been doing all impossible for the benefit of everyone coming his way?' said Devika.

'He must be knowing all what is happening, where and even what would happen in near future. Didn't he tell you, Agastya and Devika, to come to Lucknow with me or I may get fainted here, seeing these four persons? And if you remember, he also told us all that besides Rohan, we may get one more as surprise here?' said Priya.

'Strange! Who this man can be? This is unbelievable. Must be traced out. Justified action has to be taken. Do the needful, DSP Balrampur,' said the DIG. He further said, 'Here condition of these people you must have seen. This was beyond hope at our level, and we had decided finally to send them to Bareilly Mental Asylum for at least four months. But then at the final moment this nice girl, Priya, had come to our help with her friend and colleague, this psychologist. In one week they transformed them into sensible human beings. Her principal has extended good help to these two girls. Whatever you are seeing is her just one week's efforts.'

Everyone saw Priya with gratitude and praised her. Her father there felt honoured and proud of her. He understood the price Priya had paid for her social service and the value of her work. Agastya and Devika also felt regard or respect for her valuable social service and were proud of their friend.

Besides the above, they could well establish the identity of Rohan. Devika and Priya were happy that they got Rohan, their lost friend, back, whom Devika had accepted as her life partner, and now also she loved him. Though now marriage had become secondary to her. Agastya also felt happy, feeling as if their mission was accomplished. But the identity of all these four would not be disclosed to anyone.

After confirming the identity of these four rescued men, especially that of Joshi, the police team, the commandant, the range officer, etc., all left for their return journey. Jagannath also left for Gonda after meeting Priya, whereas Priya, Devika, and Agastya left for the place of Priya. They all wanted to go to Dera to see the fate of Joshi there. But Priya had committed here to the police to attend to the four they rescued. In her newly started service, she might not get any more leave. She couldn't even ask for it so begged for an excuse. Instead, she requested Devika and Agastya to say sorry to Joshi for her not coming. Devika and Agastya decided that they would go to Dera to see Joshi. Since the police party would be going non-stop from here, they would reach much earlier and arrest him. They would be able to see him at Balrampur in custody, so the two decided to go next day early morning.

At night, Devika and Priya stayed together in a close-by hotel. They were confident that the Rohan and Joshi matter would soon be settled. And now Priya had made her reach to these two. She had a say in police department. With this in mind, Agastya and Devika left for Balrampur early morning. By noon they were at Balrampur and contacted the police to know about the fake Joshi. Getting no information and without waiting for any more time, they left for Dera. On the way also, they didn't come across the police party and reached Dera at the house of Priya. There they found the guest house and the attached servant's quarters, the residence of Joshi, were cordoned by the police force. But there was no sign of Joshi. Mangloo was also in the village, having no idea. The corps (soldiers) had taken their positions in the forest, away from common men's sight but looking at the guest house. Seeing all was clear, Agastya,

Devika, and Mangloo went to the guest house side. There they saw Joshi coming from his residence with his keys and opening the guest house. They saw him entering the guest house. Seeing him, the police had also come close. The police asked Mangloo about Joshi.

'He is in the guest house, just entered in,' said Mangloo. The police took their position, alert, and entered the guest house; with the police went in Devika and Agastya and Mangloo. The police searched every nook and corner but found only a paper, which read as under:

> Trying to catch me, no use. Give up your futile attempts, I'm so close to you. You need not go anywhere for me. And I'm so far away you can't reach me. Look into your heart, you will find me. In the necessities of honests you will get me. In the honest efforts of sincerest, you will find me. I'm always restless to help deserving and to console deprived. Don't feel sad on my turning invisible. Don't shed your valuable tears on my parting away. I had been to heaven. There was eternal peace around. No bodily pain, hunger, or thirst. No longings, desires, urges, fear, or anger. No sorrows, no sufferings or happiness. No sadness of parting and happiness of meeting dear ones. No tiredness, sickness, or zeal and enthusiasm. Always in the same state of meditation, calm and contented

under strict hierarchy and its privileges. I thought what this life is about. This made me restless to experience the mortal world. Here, if there are sickness, body pains troubles, there are efforts and happiness to regain these. Longings, desires, urges, fears, anger, making human beings active, thoughtful, keen to rise to sky heights, glorious life, happiness and satisfaction to live it.

If there is sadness on parting, there is desire, hope of meeting, and happiness, jolly time in meeting dear ones.

There are spices of change—everything changing: changing seasons, weathers, rivers, mountains, landscapes, villages, cities, moods of oceans—earth and skies, flora and fauna, human beings, moods, lives, relations, and whatnot.

Silvery shivering snow-covered cold desert, blinding sandstorms, but also shading cool oasis, drizzling and snowing clouds, murmuring struggling streams, gorgeous rapids and waterfalls, and blooming, freshening vast greeneries. Valuable metals and precious stones which decorate even gods.

Everything that can be thought of is here in this physical world. If lived wisely, this earth is much better than heaven. Thinking all this escaped from the heaven, for my dear ones on earth. I'll ever be with you. Join together to make and keep this world a worth-living-in habitat.

Every time with everyone to their help,

Sincerely,
Joshi, Kālu Ram

'What's this paper? No use to us, we don't want paper. We want that fake Joshi. You may keep it. It does not give any clue of anything,' said the police officer. Agastya took it, touching to his two eyes and forehead. Devika also took it and touched with her forehead.

'My paper looked misleading and useless to you. I too would be misleading and useless for you, irrational man, and all alike you. But a true friend, philosopher, guide for gentle persons, respecting others' individuality . . .' There came this voice from behind the guest house.

All of them looked towards the origin of that voice and saw the back of a man. Suddenly Devika said aloud, calling Agastya, 'Joshi.'

Joshi was going away deeper towards the forest. Devika, Agastya, and Mangloo, also following behind the police in the jungle, were not far from Joshi. Hearing Devika cry, fast-going Joshi turned his head back and waved the fingers of his raised hands to these three. He might have seen the tears rolling down the cheeks of these three. He could simply say, 'No, no'—touching both his cheeks and wiping these—'bye.' He turned his face front and walked faster than the fastest of the policemen.

The officer said, 'Don't worry, where he will go, would be caught soon.' He further said, 'Joshi, no use running away. Can't escape. Come to us, we will save you. You are not a criminal.'

But he didn't look back. He kept on going till he reached a big old banyan tree. He easily climbed it and stood on a big fat branch of the tree before a tree hollow. From the tree he saw with grave face the police personnel and his three weeping friends below.

The police officer said, 'Exactly the same look of Joshi. We are going to catch this fake fraud man. Joshi, come down. We'll help you. You are not criminal. Otherwise, also now you can't go anywhere. Come down.'

There was no response from the other side. He kept standing on the branch, and the police officer, all his force, and the three sobbing friends were all looking upward, standing there down the branch. Suddenly Agastya took out a Kuhar Lake visit photograph, which was shot by Devika, taken with Agastya and Joshi, the lake in the background. But in the print, there was no Joshi.

Seeing it, Agastya said, 'We lived together, you helped me so much. Now won't have even your photo for remembrance and respect. Devika, you clicked us two in this picture, but he is not there.'

'He wasn't like us, he was a divine soul. And souls don't come in pictures,' said Devika.

Both were looking at the photograph; only Agastya was there. They kept watching the blank place of Joshi and feeling sad.

Exclaimed Agastya surprisingly, 'Devika, see, his photo print has come in the scenery. He is there by my side.' Both saw him surprisingly on the tree with a smile.

Joshi also became light and smiled, saying, 'Good, this was the cheerfulness and smile on your faces I was waiting for.' Raising a hand, he said, 'Bye.' Then he looked front to the tree hollow, bent on his hands, crawling, inserted his head into the hollow, and slowly took his body in. This was the last look of him they could have. There was now peace all around, as if nothing had happened. All kept peacefully standing on the ground without understanding as to what to do.

After some time, the officer ordered a constable to climb, to see, and to bring him down, pulling him out of the hollow. He reached the hollow and kept standing outside; he could not dare to put his hand in, and he asked his boss, 'Saab! He might be sitting with pistol there, or there may be some poisonous thing there in the hollow.'

'What fearing policeman! Hit the hollow with your bayoneted rifle, let him be injured. He hadn't listened us. He himself would be responsible for any such thing,' said the officer.

'Not needed, I am coming. I'll take all risk, and if he's there, I'll catch and bring him down,' said Agastya as he tried and climbed the banyan tree.

But before Agastya could reach them, obeying orders, the constable had tried his bayonet. He hit aimlessly in the hollow; there came a painful shriek. 'Aai!' On pulling back the gun, they were seeing a stained bayonet with thick, fresh blood. The faces of them all turned, squeezed with the feeling of pain. Devika covered her face with both hands, Agastya got stunned, and Mangloo too felt like weeping. Agastya, with courage, went ahead close to the hollow. He put his right hand in it but didn't touch anything; he also put his head in and could see nothing. The hollow was not deep, nor very big. It could be seen in full. 'There's nothing here. It's all empty,' said Agastya.

The officer, not satisfied, asked the sepoy to look in. The sepoy, feeling safe now, got close to the hollow, saw in from outside, seeing it clearly but for a deep bayonet mark on the front-face wall. He put his head in. But suddenly he got stuck up by a hand-like thing. He tried hard but couldn't get free. He started crying, got nervous, and started restlessly throwing his legs, dangling in the air. Agastya, sitting by his side, didn't understand as to what was happening there. At last Agastya went forward, saying, 'Let me try to help the man.'

And the sepoy also in his heart felt sorry for the disrespect and the bayonet attack. He cried, 'O God! Save me.' Agastya caught his head. The sepoy found it totally free. He sat quietly there, feeling grateful in his heart. Again he looked in with respectful eyes, putting his head in. He felt nothing. He searched with his hand inside; it didn't strike anything. He looked down at the officer, telling him, 'Sir, here, there's nothing.'

'Okay, come down,' said the officer.

Then Agastya thought to pay one last respectful visit to the hollow; in fact, he wanted to pay a tearful bow to his departed friend. Sitting out, he bowed his head in the hollow, touching the hollow floor. He too could not see anything but felt a soothing touch on both cheeks and face in the fresh fragmented flowers. He remained in the position for some time. Down below, someone started saying, 'Oh, see, hope he too is not got stuck.' But it was nothing to him; he quietly took his head out and up.

He picked up the flowers in both joined hands and got down, followed by the sepoy. He later distributed those flowers to Devika, Jagannath, and Mangloo, keeping some for Priya and himself. That sepoy also requested for a flower, saying, 'Kindly give me also one. I'll be paying respect to it daily.' Agastya gave him two. Thus the banyan tree and its site had become a place of worship.

AGASTYA WINS
MIDTERM POLL

They were still there that a messenger came running there and handed over a letter to Agastya. Agastya made the messenger feel comfortable and, with curiosity, opened the letter he just got. It was urgent, from Dina Nath, informing him that as a god sent opportunity, one seat of the Gonda Legislation Assembly of the state had fallen vacant for a midterm election. And that they both, Agastya and Devika, should immediately get to Gonda, where Dina Nath was waiting for them. They both bowed to the banyan tree hollow and, thanking Mangloo, moved to Priya's house. From there, they hurriedly started for Balrampur and further to Gonda to join a prearranged meeting there. In the meeting, with one voice it was decided that Agastya would be the party candidate for the forthcoming midterm poll.

And in the auspicious hours of the fifth day from the day, with a full crowd of party workers, friends, and relatives, with a band and all possible cheering, Agastya would go for the registration of his name in the collectorate. Though Agastya proposed Devika's name, even Devika preferred Agastya. And it was final. Priya was also invited to the big event of registration. And on the stipulated day, it was successfully completed as decided.

Now was the time of the real test. Everyone except Dina Nath was unexperienced. And Dina Nath, being a counsellor at the top level, was not in touch with ground realities. Everyone was working with utmost sincerity, but no one knew how the things were happening. Ultimately, Dina Nath called top party workers and expressed his satisfaction on canvassing. He informed them that he had come to know that on ground grass-roots level, there were several workers in each, even small hamlets. Election too was over with full satisfaction. And finally the counting day arrived; in spite of breath-stopping situations several times, Agastya won with a big margin of 150,000 votes. It was a big day for the party, and the party celebrated it in a big way, giving due credit to the persons making the party candidate win.

First of all, they all went to the temple with a band and a lot of hullabaloo. There the senior leaders got the worship performed through temple priests and offered sweets, flowers, and garlands to the deity. And then there were the workers, relatives, and friends to garland him and share their happiness with him. Priya garlanded him. Enjoying the scene, Devika joked, 'Bahini, don't be in so hurry, band's there, all relations and friends are there, sweets and big dinner's arranged, 'as already garlanded in temple. Why in so hurry? Go easy and don't deprive us of another enjoyable opportunity. We will start celebrating fifteen days earlier. I'll join on your side.'

'I'll call Rohan on my side, we two will bring you too, along with Priya,' said Agastya.

'That's right, first my dear sister, afterwards me,' Priya said, laughing. Devika turned a bit serious.

They stopped the topic. Agastya called Devika, saying, 'Come on, we have to go to Dina Nath-ji.' Meeting him, Agastya said, 'Guru-ji, with your blessings and guidance and wholehearted hard work and support of these untiring, willing supporters, this big miracle has happened. But your blessings will not be up to here only. Lifelong we'll be needing you.'

'Sure, I'm with you, challenging time is ahead of us. Bigger the tree, more storms it suffers. Each one of you, prepare yourselves for everyday challenges now onward,' said Dina Nath.

One of the party workers arrived with a carload of sweets. Kanshi Ram, with this load, took out a packet to Agastya. He first offered this to the temple and the priest, another for Joshi in the temple. Someone spoke from the crowd, 'Come on, sir, who knows who all worked with you and who are sharing sweets on joyous occasion with you?'

'Wish your words are true,' said Agastya, Devika, and Priya in one low voice. Kanshi Ram offered sweets to the trio and Guru-ji. It was the time all were collectively enjoying the victory and sharing sweets. Suddenly there arrived a car there. The rear door opened, and two persons appeared, followed by two police constables. They came closer to the temple where Agastya and the others were standing.

Seeing them, Priya exclaimed, 'Joshi, Rohan, here! How did you come?'

One of the constables said, 'Ma'am, they and we heard election result, and they knew you would also be here. They both insisted to come for few minutes and join at this joyous moment. Then saab arranged it under security and deputed us with strict instructions to reach back by midnight. Soon we would be going back.'

Priya, Devika, and Agastya expressed their happiness. They talked of their improvement. They and the constables were offered sweets. For these four persons, immediate and urgent dinner was arranged. Kanshi Ram was searched for this. But he was not traceable anywhere. Agastya himself ensured their comforts and dinner. After dinner, they offered to leave and soon they left.

After this, the band played, crackers were busted, and the office was lit with decorative lights. Some workers, ladies and gents, danced to the beats of drums and the tune of the band. This *hungama* went on for hours, which ended at the place where community dinner was arranged.

Dina Nath and Priya were requested to stay for another day for a meeting the next day for future plans. And it was conducted the next day. At the same time, there was a special message from the secretariat for Agastya to report there. And the four, including Dina Nath, reached Lucknow. Before leaving for Lucknow, Balendu, Nidhi, and Kanshi Ram Joshi were requested to stay back and meet Agastya and the others in Balrampur after they came back from Lucknow. Devika, Agastya, and Dina Nath stayed in the MLA's accommodation provided to Agastya. Priya also went to see this. Devika passed a jolly remark onto Priya. 'Come and see your house, now onwards it would be your house.'

Priya smiled and counter-remarked, 'Mine or yours, you would be using it more.' She further eased it on Devika's mind. 'It's a political base. I'll be here because of you.'

After settling down, Agastya and the others went to the secretariat, where Agastya reported. He and Dina Nath were welcomed and congratulated by the secretary and the chief minister. Dina Nath introduced Devika, vice president of the party, and Priya, assistant professor and a high-ranking party and social worker. They too were welcomed. A simple oath ceremony was administered. All present there congratulated the two and wished them the best of luck. A well-equipped site office with literature and a personal staff, like steno typist, and personal assistant (better understood as PA), were earmarked. The chief minister gave his advice to him and then said, 'What advice I can give you? Even our political teacher and sincere adviser, respectable to all, Dina Nath Attri-ji, is with you.'

'Thanks, sir, so nice of you, I feel greatly honoured. Under able and successful person like you, he will learn a lot and would have a good experience,' said Dina Nath.

'Wish I'll get his valuable support and he proves himself useful to the country and the society,' the CM said.

After high tea, he got a time schedule and period of sessions. Agastya said to the CM, 'Sir, before I get busy here, I would like to go to the public—a hurried tour of the area and meet and say thanks to the public, who sent me here.'

'This is good, a healthy tradition, you should go to the public, thank them, and ask their difficulties and highlight these here in the House,' said the CM. They left the secretariat, paying due regards to all. Dina Nath was seen off at the railway station, and the three came back to the accommodation of Agastya. The two ladies set the house to the ladies' taste.

In the evening, taking time from the DIG, Agastya, Priya, and Devika went to see him with packets of sweets. There the DIG and the DSP congratulated Agastya and welcomed them. At the happy meeting, in chit-chatting, the DIG said, 'We were thinking the three social workers have been helping us. From now on, we'll feel that political personalities are also helping us for the good cause.'

'Very true, sir,' said the DSP.

The four rescued were also there. They too felt happy seeing Priya and the others. Seeing them, Priya asked,

'Hope they reached back safely yesterday night. What time the two, Joshi and Rohan, reached back here? We freed them after hurried dinner by 8.30 p.m.'

The DIG and DSP saw each other, and the DIG said, 'Dear daughter, what are you saying? I'm not able to make out. Where could have they gone? They haven't even asked. Had they asked, I myself or the DSP could have taken them to you. You aren't less responsible than any one of us. But neither had they asked, nor did they go anywhere. Which place you say they were there?'

'The two, Joshi and Rohan, were there with us at a temple in Gonda. Two constables, with name tabs Dinesh Singh and Ravi Kant Tiwari, escorted them in a private ambassador car. They garlanded us and shared sweets. We arrange for a quick dinner for all the four. And after that gave them a box of sweets, one-half kilogram one of M/S Shukla Sweets, Gonda, and saw them off for coming here. Their cheeks too got red.'

'Yes, they were with us for about an hour,' confirmed Agastya and Devika too.

All of them looked towards them. On their right in the dustbin, the DSP saw a half-kilogram box. Going close, he found it was really a sweets box, with the said 'Shukla Sweets, Gonda' print. He couldn't say anything but kept watching each other.

'We can't even think that Priya or persons like Agastya and Devika would speak false. By look, sometime some person may give resembling look. And a person could be mistaken for someone else. But living and working with direct contact with our two constables. And they have given correct names and identity. For last ten days, they are on leave to their homes in MP. On this big restricted campus, no one can bring this sort of sweet box. What's this? This is beyond my mind.'

'Yes, sir. We were very much here with them. Could've thought different had we ourselves not been here with them,' said the DSP.

'Our doubt could have gone to some security person etc., and undoubtedly this could have been a case for enquiry. But it's dead certain that they were here with us. And same time four persons, Joshi, Rohan, and two constable with them too,' said the DIG. He further said, looking at Priya, 'Priya-ji, these persons, not a single one of them did go anywhere. And the four persons who were there with you might have been all the time with you on different occasions, in befitting forms suiting to the occasion, serving you quietly. How many more miracles we'll have to see? Miraculous men. We fear their miracles don't take away our services and livelihood. May God help us,' said the DIG.

'Once again Joshi and party 'as shown us they are superb. Our success has been for them. How cleverly they came and shared in our happiness. One thing is sure, these divine souls are always around us, doing good to us. We may not see and recognise them. But they find appropriate time and the ways to help us, provided we are actively on our move. They keep us showing right path and help us in our pursuits.'

'Absolutely correct, DIG Sahib,' said Agastya in a pensive mood. He further said, 'Now let us accept what has happened and go ahead with our schedules.' Thus, after a short get-together Agastya and the others got up to leave and left for their places.

One afternoon in Lucknow, Priya and her colleague, the psychologist, were with her group; they were happily busy in playing way reformative activities. Suddenly Joshi, in his game of hide and seek, slipped to some side and got injured badly, shrieking in pain. All rushed to the spot, attending to Joshi, and found a long, deep cut on the outer side of his right thigh. Even his pants were torn with a cut mark. Inspector called the DSP, and the DSP the DIG. All reached there in no time. They saw Joshi and his wound. They asked each one; no one could say anything. No one had seen anyone. The DIG speculated some conspiracy and hand of some gang member. He ordered an enquiry in the case, a review of the present security, and further tightening of it. He said, 'Thank God he escaped attempt on his life and he is safe.' The DIG and DSP left with a sigh of relief, leaving instructions and verbal warning to the inspector. But no one had doubt on Priya. However, Priya introspected on her way of working. How it happened. Both the teachers were speechless on the unbelievable incident and the lurking danger on these four. She gave a thought to it, if she should continue or should stop this social service which may endanger her integrity and make her liable to explanations and enquiries. But seeing the improving conditions of these, she decided to keep it on.

At Balrampur, the inspector, DSP, and SP prepared the report as it had happened and, in support, sent the blood-stained bayonet to the headquarters of the state police in Lucknow. Here at police headquarters, the DIG constituted a committee to thoroughly go through and consider this report. And the bayonet was sent to the lab for a study of the blood on it.

The Joshi Case Finding Committee prepared and submitted the report. stating as below:

> The members reached on a common consensus and the report prepared and submitted as under—

> . . . in this age of advanced science and technology and modern education, the committee had never thought of submitting a mythical report. But based on scientifically proved documents and witnesses, the committee accepts the report submitted by Balrampur Police Headquarters. Also going through the whole track record of the events connected with the second fake Joshi, the committee could not find any action by him against any person or community; rather he has been found a big help and support to all. At the same time, he got a big international and interstate gang of criminal busted and saved the nation from a big disaster.

There has also not been any charge of any misuse of any fund. The big amount of money award given to him has also been, though miraculously, deposited in the right person's bank account. And similarly to the penny, the salary of Joshi has been going to his family regularly, saving the family from starvation and a miserable life. In the absence of the genuine Joshi, for a long period of about two years, a fake person could have easily been tempted, embezzled the whole money, and could have taken innumerable undue advantages. But nothing such undue has been committed by the fake man.

The committee also put on record that there was no lapse on the part of the Lucknow police in connection with the injury of Joshi. It was part of the mythical story. No one should feel sorry at Lucknow, and the Priya team has been doing commendable work. Keeping all above facts and realities in view, the committee opines that the fake Joshi has been faithful and sincere to humanity and the country. His arrest process and case may be closed in larger interest of the people of the country. The report is being sent to the IGP, Uttar Pradesh, Lucknow, SP, Gonda, and Police Headquarters Balrampur.

There was no Joshi in Dera Chowk, the guest house. Mangloo, with wet eyes, had been managing and taking care of the guest house. His eyes had been every time searching for his Joshi godfather, who had made him, a pauper, into a respectable rich man and a forest department representative in the area.

Now there was only one Joshi, and he was in Lucknow. His condition was every day improving with his other fellows. It was hoped that in a month they would be perfectly all right to give their statements about themselves and about the incident of their falling in the trap of the gang, and also about activities of the gangsters.

The DSP, with a copy of the report, came to the college, to the principal's office, and asked her to call Priya and the psychologist. On the arrival of these two, in an informal sort of meeting, the DSP showed the copy of report on the Joshi episode and said, 'Ma'am, would you believe, in this scientific era, some divine soul came and lived with the people for so long? Saved the family of Joshi from being perished by serving for real Joshi? And then not only saved these four, his friends, from the gangsters but also the nation from a disaster? At last, when everyone had come to know about him and police chased him on the arrival of real Joshi on the scene, he disappeared in big hollow of a banyan tree. Our one sepoy hit his bayonet inside the empty hollow there, the bayonet was stained with Joshi's blood. I was thinking, Priya was feeling sad because Joshi got hurt when he was under her charge. Even then, she couldn't say a word how it happened. We had failed to believe that she didn't see anything. Rather we felt that she was protecting and shielding someone at the cost of life of these four poor persons. Ma'am, I'm sorry to you all three. You would agree with me, we people are very suspicious. Our work is such. And in this plain case, anyone could have thought alike us. Kindly don't mind. I beg your pardon. And I'm happy to inform you that here is the report, the special committee has commended your work. In such a short time, you have performed this wonderful work. These people are happy and welcome you on your going there. On your coming back, they feel sad. I congratulate you on your successful execution of this project.'

Priya was wiping tears off her cheeks; still these were continuously rolling down in a streak. All tried to console her. But no use. The DSP, thinking something might have gone wrong on their part, feeling sorry, said, 'Priya, it looks you haven't excused us for our asking you to explain the incident of getting Joshi hurt in a game. Please don't mind, it's part of life. You see, in front of you, I even warned the inspector. You know we are the custodians of the lives of the people, have to become harsh at times. Feel happy everything has gone so well, the chapter is closed.'

'No, sir, nothing as such . . .' said Priya.

'Then? A person like you, weeping for our behaviour.'

'No, sir, it's not that. All may feel happy on the close of the chapter. But for me, it's a big pathetic and tragic ending. I've lost a sincere friend. Sir, you haven't seen and met him. He was so helpful for all. To my dad, he had given new field of work and source of earning. We have lived together. He 'ad been my fast friend, an elder brother. When he was with us, didn't know he is some supernatural. And now he 'as left for good in my absence. Couldn't even meet and see him.'

In the meantime, Agastya and Devika, asking for permission, entered the office. Greeting everyone in the room, Agastya said, 'Now here's your Joshi.' He took out a red-coloured cloth pouch from his bag and took out some flowers from the pouch. The entire chamber was filled with the sweet fragrance of the flowers, as fresh as those on the bushes and plants. Everyone was surprised. He gave four flowers to Priya, saying, 'Take these and keep your Joshi with you forever.' She took these in both her hands and touched these to her eyes and forehead. He also gave one each to all present there and narrated, 'Me and Devika, we both were there with the police. Joshi was going in front of us, but no one could reach him. Reaching a big banyan tree, he climbed up and, entering a small hollow, disappeared. The sepoy hit the hollow with rifle bayonet and tried to see in. But his head was caught so badly that everyone there had given up the hope for his life. At last, he said, "O Gad, excuse me and save me." I caught his head and saw there in. There was nothing, his head was free. Then I put my head and bowed inside the hollow. I couldn't see him, but in his place I got these flowers. At the last moment he kept standing before the hollow, kept on watching our weeping faces. Then I took out the photo album, saw the snap which Devika snapped for me and him. But then in the print he wasn't there. I just saw and said, "Wish you could've been here, at least could see you." At once his image had come up in the print. Devika too saw it. We got happy with cheerfulness on our faces. And expressed our gratitude. He looked last time on us. He too was happy with us and saying, "Good, this's what I wanted to see, you happy and smiling on my final departure." Then turned to hollow, entered in that small hollow, and disappeared. This is how we lost a good friend and well-wisher forever. These flowers were this much only. Had been distributing to so many so far, even then that much. We two felt, keeping some for us, will immerse these in the holy sangam (confluence) at Prayagraj in Allahabad. We here on our way to Prayag, thought of making Joshi's dear sister meet him.' To Priya, he said, 'You too can join, if can.'

Hearing these last words, Priya, weeping bitterly again, touched these flowers to her forehead, saying, 'Oh, dear brother, you left me alone here!' Everyone's eyes were wet. All of them were using their handkerchief and, with blurring eyes, were looking at Priya, who bowed to those flowers. Suddenly, they were all left wide eyed, gaping in surprise, seeing that Priya's hair was seemingly being pressed, as if somebody's hand was put on her head, and her side locks were set right. Feeling the presence of someone close to her and a hand on her head, Priya, with eyes open, looked upwards, where she expected that the face of the person could be. But none was visible there. She sat quietly for a while and then, looking towards Agastya, said, 'I'm busy here with real Joshi, Rohan, and others and have other works also. You please carry on alone to Allahabad. I would like to go home, Dera, and worship him at his sacred hollow, the banyan tree. If permitted, I'll accompany you on your return.'

'Oh, sure you can. I'll manage for your work in the college. Special leave to you for a week,' said the principal.

'Good. The real Joshi and party, I'll manage. Don't weep. This is what your Joshi Bro too likes,' said the DSP. And touching the flower to forehead and keeping it in his purse, he further said, 'Came to know a lot, my good luck, got the Joshi's flower too. I'll keep it with honour. Now would like to go, thanks to all.' And he left.

Priya also asked the principal, 'Thanks, ma'am, anything more for me?'

'No, nothing. Thank you. Put up leave application,' said the principal. The three friends, Priya, Agastya, and Devika, left for Priya's residence. There they talked about all that had happened over the past few days. And what they were planning to do. They were sitting and talking. By night train, they were scheduled to go to Allahabad.

They also decided that, since Agastya and Devika would be in Allahabad for three days, on their return journey, Priya would join them on the station in the morning of the coming Saturday. They would straightaway go to Dera without wasting time on the way.

By next morning, Agastya and Devika reached Allahabad and then the sangam. Here they offered the Joshi flowers to Mother Ganga in the confluence of Ganga and

Yamuna with all the Hindu rituals. And they performed their worship.

After their sacred duty, they went to the place of Dina Nath. Here they didn't talk about the Joshi episode but simply said, 'It has been quite some time that we had not met. And we have come to see you and take further instructions.' They discussed various party matters and returned to their place of stay. On their return journey, at the Lucknow Railway Station platform Priya joined them, and they proceeded further for Balrampur. Reaching Balrampur, they visited the party office, hurriedly finished important pending work, and started for onward journey the same day.

It had become late. They wanted to cross Rapti before it got dark and hired a taxi for Kishanpur Ghat. Crossing Rapti, they hired horses, but there were only two horses. So Devika and Priya rode together on one, and Agastya on the other. Being night, they hired some extra men to escort them to safety. They moved on with fodder or food for the horses and dinner items for themselves and the escorts. The men carried bamboo sticks, diesel country torches, some sharp-edged weapons, and continued non-stop, reaching Dera at the house of Priya at midnight.

Jagannath opened the door. All in the family were surprised to see them. On meeting them, they expressed their happiness, supressing the pain of the Joshi incident, and didn't initiate any talk about Joshi, because they knew Priya would start weeping. So they talked on different matters, had a light dinner, and retired to their beds. Devika and Priya slept together in one room and Agastya in a separate room.

Next morning, all family members got up early as usual. But the three got up late. After getting fresh and bathing, Priya refused breakfast and desired to see the hollow tree, offer her prayers for Joshi there, and see the tree hollow. Jagannath couldn't help but to help her to her wish. He sent some two, three men to escort her. They also carried a long bamboo ladder, to help her climb up to the hollow. A plate for worship was prepared with items like flowers, wheat flour, sugar, turmeric, purified butter, a jug of water, milk, sweets, earthen lamp, incense sticks, camphor, and vermillion. The three friends started with the escorts. First they reached the guest house and the room where Joshi used to live, which looked deserted and repulsive. They looked at these accommodations, crazy to see Joshi, but he was nowhere. There was heart-sinking silence. They couldn't stand for long there, where they had been staying and enjoying for days and nights, had enjoyed long evenings sitting there. They went ahead through the dense forest. After about half a mile they reached the tree. She stood under it for some time with closed eyes, thinking of Joshi, having his image in mind. Then she cleared and cleaned a small land surface (about two feet by two feet) and made holy symbols, like the swastika, om, star, on it with wheat flour, turmeric, and vermillion and rice. She placed flowers, burning lamp, incense sticks, and camphor on it and offered water, rice, milk, sugar, and sweets to the departed divine soul. After the worship, she desired to reach the sacred hollow. The ladder was placed by the branch of the hollow; she reached the thick stem-like branch, and she sat there before the hollow and looked there inside, bowing her head. She felt the loving touch and could see some flowers. She took these flowers, paid her respects, and came down. All were having heavy hearts and choked throats.

By the time they were about to leave after worship, the police sepoy also arrived there with his family to offer their respects to the divine soul which had not only spared his life but had also showered his blessings on the family. The flower he took on that day was kept in his worship place in his house. It appeared ever fresh. The serious chronic ailment of his wife of joint pains and swelling got cured without medicines, which were long back discontinued. His long-standing claims with the department reached him unexpectedly, and his son cleared his exam with good marks, who was expected a sure failure. So they decided to come here and pay respects at the tree and hollow. Yesterday they could reach the contractor base and arrived early morning on the day. His wife felt sorry why the police made such a figure disappear. But then it was good also; this way, they could know about the divine soul and could get his blessings. Her husband had been fortunate at least to see him. The reason might be any. This place had become a place of worship, especially for the people of nearby villages and for those who had experienced the change in their lives after visiting this place.

The three friends arrived back at the house of Priya. Missing breakfast, they had their lunch. After this Agastya and Devika planned to go back and asked Priya of her plan. She said, 'My purpose of coming here is accomplished. Now don't understand what to do here. Days here look very long, and time stagnant. Here there is no work but time and time. There in cities, no time, only work and work.'

'Don't find excuses for going back. Stay with us, we too will stay for you. Here too you can create work as much as you want. Moreover, you can take it as necessary change. After spending a week here, you can go refreshed and recharged to work more efficiently, and you would be able to do more work. So don't consider it a waste of time. Time spent in hospital is not wastage of it but a necessity, though a curse. This type of energy recharging can save a person from spending time and money in hospitals and its mental agony. Take it as your natural hospital. We would plan for a week,' said Devika. By the way, they were tired, so they relaxed. In the afternoon, they jointly planned for a week to make this a purposeful stay. Mangloo had been visiting and meeting them.

Next day, as per their plan, they left for door-to-door visits, meeting people, asking about their sources of income, amount of income, and problems related to health and education of children and other such things, like at least a primary school and health centre for every thousand population. They collected thumb impressions or signatures of the people of the area and family-related data. Thus, they lived together for one full week. Several times they visited the guest house and the banyan three. They visited all the villages of the area and the labour bases of gravel extraction and catechu centres. They had even been to Kuhar Lake and the village of the name. They also interviewed the government and NGO workers working in the area and noted down their difficulties and suggestions.

In a week's time they covered some thirty villages and thousands of persons. They analysed the information so collected and listed the main requirements of the area and suggestions for the improvement of living conditions and economy of the people of the area.

On the last day, they completely left for their stay at home with the family. During the week, two times they visited the house of Devika also, and one night they stayed there. But the last day, they spent at Dera for complete relaxation and an easier return. After a week, on Sunday, they left for Gonda. There they had a night's stay. On Monday, early in the morning Priya left for Lucknow. And Agastya and Devika, after finishing their pending work, got back to Balrampur. There they prepared the demand of ten primary schools and ten primary health centres in the area and submitted these to the health and education departments with the list of signatures of the people. Soon there was a sanction for five primary schools and one mobile health team for a group of eight villages. Dera was one of the places for the primary school, and the health team too would have its base at the Dera guest house till such time their own buildings were completed. This could be possible in the current budget. The improvised shades and accommodations would be provided before mid June, the onset of monsoons. Agastya informed Priya also of their achievement and good work done in the area and also that this was the child of her one-week stay in the rural area. Now she could have more such happy stays here and more such children. After some time, she sent a message to Agastya. 'Congrats on getting good long-awaited child, wish many more such children in justification of your hard work and for welfare of the area. Here, there's much scope of work.'

THE WAVE OF PROGRESS
COMES TO THE AREA

The Forest Department, on seeing the developmental works in the area north of Rapti, realised that the area was gaining more and more significance. The completion of Rapti Bridge and the two roads would be further impetus for the influx of population here, and they decided that the welfare of the people of the area, especially better economic opportunities, needed to be provided to them so that they didn't damage and exploit the forests for their livelihood, which was their right. To meet these requirements, the Forest Department also introduced various environment- and people-friendly schemes in the area, like local craft training centres in mat making, education, paintings, wee caps, carpet weaving, local shoemaking, and woodcraft and yoga and nature cure health and spiritual centres.

With the coming of these, a total and strict forest preservation and conservation would be implemented.

With this started the influx of many people in the area on construction works of posts, guest houses, towers, staff quarters, resorts, training centres, and embankments and dams on seasonal flows and small streams, with activities, movements of the people, and construction material many local people provided, and other domestic help to the outsider officers. Many people found work on construction sites. They also opened small provisional shops and started more production of fresh milk and vegetables. Everyone looked busy for whole days, be it a lady or a gent, doing one thing or the other.

Months after, Devika called Priya for help for at least a ten-day tour together, and she reached there. In this changed atmosphere, the three started a sweeping tour of the area. Priya was surprised to see the newly active and vibrant whole area. She felt the backwards area so far was now changed into a vibrant area full of activities and life. She humorously smiled and passed a remark to Agastya. 'You got so many children now, these will certainly be the happiness of your courtyard.'

Devika didn't get sense of the children, so she said to Priya, 'Get married first, or are you in so hurry for children, want them before?'

To this Priya replied, 'Your friend is very fond of children. He has been asking me to go for . . . He looked in much hurry. So I told, "Okay, I'll try at Lucknow,"' said Priya. And all three burst into laughter.

Priya further said, 'Now so many works are coming up in this area. People think we brought all these. So many children of others are coming running to you. Let's make a rushing tour to the area to allure these before any other one. Earlier also we have been to almost all villages. People must be recognising us. This time we'll say, now your own persons are contesting election. Make them win for more works and more prosperity in the area.'

'That's right. That's why I called you,' said Devika. 'These are all government works.'

'Government is ours, so no harm for taking credit for government's works,' said Agastya.

The three, with the in-charges of the areas and some other members, made a hurried tour to all villages, especially north of River Rapti. Wherever they went, they were given warm welcome as very close familiars. People were thanking them as their own and were feeling obliged. They not only assured them their own personal vote, stamping on 'Arrow', but they assured their full support and canvassing in their favour. Thus they toured the whole constituency. But north of Rapti looked to them totally theirs. In fact, this was their advance preparation for the state elections, which may come their way. After the successful tour of the area, the three friends returned to Lucknow.

They lived there the whole day, and after seeking time from the DIG, in the evening they reached the police headquarters. The DIG and the DSP welcomed them as a winning team and congratulated them, addressing them, 'Congratulations, sir, and to you too, dear daughters, hope you won't mind calling you by short name. Devika much smaller to your social and official stature,' said the DIG.

'No, not at all, sir, you have honoured us. With your blessings, we will grow. We feel protected and fearless with your hands on our heads,' said Devika.

'This is your greatness. All of the people consider you as their own.'

After they settled down at their comfort, Agastya said to the DIG, 'Sir, here in Lucknow at the moment we don't know anyone except the police headquarters officers, college principal, and staff of Priya's department, her friends and relatives. This is our workplace now, to widen our familiar social circle here, if convenient to you, tomorrow we meet at lunch with our these four friends, the victims of the gangsters, at convenient and safe place. What would you suggest?'

'We would be happy to be with you. Regarding place, it may be our campus. All arrangements would be made by our staff in our mess,' said the DIG.

Agastya thanked the DIG and, after chit-chatting for some time, left the place, to meet next day

The next day it was a big celebration. All important persons from the city, police officers with their families, and college staff enjoyed it. But the persons enjoying this most were the four friends. Now they were perfectly normal persons.

At the lunch, Agastya and the DIG were talking. Priya and Devika were also close by. Agastya asked the DIG, 'Sir, may I request you for a favour?'

'Yes, yes, why not you just order, sir?'

'All these four victims have long been away from their houses and families. Their family members must have taken them as dead or lost forever. Please try to finalise the matter at earliest and give a happy surprise and new life to their families. I don't know anything about others, but Rohan's family has taken him as dead. His sister is of marriageable age, had not been marrying for being her brother lost. Somehow, family convinced her. Shortly her marriage will be finalised. On her marriage day, if you can give a sister the wonderful gift of her life, her brother. We would take Rohan with us for her marriage time, would keep him with us. And would bring him back here with us.'

'Oh, surely, sir, you get the date schedule for two days. You come anytime, just inform us two hours in advance, everything would be ready,' said the DIG. And calling DSP Alok, he ordered him there and then in the presence of Agastya, 'Alok, see, whenever you get words from Sir Agastya for taking Rohan along with him, arrange to send Rohan with him for two days under tight security, in safe police vehicle. Ensure they don't face any problem on this account.'

'Right, sir. Will be done.' Turning to Agastya, he said, 'Right, sir, just inform me. Within two hour, Rohan will be ready to go with you.'

Thus the big party was over on a happy note.

RUPESH OUSTED FROM HIS SCHOOL

Over the past sometime, Agastya had been very busy away from Balrampur, in Gonda, Lucknow, and other parts of the country. He could not take care of Rupesh, the boy he had been taking care of like his younger brother. And taking whom on his engagement day at Balrampur, he humoured with Priya, 'Will this boy do to show you as mom, to impress up on parents?' Nor could Rupesh approach him. Rupesh was the son of a poor man from a nearby village supplying milk to them in the city. At times, the young boy, Rupesh, had been coming to their house in the morning with his father. Agastya, seeing the boy not going to school, arranged for his studies. And now he was in IX class.

As usual, that day also he went to his school but was told that for non-payment of fees, his name was struck off and he could not attend his classes. Seeing no other way, he got back for home but decided to pass the day somewhere on the way in the jungle. On his way back, going on his pedestrian trail yet quite away from his village, he sat down under a big shady tree near the bank of Sheela River joining

Rapti a short distance down from there. At a short distance from the tree, a parting trail from this leading to his village was descending into the river going across it. Sitting under the tree, resting his back on the stem of the tree, Rupesh had been enjoying the nature—sandy banks, quietly flowing crystal-clear blue water deep down in the riverbed, green fields around to the distance. He could see birds flying and chirping, occasionally people coming and going, crossing the river. He was seeing the coming people gradually becoming bigger and distinct and the going ones getting smaller and fading away in the brightness of the day. He was not bored sitting there. It was turning to noon. The sun had become hot. He was feeling like taking his tiffin.

He took it out and in front saw someone rising up from the depths of the river on the trail, coming to his side. In his normal way, the boy, Rupesh, not caring, opened his tiffin, whatever simple food he had, and took it out. In the meantime, the man, with a shovel on his shoulder, also arrived there and said, 'Oh gad, you are great.' Stretching his body, he sat down under the tree for rest. Soaking sweat from his face with a part of his loincloth, he breathed deeply and, looking at the boy, asked him, 'Hi, son, who are you? What's your name?'

This made Rupesh not start with his tiffin and look at the man come there.

'Rupesh Kumar.'

'School bag with books in? You look to be school student. You should have been in the school this time. What doing here?'

In the meantime, without caring for the question and answers, he took out his meal and extended out to him. The man, without moving his hands, looked into the face of the boy, then to the food. He took a little in his hand, saying, 'God bless you, my child.' He touched his forehead and placed it in his mouth in one go, felt relaxed, and said, 'That's enough for me . Long live. You have it.' Rupesh started taking his. While he was taking his food, the man asked, 'You didn't answer. Why here in your school hours?'

'Yes, you are very right. I'm a school student of Ram Nagar School. I went to school, but for non-payment of fees, my name's struck off. Not allowed to attend classes, so had to come. Going back home in school time, whole village would have seen me. My parents would have felt demoralised and embarrassed. I'll go in the evening, no one will notice anything. And in the night after dinner, I'll tell parents, "I'm not keen, so discontinuing my studies. Not going to school anymore." Whole blame would come on me.'

'Otherwise, how are you in studies?'

'I'm good in studies. Come 1 or 2 in the class. And I'm interested too.'

'Would anybody believe you turned duffer, no longer interested in studies?'

'What else I or my parents can do? Many poor intelligentsia go without schooling. Or if somehow could complete schooling with credits, have to drop before going to colleges.'

'Very painful. Deserving don't get.' After a brief pause, the man asked, 'So what would you be doing now?'

'Nothing, from a labour-class family, me too a labour—a child labour, to start with. Rest up to God.'

'You are sitting here so close to the cremation ground. Don't you fear ghosts?'

'What would I fear for? What can ghosts take away from me, me—a poor boy? I have books only. Don't think any ghost would be interested in. Rest nothing. A poor is as good as a ghost. Who wants to come close to poors? Though exceptions are there. Agastya, in fact, had been helping me. He only supported me fully. For him I could come up to this level.'

'Then why he stopped helping at this stage?'

'For past several months, he's not seen around in this area. Busy man. Lot of commitments, responsibilities. I also couldn't meet him. Sure, if he come to know, he would get me readmitted.'

'So sure of him.'

'He's so nice, treats me like his family member. He only saved me from child labour and brought up to this level. Maybe my—this problem's for the time being. I'll soon see for him.'

'Maybe you won't need his help any longer. God's great.'

'May your words come true.'

'Amen. By now quite a good time 'as passed, sitting with you, feeling thoroughly relaxed. By the way, you're sitting here doing nothing, just passing time. I'm thinking of doing small social work. Can you help me?'

'Sure, if could and within my school timings. Then I would be going home. Otherwise, parents would be worriedly searching for me.'

'Don't worry. Hardly one, one-and-half hours' job. Here only. On this very trail you came by.'

'Okay then. Let's move. Why to waste time? My good luck. Doing social service.'

'Good, follow me.' After going a short distance, he stopped near the cremation ground and said, 'Rupesh, my child, I'm an old man. Here's this shovel, taking this, dig it here as I say.'

First Rupesh thought, *What sort of social service's this, digging the foot path?* Soon entered another idea into his mind: *Maybe Old Man's giving me old buried wealth.*

It did not require much effort; he might have dug about a foot only that they saw upper edge of an earthen pot. 'Now cautiously. See old earthen pot doesn't get broken.' Then they worked carefully on it and took the pot out. The pit so caused was filled back and levelled. Now Rupesh was sure this was having old treasure. The old man picked it up, touched it with his forehead, and handing it over to Rupesh, said, 'Done a good job. Now pick this up and follow me.' And he took the boy a little up the crossing site of the river and asked him to empty the pot into the flowing water. Hesitatingly, he obeyed, upending the pot and opening its mouth to the flowing water. Burnt bones and ashes were immersed into the river. 'Fine. For so long people have been walking over these with dirty shoes and feet, dishonouring these. Now these joined the eternity, joining tributary of Ganga. In a way these have gone to Ganga.'

Somehow a thought struck the boy's mind. *How did he know what was under the earth?*

That was when he heard, 'Don't trouble your mind for unnecessary things. And follow me.'

In his mind, he exclaimed, *Oh! Would I be digging these old buried deads today?* But he followed, obeying.

Now he took the boy to about half a mile away into a thick grove of trees, bushes, weeds, and wild, long grass. On one side of it was a totally razed-to-the-ground mud house. Some totally weathered-out wooden roofing material was lying around. Here he asked Rupesh to come to a place which must have been the inside part of a house and asked him to dig. For some depth, it was soft, being the fallen walls, but it became quite hard to dig further deep. When they were digging, at some distance he saw someone working in the field stopping his work, trying to see these two. The old man walked some steps towards him. Rupesh also stopped digging, standing to rest, and saw the old man going to the man. But why? The terrified working man, throwing away his implements, was running away, crying (not audible clearly for a distance but sounded like), 'Help me, save me!' Rupesh could not understand what frightened him. He could see only the back of this man. Rupesh again started digging, and after some depth, he again got a big old earthen pot tightly covered by an earthen plate of the size and tightly secured by a covered cloth and roped around. The man took it out. He opened it and, clearing a small surface, emptied it on the cleared earth surface. Now Rupesh got a real surprise; there were silver coins and gold and silver jewellery. Golden were only three, four; the rest were silver ones. And about a hundred old silver coins. He took the ornaments in hand and saw in great emotions, felt like weeping. He looked at these one by one, taking his time, perhaps remembering the lady these might have been associated with. Then he called Rupesh with his bag and asked him to take his books and copies out. Then he put the coins in it and then the ornaments. He handed over the bag to Rupesh, saying, 'Now these are yours. May this prove lucky for you. Riches belong to none, keep on moving.' Rupesh was hesitant, but he lovingly insisted and forced to give these over to him, and he asked the boy to fill the pit back, which Rupesh did. After all this was over, he asked Rupesh to walk on and lead, that he would follow. Following Rupesh, he went on saying,

'There was a time here in this small village, this was a big house full of life. But things changed to this state saw today. Hadn't ever thought of it. I was rich village head. How many had so much riches and that status?'

'Now you have gone to some other place? Take away these with you there,' suggested Rupesh.

'We all have gone to the place where none of these can be taken to. So it's yours. Ask your father to purchase some cows and oxen. This'll improve your agriculture and economy. And you'll be able to study up to any level. I may come sometime, to see you a highly placed big scholar.' He further continued, 'Thanks, dear Rupesh, you solved my two problems. From here you go straight to your house.'

'Two problems! Which two problems?'

'My hard-earned wealth I was guarding for so long 'as gone to right needy person, where it will be put to good use. And I'm happy and free now.

'And the second one was, for so long, people had been walking over my ashes, my body remains, with dirty shoes, disrespecting me. Now with your help these have gone into the lap of Mother Ganga. In fact, these were my ashes.'

Now it struck Rupesh, who cried, 'Your ashes! Your body remains?' And he turned back to see behind him to the man. Rupesh could very well hear, 'Yes, mine,' but could see none behind. By now stunned Rupesh had reached very close to his village. The day was over; darkness had started covering over. Other students had also reached their homes. Reaching home, he closed his entrance door. And reaching the innermost corner, narrating the whole story of the day, he handed over the bag to his father.

His father, assuring for only good use of the wealth as suggested, thanked the divine ghost.

On the other side, in the village, the man who fled from the field, seeing the ghost, was lying in semi consciousness in high fever, still crying in fearfulness of the ghost. Rupesh asked him about its place and type. He described its big wrinkled face, long outward teeth, big burning eyes, and fearful bony face near the tree grove near Sheela. Rupesh understood the ghostman did not want anyone to see him taking wealth out. Rupesh suggested to him to say sorry for disturbing him and to pay respects to the soul. On doing so, immediately the fearful image of the ghostman changed into a friendly one in his mind. His fever and every physical problem was over. He thanked God and the ghostman. The next day, Rupesh was again a regular student of his Ram Nagar School, chasing the dreams of his life.

———————◆———————

KANSHI RAM JOSHI
GETS HONOURED

After the party in the police grounds, Agastya and Devika reached Agastya's official residence. They stayed there for the night and reached Gonda next morning, where Balendu, Nidhi, Kanshi Ram Joshi, and other workers met them. Agastya appreciated the work of Kanshi Ram and asked him to go on leave for total relaxation, to meet after the New Year celebration on 2 January. Accordingly, Kasnshi Ram left the place for some time. Priya was staying at Lucknow. The party organisers knew this development. So they organised a meeting in their Gonda office before Agastya and Devika went to Balrampur.

In the meeting, Agastya said, 'Friends, thanks for the untiring work you did for the party and the country. Now election mood must be over. Relax and think afresh, for still harder work for bigger responsibilities to achieve success in main election and social works. I'll be doing MLA's duty to the satisfaction of the public—the voters. Secondly, we have to go for public contact, visit the areas, especially from where we expect our other prospective candidates to contest coming main election about three years from now. And the third priority is strengthening the organisation, workmen force, which's our real strength, to work on these three fronts. Our line of action would be around this theme. And we all will concentrate on these fields of work. Now we would disperse to meet again afresh in the New Year.'

A party worker stood up and suggested, 'One more thing here, sir. Everyone has worked so sincerely in this election. We are all party workers. But there were many more guest workers, your friends and relations, and many more whom we don't even recognise. We must give recognition to their sincere hard work by giving them some incentive, some appreciation in the form of some memento.' Everyone praised the idea and agreed for mementos to some such persons. For Priya, mementos could be sent to Lucknow. But for Kanshi Ram Joshi, Basti, his home address, was just forty kiloyards from here, the next station by mail train. Some party workers might go and honour him in his family and locality. These suggestions were accepted by all.

The party memento for Priya was taken by Devika. And the other memento was given to Paras Nath Dwivedi; a group of four persons offered to go and honour Kanshi Ram Joshi. Someone from among the people sitting behind said, 'What, going and honouring there? Why don't you honour him here when he comes back? See, you don't lose a friend and sincere worker.' But the meeting did not pay heed to it

After three days of the meeting, the group for honouring Joshi in Basti left to honour him. Reaching there, they located the house by the address provided to them by the party office. There they were happy to see Joshi, who welcomed them and made them comfortable. Some neighbours had also gathered there. The leader of the group honoured him by presenting the memento and garlanding him. The team members saw the house and asked, 'Two families live here?'

'Yeah, one mine, in this portion'—pointing to one side of the house—'and in the other portion is my brother, Kālu Ram Joshi. He had been serving in the forest department. Presently posted as caretaker, guest house, Dera Chowk. He has been coming for an hour, giving his salary regularly to his family and going back same time for last two year. Some time back he helped busting a big international gang of criminals and was awarded one lakh rupees, which he deposited here in the bank. Money has been credited in the account.' Telling all about his brother Kālu Ram, Kanshi Ram prepared and served tea and snacks to his guest. He kept his memento and bouquet of flowers in his inner room. And coming to the sitting room, he sat down with the group members and further continued, 'See, some people say my brother, who has been coming and giving his salary income to his wife and who came to bank, was not my real brother but a ghost and my real brother was kidnapped by a gang of criminals some two years back and at present he is in Lucknow in police safety.'

A group member asked, 'Where's your family?'

'Gone to hospital,' replied Kanshi Ram. And he further asked, 'Does it sound acceptable, my brother a ghost, coming regularly to give out money to family?' He further said, 'But I don't bother about all these things. Leaving these aside, I express my happiness and gratitude to Agastya saab, Priya-ji, and Devika-ji and all others for considering me worthy of this honour. Kindly express my hearty feelings to them. I'm also grateful to you for gracing us. Indeed so happy.' Suddenly, he said, 'Please excuse me. Just coming.' He left the place to get inside the house.

Outside, an auto-rickshaw arrived on the main entrance and stopped in front of the main door. A lady came out of it. And what they saw now was astonishing to all. The lady supported a man coming out of the auto, with a fractured leg covered in foot-to-knee plaster. With the help of the lady and the auto driver, he came in. He saw the guests, paid regards, and introduced himself. 'I'm Kanshi Ram Joshi.'

The guests introduced themselves. Paras Nath said, 'We had come here to honour our party worker Kanshi Ram Joshi, and had honoured him for his commendable untiring election work. By the way, are you twins, having exactly the same looks? But twins are never given the same name. How come you both bros have same name? Kanshi Ram Joshi?'

'No, not at all, I'm all alone here, my elder brother Kālu Ram has not come home for several months,' said Kanshi Ram, and he further asked a neighbour there. Had he come today? Was he inside? Whom have they honoured?

'No, we haven't seen Kālu Ram. Strange! It were you. We thought your plaster got removed. You were here. Received a gift, got garlanded, served tea,' said the neighbour.

'Where's he? And who is he? I'm in plaster for last one month.'

'He went in, in the room,' said two or three in one voice. They further said, 'See it yourself, where can he go? No one can escape from here. On the main entrance we so many are sitting.'

Some two, three persons went inside. The rest were all sitting in the main entrance room. They saw in the rooms. He also went in, looked at each and every room, the bath, the restroom. The staircase was locked on the roof but was then opened, and they looked around the roof and every inch, but no one was there. Only the garland was there in the main room.

'You all must be correct. Why would you tell lie? I'm sorry I couldn't see my lookalike fellow,' said Kanshi Ram.

'You couldn't have seen him. Exactly at your appearance, he disappeared. He worked in your form in your absence, ghost of Kālu Ram in your form, disappeared on arrival of real Kanshi on the scene.' Paras Nath recollected and, looking to his fellow, said, 'Do you remember, someone warned in our meeting, "Why you are going Basti, his home? May lose a friend, a sincere worker." Who could else know the reality of a ghost except a ghost? But to some extent it had been good. At least truth and reality has come before everyone. Though we would surely remember him and would miss him. It's also good that we could respect him, honour him. Humans could have been missed, but souls must have been honoured. They will be happy and bless us all. Knowingly or unknowingly, we have in a way done a real worship.' Tea was over. 'Now we must make a move for going back.'

Before they could move, another man said, 'One thing isn't clear. Why did the souls assume the forms of you two brothers?'

'Can't say. The souls may reply better. But in my brother Kālu's case, the ghost took form of my brother who had gone lost and served for him wonderfully and saved our whole family of starvation. In my case, may have served your party or even my house today in my absence,' said Kanshi Ram.

Standing at his side, the wife of Kanshi Ram Joshi, shyly looking at Joshi, said, 'Aye-ji, thank God you were never absent in the nights.'

Everyone burst into laughter. The group members stood up to move. Kanshi Ram asked them to stay at least up to lunch, but Paras Nath said, 'It's okay, had nice time and a wonderful experience. Would come some other time. We wish you quick recovery. Be healthy soon and now you work in the party for the ghost.'

Kanshi Ram thanked them and assured all possible help and support. But the news spread like wildfire and had become common man's topic of talk soon in the whole city and the area. People started fearing talking to any other person. How to differentiate and know if they were talking to a real or supernatural one had become difficult. People even started saying ghosts had cast vote for Agastya and made him win. 'All the time ghost remains with him. He's a man of ghosts.'

After a month, Agastya came to Gonda and Balrampur. Many were not going close to him. When there were people with him, in justified way people would touch them. Some were taking advantage of the Indian tradition of touching feet of the respectable, were testing him for real by touching his feet pressingly.

Paras Nath met him and narrated everything he and his group experienced in Basti. 'Which date you are talking about? When did you go there?' asked Devika.

'It was on 28 December,' replied Paras Nath. 'One of our man visited the Banyan tree and the Joshi hollow. On that date at about eleven he saw Kanshi Ram sitting on the tree on the hollow branch, and his memento is there in the hollow.'

Realising the popularity of the tree and the hollow, Agastya and Devika realised that since now so many people were visiting the tree and climbing to the hollow, they got a permanent steel staircase, and a small platform on the top fabricated there on the tree. They had offered their worship and had a look at the hollow and found the memento given to Kanshi Ram Joshi there. They also offered flowers and sweets, incense sticks, and camphor.

When Agastya and Devika were discussing these things, there came a man. He offered that he, with his friend, would provide worshipping and other items of common use the whole day.

He said, 'Let some shopkeeper put these things. I'll sell these whole day.'

Then Devika asked, 'What will be your earning? How'll you earn your living if you'll be selling other's items and return the whole proceeds to him?'

'My earning will be my worship to the banyan tree. Moreover, we are three, four friends. It'll be a side work for each one of us,' said the man.

'Now the question is, who will keep these items there?' asked Agastya.

Here Jagannath came forward. He said that at the moment, the flowers may be wild. Rest of items, he would provide. No problem of account. 'I won't need proceeds, all up to this man. Later we'll encourage some farmer to start floriculture and to sell flowers to us for the tree.' Thus, the place turned into a popular place of worship. There they cleaned some area and put a thatched shade; under it, on a platform the worship items were kept for the public. People had a feeling that, that was a haunted place. But they also knew this: that in the area, no one faced any problem. If anyone was caught in some trouble, someone would arrive to get the person rid of the problem. So you can see even a single lady or gent resting there under the shade near the banyan tree in the dense forest. It had become a place of faith of people of all religions and places. After some time, even free meals started there, morning till evening, and no one knew who was doing all this. And from where the things were coming. But there were no drinks, meat, fish, or eggs. No sacrifice of any type of life, animal or bird—a totally pious atmosphere.

RESCUE OF CHILD

Even Agastya and Devika didn't understand what this all was happening. How were things going on there? Where was the ration coming from? Who was cooking? Where were the stores? But he let the things go on, with the addition of his shares. So long as these were helping and improving the behaviour of the people.

Once, a couple with a four-year-old child came to visit this place. Crossing the Rapti, the child started playing with the water. He bent so much that he rolled on into river. People shouted but could do nothing. The boatman told them he couldn't risk fifty lives for not sure to get the child in this big river. The rowing boat wouldn't come back here against the current if taken down the ferry point with the current, looking for the child. Fainting, crying all the way, the couple, with the help of others, reached the banyan tree. The crying parents, reaching there, sat down under the tree. People offered water and some eatables, but they simply cried.

A person came and asked, 'But why are you crying?'

Some fellow said, 'They lost their only child in Rapti.'

'Would you go and see a child that side if that's yours?' asked the man there.

'No use seeing children. Our child can't be saved, he disappeared in fast deep water in front of us,' said the weeping father.

'You at least may see it once. I fished the child out from deep Rapti. I saw from distance a child falling off a boat crossing river. And left my horse in the river down the current, in clear water, as it's these days. I saw the child flowing underwater, fished it out, and brought here, fastening on my back,' said the man. Somehow they agreed to look. They went to the shade. From a distance they saw the child happily eating biscuits. Both husband and wife gazed at each other, didn't go to the child but ran back to the banyan tree and climbed to the hollow.

After offering payers and worship, they came down to the child. The lady picked the child up in her arms and wept bitterly, saying, 'It's not possible. Without asking for, without any request, before us the child's here. It can't be, it's a miracle.' The couple lived for two days in just the open in the dense forest, offering prayers and worshipping.

A visitor staying in the guest house was lost in thoughts of 'Who is taking care of these with small child, simple lady, and gent amidst dangerous animals all-around? People put their lives to such big risks for the sake of faiths. Who keep up their faith? Who saves them from all risks? It is further a matter of self-confidence and faith. This is above every logic, scientific theories, thinking, and approaches.'

God help the people.

GHOSTMEN NIGHT

Agastya and Devika, on their tour, stayed for a night in the Dera guest house; Balendu and Nidhi were also with them. In the evening, they met Jagannath and other people in the village. After an early dinner, as mostly taken in villages, they walked a little in front of the guest house, listened to the news on the transistor, and retired to their beds. By midnight, Agastya's sleep was disturbed. Agastya got up, came out of the room, went to the table, took a glass of water, and took a turn in his room to go back to his bed. Through the glass panes of the forest-side window he saw some lights at a distance. He got close to the window panes. He was surprised. There were country-made torches all around, spreading dazzling light all around. In the light, a big number of people were dancing, singing, eating, and enjoying. It looked festive there.

Agastya quietly asked the others also to wake up and watch with him without making any noise. They also saw and confirmed it as some festivity near the banyan tree. They decided to come out and see. Slowly, slowly, they walked towards the light and stayed at a distance and gazed at the celebrations. But soon two men and a woman got to them, caught them by the hand, and took them to a sitting platform under the banyan tree. They brought four plates of eatables and offered them, saying, 'We knew you would come. Your four plates were already prepared. Don't hesitate, we are all your people. Avail it. It is rare opportunity for us. We want you eat with us. We keep on taking with you very often.' After offering sweets to these four fellows, the men and woman again joined their group of celebrations.

These four fellows looked at each other and at the plates. The plates were well arranged, with sweets and salty items, even freshly fried items—cooked in a cooking medium, these were skilfully served.

Agastya whispered, 'They are our people taking their meals very often with us. What all is this? Is beyond my comprehension. Better let all this go on uninterrupted. I think we can't disturb them. But they are surely disturbing by keeping on coming in our lives and working.'

Immediately, in continuation they heard, 'You too can disturb our living and working. By nature, man is inquisitive and destructive. His is physical world. His curiosity and greed keeps on compelling him disturb even nature and others. Ours is a different world, same as yours but in different space. You have cleared peaceful forest land, river basins, and transformed vast areas into crowded, noisy, polluting industrial areas and urban centres. We had to leave such places. We don't want clashes with your world. After all, we are from amongst you. Our near and dears are still in your world. We are peace loving. Live away from crowds, but we also live and move with you in your world. Think if you make a resort, a hotel, or a tower, a factory near banyan tree, we won't be stopping you. But how would we be gathering and enjoying in such place?'

'I assure you, in this area of about ten square kiloyards, around banyan tree will never be disturbed.' Looking to Devika, he said, 'Devika, please keep in mind and aware the people around here to never let any big manufacturing and deforestation come this area. Cottage industries are equally productive, engaging large number of people. This banyan tree is our tree area, a sacred place for all of us, abode of our dear Joshi.'

There were shouts of joys, with clapping and slogans. 'Victory for Agastya, Devika, Balendu, Nidhi, and party, long live these friends!'

Some voice said, 'Oh, you left Priya, though she is not here today, but she is our very close.'

Then there were loud voices. 'Very true, victory for Priya, and happily long live Priya.'

This continued for hours. The four friends kept on enjoying the celebration. Then shouted a voice, 'Well, friends, hope you all have enjoyed the night. Now the time of our Lord Shiva is fast approaching. He himself start taking round of the whole world in the holy time, Brahma Muhurt. [Very auspicious time, from 4.00 a.m. to sunrise in Hindu mythology.] That's why people perform religious rituals, worship, holy baths, or visiting religious places or reading holy books in that early-morning period.' The voice again said, 'Now we would have meeting, would take the account of the last week and finalise our activities for the next week and next meetings here.' The voice called, 'Shivdayal, please go to the honoured guests and escort them to the guest house.' A loud direct voice said, 'Excuse us, sirs, ma'ams, this being our top secret from the mortal world, we have to have it in our own way.'

'Okay, thanks, had a nice time with you, dear friends. Hope to live in close and pleasant harmony.' All came to a standstill.

'Fare thee well, dear friends. Bye-bye,' said the four friends, raising their hands.

Agastya again said to the voice, 'Please, you continue with your programme, we will go on our own.'

The voice said, 'No, no, he will go with you.' And an unrecognisable form walked with them.

Agastya said to the form, 'If you don't mind and your world and system permits, may I ask you something?'

'Yes, you can, there is no restriction on your asking. Answering would be up to me, my ability, my system, and also to the extent it is in the interest of the people,' said the form.

Agastya asked the form, 'What's your past, your name, and address, etc.?'

'My past or future is mine, it's no other person's concern. Nor this knowledge would benefit anyone, rather may create problems. Suppose I'm very close of someone from 23 August 1958. It could be problematic for them all. So no answer, ask some other thing.'

'Okay, how can anyone know about your world?' asked Agastya.

'To some extent, by chances, like you could see some of it today. Or by the study of parasciences and to any extent through yoga meditation, transcendental meditation, intuition, worship to Lord Shiva and his blessing, or blessing of any main trio gods, Brahma, Vishnu, Mahesh, the trio goddess, Sharaswati, Laxmi, Parwati. Other gods and goddess, holy angels can enable you to peep into this world. We live to their blessings and orders. Or by other holy methods of other religions.' The form further continued, 'But so long as you think doing good to others, work for benefit of others, benefit of the masses. We automatically, on our own, would come on your side. Neither you will recognise us nor would we be under your command. But we work and support you in full for your mission. In that case, we'll help and support you for your personal gains also, to make you successful and strong enough to meet the challenges and do well to all. So long as you are good, positive, and have faith in God, we and our all force is with you. But the moment you become high headed, selfish, and negative thinker, harming others, we leave, because you come under Satanic forces and his men. They take such people to their world of miseries, pains, and sufferings, however rich or strong a person may be. So thinking and actions are yours, as per teaching you get. Your impression [sanskaras], the blessing of your well-wishers, and our support are always with if you deserve.'

The form further continued, 'The negative sphere of our world also works the same way but for negative people, presenting themselves fearful and strong, aggressive, aiming they will gain the powers to rule the masses. They feel happy in trouble of others. Consider people their resources and wealth. And try to establish rule of terror. But soon they meet their end and get perished.' He further said, 'The people of positive thinking worship the ultimate supreme power, the god for good wisdom. The mind and soul always submitted to him. Riches, power, and strength to serve the needy, poor, and weak, not to build up empire. God and we remain pleased with the people abiding by law of nature and submitting to the common cause, feeling pain and disturbed in the sufferings of others. People are capable of deciding their fate themselves. So strange is our world, so close to yours, we are always with you.'

By now they had reached the guest house; it was going to be four in the morning. They thought of going to bed to sleep, but the words of the voice came to their minds. *Lord Shiva's time has come. Let us feel his presence rather than going to bed. At least to remember him.* They had reached the state that no one was feeling sleepy, drowsy, or tired. The refreshment they ate there was so energising, refreshing, tasty, and so light. They were full of energy and full of good thoughts. Balendu thought and thought; aloud he said and asked all of them, 'What was the date he gave?'

Nidhi recollected and said with doubt, '23 August 1958.'

'Yes,' confirmed Devika.

'Why he gave this date? His voice-voice was appearing very well familiar to me. And the time the form was with us, saw towards me maximum times.'

'Yes, that is true, it must have some significance,' supported Agastya.

'Oh yeah, got it. How unfortunate I am. I didn't have the slightest feel. I had spent the whole night with my favourite uncle. I walked with him. I talked to him. Yet didn't recognise and feel him. He had even told me. Given the date of his passing away. Hint after hint he gave. Kept seeing me. Expecting me, I would recognise him. But till last, I even didn't try. My mind didn't work on that line. Now tried and got it but no use.'

'It is of very much use. I'm happy seeing you grow up into a nice young man. And that you are in good company. That's why you could not only see but could even enter and enjoy the supernatural world. Though some others were also there but didn't have the slightest feel of anything happening there, not even your going and staying there. Seeing you in mental tension, I had come, but don't make it practice. Don't repent for past. Look forward. Forget the past, enjoy the present, and keep prepared to welcome the future. May God bless you all. Bye-bye, my children.'

It was going to be about the breaking of the dawn. Devika thought of changing and playing the cassette of the morning prayers. She went to insert the cassette in the player but found already there was one. She rewound it and played from the start. It started playing and voiced, 'If you don't mind and your world and system permit, may I ask . . .'

She stopped it, saying 'What is this?'

'What? Play it again,' all said. She rewinded a line and played it again from the beginning; it voiced the same thing. 'If you don't mind and your world and system permit, may I ask you . . .' There was the complete talk of Agastya and the voice of the form escorting them to the guest house and then the voice of Balendu. The voice was heard by all addressing to Balendu till 'Keep prepared to welcome the future. May God bless you all. Bye-bye, my children'.

The voice further added to it, 'You can play and hear it only three times. It's up to you on which occasions. Hope it would benefit the people interested in divine powers. Any worldly person can hear it, as it may shape their thinking and thereby their lives. May everyone have satwik Buddhi [intelligence dedicated and submitted to God and his creations].*"

---

* Three types of mindsets:

Satwik - submitted to God for divine knowledge, simple life, and simple fresh food.

Raajsi - aggressive, worshiping for power, tasty, spicy food, very active with pomp and show.

Taamsi – worshiping witchcraft, lethargic, shabby living, taking stale food, etc.

'Oh, divine voice, you have given us richest treasure of our lives. We bow to thee with our deepest regards from our hearts,' said Agastya, and everyone joined him. All were under the strange feeling of astonishment.

'Oh, Uncle, you have given me the richest gift of my life,' said Balendu.

They, from the cores of their hearts, were thanking the ghost. They remained confused by the mix of the natural and supernatural worlds. They remained sitting and thinking all this. Devika and Nidhi got into the kitchen, prepared tea, and served this to all. After breakfast, they thought to go to Jagannath, to find the progress of the floriculture. But soon, Jagannath arrived there with a farmer. Jagannath had explained to him everything. The farmer was ready to grow flowers on his two bigha-sized field. But the farmer was not well, nor did he have bulls to plough. They were sitting and talking outside the guest house.

<hr/>

FARMER'S FIELDS CROPPED

The same time, two persons with bulls arrived there, saying, 'Saab-ji, we are in utter difficulty, we are from lower flood-hit area of Rapti. In the monsoons our field remained underwater for three months, with no winter crops, cereals, and fodder. We are now roaming village to village, labouring and ploughing field of others on crop-share basis, i.e., on the crop getting ready or on its sale, one-sixth of the produce. Here we get our food and fodder for our cattle in this area. We have some seeds of rice, wheat, peas, veg seeds, and flower seeds. May we get some work here in this area?'

'Yes, surely we'll get you work. You prepare flower beds along the guest house, this caretaker quarter, and places you feel suitable aesthetically. Besides this, beautify the area around banyan tree in this jungle. But a first-priority work at present is helping this farmer. We accept your term of one-sixth of crop in cash or kind. On a two-bigha field, he wants to grow flowers,' said Agastya.

'Surely we will help cultivate field on crop-share basis. It is only two bigha. The owner may also join us, we would become three. Today only we will finish the whole work, the field is suitable to plough. Soil is moist, and by afternoon the total work would be over.'

Agastya had asked Mangloo to cook for all. Devika and Nidhi helped Mangloo in cooking as well as the farmers for preparing flower beds and sowing seeds.

After the fieldwork of sowing seeds, the labourer approached Agastya and said, 'Saab, the work is over, now we go in search of work elsewhere. We'll come again to see the crop growing and would do necessary work required at that time. Till then any available person can water the plants and take out wild weeds from fields. Hope you'll have good crops. Now permit us to go.'

'Before you go, please tell us your labour charges for flower beds in the guest house and around the banyan tree,' said Agastya.

'Banyan tree is ours too as of yours. We won't take anything for that. Guest house is also for all. In the field, we'll share the crop at harvest. So we owe nothing to you. Just remember us and help us in need. Thanks,' said one of the labourers. And the two labourers with the bulls left the place on their way to a place only they knew in search of places of their choices. The farmer was in his field, and Mangloo at the guest house, and the banyan tree started looking after the flower crops.

Agastya, Devika, and the others left the place for going to Balrampur. After reaching there, they all got busy with their different works.

There in Dera, in the flower beds, the flower plants were growing fast. The farmer and Mangloo were taking full care of the plants. Even the flower plants were spreading their fragrance all around. People were coming, asking about the plants, their names and varieties. But no one was able to tell. These were rare plants, never seen before by most of the people. The two labourers, people say, were at times seen passing by, adding manures and taking care of the plants. Soon the flower beds and the crops in the field stated blooming. The flowers and their fragrance were superb. The pattern of the flower bed they prepared before the guest house was wonderful and changed the look of the guest house. Similarly, the people coming from distances to the banyan tree felt relaxed and refreshed with the nostalgic fragrance and eye-soothing look of the colourful flowers.

Though the banyan tree itself had plenty of wildflowers around it, these were not plucked. The farmer who had spared his field and started the floriculture for the purpose was requested to supply flowers to the place. Every day in the morning, with the information to Jagannath, he had been taking flowers to the banyan tree shop. At the end of the month, he had been getting a handsome amount. The two labourers who made floriculture possible and were to claim their share from the income of the farmer from flowers were never seen again after the flower crop started seeing the shop. The farmer waited for some months, and then a year. He had kept their share separate. But one night he heard someone say, 'We won't take any money from the banyan tree shop. You may keep whole income. It's yours. Keep on supplying flowers regularly.'

One fine morning, the farmer took flowers to the shop. There he found two persons worshiping; they had a tractor attached with a hero and plainer with them. After the worship, they started the tractor for going back. They asked the farmer if he was also going that side. On the farmer's yes, they took him also on the tractor. Coming to the village side, seeing the unused and untilled land, they asked him, 'Whose fields are these, lying like wasteland in crop season? Why's he not cropping these?'

The farmer replied, 'These are mine. I fell sick in working season. And now these have become hard for our simple country plough. Now for a year these'll remain waste.'

'Oh, ji, why waste land? It is national resource, producing agricultural wealth not only for farmers but for country. We are in hurry, you go home, prepare lunch for us. Here we see this small piece of land, hardly an hour's job.' Sending farmer home, they started tractor work on the field. Completing the work, they reached the farmer's place, asking aloud, 'Got lunch ready?'

'So soon? I could hardly prepare simple rice and pulse only,' said the farmer. And he didn't ask for the fieldwork, thinking, *What could have been done in so short? But anyway, otherwise also these 'ere lying waste.*

But the tractor man declared, 'Your fields are done. We had some seeds, enough for that small field. Everything's done. Now you take care of these.'

'But I couldn't do my work. Only so simple undercooked lunch.'

'A thing done in time is a thing done. And this's food, God's grace. You just bring whatever's ready. Have to go long way.'

The farmer hesitatingly served whatever he could. And the two ate it to their full satisfaction, praising it so much. The more they were praising, the more he was feeling embarrassed. Seeing it, one of them soothed him, saying, 'It's not a false praise. You can taste it yourself. At least we enjoyed it. And now here we go. We worked on your field. What work, only ran a machine for some time God has given us. But you worked much longer for us, prepared food. You worked more for us than what we did for you. So no giving, taking of anything but good wishes.' And they left for their further destination. On their way back with the planer, they cleared and levelled the way from the banyan tree to Village Dera, passing by the side of the guest house. Near the guest house, they met Mangloo, exchanged their good wishes, and asked Mangloo as to how he was.

'I'm fine, saab-ji, and flowers are wonderful, where did you bring these unique varieties from?' replied Mangloo.

'We? You know us?' exclaimed one.

307

'I'm sure you are the same who sowed these flower beds.'

'But how did you recognise? We are in different look and on tractor. Tractor had been further misleading. And for God's sake, don't tell anyone else.'

'The way you have come here in the forest to help us all. Who else could you be?' said Mangloo.

'Don't say so. We have done nothing. Okay then, Mangloo, now we go,' said one of the two.

'Right, Saab, keep on visiting,' said Mangloo.

The farmer, not caring for the fields, went to that side the next day. He was surprised to see the fields were done. A major portion of the fields was cropped with multiple intensive seasonal crops. And some smaller portion for various vegetables so that the farmer got daily as well as bulk of crop at the end of the season. At the same time, his family would be getting home-produced, balanced, rich food daily.

The farmer two days later saw Mangloo there on the field's side and asked in a low voice, 'Did you see who the two tractor men were?'

'Yes, why not? They were the same who came last year with bulls. This time for you, came with tractor,' replied Mangloo.

'They came for me, but I, being a fool, didn't recognise them. It wasn't possible for me to crop these dry, hard fields. Why are you so pleased on me? I have never served you, oh my lord. You have been so kind to me. I'll take care of your crops. I'll serve you as much I can.' He was happy to see the fields. There had been occasional good rains. In three months, his tomatoes were ready, giving crops. Green chillies, carrots, lemon trees had come up in good size; harvesting would take time. Wheat, gram, mustard had grown to their full size. One whole big acre of field was full of wheat and totally yellow with mustard flowers. The rows of potatoes were full. He started sitting on the field to protect the crops from the wildlife. Early morning he would come, and late night he would go. His wife was also very happy. She had been bringing his meals to the fields. The whole village people felt strange about the miraculous help to him. The farmer had been helping people in his own way. His house became small to keep these rich crops. However, he made arrangements to sell these. Wealth was showering on him. The more he started giving to the tree shop for free help to the public and helping his village fellows, the more he was getting.

The stories of this success had reached Priya, Agastya, and Devika also. They were happy, and with him they were trying hard to change the shape of the village. Now occasionally they had been coming to the village.

———•———

AT THE SITE OF ROAD CONSTRUCTION

The work on the Rapti Bridges—seasonal at Kishanpur and permanent at Bijlipur—and roads was going on in full swing. These works had provided good job opportunities to the local people, especially for menial works. On the road parallel to the Nepal border, work was going on some two miles east of Haati. At the work site, the work supervisor got a temporary thatched hut raised for him to take shelter against the rain, the scorching day sun, and of course, the wildlife. In the hut, they kept a table, some benches, a stool or chair, a folding bed, a bamboo running across its width to hang his clothes or other things, like umbrella or bags. Besides, it also served as the record room for account books, registers of labour attendance, cash disbursement register, and other necessary items of their daily requirements.

In the evening, after the working hours were over, in the pleasant evening, the contractor's person got his chair and table put out on the road. In the drawer of the table, he kept all the money, and the attendance register was on the table. He asked the labourers to come one by one in a single line and sign or put thumb impression and accept their daily wages. Since women enjoyed an equal and respectable position in their tribal societies, the labourers started coming in a mixed line. But the supervisor said, 'No, no, women and girls at the last, men first.' After all the men had been paid their due, many of them left for their homes while some went and sat down to the side. As was his practice, the supervisor would pay a few rupees less to each of the women workers, to splurge this money on wine, meat, etc. The women labour started coming on their turn. Then he said, 'Only those whom I call.' He called, '*X, Y, Z . . .*' They came, took the wages, less as for all others, and went on, leaving the site—alone or with their husbands. Most of the people had left the site. Only a few were left who lived close by. Some were there for security reasons, and then there were those two or three beautiful young ones whose names were yet to be called. Then he said, 'Sufficient time has gone, it got late, we can sit in the hut.' The cunning man took the table and chair to the hut, called one of the girls left behind, and it took a good amount of time before she came out with some currency notes in her hand. Except the actual act of sex, he had done much against her wishes. Then he called the next. She was more beautiful. Only the most beautiful one was left out, sitting and waiting. The supervisor was engaged in his nefarious activities. Some voices were coming from inside the hut: 'Oh, what's there, and you will get double the wages', 'Oh no, you keep my wages too!', 'Oh no! Don't!', and all.

Finally, the last of the girls, Gauri, was called for the wages to be paid. The supervisor looked at her wickedly as she approached the table. He was going mad with carnal desire.

Suddenly, the usual voices of the area were subdued by the mighty roar of, apparently, a lion. Everyone was shocked and rooted to the ground for a few moments. As the reality hit them, everyone took to their feet and ran helter-skelter to whatever safety that they could. The majestic animal, a lioness, with its eyes fiery red in rage, emerged from the western side of the jungle and came running straight towards the hut. It crashed through the flimsy door and pounced upon the supervisor. Gauri escaped from the clutches of the supervisor. Shivering and frightened, she ran towards the deep forest and hid alone behind a bush. The lioness sank her teeth in the chest of the supervisor, mostly getting stuck in the thick winter clothes but managing to pierce his chest as well. He was caught in a strong grip, thrashed and banged left and right against the fragile wooden wall of the hut, which was getting broken and razed. He was almost like a rag doll under the front limbs of the ferocious animal. With him hanging limp from her jaws, the lioness took two, three jumps, dragging him ruthlessly. The labourers, with bamboos and sticks, ran towards the lioness to get him freed. The lioness dropped the supervisor on the ground but, standing upon him in complete fury, opening her big, wide open jaw, roared and gazed at the labourers as if she would attack them. They came to a standstill. She again picked him up and in two big jumps was near the girl hiding behind the bush. She dropped the supervisor on the ground, close to Gauri's feet; she circled around the frightened girl and the supervisor, gurgling, roaring, and looking towards the other people standing some distance away. The terrified girl again ran and hid behind another bush. The lioness kept circling the half-dead supervisor lying terrified. None else dared approach him.

The lioness took another look at the supervisor and again reached him. It placed its front paws on his chest, raised its head up, gave a blood-curdling roar, and took a long leap, landing upon Gauri, who was hiding behind the bush. Gauri was petrified and couldn't even cry. She, pressed under the heavy lioness, felt half dead and lay with her eyes closed, awaiting her death by this ferocious lioness. She passed out in fear. But then she heard a friendly and familiar laughter in a girl's voice. She opened her eyes, still trembling with fear but hopeful of help being here to rescue her. She was astounded to find that the lioness was nowhere to be seen. She could only see a pretty young girl. It was Divya, the girl who worked with her every day at the work site. Divya joked, 'Not able to bear my hug, are you?'

Gauri, still pinned underneath her, screamed in delight, 'It's you!'

Divya, the lioness girl, said, 'Rascal! He was troubling you. Thanks to the timely intervention by that ferocious lioness, now won't dare touch any girl. If he ever tries again with anyone, he will surely meet his death. As for you, my dear, if I had not come, the lioness would have eaten up you.' And they both laughed aloud.

The people standing at the edge of the forest were weeping, assuming that the contractor and the girl both had surely died. They were surprised upon hearing the laughter behind the bush, where they expected the girl lying dead. Divya picked Gauri up by hand and said, 'Come on, get up. Let's see the lover boy.' They reached the supervisor, lying terrified, where others still didn't dare approach. The two girls bent down upon him, held each of his hands, and tried to make him stand. Divya said, 'Hey, saab, nothing happened, we've chased the lioness away. Be brave, won't you come to the hut?'

'What hut? My mistake! I sent everyone away to flirt with the girls. Now won't even look towards the girls. Oh, my sisters, my mothers, save me!' begged the supervisor.

'Oh, you are already saved. Come on, stand up. Come to the hut,' Divya said.

'Don't say hut. I'll keep several people in the hut now on,' said the supervisor.

'And our today's wages?' asked Divya.

'Go take as much as you want from the drawer,' the supervisor said.

The two girls picked him up and took him to the hut. They also called out to the people standing away. In the presence of all these, Divya went to the drawer with the other girl, picked out a handful of currency notes, and passed them on to the girl, saying, 'Come on, take these all. You have suffered a lot today, remained so much terrified for so long. Thank God you didn't die. I would have felt guilty of not helping a girl and taking her life.' She further said to Gauri, 'But I wouldn't have, in any case, let you die. That was the peak of your fear when I jumped on you and tried to comfort you. Now that you're safe and out of fear, would you be my friend?'

'Your friend? No, no, I can't be. I would ever remain in your service. You are some goddess. And I can't take any extra money also. Only my dues,' said Gauri. And keeping some of the money to herself, she returned the rest of the notes to the drawer.

'Now come on! Don't speak like that about me. I too have carried loads of earth and stones with you whole day. I'm a simple girl like you. If you don't like me for friendship, it's all right. But I'll remain yours, and even without calling me, I'll reach for your help,' said Divya.

'You worked like me whole day, but you didn't take money. You had given all your money also to me. You can assume any shape and form. I'm a poor girl, you are goddess. I worship thee and thank you for such a timely help,' Gauri proclaimed.

'I can't help what you think or speak about me. But I take you as an equal to me, my friend,' said Divya. She further said, 'Okay, feel happy! Bye.' She walked away and, after a short distance, disappeared. This girl was astounded; where could she go this side in the dense forest? There was not even a trail, no village this side for miles and miles. No person ever went this way. Then she murmured, 'Let her go, what I can do? She is strong enough to manage her matters.'

The people—men and women still there—were attending to the shocked and injured supervisor. They offered him hot tea from the thermos and helped him come to normalcy. They then helped him go to the nearest village, Haati, with all his luggage except chair and table.

The supervisor was saying only one thing. 'Where did the lioness come from, and where did it go? Why did it leave me alive?' Except for thrashing and banging him against the wooden structure of his hut, it didn't give even a scratch. His was likely to be sure death today. She was so powerful, even so many men couldn't distract her.

Gauri was thinking even more. Who was she? Who were the others like her working with them as labourers? And why were they working, and for what? The attack of the lioness remained the topic of the day. And everyone was thinking the same way for next some days.

The next day, the supervisor was in trauma, and at least for some days he was not in any position to do his normal work. Another supervisor was sent in his place to ensure the unhindered progress of work. This man was even more crooked than the earlier one. He told the contractor, 'The forest is full of wildlife, there are unsocial elements and criminals hiding and finding refuge and shelter here. We work with good number of young women workers and also keep money with us. So for safety of the workers, as also of the money, to keep up morale and a sense of security amongst the labour, two armed gunmen be provided as security guards.' The contractor was compelled to provide the gunmen as requested by his site supervisor. This crook went to the work site escorted by the guards. He got his office permanently set up inside the hut. He scrutinised the list of workers in detail to see who were working among the labourers. He was particularly pleased to see that the list included a large number of women. So he thought, why wait till evening for the wages disbursal time? Why not enjoy the fruits of his position through the entire day? He called two, three labourers and told them, 'I'm not well. I had to come to the site because the injured supervisor hasn't recovered yet. I would prefer to rest. Prepare my bed in one side of this hut itself.' After things were ready, he sent the men back to work. The guards were posted outside the hut.

The supervisor settled comfortably in the hut. He took out a bottle of rum that he always carried in his baggage, some light dry snacks, and started enjoying the drink. It took him less than half an hour to send four large pegs down his throat. In his high spirit, he came out and went around the entire stretch of the work site, which was about 200 yards. He had directed the men to be employed on the farthest end, citing the safety of the workers as the reason, and women much closer to the hut. As he passed by the workers, he enquired about some of them, asking their names, villages, etc. If it happened to be a woman, he also asked if her husband too was working there. If so, who was he and where was he working? If working close by to her, he would immediately be despatched farther away.

After setting up the work site to his liking, he called two of the women workers, talked to them cheerfully, and asked them to follow him to the hut. He reached the hut and told the guards, 'Keep standing alert and watchful towards all directions and ensure nothing wrong happens to anyone. And beware of wildlife. A very unfortunate thing has already happened yesterday, two of our people could have died. Don't know why that supervisor did not ask for guards earlier. Don't relax, you haven't come here to sleep in the cool shades.' Saying all this, he got inside the hut and murmured, 'How hot the sun is!' He took off his shirt and the trousers, put on a loincloth (*lungi*) around, and seemed pretty excited about his perceived adventure. As both of the women reached the hut, he called them inside. 'Come in.'

The women saw him lying on the cot as they trooped in. They exchanged uncomfortable glances, feeling afraid as well as guilty. They were wondering why they had been called and why they agreed to come in. Even as he lay down on the cot, he said, 'Don't worry, come closer, I'm not well. I just want you two to massage my arms and legs.' Pointing to one he said, 'You please do my legs.' While pointing to other one he told her, 'You come and massage my shoulders.' The women were hesitant. This was definitely what these never wanted to do. Sensing their reluctance he said, 'Oh, what is this! Just a little massage to ease the pain that I have been suffering from. And despite that pain, I am here, standing in for your injured supervisor, to ensure your safety and comfort. Am I asking for too much?' One of them, apparently elder to the other, replied, 'I will step out and send some of the men folk, they would be much stronger and will give you a better massage to take care of your pain and discomfort.'

'Oh, what are you saying? They don't have hands, it's rather like rocks. They'll do more harm than good. They will break my muscles, and my body would ache even more,' said the supervisor.

'That's what it should be!' whispered the second woman.

'Don't worry, you won't have to lose out on your work. You'll get more wages than the usual. And here you would be relaxing in shade rather than sweating it out in the sun,' said the supervisor.

'We would prefer to go without wages than indulge in this nuisance.'

But upon his repeated insistence and finally the unveiled threats to them as well as their family members being rendered without employment, they relented, saying, 'It's sin to be here for women.' They took their position. He looked half naked and was constantly trying to expose more and more of himself to them. The woman working on the legs had to keep picking the loincloth to cover more of his parts again and again. The lecherous man had been touching and caressing the sensitive parts of her body. On his upper side he had been moving his palm all over her sensitive parts. The women, without saying anything, had been tolerating his misdemeanours, thinking that they were there only for minutes. They could hardly afford to annoy him. He had the capability to trouble them in different ways. Without even looking towards the scoundrel, both of them were going on without seeing where he was being pressed, where not. After a while, noticing that they were absolutely indifferent to him, he said, 'Hey, what you both are doing? Are you like cutting the grass for your cattle? Now go and send that girl of yesterday. She has suffered a lot. Let me check up on her.'

Heaving a sigh of relief, they hurried out of the hut, murmuring, 'Why don't such people die! We were two of us and even then suffered so much. Except sex, he has done every possible mean thing with us.'

'For that he has called that girl alone. Poor girl doesn't know what all she will undergo. This is a crooked fellow, would keep her whole day. She is young and beautiful.'

'Yesterday she got saved.' said the other one.

'Yesterday it was different. That earlier supervisor was just enjoying while disbursing the wages. Today this rascal is lying with full intention, with whole day and full preparation. God save the poor girl,' said the first. Passing by Gauri's side, the elder one said, 'Hey, Gauri, we've had our share. Now you go. You have been called by the new supervisor. He wants to express his sympathy on your sufferings of yesterday. (In low voice) God save the poor girl.'

Gauri got panicky and was stunned. Divya was working by her side today also. She said jokingly, 'Why are you worried? Your new lover has called. Go happily.' Addressing the two women, laughing, she said, 'Hope you both are not mistaken. He might've called me. Be sure whom he called. Wasn't I whom he has called for? May I also go? No one calls me. I would've to go on my own.'

The elder one of the women remarked to her companion, 'She hasn't been called yet, that's why she is saying like this.' Then she turned to Divya, who was still laughing, 'If you get called inside once, then we'll see how you speak and laugh. In fact, you will not be able to speak at all. You are lucky that he hasn't set his eyes upon you. Where were you hiding yourself? You should have been the first to be called.' Addressing Gauri, she finally said, 'Don't worry, we pray that you be safe! Now before he gets angry, please go to him.'

'Have no choice! I guess I do have to go.' Reluctantly, Gauri stopped the work, looked at Divya by her side, and walked slowly towards the hut. When passing by the guards, they looked at her with greedy eyes and twirled their moustaches. The two women kept standing on the spot, seeing her going to hut, murmuring, 'Because of her we're saved. May God be with her.'

Sensing the things to get worse in the hut, Gauri said to herself, 'Showers would be no use if the crops get dried up.' Seeing the girl get in, the supervisor called her close. She appeared reluctant and wasn't getting close enough. So he, getting up a little from the bed, caught hold of her arm and pulled her towards the bed.

But suddenly, it was as if the rug was pulled out from under his feet! Following a sudden commotion at the door of the hut, there appeared a large and fearsome-looking dacoit—tall and hefty, copper coloured, rough small-poxed face, big bloodshot eyes, thick black moustache, dusty rough hair hanging down to his shoulder blades, a shabby red two-inch-wide ribbon tied around the head, thick steel chain around the neck, a thicker iron chain around the waist, and a belt of cartridges, along with a shotgun, hanging on the shoulder. With his large muscular hands swinging freely, he walked in with long and forceful strides. He was flanked on both sides by two equally fearsome men, one on each side. They appeared to be his assistants.

All of the labourers had gathered outside the hut, most of them trembling with anxiousness, someone whispering, 'Where has this deadly storm come from?'

As these rugged men had reached the hut, one of the assistants had caught the gun of one of the guards by the barrel, looked towards the other guard, and menacingly shouted at them, 'Rascals! You are guarding a crooked man committing the heinous crime of trying to rob the honour of a girl of character. Why didn't you kill him first? We aren't killing you, cowards. But run beyond the range of our guns and our sight if you want to live,' The two guards scrambled away as fast as they could till they disappeared into the forest.

The three dacoits, roaring, entered the hut and saw the supervisor on the cot, pulling the girl upon himself forcibly. The dacoit roared like thunder. The labourers outside the hut were terrified. Someone remarked, 'Surely Supervisor will be dead today and whole money will be looted away. Yesterday that man could survive attack by the lioness. But today this man will surely go.'

The dacoit caught the neck of the supervisor in his large right hands and dragged him out of the hut like a rag. He lifted him up over his head in stretched straight-up arms and in a swift movement flung, threw him away to a nearby pond filled with more of mud and less of water. It was full of small insects, crabs, small fish, leeches, frogs, and aquatic scorpions. The portion of the body of the supervisor out of water was a dry island for them. In a minute hundreds of insects were on his body, leaving him in terrible shock and pain, as was evident from his painful shrieks. The dacoit still stood on the bank of the pond, barking at him, 'You are alive only till you are in the slurry of the pond. Bastard, coming out of this pond will surely take you to a painful death.'

The supervisor cried and cried for mercy, 'Kindly pardon me. Be kind to me. Spare my life. I'll die here, these insects will kill me.' In tremendous pain, which was accentuated by the venomous stings of the insects, and shivering with fear, he had been pushing insects off his body. But more and more of them had been creeping upon him.

The dacoit again roared, 'Idiot, I've spared your life, that's why you are still alive and talking. You are disgrace to mankind. Even we criminals, dacoits, honour the women of good character. You were robbing a helpless girl of everything that she treasures. Now remain here and pay for your unpardonable sin.'

He turned towards the hut and entered it. Inside, Gauri stood terrified. The dacoit pulled the girl in his arms and embraced her. She, out of fear, kept both her hands in between them, palms pressed against the chest of the dacoit, and murmured, 'Please spare me. Let me go.'

'Surely you'll go. But let's enjoy for some time. I know you aren't my friend. But I can die for you,' said the dacoit.

Gauri pleaded, 'What's the difference between the supervisor and you? I'm going to be robbed off in both cases.'

Suddenly, instead of the rough manly chest, she felt soft well-developed breasts pressing against her palms. 'Oh, darling, there's lot of difference between the supervisor and me. Wish I would've been a man and you my loved one.'

Gauri opened her eyes and looked upwards, towards the face of the dacoit. She exclaimed in joy, 'You! It's you again? Why . . . what all have you been doing for me?' It was Divya, the same girl who was working by her side and was joking at not being called by the supervisor. She was also the one who had appeared as her guardian lioness yesterday. With tears rolling down her cheeks, she said, 'You have most certainly saved me from total ruin today as well. My limitations are that I can't be of any use to you, I can't be your friend. I'm a mortal poor girl, and you a divine power.'

'It's nothing like this. You are great, and that's why you are being saved. Nothing will happen to you against your wishes. Don't fear me! I may be far away from you, but I'll remain your friend forever. We have been working together,' said Divya, the ghostgirl. Both laughed.

Gauri asked her, 'Now how would you get out of this hut? In front is the supervisor. Seeing your beauty, you would be first to be called tomorrow by your lover. You wanted it too!'

They laughed again, and Divya said, 'See, I am going out, you too go out. The manager is taking a dip in the pond to cool himself off!' She at once turned into the same fearful dacoit, came out, and called the supervisor. His body bore the signs of stings and cuts of insects all over, blood oozing out of many. He fell to the feet of the dacoit, saying, 'Kindly spare my life. I don't want to die, pardon me for my sins.'

'Go, touch the feet of the girl and beg pardon of her,' said the dacoit.

The supervisor immediately ran and fell upon Gauri's feet and said, 'Oh, goddess, oh, my mother, my sister, please spare my life, forgive me for my sins.'

Gauri said, 'Okay, go! Don't ever trouble any girl or a woman, thinking that she is helpless. Honour the woman, always.' The supervisor touched his ears in penance. Gauri, looking towards the dacoit, requested for him, 'Please forgive him and spare his life.'

'As you please, my dear sister,' said the dacoit. Everyone was feeling astonished. All this while, they had been fearing that, saved from the supervisor, the girl was probably being ravaged by the dacoit himself. They were together inside the hut for quite a long time.

The dacoit then asked for a glass of water and asked the supervisor to sit on the ground in front of him. He took the glass full of water in his left hand, and taking a little of water in the open palm of his right hand, he sprinkled it over the supervisor. The supervisor, within seconds, turned as clean as if he had taken a full bath. There remained no sign of stings, bleeding, or any pain. He felt as fresh as he had never felt before. He could not believe the miracle he had just experienced.

The dacoit and his two fellows looked towards the direction in which the supervisor's guards had disappeared. They were making their approach from the forest towards the hut. Offering them their guns back, the dacoits moved away and disappeared into the forest.

Everyone but Gauri was astonished to see this strange incident. No one could understand what had been happening over the last two days. One of them said, 'Neither was there the lioness yesterday, nor the dacoits today. Surely these were some divine souls.'

'You are right,' said the supervisor. 'It came like a storm and passed away like a morning calm, putting us wiser.'

The two guards went up to where the women had assembled and said, 'Tomorrow onwards we will be at your service, taking full care of you, protecting our mothers and sisters that you are, even at the cost of our lives.'

Gauri too did not understand these happenings. Who was this girl Divya, so powerful, capable of doing anything?

And even in spite of this, she came every day on time, obeyed all orders of the supervising staff, doing the tough work of carrying heavy earthen load in the hot sun the whole day. She was happy that in her lifetime, she had the opportunity to have the favour of a divine power and not only had seen his messenger but also had lived with one of them. But she was confused and frightened too. She was not able to understand how she should treat her. What courtesies did she need to observe? The powerful girl seemed happy doing all favours, but what if she got annoyed sometime? What would happen? What might she demand?

They next morning, all labourers came to work as usual, and the supervisor too was back on duty. He treated both these girls nicely, showing no anger or contempt towards them for whatever he had suffered the previous day. After some time, he called both of them to his hut office. Some workers thought he hadn't mended his ways. The two guards also got alert. When the girls passed by them, they said, 'Don't worry, we are with you. On slightest sense of any wrong with you, we would come and thrash him.'

The two girls went inside. The supervisor made them sit comfortably and very politely said, 'I don't know who you two are and how the incidents of past two days are related to you. But I take you to be common girls. Please work in easy manner, to your capabilities. You can tell this to other women workers too. All of you are equal and respectable to me. I know whatever I did yesterday is not excusable, yet I hope you will forgive me. Please tell me what I should do as repentance for my act of shame.'

'You have realised your mistake and you have mend your behaviour, that's enough. We don't have any anger or hard feelings for you in our heart. With this change in you, we have forgotten and forgiven all that happened. You may please treat us alike, with no extra leniency,' said Divya. She also said thanks to the supervisor, asked if there was anything else for them, and then both of them left the hut. On their way back, the guards said, 'Today we think he behaved well. Otherwise, we were ready for the worse.'

'Yes, he was okay today, behaved like a gentleman,' said Gauri.

'Sister, about lioness, we had only heard. But yesterday we've seen. Who could be the dacoit? He didn't touch the money nor harmed anyone in any way. It seems he knew the supervisor would call you to abuse you. And how sharp he was, precise to the seconds! Even a delay of a minute could have ruined your and his life. Surely he must have appeared from here only and disappeared too here in this very jungle. Yesterday it looked as if our lives are gone. We got so frightened and ran breathlessly into the jungle . . .'

'Where you were saved from a bear attacking you by another bear and were made to run back to reach here in time. This is all you'll tell. We have listened the story. We are in hurry, please don't mind,' said Divya and both moved away.

She looked with an unexplained pain in the eyes of her friend, the pretty little Gauri, and said, 'I feel my presence with you is creating many confusions in your mind.' Both remained standing, facing each other, speechless. And begging her excuse, Divya slowly walked away and went behind a thick tree. The girl kept standing, waiting.

The guards also said, 'What's matter? She went to the back of this tree. There was nothing here. No lion, bear, who else could have taken her away?' The guards and some two or three ladies who had seen these two girls standing and talking came and helped in looking for the girl, but it was no use. The supervisor also heard people talking loudly in worried tones. He also came out. Some started going back for fear of him, thinking he would scold them for leaving the work, coming there and talking. But he called them back like a gentleman and asked calmly what the matter was. Upon hearing what had just happened, he called some more men and asked them to look around.

He took Gauri with him to the tree. He bowed to the tree and touched its root, with both hands folded, saying, 'It was our good luck we lived with you and could see you with our eyes. We could talk to you. I know you are gone, not to come back, like Sita Mata. Your work here is complete, you have taught us dignity of labourers. You've been carrying heavy earth load on your head the whole day in the hot sun. You have also taught us to lead the path of gentleness and equality. You were surely some goddess. We are human beings, the effigies of mistakes and sins. Please forgive us and keep showering your mercies and blessings upon us all. We'll follow the path you have shown us. Your godly image will always remain as fresh in our heart and vision.' With folded hands and closed eyes, remembering her, he remained standing there for some time. After some time, with a heavy heart, he returned into his hut, saying to himself, 'Ten minutes ago she was sitting before me. I'm fortunate I called her. At least I could beg her pardon. I could see her at parting time.'

One of the guards said, 'Surely she was some goddess. She has told all that had happened with us in the forest yesterday. We hadn't told to anyone.'

The more and more people talked of her, the more bitterly Gauri was weeping. All the men and women were consoling her, saying, 'You are so lucky. You've lived with her so long. She has helped you in such wonderful ways. She has been your friend.'

On hearing such words, she felt more pain and wept aloud, remembering her. 'Now it looks as if she was never with me. I came to the office with her and now returning alone, losing her. I have nothing to say it's her remembrance. Where and how can I see her again?' The moment she said these words, a full-size, bright-red chunni (head cover cloth used by women) with embroidered border and designs all over it in golden and silver work appeared on her shoulders, draped around her neck.

All people close to her saw this miracle, and immediately they shouted, 'Goddess has sent her gift even from the distance.'

Someone ran to the supervisor. 'Sir, come and see. Goddess has sent her gift.' He too came running and saw the wonderful thing. He took its end in both his hands and touched it to his eyes and forehead; tears rolled off his eyes down on his cheeks.

Suddenly they heard a girl's voice. It was Divya undoubtedly. 'My dear friend, I'm your friend. Hope you would accept my small gift, the chunni, it would never turn old or fade. No one can steal it. You can use it in your marriage . . .'

Gauri angrily said, 'You won't change, even from up above you are joking and teasing me.'

The voice again continued, 'Okay, okay. Now don't cry, it would pain me. My parting time had come. In fact, I got late due to talks in the hut and then with guard brothers. I'll always be helping you and others. I'll always be with you, except for the time you would be with my brother-in-law in your happy moods.'

Gauri again said, but now smiling, 'Again you are back to your playful nature, teasing me.' And she fell calm.

The sky boomed, 'Okay! Bye, be happy, all of you.'

People there were left awestruck and chattered away at having been lucky of a heavenly experience. But soon, the smiles and laughter turned into sobs of gratitude and longing.

No one felt like working that day. Even lunch did not seem palatable. The whole day there was an uneasy silence on the site. The condition of Supervisor was also the same. He didn't insist on anyone to work. Rather, he decided to pack up early that day. He called everyone to receive the wages and to go home early. Everyone thought they would get one-fourth of the wages for the day, as no one had worked. But the supervisor paid each one full wages. They felt that now he had become so kind and saintly. As they took the wages and started to go back, the condition of the work site left them dumbfounded. They were astonished that more work than marked for the day seemed to have been done, without anyone actually doing it. They all muttered silent prayers and left the site in a pensive mood, as if they had lost a big treasure.

With only a few of them left at the site, most of whom walked to work and back with the two girls, they saw Gauri standing and looking sadly at the work site. Not wanting to leave her alone, they waited for her to join them. After some time she turned her back to the site and started walking towards the village. From behind them, they heard the sound of *clip-clop*, *clip-clop* becoming louder and coming closer. They recognised the man riding the horse as the village headman, who saw Gauri and said, 'Going alone today, left your friend on the site itself. Why? Would she come late?'

Gauri listened to him in astonishment and asked, 'Where and when did you see her?'

The headman replied, 'On the site, near the hut on the chair. She was talking to two persons on bench! Yes, there were three of them.'

'How long back did you see them?' she shot back excitedly.

'Only the time my horse took in coming here, back,' replied the headman. 'The three were discussing something. I asked her why she was sitting alone till so late. She said that she would be going soon to some other place and that she wasn't alone.'

Gauri stood still, listened to the headman, and started running back. The accompanying people tried to stop her, saying, 'It has already got late. Goddess might have left, and once she has disappeared, she wouldn't meet you now in that form. In daytime the goddess could have appeared. How can she meet you now? Don't go to see her. It would pain her. She would feel helpless in meeting you. Leave everything to her, to create the situation for her meeting you.' Gauri stopped running, looked longingly towards the site, but realised that they were right. She wouldn't find her there. She turned back and walked pensively towards the village with the crowd.

There at the site, two elderly figures were sitting on a bench, and in front of them in the chair was Divya, the ghostgirl. One of the two elderlies said, 'So you've shown your childlike nature. In spite of living like a common person, you had started playing miracles, as if we are magicians.'

'What miracles I have played?' asked Divya.

'Lioness, dacoit, first got the body of the supervisor cut by swampy souls, and then curing with freshness, making the girl feel that the lioness or dacoit were none other than you—some ghost. What are these? There were a dozen more like you down there working with all, could anyone even know if any ghostman was working with them.'

'All this was necessary to set the wicked fellow right, to save Gauri, and to bring her out of the fear of the lioness and the dacoit.'

'It wasn't necessary. But it was necessary for you to get the status of goddess in their hearts.'

'Now stop this discussion. Think of the poor little girl. How should we get her mind back to normalcy and how to send her back to her place? In this state, neither she can go back nor would she be able to lead a normal life.'

'We have to do something. But for God's sake, don't play those games this time.'

'Okay, go ahead, I'll take care.'

The three discussed something deeply and disappeared.

GAURI MEETS ANIKA

It was late in the night. In the of village of Gauri people had had their early dinner, as was the routine in villages, and got confined in their houses. The village was enveloped in darkness. Only in one house there was light, and some people, the family members, were talking. It looked like someone was either sick or not having the meal, and others were insisting on eating.

Out in the village, an aged man with a girl roamed the village lanes to find a suitable house to spend the night. Seeing the light in the house and people still awake, the man knocked at the door. After a wait, the door was opened. A girl appeared in the door and looked for any signs of recognition in the faces of the man and the girl who had knocked the door. The man and the girl also looked at the girl looking sickly, tired, and weeping with puffed eyes. She asked the man, 'Yes, what can we do for you?'

'Dear daughter, we have come for some work in the area and got late.'

Hearing someone talking at the door, the father of the girl also reached the door and asked, 'Who's there?'

The girl told her father, 'Someone with a girl want to stay with us for tonight.'

The father said, 'Oh, yeah, yeah, why not! Come in. You are welcome.'

The man said, 'Sir, we are carrying our food with us. Please allow us only to spend night in your house.'

'Don't worry, come on in. Do feel at home, take this as your own house.' They were taken in and were made to sit comfortably. Water was offered, and they washed their faces, hands, and feet. After settling down, the man and this daughter went to one side of the room and took out a small cloth pack to open. The house owner saw them and said, 'What are you doing, sir? Whatever you have, keep it with you. We too haven't taken our meals so far. Please dine with us. It's ready. The only delay is, this girl's not taking anything. She hasn't taken even water since she came home from work.'

'Why? What's matter?' the guest girl asked.

'What can I say? One of her friends has left her. In fact, she has disappeared, giving a gift to her. She says she was some divine girl who has saved her life at several occasions. Since the time she came from her work has been weeping and weeping.'

'May I go to her and try?' asked the guest girl.

'Oh sure, come, she's in the worship room,' said the father. The guest girl took the dinner plate, looked back at her father, who reached out and told her to act wisely. The girl looked at her father, the place of worship, and noticed the red chunni placed near the worship place. She got close to the girl, who lay covering her face with a coverlet. The girl, with plate in hand, asked her, 'Hello, friend, get up.' She removed the cloth from her face, and the girl, Gauri, opened her eyes. 'Have your dinner.'

'I'm not feeling like taking anything. You have it,' said Gauri, lying in bed.

'How can we eat where my hostess is not taking anything? We won't take even whatever food is with us. My morality directs me to live here as our hostess is living or to leave the place. Should we leave the house to go somewhere in the jungle, or sleep hungry? Actually, I'm feeling very hungry. Haven't eaten anything since morning,' said the guest girl.

Gauri had no answer; she got up and, looking at the girl, murmured, 'Very clever. By which name can I call you?'

'Anika. You can call me Anika,' said the guestgirl.

Both smiled. 'I'm Gauri,' said the hostess girl. The guestgirl took a little food in her fingers and tried to put in her mouth. Gauri stopped her hand and said, 'No, the guest first.' She picked up a piece of bread from the plate and placed it in the mouth of Anika. Anika also offered a bite to Gauri, which she now accepted. With the first mouthful, Gauri wondered with eyes wide open, 'Hmmm, it's really so tasty. But it's not the same as what my mom cooks every day, surely there's something in your hand.'

Simultaneously, Anika also exclaimed, 'So tasty, must be miraculous mom and something in your hand.' Both made each other eat and took three course services.

'Would you be my friend? I'll remain yours,' said Anika.

'This time, I won't hesitate. Would accept the offer surely for life long,' said Gauri.

After dinner, the father and the mother of Gauri felt that 'God has sent these guests just for our Gauri and us all, in no time she got normal.'

The food was flavourful and very tasty. And so was the sound sleep they had for the whole night.

The next morning, they got up early and got ready to move after breakfast. Gauri's mother packed the lunch for her daughter and also for the two guests and also gave them a bottle each of drinking water.

After breakfast they all were sitting in the sitting room. The father of Gauri asked the guests for their further destination. One of the guests said, 'I work in the forest for a contractor, gathering medicinal plants, soon we would be establishing camp near Dera. Anika is left alone at our place, she insisted to do some job wherever she gets. Someone suggested us to contact on a site near this village. Yesterday, we should have stayed at Dera, but wrongly we proceeded further to this village. Luckily, in the night we got your house. Otherwise, we would have been in trouble.'

'You can never be in trouble. You remove the troubles of others,' said Gauri's mother. 'You haven't come wrongly. God has sent you to the right place. He sent you for us. We all were in trouble. We had done all possible for our daughter. But she wasn't even taking water, and we had no hope that any one of us would take dinner. Whatever we all couldn't do whole day, your daughter had done in minutes.'

SOCIAL WELFARE
STARTS IN THE AREA

'Now I would like to go with your daughter to the site and try to find some job for Anika there. Heard Devika is from this place, and luckily, she is there today. Can we meet her?' said the father of Anika.

'Surely you can, if she is there. I've no idea about her. I had been out. On your way, you can go that way,' said the host. And they all four started on their way to the roadwork site. While going to the site, on their way passing through Haati Village, they reached Devika's house. At the knock, her father, Surya Dev, opened the door. After an exchange of morning greetings, Surya Dev made them sit comfortably in the sitting room. After some time, Devika got to the room, ready for going somewhere. She asked these people the purpose of their coming to her.

The father of Gauri said, 'These are some nice people. They had come last night to us. He wants her daughter, Anika, to get some work at the work site. We have come to you for this reason, if you can recommend her to the supervisor.'

'I'm going to the site to see the progress and problems there. Hope the labour are treated well there. Their proper care is taken, especially of the women workers. You can also come with me. I'll see if it's possible there,' said Devika. She called one of her attendants and asked if everything was ready to move. The attendant confirmed, and they all left the house and, after about one hour, reached the work site of the road.

The supervisor got information from the persons, and it reached him in advance that some big person was to come to the site. He at once put some labourer to make things presentable and got his office set right, and seating and tea arrangements for the visitors were done. After doing all this spade work of giving a good look, he reached the points the guests were expected to arrive at. There he, with his labourers, received the guests, Devika and the others with her.

Devika took a round of the work line or area under work and discussed the progress of the work with the supervisor. She also talked to the labourers. The labourers informed Devika of the difference in working conditions a day before and now. They also told her about the two incidents of the lioness and the dacoit and also how the ghostgirl disappeared there and her friend, Gauri. Devika was moved upon hearing about the incident of the ghostgirl. She went to the tree where the ghostgirl disappeared. There she,

Gauri, Anika, and some others went and saw the spot. She stood there quietly with closed eyes for some time. They all saw some flowers were placed there under the tree. Devika asked, 'Where the flowers have come from?'

Supervisor replied, 'I offered these flowers here. I worship her. She was a divine, pious soul. She has shown me the path of righteousness.'

'Good, very good, you are saved of many miseries. But many have paid heavy cost for your benefit,' said Devika. Seeing a big hut shade erected there, she asked, 'Why this second shade?'

'I got it done for labourers. It's their first-aid point. Also, I want to appoint two tender-type, soft-spoken, caring girls or women to keep young children of working women here. And to help the workers in their time of necessity. Till yesterday I had two such girls here. But one of them has disappeared. Other one, this Gauri, also didn't come today so far. She's here with you, ma'am. I've identified her for this work. If she's willing. Are you willing to work as welfare worker, Gauri?'

She willingly consented.

'How would be this girl for your second one?' said Devika to the supervisor.

'Very fine, ma'am, you have solved my big problem here in the forest. Right from today, she would be on work roll. These two girls need not go for any earth work. They will remain here for work in this new hut from today only. They would also interact with the workers to know about their personal problems. And would be attending to them to help them, counsel them, to guide the ladies in their personal and professional matters, to keep up their morale high, and to make their lives more meaningful, to develop creativity in them. These ladies and gents would be made aware of how can they live a better life while working here and after this.'

Devika was happy with the idea; she said, 'This is nice idea. Monitor it properly see the progress of your project and its result. Though this is not part of your duty, but it is good for the community and the country. I'll also help you. Time to time, I'll meet you to see its results. I want that you three persons remain in the area with this project as paid personnel. You would be shifted to a better central location after some time.' After refreshment and tea, she got up to leave the place. She met the two girls and asked them to work sincerely in the benefit of the community under the instructions of the supervisor, taking their own initiative. The girls were also happy, and they assured her of their good work. Thus infusing a new life among them all there, Devika left the place. And the two girls assumed their new assignments.

After putting the two girls on their job, the supervisor returned to his office and, getting into his chair, holding his head in both hands, sat quietly, murmuring, 'What an unnecessary additional heavy duty I have put on my neck. Became over smart just to please her. I have spoken so highly about this small work. Thinking of doing on my own as voluntarily service. Now this has become my main heavy duty. The ladies of the area may not create new venues for them, but I have surely created big new problems for me. I may be slack in my main road construction work, but for my self-created problem, I've to maintain weekly progress report of this my so-called "tertiary turned into primary" work. May God help me in my foolish venture!'

The supervisor had been treating the welfare service point as his unwanted pregnancy and had been helping the two girls, so to say, guiding them reluctantly. But with their initiative and sincerity, the two girls had made it very popular among the people. And with this, the girls had become very popular and highly welcome figures among the people. An appreciation letter was given to the supervisor for his commendable work in social service. After this he started realising that he had been getting credit and recognition for others—the girls' efforts. On the grass-roots public level of social work, the two girls had been popular and well sought after. But in upper official circles it was the supervisor who was known. This had enabled him to reach and move in the higher official circle. Heart to heart the supervisor felt himself obliged to the two girls for being lifted to a high position from being merely a contractor's private supervisor to a well-recognised person among officers and politicians. He had been directly reaching out to Devika, Agastya, and Priya for even personal favours for his works. Now he felt the importance of this small work he started. And in a way he turned into a real social worker.

GAURI VISITS ANIKA'S HOME

The two girls had been working together so friendly that the people had come to recognise them as the duo girls. Several times, Gauri had been taking Anika to her place. To some extent Gauri had recovered from missing her godly friend. Of course, she had been remembering her sincerely and had honour for her and her gifts. But in her day-to-day life she had become normal, taking to her work with all sincerity. One day, Gauri insisted that she would go with Anika to her home in the evening, after work. Anika started thinking of how to handle this situation. She put up the problems to her so-called father. He suggested, 'You better call her on any Wednesday. On this day, mostly we all from this area live together here at our place. Otherwise, we have our weekly schedule. On Thursday we spend the night at Joshi tree. On Monday we visit Shiva temple. On Tuesday Lord Hanuman temple. Thursday and Friday are spent in tombs, graveyards, and cremation grounds. Saturday is reserved for Lord Shani's places, and on Sunday some of us visit churches.'

On Monday itself, Anika told Gauri to be ready and to come prepared on Wednesday to go with her to her place. On the fixed day, after the work was over, though Gauri had complained about some body trouble, felt feverish, and acute body ache, she decided to accompany her. And both walked together on the narrow forest trails and reached the place. Gauri was happy to see the small village amidst the thick forest—neat and tidy, small, small houses, no dust, and no smoke. No sign of any professional work being done, no cattle heads, no milking, and no food processing. People were meeting one another joyfully. In a place, several people were sitting together, enjoying gossip and some game. Gauri felt strange, thinking, *What sort of place is this? Never seen before, this type of village. People were looking cheerful and jolly, talking joyfully in a high pitch.*

Gauri was not feeling well, and the long tough walk made her further more sickly, and she was feeling totally exhausted. She was thinking, reaching Anika's home, that the first thing she would do would be to lie in bed and rest for the night. But reaching here, she totally forgot to rest or to have something to eat; she felt neither any sickness nor tiredness nor hunger or thirst. Even then the two friends went to a room and retired to bed for some time. Then Anika brought water and some eatables with her. The water was very refreshing, and the eatables very energetic and tasty. Gauri asked, 'Why this village is just like transit camp? Do the people not work? There are no sign of people doing any work, no cattle and no agricultural implements.'

Anika replied, 'This is simply because all the people and their families remain out for their work. Here, no one lives who would take care of the cattle etc. That's why I asked you to come on this fixed day. People come here only to meet each other on fixed day.' She further said, 'It would be better that for some time you take a short sleep or nap. Then we will have dinner and will also go around to see the village to meet people and see a cultural programme. It will be a whole-night programme, you may not get to sleep in the night. It would be possible only in the pre-dawn for a very short time to rest.'

Both of them went to bed and went to sleep. After about two hours, they woke up, got fresh, and sat down for dinner. As her mom wasn't there, a woman neighbour had been helping Anika provide and serve dinner. 'Delicious!' exclaimed Gauri. It was all vegetarian food with fruits, rice, pulse, vegetables, and chapattis and sweets. Having had the dinner, they both again had rest for a short time and got ready and got out to meet the friends and see the village. Anika took Gauri around and introduced her to her friends and the other village people. Gauri was very impressed. She felt like she was moving in a dreamland. Gauri and Anika took some time visiting the village. In the meantime, people had started assembling at a common place. Lit torches were fixed all-around and at the main entrance. Proper seating arrangements were made. Gauri and Anika arrived there and occupied their seats.

After about one-and-a-half hours came, the programme coordinator went for permission from the head of the villages and informed them of how many persons had reached there and that there were four guests who were sitting along with their hosts in the separate area marked for guests. There, mostly people were standing, moving from person to person, sharing information and light jokes. They were taking some refreshing drinks. Gauri and Anika also got a glassful of sweet refreshing, tasty juice. And then started the music, and dance with songs. This continued till a little before the break of dawn.

The programme came to a halt. The head of the community thanked the guests, all the people who joined the programme, and those who took part in the performances. He thanked and permitted the guest, their hosts, and all others who were not keen to attend the meeting that was going to follow shortly after to leave for their houses.

It was this time Gauri and Anika left the site of the gathering, reached home, and went to sleep. Gauri got up a bit late; by then Anika had made all arrangements for breakfast and packed lunch. After Gauri woke up, she got ready hurriedly, and both of them had their breakfast. Lunch was packed for both. At the time of their coming for duty, Anika's father gave a gift-wrapped packet to Gauri. Gauri resisted to take the gift. She said, 'Uncle, it is not required. You had taken so much of my care, gave me so much of love. That's my gift. Kindly give me your blessings, and nothing else.'

But he said, 'Dear daughter, you are a nice girl, a dear friend of Anika. You are just like Anika to me. My blessings will always be with you. This is nothing, please accept it on your first visit to us, for remembrance.' And she had to accept it. Thereafter, both of them left the place.

On the way, Gauri had been telling Anika, 'What was the necessity? Why didn't you tell Uncle not to go in for this formality?'

Anika said, 'Why should have I told? What difference does it make? What's harm if he has given something to his other daughter?'

Gauri kept quiet, but in her mind there were many questions and doubts about the unique and strange experience she had in visiting the village. But she preferred to remain quiet with her questions.

The two girls worked together as social workers from their office, shifting from place to place on the road under construction, with the shifting of the work site as the construction progressed. Every month, the work site was going about a mile farther away from the village of Gauri, and her travelling distance was increasing. She was at the verge of submitting her resignation that Agastya and Priya came on a tour of the region. Agastya was very happy with the project. This project had given very encouraging results, and therefore, Agastya and his party gained popularity beyond expectation in the area. Agastya, who wanted to take up this project on wider scale, took the supervisor and the two girls out of the road construction work and transferred them to another new public welfare project at Kuhar Village, in a permanent location. Under the expansion of the scheme, Kuhar Village was made the regional centre, with a training unit for cluster centres—one centre for each group of five villages.

Supervisor had become the regional officer and the two girls the assistant regional officers. But Anika expressed her inability to accept the offer. She said, 'I would work for full time like Gauri, till such time I fully train a girl to work in my place. But I'll be working as honorary worker, not taking any government portfolio or a post.'

Priya, feeling in heart the helplessness of a girl and fearing the loss of Joshi and Kanshi Ram, convinced Agastya to appoint another girl from Khairi Village. She said, 'I know there is a well-qualified graduate girl, Naina, graduated from Balrampur.' And the girl was appointed in the first upper row. Anika was appointed as voluntary officer with Naina till she was fully trained to work independently. Thus, at the regional headquarter the team was regional director, two assistant regional directors, and Anika, a voluntary officer. For the road construction site, the contractor was asked to appoint another supervisor and two other girls or women workers for the welfare of the labourers there. The entire social welfare team was restructured, and the whole area was undergoing metamorphism in all respect.

Agastya, while leaving the construction site, was deeply perplexed and in a pensive mood. He had felt a strange flow of energy surrounding them while he had been talking to the supervisor and the girls, Gauri and Anika, in their office. In particular, he felt an instant spiritual contact with Anika.

He could not recall that he had ever met or seen her before. Yet there was something familiar about her. What it was exactly remained a suspense in his mind. Was she someone whom he might have seen in his earlier trips to the region? Could she have been an acquaintance through the villagers whom he had stayed with or worked with in the area? Was she involved in party work or in the election campaigns? He wasn't sure of anything except the fact that Anika had something in her that seemed to draw him towards her in a very unique way.

On their way back Agastya and Priya went to the banyan tree, paid their respects, and inspected the work done there. The visit to the tree seemed to calm Agastya, and he suddenly felt lighter.

Then Priya asked him, 'This approach road is good. It will facilitate people approaching the holy tree, but it needs to be surfaced. This shouldn't cost much.'

'You're right, it must be done. Otherwise, it would be covered by wild growth. I'll talk to the road contractor. He will do it. In the next phase, I'll see to it that the road comes to the village,' said Agastya.

'That will be good, and it will be wonderful if it could go up to Haati, joining the parallel road to border, it will serve this heartland, providing quick reach and quick movement on the border. It would be great strategically. Haati would turn into an important business centre and defence base,' said Priya.

'This link road will facilitate me too.'

'How would you be facilitated?'

'It would be easy for me to bring big marriage party to your place.'

'Marriage party to this village! Good joke! You already got married. We'll be good friends now, you a politician and me a social worker. That, too, if you would like to keep me as your friend, because choices of only big ones are met out,' said Priya.

'Me, married? What are you saying, ma'am? And how are my choices different from yours? Moreover, if you know that I got married, you must also be knowing who my bride is. I got married and I don't know.' Agastya simply laughed.

'You very well know, dear, to whom you are married. Your priorities, your interests, your politics, and your friends,' said Priya.

'You too have your priorities, your interests, and your friends. In fact, you remain more committed to your priorities. You have forgotten every other thing and everyone else. As regards friends, Devika and others are there. Oh, ma'am, that way you too are married. Not only married, but you have children also.'

'I have doubts about your intentions right from the very beginning. Doesn't matter. You carry on with Devika, a better person suiting your work and interests,' Priya complained.

They went on talking in light mood jokingly. But in these light talks, somewhere Priya had hinted on the feeling she might have had somewhere in her mind. Their subject-oriented talks were turned into a light humorous one. And Priya overheard two persons sitting and talking. They were talking about Kanshi Ram Joshi. She quietly alerted Agastya also to listen. Both got a little closer, showing themselves as if not paying attention to overhear them and talking about something else. They heard one of them saying, 'This Kanshi Ram Joshi has worked wonderfully in the election.'

'That's right, he has done his work very well, and how cleverly he has made his place close to Agastya and controlled his whole constituency so efficiently that he looked everywhere. He turned all voters in his party favour,' said the other one.

'Agastya deserved it, he is nice. His fellow party leaders are also good. They recognised his work and honoured him,' said the first one.

'You also have worked tremendously. The only difference was that you worked in low profile and he was in front profile. Everyone recognised him,' said the other one.

'And you, you worked more than me. You were directly every time with Joshi. Recognition, we don't care about. Rewards, recognitions, these have no value in our world.

We all are happy. We enjoy only working for nice fellows. And in that last-day function, how we all enjoyed with Joshi Brother. We had brought even their real Joshi and Rohan there. Two of us were in the police uniform. In fact, in the meeting, I told also not to go Basti, Joshi's place, warned that they may lose a sincere worker. But no one listened. That's the weakness of mortals, they are governed more by logic and their whims.'

'The other day, poor Kanshi Ram Joshi had to play many tricks, real Kanshi had arrived at the scene. Thank God he could save the situation. Had to run right from inside the room with memento, which he placed at his place on the banyan tree,' said the first one.

'Where is he now, and what's he doing?' asked the other one.

'Didn't you know? He is there only. Doing nothing but the same as we all do, waiting for suitable opportunity and planning for availing that. He will surely go soon. He is very fast front-line worker. The main election is fast approaching. They will soon be starting their long-term campaign.'

Agastya and Priya got clear picture of their success. Both stood under the tree, thanked these two persons from their heart for their services, and requested them to tell them the way they could pay back their due regards and true remembrance to them.

ROHAN VISITS HIS HOME

From Dera, Agastya left for Balrampur, whereas Priya stayed back at home for another two days. At Balrampur, a messenger informed Agastya that the marriage of Rohan's sister Monika had been fixed for the twelfth of January, ten days from the day, in his native village of Bharai on G. T. Road, some fifteen miles short of Aligarh. Agastya discussed the matter with Devika, who was already in the station. They prepared a plan for taking Rohan to his sister's marriage and maintaining the complete secrecy for not risking their lives.

In advance, Agastya informed the DIG at Lucknow, who further directed the concerned officer for the needful and also to take a complete search of the village and the area to avoid any untoward incident.

On the fixed date, Agastya, Balendu, Nidhi, and Priya reached the police headquarters in the morning and met the DIG. And under security cover of four armed, well-trained police guards, Rohan and all these four friends left for Village Bharai at about 11.30 a.m. On the way, they halted for lunch. And covering their long distance carefully, they reached the destination by 6.30 p.m. All around there was strict security. No one knew the reasons for this security. Not even the local police. Everyone thought that might have been against the dacoits. But seeing the police van and police guards, the police could understand that some big personality had come.

Unaware of the development, the parents of Rohan had been performing the marriage rituals in their normal way. It was evening and the garland ceremony was taking place. The village people started gathering around the place of marriage. Some saw Rohan and ran to the family, shouting Rohan had come. The police had brought Rohan. By this time the bride, Monika, with tears in her eyes, escorted by her friends and family ladies, had started with the nuptial garlanding ceremony scheduled to be held on the main entrance door of the house. Missing her dear brother, she was doing all this against her wishes. She had come to garland her going-to-be husband. Both were standing facing each other. At the back of the groom were his friends and members of the marriage party. And the bride was supported by several girls and family ladies. The door and the room, even the balcony above, were fully packed with guest and visitors. This was the main and crucial time of the marriage ceremony. Not to miss this occasion, without meeting family and parents, Agastya hurriedly took Rohan to the place. On one side of the groom close to him, in front of Monika reached Rohan with Agastya and two girls, Priya and Nidhi, with the armed guards at their back. Rohan and party stopped there, to the extreme of their happiness that they arrived on time. They were successful in their efforts, and they would be meeting the family after the sacred performance. The final moment had come. A big, very well-prepared, beautiful garland was given to the bride to garland the groom. She, looking down, held it in both hands, breathed deeply, gathered courage, and slowly lifted up her face and eyelids to garland. In doing this her eyes fell on Rohan, standing in front of her, who was also watching her with a cheerful face. And now both were seeing each other eye to eye. She failed to understand and react anything, turning into statue type. The groom saw her watching so intensely a young boy, leaving aside garlanding him. He too didn't understand anything, felt insulted, and was getting annoyed. All three got to a standstill. Her upward-going hand, face, and eyes got stuck statue like. Seeing his sister looking at him, a smile ran on the face of Rohan, tears rolling down his cheeks. He could only utter 'May God bless you, Monika'. Hearing her name, 'Monika', she got confirmed that he was Rohan, her brother. She, forgetting everything, cried, 'Rohan!' And leaving the garland, she ran to Rohan. They clung to each other. By then his mother, father, other family members, relatives, and villagers also rushed to the site. The police kept them away. Every family member was weeping with happiness. Seeing this, the groom, not understanding anything, mistook it as a love scandal. As if her lover had arrived with the police.

The groom left the place in anger and told his father, 'What's this? Why we have been called when she was to be married with someone else?' They all gathered and walked away to their place to talk about why the parents of the bride did all this.

Rohan's mother met him, embracing him. And so did the others. Mother told Rohan and party not to come forward but to remain standing where they were. She would welcome them with the purified-butter lamps, sprinkling rice and flowers on them, performing *aarti*. She came with a plate of lamp, vermilion, flowers, and rice and put the vermillion on the forehead of Rohan and the others. She showed them the lamp and offered rice grains and flowers to them.

While she was doing all these, the groom, his father, and others had also arrived there and started asking the father of Monika. 'Why have you called us all here, troubled us so much, and insulted in front of our all relations, when you were to do all this with other boy?'

'You all are our honoured guests. We have invited you for marriage of my daughter with your son,' said the father of Monika.

'But why the marriage ceremony was stopped, and leaving the ceremony, she ran to this boy? Her mother has performed this ceremony with him,' said the father of the groom. Most of the bride-side persons laughed. He further continued, 'What's there to laugh at? Am I wrong?'

'Yes, brother, you are very much wrong. These two are real brother and sister. How could you think so? In fact, we don't know where he had disappeared. Even government couldn't do anything. And after waiting for about three years now, we all had taken that due to some accident, he is no more. But the almighty God is so merciful. Who are these angels for whom we could get our child alive back? In fact, it is for your lucky feet. You have brought us our good luck, our child back to us. We can only thank you for bringing us this good fortune,' said the weeping father.

'You are right, Uncle, it is for them. We have tried so hard to bring Rohan on this sacred occasion to give our sister Monika the most valuable gift of her life, on her marriage, her loving brother, Rohan,' said Agastya.

Monika came forward and touched the feet of Agastya and Priya. But Priya lifted her up, saying, 'No, not needed, you are our loving younger sister.'

'Brother, please excuse us. We are sorry we didn't know. We are happy. In fact, now it would be real happy occasion. We would be taking away with us our cheerful daughter, who had been all the time weeping so far. But you didn't tell us all this. You said you have lost your grown-up son. How had it happened?' said the father of the groom.

'We don't know anything about him. We are seeing him right now. As you see, these fellows who've come with must be knowing details of all this progress,' said the father of Monika, the bride.

One of the policemen said, 'Actually, sir, Rohan had gone to the Tarai Forest tribal area beyond Rapti for his study project. Had been staying in a guest house at Dera, village of this girl, Priya. From there he was kidnapped forcefully by a big international gang with their base near Nepal border for engaging in their illicit trade activities. He did not agree, they kept him on drugs and tortured to agree for their work. For that he lost his memory. These were four victims now rescued, are under strict security. Only due to the efforts of Sir, who is our MLA also now, and Priya-ji he is brought on this special occasion of Monika's marriage. All the four will be under police protection till the whole gang goes behind the bars. Devika, vice president—Ra. Ma. Dal, couldn't come today. These are all close friends. These three saved their fourth friend, Rohan. They did what government had given up and closed the file.'

'We did not do anything for anyone. We got our friend Rohan freed from the clutches of the gang,' said Agastya.

'Now you all four with Rohan would see my daughter's doli [departure carriage of bride] off,' said the father of Monika.

'Surely this is exactly what we came here for. We are sorry for the interruption, already it has gone so late. Please resume the ceremony,' said Agastya.

The father of the groom, on behalf of his party and self, congratulated the parents of Monika and thanked Agastya and his friends for their wonderful work.

Monika took Priya and Nidhi along with her to join her other friends and family. The nuptial garland ceremony was resumed. This time, Monika looked more beautiful and cheerful. The whole atmosphere, charged with energy and happiness, was totally changed. Rohan had joined his family, but the police guards remained everywhere with him. After the garland ceremony, dinner was served to all. Rohan, Agastya, and Balendu were served the food, tested by the police guards in a separate place. The dinner was followed by the main ritual of marriage, going around the fire god, followed by other ceremonies. The whole night, these continued. But after dinner the main crowd had gone to rest and sleep. Only close related persons were busy in required work.

It was past midnight; necessary ceremonies and rituals were going on. There was pitch dark all around. People heard clip-clops, neighs of horses, loud laughter, and fearful voices coming closer. The police posted in the village and the escorts of Rohan got alert and took their automatic arms in ready-to-attack position. Everyone got panicky. People started running for safer places here and there. But no place looked safe at such time. Women, crying and trembling, calling for their children, ran here and there, hiding them and themselves, forgetting everything else. The police people said, 'You don't worry, we are there.' But no words looked enough for safety to the people. Suddenly over-enthusiastic dacoits opened fire in the air to frighten the people, to get easy heavy loot. On their firing, police opened fire, the automatic weapons taking aim towards the general direction of the dacoits. These hundreds of rounds in a few seconds from wide front fell like drops of rainwater on the fast-approaching gang.

Soon shrieks of pains, cries, and neighs of horses were heard there. Some thundering voice shouted, 'Run back, return fast, there looks like a big ready force. There is sure death today. The dirty fellow did not tell about this full tight security force, only said about the big marriages of rich party. I'll kill the bloody informer, has sent the whole gang into the jaws of sure death.' A searchlight was thrown on the gang. They looked panicky and nervous, turning back on their heels. The turning sound of horses was clear. Whispering voices said, 'Pick up the injured and hurry up.' Some more firing by the police ensued, and they, leaving behind some bodies, galloped away.

There was calm all around. The police announced, 'No danger now.' All came out of their hiding places, saw one another, and felt a sigh of big relief. Everyone was sharing his or her condition under fear and panic and techniques of hiding with joy now. All were thanking and praising the police for saving them. 'Very good police. Very quick action.' A searchlight was thrown. In seconds, that open area close to the village turned into a battlefield. A seriously injured man in a coma was lying there. He was profusely bleeding. The police station was informed. The superintendent of police at district headquarters was informed. Some policemen had taken positions around the body and the field. There were patches of blood here and there, and thick lines of blood trickling down were leading them, exactly the same way as the Urdu verse of (Quawal) Habib Painter had very touchingly depicted: 'Apnaa hi khoon dushman ban gayaa, raastaa bataane ke liye.'*

---

* 'A hunter shot an arrow at a lion,

It wasn't killed, got injured and ran away,

Within an hour more the police force arrived there. The dawn was about to break. Darkness was bit less now. The superintendent of police, two inspectors, and a big force were there. The dead man lying face downward was turned to face upward. Seeing him, every officer and policeman shouted with joy and greeted each other. 'Oh, what a big success, got so suddenly, unknowingly. Has he come to die himself?' It was big headache for the police. Big gang leader Chakra, a rupees-one-lakh-rewardee dacoit, was dead.

The SP and the inspector came to the house, where the marriage ceremony was about to be over. He called the father of the bride. The SP shook his hands and congratulated the father of the girl and said, 'Hope everything has gone well. This marriage had been very lucky for us and for lacs of people of UP, Haryana, MP, and Rajasthan. For years this big-rewardee, notorious gangster dacoit has been failing our all efforts. He has even killed several of our police personnel. But here so suddenly, without even sweat to anyone, he is lying dead. His gang is busted. Others will surely be caught. They can't hide the amount of blood left, the thick trail leading to them. I've sent the party to chase them. They won't be going to big distance, it was only an hour back they started back from here that too most of them

---

But hunter, following blood trickled down,

Reached the lion and killed. The dead soul

Felt,'to guide the hunter,

The enemy was none, but blood of my own.'

seriously injured. We consider ourselves lucky. Actually, for the brainchild of Agastya-ji. He approached the police headquarters and got this arrangement done for your safety, which has become safety for crores of people.'

'Thanks, your staff is so nice and so quick. Their alertness and presence of mind has made all this possible. We are obliged to you for your efforts. The marriage of my daughter has gone uninterrupted. Mr Agastya is here only,' said the father of Monika.

'He is here! I would like to meet him,' said the SP. A boy was sent to inform Agastya.

'Here he comes,' said the father of Monika.

The SP called out, 'Good morning, sir, and double congratulations.'

'Good morning to you and thanks for congrats. But why double?' said Agastya.

'One is for the undisrupted marriage of Monika, and the second one is for busting yet another big interstate gang of dacoit. Chakra, he is lying dead there. Only you and DIG police headquarters planned this. It's a big success for police. Dacoit, of rupees one lakh on head, is lying dead there.' They were talking when at the same time the sound of distant firing was heard. The SP further said, 'Surely our chasing party must have overcome them. Must be encountering there. I know they were not left fit to go long distance.' Addressing the father of Monika, he said, 'Uncle, our best wishes for the newly wedded couple. We would like to go now. Thanks.'

'Stay for some time, it's morning time, have a cup of hot tea,' said Agastya.

'Have to see there, firing is opened on another front. Have to monitor all this. It's a big day for us. Kindly congratulate DIG, sir, I'll too talk to sir. It would be a celebration day for us all,' said the SP and he left.

At Monika's home, the atmosphere had turned serious. The departure time had arrived. Monika was meeting her father, mother, uncles, aunts, friends, brothers, sisters, people of the village, relations, and finally, Rohan, Agastya, Balendu, Priya, and Nidhi, whom she had been meeting again and again. She was weeping and bursting into tears. Everyone was weeping and slowly, slowly were taking Monica to a well-decorated car. And finally they made her sit in the rear left window-side seat so that everyone could see her off and could meet her at the parting, blessing her, putting their hands on her head. On the final step, Priya and Nidhi were close to her door. Monika was holding their fingers through the car window. Rohan, Agastya, Balendu, and the father of Monika were pushing the car (as customary. Though the engine was running, it was at dead slow speed). A final look back of Monika on all and her village with running eyes and nose. Her husband was in her right-side seat. The car was gaining speed, and all family and relations were being left behind. They all stood still, looking at the fast going-away car till it disappeared. And all these turned back.

Reaching back home, they all assembled. Out-station relations started going back to their places. Agastya, Priya, and Rohan also asked to return to Lucknow. Rohan's mom said, 'My children, you have given us a new life. We can't express our gratitude. But we were busy, couldn't even see Rohan to satisfaction. Can't he stay for some more time?'

'Aunt, now we have to go, even this much was not possible. He is under government care. Think if there were not so much police yesterday. What reply DIG could have given to the public? Now whenever you want to meet Rohan, come to Lucknow and reach her place,' Agastya said, pointing to Priya. 'She will take you to Rohan or would get Rohan at her place. She will inform me also, if I'm there in Lucknow at the time. You needn't worry. His full care is being taken. Think as if he is with you. You all are tired. We are going. You take rest and some sleep. Now please arrange a cup of hot tea. And we go after tea.' He pointed to a policeman. 'Please call the driver also, who had been sleeping whole night.'

Family members and relations of Rohan were coming and meeting him. He too was happy to meet them all. Fresh hot tea had come and was served with some salty snacks. Mom called the store in-charge and told him to pack some sufficient quantity of eating items for the journey time for them, individual packets for each one of these, and also a spare one for Devika. She had sent a good gift for Monika. 'Would have been good had she also come, we could have seen her.'

'Mom, she's not the same Devika of past. She has become big and busy personality now,' said Rohan.

'Not bigger than own persons and friends. You are in no way less. All are equal friends,' said Priya.

'I, I have to start afresh, a new life. At the moment, I'm nothing. Even my final-year studies are incomplete, neither could I complete my project, nor do I know my college position, what would happen,' said Rohan.

'Don't worry, it was unfortunate incident. Ups and downs, accidents occur in everyone's life. One shouldn't be discouraged by such things. Think you've come out successfully. Whole life is ahead. We are all with you, not going to leave you on road as it is. Take it bravely and start from where you are. Thank God he is there to look after you,' said Priya.

'I'm saved by you, and you have given me this new life, that I'm here. I can think of my past and future,' said Rohan.

'Don't make us gods. We are very common men, not other than you. We haven't done anything for others but for ourselves. We were worried for you. So don't think other way,' Priya said.

Tea was finished in gossip. Their packets were kept in the van. They all moved to their van. Sitting in, they started on their way back to Lucknow. All kept seeing them and waving their hands till they got out of sight. Turning back, said the mom, 'This was another a painfully departure. See off. Don't know when would come home to live with us normal life.'

'Will surely come, see what type of persons are working for him. Could we do anything for him? We had sat quietly, accepting him as gone forever. Yesterday seeing him was unbelievable. When someone came running, shouting, "Rohan has come, Rohan is there," I didn't believe nor tried to go that side. We couldn't have got him even treated. And see how the so-dreaded dacoits had come in the night. Marriage would have surely been finished, and can't think how many of us would be lying dead and how many injured. Life of survived ones would have also been hell. This place could have become dreaded hell. It were these who have saved us in all respect.

'Dacoits could have taken away bride. Thinking of that, I shiver, turn mad. Thank God he has given well-wishers like Devika, Priya, and Agastya. An MLA had been working for us whole night. All these three had thought so much that a brother should join at sister's marriage, and they themselves, at their own risk, have brought him here. Who does anything for anyone? They have made this marriage ceremony a real joyful. May God bless them all. Now we both would go Hardwar for bathing Ganga,' said Rohan's dad.

'Yes, you are right, impossible has happened in our life. We must go and thank Mother Ganga,' said Rohan's mom.

On their return to the police training centre at Lucknow to hand over Rohan, the vehicle, and, the police guards,

Agastya and Priya sent word for the DIG and the DSP. But they found extra security and chaos on the campus. On their message, somehow almost running, the DSP came, congratulated them, and took back Rohan and other things and also the sweet packet sent by the parents of Rohan. And thanking them, he hurried back, saying, 'See you soon.' But the DIG took time to come to them. He was also quite tense. Agastya asked if there was any problem.

'Not small, sir, big problem. Fifteen guns are missing from tight-security quarter guard. Where can be more safety? And you know, I, being a police officer, won't care that much my wife leaving me, but can't afford gun going away off me. Also, if gone to wrong hands, of which there are 100 per cent chances, no gentlemen'll take away these from here, these will be used on us, empowering criminals.'

'Sir, hope ma'am's not close by, listening you,' Priya said.

'She knows what missing of gun's for a soldier—court of enquiry, maybe even dismissal with disgrace.'

In the meantime, a sepoy came running. 'Sir, all guns are intact there, even some more, like some blood-stained spear, dagger. Only some ammunition, cartridges are not there.'

'Thank God. Great relief. That can be managed. At least now can celebrate the big success. Come on, feel relaxed. Would sit in my office.' Moving to his office, the DIG also sent for the DSP to come there. On his coming there, the DIG ordered him, 'As a security on the way and in the village around, prepare deputation of fifteen cops by our vehicle with not recorded out or in past two days. And do it in back date. This require my signature only. To get all credit and to justify utilisation of the ammunition, has to do this much. Also get the blood report of Chakra from that station to match with the one here on these weapons. Here our doc can do this. From there, get the report text on phone. And report to me soon. Also check if some cartridges are there in the guns. Ensure every gun's unloaded.'

'Sir, when we went to see Chakra, from that area also I got some empty covers of used cartridges and gave to one of guards went with us,' said Agastya.

'That's good. I'll get these,' said DSP, and he left to carry on as directed. Here in the office, Priya passed on a packet given by the parents of Rohan to the DIG. And they had hardly finished with their tea and chit-chat when the surprised DSP reported, 'Sir, here is the movement order for fifteen corps and a vehicle for your signature. And these are the blood reports. It's strange the two blood sample are matching. And the sepoy gave three empty covers, these too matched with those in our store. Two we got from the guns, these are also matching. Now we are short of thirty-five cartridges. It's confirmed that our guns and ammunition has been used there.'

'Yes, that's good. But not for killing Chakra. He's not killed by gunshot but by some none policeman fighting with sharp-edged weapon now in our store. Now all problems are over. Enjoy and get Joshi party also here. Let them also enjoy with sweets.'

On calling them, they all came normal in happy mood. But Joshi was abnormal in anger. 'What a tough man! How dare he thought of looting the family and spoiling the marriage of the sister of our friend? She's our sister too. Killed him with spear, and in close fight used dagger also.'

'Thank you, Joshi-ji. We got it. Now rest and let these bros also enjoy the sweets of the marriage of our sister,' said Agastya.

The very next moment, Joshi was quite normal, asking, 'Why are you all looking at me?'

'You were saying something not relevant to you,' said Priya.

'Me? Sorry, but I haven't said anything. No idea when and what have I said,' Joshi replied.

'It's all right. Don't bother, enjoy it,' said Priya. Rohan distributed sweets to all, and all enjoyed the party. After these, all left. The DIG, looking towards Agastya, said, 'Now everything's clear. How many credits and successes you and your ghostmen would give to us?'

THE DIG VISITS DERA AREA

The DIG kept all these reports secret, known only to him and Agastya. So that it did not become confusing media topic. Only those who could peep into the world of ghostmen knew this reality. And this time, all six—Agastya, Priya, Devika, Joshi (the real one from headquarters camp), the DIG, and on the special request of Priya, Mrs DIG— went to Dera. They stayed in the guest house. So long as they were there, Priya had invited the team to her place for dinner. In fact, the DIG had planned it only for one day. But the thick forests and enchanting peace compelled him to extend it for another two days and stayed there for three days and relaxed fully in the peaceful and refreshing atmosphere away from the madding crowds, dusty and smoky air, and deafening noise of teeming, crowded metro cities. The BSF camp commandant was also invited on one day. He too invited the DIG and all the others one day to lunch at his place. The DIG was also taken to Devika's house. She had made special arrangements. Food included special local cuisines in the lunch. The DIG and Mrs DIG were given token gifts, mementos of local crafts, showpieces. Several times they had been to the Joshi banyan tree. The

DIG and his missus sat under the tree with closed eyes. They felt as if some atmospheric power was giving them a soothing effect. They went up to the Joshi hollow also and got lost in a different world.

One day the BSF commandant himself went there and went to the Banyan tree. He sat there for some time in meditation posture and could have the joy of a different feel of this place. He said, 'We, including our staff and soldiers, have made it a part of our routine to come on a visit to this place, the banyan tree. We not only get mental peace but also feel as if someone is going with us to help us and solve our problems.'

'I feel, besides innumerable other things, Joshi has given us two big successes which have made history of our department—busting of this big international gang here and killing of Chakra and, over and above these, this place of worship for all,' said the DIG.

On another day, Agastya and the party accompanied Mrs DIG and the DIG to Kuhar Lake. But now besides the wooden dugouts, beautiful colourful paddling and rowing boats were glittering in the bluish crystal-clear water. They enjoyed the trip with tea and pakoras on the boat.

The visit of Kālu Ram Joshi to this area proved to be rewarding. As soon as the party had reached Gonda, Joshi showed his familiarity to the place. He slowly said to Agastya, 'Some forty miles is Basti from here. For mail trains, it's next station only. By road, one hour.' Maybe it was his urge to see his family that made him say so.

'We'll go there some time, today we are going to Dera,' Agastya told him. Joshi didn't say anything, looked somehow submissive. Then they proceeded further to Balrampur. This place also looked very familiar to him. From here they took a longer route, of a surfaced, metalled road via Bijlipur, Tulsipur, and Badhni. Tulsipur was also the railway station on the Gonda-Gorakhpur metre gauge loop line. At Bijlipur their cars crossed River Rapti.

Here, surprisingly, Joshi said, 'In rainy season, sometime this road submerges in Rapti floodwater and traffic get disrupted.'

Reaching Dera Chowk, Joshi became active, as if he were perfectly all right. Even about his kidnapping, he told them, 'Date and day I don't remember, but it was afternoon of November 1958. I had come from home after celebrating Diwali. I was sitting under'—he pointed to a tree—'this tree, some six, seven sadhus [saintly looking men] came. I offered them water. They sat down and smoked their smoke clay pipe [chilam], leaving clouds of smoke, and asked me, "Smoke* this, my child, you will be happy." And put some powder-like thing on my right palm. I didn't take it and threw under a plant. Then they four grabbed me and put that powder-like thing in my mouth. Soon I started losing my senses. I reached the actionless dreamy world.'

Thus enjoying the time, they passed three days at Dera and the final day of departure had come. Mrs DIG

---

* Statutory warning: Drugs and smoking are injurious to health.

and the DIG were seen off with several gifts of local crafts. Some mementos were given by the BSF camp also. Mrs DIG expressed, 'Priya had made my ever-memorable tour possible. It was for her that I could have this wonderful experience. Wherever we may be, I'll make it a point to visit this place again. A wonderful place, and the abode of Joshi. May we all keep on getting his benevolence. Thanks.'

'Ma'am, make your next visit soon. Actually, this is the best time here, October to mid April, water and greenery everywhere. Summers are hot and dry. Come during winter months up to April with more time,' said the father of Priya.

'Surely I liked the place. We'll come. You too come to Lucknow and do come to us. Bye!'

'Thanks, ma'am. See you. Bye. Bye, sir,' said Jagannath.

Both the cars—the DIG and his missus's and that of Agastya, Priya, Joshi, and Devika—left together on their return journey, following the same route they had taken for their onward journey.

Reaching Gonda, they stayed there for some time. Though Priya insisted on taking them to her place, the DIG said, 'No, don't bother, suddenly reaching home won't be good. Also it would be taking too much time. As rightly desired by Agastya, it would take only three hours, we can make Joshi see his family. We would see and note his reactions. It may help him come up soon, like his seeing Dera Village and his guest house. Someday we can bring Rohan to his college. Let him get free from his hearing dates of courts. We will free him. We will also call the family members of these all four and would hand over them, with instructions to their local police stations.'

Thus they had been talking. The local superintendent of police had made their stay and lunch arrangements. Further, the superintendent of police of Basti was also informed to get their stay arrangements in the circuit house there and to meet them there with the inspector.

Soon after lunch they left for Basti and, in about forty minutes, arrived there. The inspector had already located the house, and the family was told to keep ready to receive them. The whole party except for Mrs DIG went there with Joshi. Joshi himself led the party to his home. There he first met his brother, sister-in-law, the children, and his wife. He asked the well-being of them all. But meeting his wife, he failed to control his emotions and wept bitterly, with tears rolling down from his eyes. His wife and children were also weeping, and all the others turned serious with wet eyes. After quite some time, he asked his wife, 'How you and children had been living all these years? I had given up my all hopes of seeing you again, but it's because of these ma'am, saabs, and sirs that, alive, I could come back home to my family.'

But weeping, his wife said, 'Aye-ji, but tell me first, you are original or duplicate? Hope you're our real one. The duplicate one was also an angel. Had been coming to give money only for short time. Never stayed for night. Which one are you?' Everyone had wet eyes and choked throat but burst into laughter.

Somehow, controlling his hard laughter, the DIG said, 'Don't worry, Mrs Joshi, but this time we all assure you, we brought the original one.'

'Then it's all right, sir-ji. I was telling papa of my children we had no problem here. Brother, sister, all these children were here. But how could he live in all those miseries? Our bank account has sufficient money. Someone exactly like him had been coming to bank for depositing money. He had been paying short visits in banking hours, meeting brother and children, not me. I didn't understand then why he had been coming from such distant place for so short of time. Now we are told he was some ghostman doing our welfare and taking our care. Some days back also some other ghostman had come for your brother too. People say he also had done some big good works, big men from Gonda came to honour him. But then our real brother had come, and he disappeared from inside our room,' said Mrs Joshi.

'Don't worry. I'm very much real. Get tea and something for saab-ji. We would be just leaving for Lucknow. There I'm under treatment and for court matters have to be there. Soon I'll be back to my family, with you,' said Joshi. Joshi also recognised his fellow friend and neighbours from the city and met them cheerfully and asked about their well-being. Soon he was an active normal man, with his full confidence back in himself.

THE CAPTIVES JOIN THEIR JUBILANT FAMILIES

The family visit of Joshi touched the heart of the DIG. He realised that the sooner these four were reunited with their families, the better it would be for them in regaining their confidence and normalcy, and also for their families and children. They had noticed the difference in Rohan and Joshi just after their one visit to their families. He discussed this with Agastya and Priya and decided to consult the courts soon. The party left Basti, and by evening they reached Lucknow after a very purposeful tour of the area, the workplace of Joshi, where a big gang was busted.

Resuming his office, the DIG started the process of their early joining of their families and accomplishment of big work project. After five days the courts too got convinced to record their statements and set them scot-free. As they had been innocent victims of the gang's kidnapping, all these had passed through unbearable tortures and sufferings for so long and have been away from social atmosphere. On priority their hearing was arranged. All four were asked to prepare their statement papers and submit. They submitted their detailed statements. This was followed by the cross-examining and questioning of each one of these four, with respective statements of each one of these to know the details of each one of these. And also about the gang's activities, because these were the only four witnesses who had seen the gang's activities from up close, and they themselves had undergone tortures and sufferings from them.

On completion of the whole process, the main finding came out that except for the initial differences of locations where they fell prey to the clutches of the gangsters, the rest of the details were almost the same: that they were kidnapped by the gangsters by their tricks, for using them in their malpractices for their gains. This proved them innocent, guilt-free, clearing the way of these four for joining their families. Now they were free to move unescorted on the campus, living like welcomed guests. Their counselling sessions were held to help them decide what they would be doing after going back to their homes. The department of Joshi and the college of Rohan were directed to take these persons back in the position they were when kidnapped. The other two were businessmen. Their families had been asked to come with the proof of their identity and to take their men by submitting required undertakings to the effect that due care of their physical, mental, and social health would be taken and that no pressure of any type would be put on them and that the person would be produced to the local police or other government agencies and courts as and when required, at their own security arrangements. And that they would not put up any claim for the losses, sufferings, and harassments the family and the individuals had undergone.

On the receipt of this sort of call letters, the families of these two became jubilant. The families of the other two were ignorant so far about the whereabouts of their men and had accepted loss of their lives. They took this as heaven's fall of sudden happiness and his blessings. They further informed their close relatives by telegram, phone, and personal contact. Big groups of their families and relatives reached there at police headquarters and got busy in making preparations of their reception in a festive manner.

The police headquarters had also arranged, in a small way, a formal reunion ceremony, which was attended and addressed by Agastya, Priya, Devika and, the DIG. In a delightful atmosphere, the four joined their families back after years.

ANIKA PLAYS A TRICK
WITH MUKESH*

Village Kuhar was developing into a vibrant centre of activities, with agencies like a tourist centre, a training centre, and a business centre. In the social welfare regional and training centre were Regional Officer Kriskan Kant Tiwari and the two assistant regional officers Naina and Gauri. Anika was a voluntary counsellor. Being a voluntary and experienced worker, Anika enjoyed a better life of mobility in the centre. She had forgone the offer of the next-to-regional officer post of ARO and helped Naina get that position. She had been the moving force in the area, meeting people, going to their houses, meeting ladies, solving their problems, and motivating them to come forward. Most of the time, she had been moving in the mobile-library-cum-exhibition-counselling-unit. The day she couldn't meet someone, they used to come, saying, 'Didn't see you for the day, how have you been? Where have you gone? See, we have done this, the way you suggested. How about now?' All

---

* Statutory warning: Self-medication is dangerous to health. Consult a qualified doctor for health problems and use of medicines.

these had become common things in the area about her and the other two.

There, a branch of the Tarai Bank was started in Village Kuhar in one big room of the welfare centre. It was a two-man staff branch. Mukesh Gupta was branch manager and Rakesh Dixit his assistant. The staff of the two organisations had been meeting frequently and got intimate to each other. Meeting, sharing jokes, having light fun, and sharing eatables had become part of their everyday life. The welfare centre, in a way, had been fetching big business for the bank. Anika, in her work and meetings, had started telling people, especially ladies, to start small savings and to take loans to start their small productive business units. Thus, Anika had made the work of the two organisations complementary to each other. Without any fieldwork or exercise and publicity, Anika had made the bank attain substantial growth. Anika had been coming to the bank with the locals, both men and women, advising them how the bank could be helpful in their new jobs and in creating new sources of income and also that they could keep their earnings safe there. Anika also familiarised the simple people of the area with the workings of the bank and banking processes.

In his spare time, the manager, Mukesh, met Anika and joked, 'Have made everyone wise against us.'

'Had to alert and make innocents aware about available beneficial schemes available for them,' said Anika.

'Ma'am, maybe we will see a board outside our bank tomorrow inscribed as "Beware of the Bank Staff". You have almost flogged us, bringing so much work all the time. Brought us so much of business! Wanna kill,' said Mukesh.

'Making board would require much money. And the bank is yours, a miser. I won't get you boards prepared. I'll ask your authorities to put up such board, with more words, especially "Young Girls, Beware of Mukesh",' said Anika.

'Oh god, where have I come? Had I known this before, that a quarrelsome girl like you is here, I would have never come here,' said Mukesh.

'Now that you have come to know, why don't you run away? So when are you going? But before going, at least do one good deed. Pass on the keys to me, especially of the strong room.' Making a jolly facial expression, she said, 'Taking over keys, I'll put up a board outside the bank—'Bank is closed forever'. This I'll get done from my own money.' Anika laughed.

'Since you are the grandma of honesty and will be doing this big social work, why don't you take this much of money from the chest?'

'Your suggestion is welcome. You needn't worry. Otherwise, also it would close, when there is a sincere manager like you. What sort of miser people have come in this place? Their home must be richer than this bank.'

'Should I give you the keys of that also?'

'No, no, that, you keep with you.' Anika became serious and said, 'It would be loss to me but would bear. Miser's things won't get digested.'

'There would be sufficient money. Hope you won't turn miser. Get some digestive powder, everything will digest. Live like princess of the bank with a big board, "Young girls, beware of gurgling bull man, Mukesh, the Miser". You'll be well taken care of. Government will take care of you. Gunmen guarding on your gate. And you'll be kept in big, strong building with strong black iron-barred gate. People would be coming to see you.'

'Me! Me behind the bars. Forget it, there is none who can do that.'

'This small fry would have to helplessly perform this unpleasant task. Going to police and report a grandma of honesty leaving me half dead, had taken away bank keys. Save me from her teeth and claws by sending the generous princess to her right place. This princess will rule there. Otherwise, who can survive this dictatorship? Someone will have to send the lioness to her cage. At least people would get to breathe easy.'

'Easy goer, guarding the wealth of others. Non-risk-taker live longer. Long live the sophisticated urban babu.'

'You too, Princess, live long. Who would be the fortunate prince to have this type of energetic life partner? My sympathies for the poor fellow.'

'Certainly not you, so don't be scared of.'

'Won't mind beating the drum hung around my neck.'

'It won't come to your neck. Will always remain a distant drum. Distant drums are always sweet. Distant pastures look greener and mountains beautiful. So go on dreaming of sweetness and beauty, which for your good luck are in plenty here.'

'Don't need plenty. Only one would be enough for the life.'

'Very good. Looks changed for good. Go on searching, we would also help in search. Hope you get some old one. That won't trouble also, rich in experience. You so rich in money. Would be ideal trouble-free couple.'

'Those having well-wishers and friends like you need no enemy.'

This sort of light-hearted leg-pulling and banter had been their everyday fun. Even in their society and friends' circle, people had stated taking them as fighter friends and had been enjoying their dialogues. While Anika remained absolutely innocent as a friend, Mukesh didn't even realise when he started liking Anika and her sociable nature. Everyone liked to meet and talk to her.

Mukesh had developed an attraction for her. He had been longing to see her every day. To remain close to her, for one reason or the other, he had been creating situations in which either he would come close to her or she could come to him. He had been dreaming of her. This thing had become a part of his life. On the other hand, bubbly, cheerful, talkative, and frank as she had been, Anika had been reaching and meeting him for official works. Also, it being a small place, officers kept on meeting each other here and there. She too had been meeting him or calling upon him but keeping a healthy distance with humour and decency, like, 'Hi, urban gentleman! How are you feeling in the forest? Must have done some good deeds in previous life that you get to enjoying this service, sitting and doing nothing. Do something good in this life too.'

'What should I do? Would you suggest?'

'Yes, why not? I'm public counsellor. But what should I suggest to you? You may not like even to listen. Doing is a far distant thing.'

'I doubt any good workable idea would come out from the horse's mouth. But do your duty without bothering others. This poor fellow would be grateful. Kindly do suggest.'

'Give away this wealth, you are sitting on to the neediest. They would be happy. You would be happy with no money left, nothing to do. And way to the heavens shall be clear for you.'

'Way to heaven or prison? Which one you are clearing for me? Ma'am Anika, in this so big a world, you didn't find any other place. Why have you come here? I haven't done any good deed in previous life but might have done all badly. That's why here got a well-wisher like you, the big fighter.'

'Come to know reality so soon. At least mend your ways in this life. Accept my advice.'

'Is this the good you are doing to me? Sending me to prison, corrupting me?'

'Me? Corrupting you? Such a big allegation you levy upon me. An innocent girl has corrupted a boy. Oh god, where should I go?'

'Don't cry. Feel pity on me. I'm a boy of tender age, living all alone. My whole life is ahead of me. Please spare me and let me work.'

'It's good.'

'What's good in it?'

'This, that you want to work and that you are all alone, still a bachelor.'

'Why are you so happy on my bachelorhood?' Mukesh was thinking of her coming on the right track to reply something favourable to him.

'Because a poor girl, if there is some, destined for you must be living happily till such time she is married to you. Later she would have to have it as her repentance. And you too must be dreaming of the most beautiful girl and feeling happy in your daydreaming. But no use dreaming impossibilities.'

'Thanks for unsolicited "advice". And for your information, I don't have to dream. My so big a dream is sitting in front of me. How can I dream with this headache?'

'Why don't you take some prescribed medicines and rest, otherwise also you don't believe in doing anything but rest. But see, too much of rest also causes problems?'

'There is no medicine which can make me rest.' Mukesh paused. 'Oh yes, there is one.'

At the same time, Naina also reached there. Mukesh welcomed her and asked, 'Are you twin sisters? So much resemblance between you two?'

'We are alike only in our looks. In human qualities and intelligence, Anika is far more superior to not only me but most of the girls. Wish I could've been one-tenth of her,' Naina responded.

'To me it looks the other way. You both are alike in looks. But in human qualities, you are much better. And in creating troubles, quarrels and to give headache to some one, there is no substitute to this goddess of troubles,' said Mukesh, and he looked at Anika, but within his heart he felt differently. *Anika, what wonderful girls you both are. What would be my life without you and your fun-filled chats and leg-pulling? May God never take you away from my life.*

'What are you thinking, urban babu? Okay, me too, going in search of sleeping pills to have peaceful time. But develop some habit of at least doing some work. Please expedite the loan case of that lady Ninya for purchasing a cow. So that she gets it before you or I go to sleep,' Anika retorted.

As she got up to leave the room, her eyes fell on a half-opened drawer of Mukesh's work table. She could see a medicine bottle almost full of some tablets. She got closer, saying, 'Arrey wah, keeping medicines in office. Come fully prepared to rest here.'

'Have to remain fully prepared. Some people come here and leave me with headache. At least in the night to have some sleep, I keep these sleeping pills. Sometime take at bedtime,' Mukesh said.

She picked up the bottle. 'Really, Manager Sahib, you have it. Great! Good, my work has become easy.' Going to one side, she emptied the whole bottle over her mouth, making it seem to a watcher as if all the tablets had gone in her mouth. She picked up a water jug from the side table, and before anyone could understand or do anything to stop her, she poured water from above into her mouth and acted as if to swallow the tablets. She had actually, very deftly, slipped the twenty-four-odd tablets into her other hand.

Naina and Mukesh were dumbfounded by Anika's actions. They were unable to think what to do with her. Mukesh tried his best to put his hands in her mouth to make her throw up and get the pills out. But he failed in his attempts. He was on the verge of breaking down, sweating and helpless, trying to save her from what he thought was her impending end. He was looking at Anika, who was, with her large and wide-open eyes, still laughing at him. 'Oh, I feel so sleepy.' She yawned with outstretched arms. She started going out of the banker's office, and without looking back, she waved bye-bye. She had been staggering like a drunkard.

As Anika was walking out, Agastya also walked into the office. He had not been able to meet the bank manager, an old friend from school, during the last trip a few days back when he had established the social welfare offices in the neighbourhood. Anika passed by him, staggering like a girl out of her senses but smiling mischievously.

Unaware of what had just happened, Agastya did not know the perceived complexity and seriousness of the situation. He simply asked, 'Mukesh, why are you so distraught? Has something serious happened?'

'Oh, Agastya Sir, you have arrived just in time, as always, my friend. Yes! That girl, Anika, these were sleeping pills. More than two are dangerous for life, and she has taken the whole bottle, more than twenty tablets. She will die soon. She has consumed full bottle.'

'What? Full bottle of sleeping pills! Is she crazy?' screamed Agastya. 'What happened? Did you say or do something to her?'

'No! I was just joking with her, teasing her. But you gotta help me, Agastya. She'll surely die within next few minutes. Can something make her vomit? Is there anyone who can treat her?' he said while sobbing hard. He had been running here and there, meeting several people in the social welfare centre. Naina also seemed nervous and helpless. Everyone who came to know of it felt afraid and concerned for Anika. Fortunately, Gauri was on leave that day. She wouldn't have been able to bear seeing Anika in that half-dead condition in which she had left the bank.

Agastya told Mukesh to wait at the bank and told him that he would go and check up on her. He had travelled in his jeep and could also take her to the primary health care centre at Dera, if necessary. Mukesh insisted on accompanying him, but Agastya reminded him of his responsibility as the bank manager, and he had to relent. He also instructed Naina and the assistant manager of the bank to attend to the complete wreck of a man that he seemed to be at that time. Mukesh, in a complete state of despair, sat down in his chair in the bank, folded his hands, closed his eyes, and silently prayed for the girl whom he had come to adore with all his heart. Naina and the assistant manager watched him, equally helpless, and they too prayed for Anika's well-being.

As Agastya neared the exit of the bank and the social welfare centre, he heard a soft hissing sound. 'Tshh . . . tshh!' He stopped and looked around to see Anika peeping from behind the boundary wall. She was grinning from cheek to cheek.

Agastya was surprised to find her right there, just a few steps away from the bank and absolutely hale and hearty. He walked up to her and asked her angrily, 'What was it all about?' He apprised her of the condition in which he had found Mukesh and Naina. Anika stopped smiling and turned serious. She told him that she was also feeling bad. But she too was helpless to tell anything to anyone else. However, she had stopped the messenger from carrying the message to the village, to avoid the entire village from panicking about her health. 'I had just played a trick.'

'But what about all these people who are worried about you? Did you not think about them for even a moment? They are all so heartbroken and distraught, feeling that you are in some kind of danger,' Agastya told her.

'I am very sorry, babu-ji! That was definitely not my intention. I was just joking with him. I did not realise he will not be able to catch my trick and things will get to this stage,' pleaded Anika. While she was trying her best to maintain a serious face, the look of mischief in her eyes and the smile that she was trying to suppress caught Agastya's attention. He was instantly drawn back to the day of his first meeting with her, and that feeling of an unexplained familiarity tugged at his heart.

It took a few moments for Agastya to register that Anika was saying something to him. 'Babu-ji . . . Oh, babu-ji! What happened? Are you also not well? Will you like some pills to soothe your nerves?' She extended her hand, upon the palm of which rested about twenty-odd tablets. Her enchanting smile and the sparkling eyes seemed to tell the complete story to Agastya of how she would have befooled the unsuspecting manager and her friend Naina.

Agastya returned a warm smile to her and said, 'I am sure you will be able to handle this situation better than anyone else. Why don't you end this game here and let them know that all's well?'

'Of course I will.'

'Well, I have to leave for an important official engagement. When Mukesh is back to his normal self, please tell him that I shall pay him another visit soon.'

'All right, babu-ji. I will convey it to him,' said Anika as she walked towards the bank. Agastya stood watching her walk away from him. At the entrance, she stopped, turned back, and smiled at him, waving her hand. That pang of familiarity suddenly returned. He watched her disappear from his view as she went into the building. Even after she had gone into the bank, Agastya stood rooted for a while. His trance was broken by the jeep driver calling out to him. He nodded to the driver and made his way to the jeep. He knew he had to find his answer. He silently wondered if that look, smile, and wave at the time of parting was any similar to Joshi's when he had bid farewell to them before disappearing into the tree. It came back to him at that instant. Though the girl bore no resemblance to Joshi, it was her smile and the expressions which were his. Agastya realised that Anika was here for a purpose. She was there helping someone—Mukesh, Naina, Gauri, or someone else?

Well, it could be anyone or it could be every one of them. As it finally dawned on him who Anika was, Agastya knew he need not wonder anymore. With her presence there, things were bound to happen for the good of whomever she had come to help. He asked the driver to speed up so that they could get back home in time.

In the meanwhile, Naina, who had left Mukesh and his assistant alone in the bank, saw Anika walking in. She was still grinning and did not seem anything like what she had appeared to be when she left the bank about half an hour ago. Anika told Naina what she had done, got slapped on her back by Naina in mock anger, and the two of them had a good laugh at what she had just done. She took Naina with her and slowly tiptoed behind Mukesh, who was sitting with closed eyes and folded hands in worshiping posture. Anika hid herself by squeezing between two tall cupboards stacked with files and account books. Naina stood behind Mukesh's chair, smiling at his state. After lot of praying quietly, he opened his eyes and said aloud, 'Oh, God, I'm helpless. You are my only hope. This tragedy has happened in fun for my foolishness. I promise before you I'll never touch a sleeping-pill. I'll never keep it with me.'

He heard a voice. 'Is it? Are you sure you'll never use it?' Anika spoke in a modulated heavy voice from where she hid.

'Truly, I'll never use it,' replied Mukesh. 'Wha-what? Who is this?' He swivelled in his chair to look at the source of this voice. It was Naina, standing behind him. He stood up and came closer to her and asked, 'You, it was you spoke all this?'

Naina burst into laughter and in that state couldn't speak anything. She pointed her index finger towards the cupboards, from where emerged the figure of Anika, laughing uncontrollably.

'Look, on your request, God has returned me from heavens. Don't kill me! Or he'll call me back.'

Mukesh, coming around slowly, could not believe his senses as he came closer to her, saying, 'Who can beat or kill you? You are not an ordinary person. You are too good for me. Please excuse me!' And weeping, he just knelt on the ground before her.

Anika picked him up, saying, 'Oh, come on! It's not like that. We are friends. We are all equals. I am really sorry that I troubled you so much. But my intentions were different, you must have understood it. I wanted you to refrain from using a drug. It may be commonly used, but sleeping pills are also injurious to health. It disturbs the natural system. You better adopt natural and yogic ways for keeping fit and sound sleep. Sleep induced by pills is a sleep borrowed for the time being, but it kills your biorhythm in the long run.'

She further added, 'And secondly, Mukesh, I cannot reciprocate the love that you have started to feel for me. You may not understand what I mean right now, but very soon you will. Please forgive me and forget me, except as a true friend who means good for you. Naina is the right one for you. She is a very kind-hearted and loving girl and.' With a wink, Anika added, 'She even looks a lot like me.'

'But that is only if you both find it possible. These were my feelings. Rest is up to you. I won't mind it in any way. This I've just proposed. You both see your likes and dislikes. Please don't accept it just because I suggested it.'

'I have understood. My troubles were no troubles at all. I was taking recourse to a cowardly way. But all's well that ends well. For a moment I felt as if for my foolishness, I've lost you forever. No one can survive after taking so much dose of these pills. You've opened my eyes. I'll never use these pills or even other painkillers or any medicine unless recommended by a doctor. Regarding my loving Naina, that would be a different matter which only time will decide. But to you I would take in very high esteem,' said Mukesh.

'Now let's come. Others must be worried. We must meet them to make them feel better!' Anika said.

'I've to send someone to Gauri also, to tell her not to come right now in these late hours. I had sent a man to inform her about your being serious,' Mukesh said.

'Not needed. I had called him back from the way. I knew when you were sending him. Gauri would come tomorrow only at her usual time. The only thing is, you get normal and relax. You had taken too much of stress and strains. Now no tension!' said Anika.

'How would I live a normal life without my food? That's my problem now. I've to see that. How to adjust with nature,' said Mukesh.

'Why without food? Won't you get food today? What has gone wrong with your food supply system?' asked Anika.

'My whole food supply system is finished. But since it is dried up and my source of inspiration is finished, don't know how I would live. From now onwards the characters would appear in different role in my life drama,' said Mukesh.

'You play your role without worrying about other's role. Don't think of those things which are not in your control. Let's all go to our places with the happy ending of this drama,' said Anika.

After sending everyone to their places, Anika tonight went straight to her place, her own village. There she went to the central-point stage. Sat down and wept bitterly. Whosoever were present there, they also gathered around. And there reached the head also, who had been living there permanently. All other ghostmen serving at different places came here to share their experiences, to discuss problems, and to seek advice. The head and counselling members advised on such issues. If need be, sometimes they called back the particular ghostman and replaced him or her or make some mutual transfers, etc. In a way this village was their record headquarters. Here, seeing this bitterly weeping girl, the head pacified her, saw her record, and praised her and asked her to speak about her troubles. She said, 'Today, I'm feeling sorry of my role play. I had been serving the people. Helping the needy. Had been inspiring the discouraged. So far it all had been going on well. I was happy and satisfied. But someone had started loving me. And loved me so sincerely that he was ready to even sacrifice his life for me. I had to cheat him. In a way, I deceived him. We teach to love each other. But if we get involved, we can't do it. We say love is divine. But we are deprived of it. We can't have the pleasure of being a sister, a wife, a mother. We can only see others enjoying the lives of relationships. We are nothing more than lifeless robots, today I'm repenting of myself being a ghostgirl.'

The head listened to her carefully, consoled her, and said, 'It's you who feels that there is life in that world. The people are living a joyful life there—'

'And I turned their joys in sorrows. The man, Mukesh, doesn't understand how he would live now,' she interrupted.

The head further continued, 'Listen to me, listen to me first, my child. He has reached this stage not for you but for his own misunderstanding and delusion, that you too loved him. How could he decide the fate of any girl without asking for her consent? The girl could have had her limitations and commitments. Nothing wrong has happened from your side. Regarding enjoying the pleasure of relationship, if these mortals have pleasure, they have much more displeasures, commitments, and sorrows too. The mortals keep on struggling their whole life in meeting the requirements of these relations. Many wisely people get themselves freed from these bindings, like Gautama Buddha, Aadi

Guru Shankaracharya, Chaitanya, peers, faquirs, angels, saints, gurus, etc., but the worldly people can't imagine their lives without these relations and social connections. We are lucky. Without any bondage and commitment of relationship, we live away from pains and sufferings of these. Yet by living close to these worldly fellows, through them we enjoy the feelings of being as a worldly people. We can enjoy the benefits of both—the material mortal world and the supernatural world of ours, souls. So there's nothing to feel sorry or repent but to cherish the advantages you have over the world of mortals. Think, had you been a worldly girl like Gauri or any other one, could you help so many people, could you save Gauri from the supervisor, which you did in such a way that their lives are changed?'

'How would I face that weeping Mukesh, who is feeling himself as robbed off?' asked Anika.

'You needn't worry. That's the fate of the worldly people. There are very few momentary joyful occasions in their lives. Most of their time, they keep on struggling, feeling sorries and repentings. They enter the world weeping and leave it too weeping. To minimise their weeping and troubles, we as their good neighbours, in our spare time, reach them to their help. You may now plan to help him come out of his painful situation. Go tomorrow as normal girls and bring him up. I have told you much. Tell me if you have any other problem,' said the head.

All the ghostmen standing around and listening to them disappeared. Anika also stood up and paid her respects and thanks to the head. She slowly turned back for her place in the village, and the head also left for his place.

That whole night, Anika kept on thinking and planning. The next morning she reached Kuhar Regional Office. Gauri had also joined her duty after availing of a leave the previous day. Both the friends met as usual and resumed their work. After some time Anika asked Gauri to visit the bank, and the two arrived there. There they saw Mukesh working as usual. He welcomed the two and offered them chairs. Gauri asked him about his well-being. He too reciprocated. Anika asked, 'What's matter, working so seriously? Hope everything is okay. Had comfortable sleep in the night?'

'Yes, very much,' answered Mukesh.

'With or without the sleeping pills?' asked Anika.

'I had a sound sleep without any pill. Taking pills, I left in front of God. And he has helped me get good sleep without these. About size of dose, now as I'm not concerned about it, I can't say anything. But I wonder, here are some people who don't get a blink even after consuming the whole bottle of it,' said Mukesh. 'Don't tell this, Mukesh. Must be already emptied bottle, with only one or two left in it,' said Gauri.

'You don't believe it? Nobody would believe. Even I wouldn't have believed it hadn't it happened with me. But it happened in front of my eyes. A full bottle with more than twenty tablets was emptied in mouth. And before terribly frightened me could do anything, the goddess took jug from my table, poured the water in mouth, and swallowed the whole lot. For two, three hours, I had no blood in my body. I ran crying here and there. Sent a man for you also to call you immediately. In the state of total helplessness, having no hope from anywhere, I prayed to the Lord and gave up taking these pills for my whole life, and I got a new life!' He further said, 'You don't have to go long distance to have a look of the heroine of the live drama. Just turn your eyes to your left and the heroine would be in front of your eyes.'

Gauri looked to her left and saw it was Anika on her left and uttered with exclamation, 'Anika! It was Anika?'

'Yes, very much, ask her,' said Mukesh.

'It was nothing. I didn't know he would get so much upset. He had sent for you also to call you. But I called the man back from the way. In fact, I came to know he remain sleepless in the night and takes pills, which is a drug. I thought of a trick and tried it. I came to him. Took his whole bottle, and showing all as if emptied in mouth, I emptied the bottle in my left hand then, keeping the jug at a height from mouth, poured water in mouth and acted as if I had swallowed the pills. Later threw these out.' She pointed to Mukesh. 'You can go and see it out there. In fact, Agastya babu is also well aware of all this. I showed the pills to him as well when he was going out of the bank.'

Mukesh murmured, 'Come and listen one more fantasy tale. Let us see this too. Okay, we may take it to see.' He, his assistant, Gauri, and Anika too came out. And they were astonished to see most of the pills out in dustbin in an undissolved shape and some white power, like they had been lying there for some time.

Anika came forward and said, 'Still have doubt? Come and check it.' She went there, picked up one tablet, and showed it to Mukesh by putting it on her open palm.

By then Naina also arrived, asking, 'What's going on?'

Mukesh said, 'Good, you too have come. Yesterday you were there when Anika swallowed the full bottle lot of pills. She's narrating a different story today, saying she had thrown out these tabs out here. You also see these here. Here is one tab picked up from there.'

'Very strange,' said Naina, smiling and winking at Anika and Gauri. 'Yesterday in front of our eyes, she had taken whole bottle of it. Her survival was no less surprising. It's yet another surprising thing.'

'We can't doubt the great soul. Whatever strange experiences she may put us in are all less. We can't think and imagine what all she can make us feel and experience,' said Mukesh.

They were all staring at Anika. Waiting a moment, Anika said, 'Hey, why are you looking at me like this? What's strange in it? Here, there are many ladies and gents practising magic tricks. There are several ladies and gents keeping the men or women of their choices as captives in the form of their pets. They create and cure troubles of the people. Every day so many people approach witchcraft doctors who treat snake bites, scorpion stings, wasp stings, rabid-dog bites, and several other problems. I don't know that much. I'm a simple girl, a friend of yours, the same as you all. There are big, big trick players here. Better you change the topic. Mukesh must be angry on me. You are all on my side and help. Otherwise, he would have killed me,' said Anika. Changing the topic and to change atmosphere, Anika further asked, 'Yes, Mukesh, what's the position of the loan for that lady Ninya?'

'That's through, she can come anytime with identity proof and two witnesses,' said Mukesh.

'That's good. At least one thing is done.' Addressing Gauri, she said, 'Gauri, Mukesh had gone under heavy tension whole day yesterday. Let's have some change and outing. Why don't we go to the lakeside and have lunch there? Both of these from bank are invited,' said Anika.

'I'm happy without your picnic. There you will show some other miracle. And surprised we would come back home,' said Mukesh.

'Oh no, Mukesh, why you got so scared? For one small thing, would we no longer be friends? Have you broken up your friendship band from me?' Anika asked.

'No, never. How can it be? The only thing is, your position is changed for me. You are no longer a friend for me but a girl for whom I have great regard and respect. I don't feel like laughing with you but feel heavy with respect for you,' replied Mukesh.

'Oh, that's good that you would obey my command,' said Anika.

'Sure, your words would be command for me,' said Mukesh.

'Then do one thing. Don't make me so heavy and old, a piece of worship from a simple girl. Please keep me in the same old position of your friend, where I would share friendship, jokes, and fun with you all, so that my life doesn't become heavy, life of scholars and philosophers. Let me live light as before. It would be a favour for me. I won't play trick anymore. Don't punish me so much for my one mistake, join us on our outing,' said Anika

'Okay. Good idea,' said Mukesh.

'How would be on coming Sunday?' asked Anika.

'It suits me,' answered Mukesh.

'It suits us also,' said Gauri and Naina both. All the three girls left the bank for their offices.

Anika begged their excuse for going some place, saying, 'Excuse me, I've to go to send message to Ninya to come and take her loan.' And she left them. She invited Ninya to come to their office with the attested identity from the village head. Also to bring two commonly known persons to the bank with her to take her loan. Only two bank officials were left working in the bank.

BANK ROBBERY AVERSION

A man, half clad in the simple tribal style of the area, reached the bank. He bowed to the manager, Mukesh, and sat down on the ground before him on his haunches. Manager asked, 'How come you are here? What purpose?'

The man said, 'I've come for some money.'

'How much you need?' asked the manager.

'Say, some two, three lakhs,' said the man.

'Only two, three lakh? What do you do?' said the manager.

'I don't do anything, nor do I have any property. That's why I need money, so that I can live comfortably,' said the man.

'Loan's loan. It's to be returned. How would you pay back or refund the amount to the bank?' said the manager.

'Out of this very amount, a little I would return. For rest, you get me some job here. A good job, it should be comfortable,' said the man.

'Then why asked only for two, three lakh? I think you should ask for some fifty, sixty lakhs. You would live more comfortably,' said the manager.

'It would be very nice of you. Then give me that much. When should I come with a big bag?' asked the man.

'You needn't 'ave to come here for this. You would've to go to a big bank. This's a small branch helping the needy and poors, farmers, and businessmen of the area. You've come to a wrong place,' responded the manager.

'I've come with a big hope. I'm sure I've come to a right place. Saab-ji, why don't you distribute this whole money among the poors here? You would be happy, free from worries. I would be happy with the money. Please call me when you distribute. I would live like a princess.'

'*Princess?* Dear, you are a man, say *prince!*' said the manager.

'Yes, yes, the same,' said the man. The manager, Mukesh, and his assistant both were now enjoying gossip with him in good humour. The man was also enjoying it in his innocence. The bank staff both were working with their files and papers and side by side were talking to him, lifting their eyes, looking at the man with smiles. The manager took out a packet of biscuits from his drawer. He gave some to his assistant, some to the man, and the rest he kept for himself.

The man said, 'Saab-ji, hope you would give me as many lakhs as many biscuits you gave me. It's a good omen.' They were talking light and the bank staff was busy too in their work.

Suddenly three persons appeared in the bank, with covered faces (only eyes open) and with weapons in their right hands in attack position, in thundering voice saying, 'Aye, Manager, if you want to live alive, hand over whole cash or you both would be dead.'

One of them got hold of the assistant. The other two caught the manager. Two of them were standing outside, shouting, 'No one should come this way, keep yourself closed in your houses. Anyone seen coming this way will be finished.' The manager and assistant were trembling like dry thin leaves of a tree. The biscuit he had bit in his mouth was falling out. A dagger was put on his neck, and the dacoit asked for the keys of the chest.

The man still sitting on the floor said, 'Dacoit-ji, saab has promised me three lakhs. Please leave that much and also for Ninya, she must be coming. I'm one of her witnesses. Manager-ji, how much is for Ninya?' But the manager couldn't speak a word. The man sitting, not understanding the seriousness, was still in his humour. He asked, 'Hope there's sufficient money.' He saw the manager in great trouble. He stood up, saying, 'I must push off. Here it appears dangerous. Manager saab, I would come again.

Dacoit-ji, please leave some money for me and Ninya, our loan.'

'We have not money but death for you. Let us send the two bankers to their places first, then see you. Your death has brought you here. Feel happy till then,' said a dacoit.

The man stood up slowly, walked to the manager, and asking the manager if it was so painful, gave an easy backhand slash of his left hand on the temple of the dacoit holding him. The dacoit fell unconscious on the ground. Then he caught the other one by the shoulder with his left hand and gave a heavy punch of his right hand, and the dacoit was seen going flying out through the main exit door, falling there unconscious. Then he went to the third one, whose pants had already gone wet. Trembling, he fell on the feet of the man and begged for his life. But the old man said, 'How dare you came here? Now have to have your share.' And he gave a hard slap to him. The dacoit, holding his head with both hands, sat down on the ground and lay down. The man picked up the two dacoits by the back collars with both his hands and took them out, dragging them, saying, 'Manager, let me see the two outsiders also.'

But they had already fled away, saying, 'We would leave even this area forever, my god, it's death in man's form. God save us.' The man ran out chasing them and was not seen again. The manager wished the man to come. At least, he could have lightened his heart by expressing his sincere thanks to him, who saved their lives and the bank.

Both the bank staffs were shivering in fear. They were unable to even stand and talk to each other. Both were sitting in their chairs, with their heads resting in their hands, unable to even pick up the keys lying on the side of Mukesh. The bank was open. The three dacoits thrashed by the man were lying half dead outside the bank. It was hardly two, three minutes when the man chasing the dacoits had left that Anika, with Ninya and the village head, arrived there with a thermos flask and some fresh, hot snacks. Also arrived there were the regional officer, Gauri, and Naina.

Anika, reaching there, patted the two and asked, 'What's matter, why sitting like this? Oh, the keys lying here. Why? Have you decided to pass on these to me? Come on, you have dealt with them bravely. They are lying on the ground. Why terrified now, after facing the main crisis? Come on, stand up, see outside. Walk fearless in the open.' Gauri and Naina also encouraged them and offered them hot tea and fresh, hot snacks. They all took tea with them. Gauri asked the village head to remove the people lying outside. Sprinkling water on their faces, he made them lie in the shade to bring them to consciousness. They were tied to a tree, and the police was called. Till then, these were guarded.

Anika said to Mukesh, 'Well done, Mukesh, Well fought, saved the bank.'

Mukesh simply laughed.

'That's like a brave man. Now have tea,' said Anika. They all sat together, enjoyed the tea, and shared jokes.

Soon they both were normal. Anika again said, 'Dear, now we'll have to have a grand picnic. For safety of the bank, we'll put a special guard. Don't know when it may strike to your mind to pass on the keys of the money to this poor girl, would've lived like a princess.'

'Today only you had said you won't play miracles,' said Mukesh.

'That's right. Have I done anything?' said Anika. Mukesh, saying nothing, simply gazed at Anika and smiled. Anika said, 'Our prearranged picnic programme hopefully stands without any change. Sunday morning, we meet at the lake dam. Mukesh would arrange for breakfast, tea, lunch, and afternoon tea there only. Food etc.—Gauri and myself. Sing songs, fun, and hungama—Naina. And here we go. If anything, Mukesh, tell us. Hope you are totally out of fear. May we go? Ninya may come later.'

'Why later? It's only ten minutes' work,' said Mukesh. He took out a form, filled in name, address, amount of disbursement, and had a revenue stamp affixed. Ninya was asked to put on a thumb impression on the stamp and three other places. Witnesses were the headman of the village, then second, Anika. Anika?

'No, no, not me. I fear money matters. You'll catch this poor girl. Better you have strong party. Naina would also be your family matter. Gauri would be right. You may put second witness—Gauri,' said Anika.

The manager inscribed Gauri as second witness and handed over the loaned amount to Ninya. Thanking the manager, everyone left the place. Only the manager, Mukesh, and his assistant were left. They both looked at each other. 'Did you notice how cleverly Anika avoided being a witness? She worked so hard. Arranged everything but last movement, got away from the scene. She was right, saved us from getting our loan document forged. She is not a real human being. She has denied such a high post and promotion. She was senior to Gauri. That is why she preferred to work as a volunteer,' Mukesh remarked.

'You are right, sir,' said the assistant. The manager asked his assistant his feelings about the incident. The assistant said, 'Sir, the voice of the man resembled very much to that of Anika. And he said the same humorous things once spoken by Anika, like "Distribute the money to all", "I would live like princess". And though we were trembling like a leaf, he was normal and fearless of any untoward eventuality. We were enjoying the innocence of the man, taking him a simpleton. But by keeping the atmosphere humorous, he was enjoying our ignorance. And surely he knew what wrong was to happen, was passing the time till the ill-fated time. He was some ghostman, a supernatural power. We have consolation that at least we treated him well, offered biscuits, etc. Surely it was Anika. She is wonderful girl. Now feel like imagining, how was she sitting on the floor in front of me, asking for rupees two, three lakh? But our pity is neither we can say anything nor even we can thank her for saving our lives and the bank. Now go on seeing without opening mouth.

'On road construction site near Haati, a girl who saved several women from the wicked fellows, on her disclosure of identity, disappeared. Similarly Joshi and Kanshi Ram had to disappear. So better to keep ignorant about her.' He further, looking up to the infinite, closing eyes slowly, uttered, 'Oh, great soul, wherever you are. Kindly accept our sincere thanks. And keep on showering your mercies on us. Never deprive us of your blessings.' He hardly completed his words when he heard, 'May your wishes come true. May God turn extra merciful on our friends.'

Mukesh opened his eyes and saw Anika entering the room with her right hand in blessing pose, laughing and saying, 'It appears as if the incident is still hanging over you people. Still going around the gods and thanksgiving ceremonies. Turned some extra religious. What's matter?'

'You-u-u. How happened to come—' Mukesh said.

'I forgot my umbrella here. It's there.' Really her umbrella was there on a wall side table. She took it, saying, 'I would be tanned walking in sun. No handsome boy would select and accept me for marriage. Have to remain careful about my colour and complexion.' She further said, 'Okay, Manager saab, see you. Sorry for disturbance, carry on with your prayers.' And she went out before manager could say 'My worship is complete and fulfilled. My deity has accepted my thanks in persons'. She had gone.

The manager and the assistant looked at each other. Slowly the manager asked, 'Did she really left the umbrella here?'

'Don't know, sir, but now she picked up from here only,' said the assistant.

'Now let the things go as these are, we would turn mad, seeing the logics and reasoning in these. Let's forget it,' said the manager, turning to his work.

———•———

PICNIC AT THE LAKE DYKE

Sunday morning, Mukesh had arranged for everything assigned to him for assembling—seating, games, meals, songs, and boating, etc. All the members of the social group were assembled. The regional officer had gone out of his station. Gauri, Anika, Naina, Mukesh, and his assistant were there. First of all, they walked hand in hand, singing group songs, followed by breakfast and tea. Then they played some games of physical involvement, like running and catching, walking or running on one leg, jumping squares, etc. When they got tired, they changed over to cards. They had a sumptuous lunch there and relaxed in the shade, enjoying singing songs and jokes, titbits, etc. With every item, Naina and Mukesh appeared to be coming closer. In the hot afternoon, they decided to go on boats and enjoy sailing in the water. Since there were only two boats, besides some paddle boats, they decided to keep one male member on each boat. Mukesh would draw a chit for a partner. The rest two would go on another boat. Three chits were prepared and mixed up, and Mukesh was asked to pick up one. He picked up; it was Naina. They both boarded a boat and sailed out into deep water, singing some duet songs. The assistant went to the other boat; Gauri and Anika were still sitting. Gauri picked up the rest two chits, opened them, and saw these both were also with Naina's name. Gauri saw Anika and smiled, saying, 'Clever enough, born to do good to all.'

The two got on the boat, sailing in the opposite direction of the other boat. The boat of Mukesh and Naina sailed in the shadows of the thick forests on the margins, with an undergrowth of fast fragmented flower-laden bushes. There were water sheets covered with green thick round-shaped lotus leaves studded with fully bloomed red flowers. It was all nostalgic to sail in these waters. And over and above all these, they murmured the love duets. Even Cupid must have been feeling jealous of them for such a lovely love setting. So they couldn't escape his arrow. The other boat was also in no loss. They too enjoyed it thoroughly. The two ladies took special care that the man might not be thinking himself an odd figure, did not get bored, and did not feel that he was there only to sail the boat for the enjoyment of these two ladies. Anika sailed the boat for most of the time, singing songs. They kept the man involved throughout the time. The sun started going down. The boat of the two ladies reached back the picnic winding-up point. The other boat too returned. Everyone was happy, saying, 'had a good joyful day'.

Gauri said, 'Boating time was good but quite insufficient.'

Mukesh and Naina supported her claim. 'Surely it was very joyful but short. Could be longer.' They had evening tea and walked back to their places. In this short time, Naina and Mukesh had come very close to each other and had become very intimate. In the night also, she felt, wished it could have been a longer time. And when would be next opportunity to meet Mukesh? Next day, they were back at their duties, looking fresher, recharged with energies, and more enthusiastic.

The manager asked his assistant, 'How was the day yesterday?'

The assistant said, 'Sir, it was jolly good day. The two ladies were so senior to me. In the beginning, I felt where I have come. But Gauri didn't give me time to think, and whole time I was laughing. Anika herself sailed the boat and kept on singing. All the time we felt lost in the world of dreams. Sir, there's no comparison with her in any field.'

'Comparison can be made in similar type of things, among worldly people,' said Mukesh.

'Sir, on your boat, your partner was Naina. You must have enjoyed. You both were same type,' said the assistant.

'Yes, her name came in my picked lot. We enjoyed very much, as never before. Wish I get many more such occasions,' said Mukesh.

'Sir, you were sure to get Naina as partner.'

'Why, how can you say so?'

'Because on all chits, only *Naina* was written.'

'What? How did you come to know?' asked Mukesh.

'Yes! After you and Naina left, Gauri picked up all chits, opened, and saw. All chits were for Naina for your boat. Then Gauri saw to Anika, smiled, and said, "Clever enough. Born to do good to all",' said the assistant.

In the afternoon, after the bank hours, Naina came to Mukesh. Both sat together at tea. 'It was wonderful day. Now feel like living together. This single opportunity has brought we two so close. I consider myself fortunate now. God has brought us two together. Whole night, I kept on thinking, had my name chit not come in your hand in draw, what would have been of me? It would have been different. Thank God I got the choice of my life so sudden,' said Naina.

'No need to worry, only your name was to come in my draw. You may thank God. But thank Anika too,' said Mukesh.

'What? What do you mean?' asked Naina.

'Yes, I mean, only your name chit was to come to my lot. All chits were of your name for my boat draw. So without any risk, only your name was to come to me. And this all was done by Anika. Even Gauri was happy and surprised to see all those chits,' said Mukesh.

'My god, such a wonderful soul. She has shaped our lives. We are indebted to Anika for our lives. There is nothing impossible for her. Now that she has brought us together. And we have come so close to each other, Mukesh, now not possible for me to live without you.'

'The same is the case with me. Naina, I can't think of my life without you. Please keep on meeting at least once every day.'

Since then the two had been meeting so frequently. Almost every week they both had been going for boating together. She had been bringing lunch for Mukesh and sharing it together. One day Gauri, Anika, and the regional officer all got two invitation cards each, bearing 'Naina weds Mukesh' and the other one 'Mukesh weds Naina', and their marriage was solemnised with pomp and show in the native village of Naina. They expressed their special feeling of gratitude to Gauri and Anika, telling them that this was the result of their efforts and that Anika desired this.

MUKESH VISITS BANGDU
BRANCH OF BANK

With the increased work and activities of constructions of roads, bridges, banks, cottage industries, self-employed workers, construction of artificial lakes on seasonal rivers and water flows, tourist centres, and resorts in this area came increased banking. And with the increase in banking, economic activities, and improved economy, this thick forested area, infested with wildlife so far, also got infested with cheats and notorious dacoits, which were already places of refuse for interstate criminals and gangsters. The contractors carrying money for disbursement of wages or for payments for their purchases had been becoming their easy targets.

Mukesh had also been managing a fortnightly counter branch of his bank in Village Bangdu to help the school, post office, primary health centre, and other functional units of the place and people of the area for money deposits and payments. On one such scheduled duty he was due to go. He had hired a horse with a horseman who would be his help and escort also. And riding the horse, he went to the village for counter 'on the spot' banking and promotion of banking activities.

In the evening, after finishing the day's work and collecting deposits of the people, the two were coming back. The manager was on horseback, and the horseman-cum-escort was going ahead, holding the rein of the horse. After about two miles, a sadhu (saintly looking man) sitting under a tree, resting his back on the tree, somehow stood up and, coming in front, asked Mukesh, riding the horse, 'Child, look, my ankle is sprained. May see it's swollen. I can't walk. Please help me ride your horse for about two miles. Here, there is none to approach for help.'

Mukesh got down, giving his horse to him to ride. He rode up the horse with his strong tough trident upright. He passed his ruddle-coloured cloth bag and head cloth sheet to Mukesh, with the instruction to hang the bag over his shoulder and to put the sheet on his head. He didn't understand it. When he was sitting on the horse, why couldn't he carry these? But without questioning, he obeyed and turned looking like a disciple of the saint on the horse. They hardly had walked about 200 yards when on the side of the track, they saw some five, six tough, fearful men armed with weapons. Mukesh heard them talk. 'When would the manager come? He had collected heavy hard cash today. We had been waiting for hours.' Then the gang leader asked a man, 'Aye, are you sure he would come?'

'Yes, Leader, he was there in the village with a man, must come. Otherwise, where would he go?' said the man.

The saint on the horse rode quite fast. After about a mile, he got down, saying, 'I think I'm feeling quite okay now.' He took his bag and cloth sheet back and walked on his different way.

Mukesh was frightened on thinking what would have happened hadn't the saint been there. The horseman was also nervous, saying, 'Saab, generally these dacoits don't say anything to people like us. But today there was surely danger to life for carrying money. You were in extreme danger and me too. In future, when coming, bring strong police with you. The saint saved us, with his items given to you, he turned you into a member of his group, his disciple. The dacoits didn't doubt our identity of saints. They must be waiting for you there. After waiting for some more time, they might go to the village. Verifying from there, they would come behind us to catch us. If got caught, that would be still more dangerous. They would not only loot but would also shed their anger on us. Better would be to run as fast as we can. The only plus point with us is, the saint has brought us to safer distance, a safe lead. But this lead may turn unsafe if they come fast, because they know our speed and our lead distance. We should go fast enough to maintain the lead, and reach home. It's getting dark also. God knows what would happen.'

They were going as fast as they could and reached Dera. From there also Kuhar was about ten miles. The horseman said, 'The dacoits might not come chasing us by this way, because Dera is a well-protected village, as well as because the BSF is also close by. The dacoits, if they came chasing us, would have to take the much longer thick-forest trails.' Mukesh was also consoling the frightened escort, saying, 'Nothing would happen, the one who has saved us would help us now also. We didn't smell the danger, were going unaware. But he was seeing danger lurking up on us and saved us. So don't worry, go on doing what you can. There should not be any slackness in our efforts. Rest up to him.'

They were almost running and reached their village by fall of darkness. Seeing the village, they looked at each other with a sigh of relief. At his residence, seeing Naina, he embraced her with tears in his eyes, saying, 'Dear, I was finished today. A saint saved us of dangerous dacoits waiting for us.' Naina took him to the place of worship and thanked God.

GET BUSY IN THEIR PROGRESSIVE GROWTH

Agastya, Devika, and Priya had been in Lucknow for the past few days. Priya had been busy in her college and social work, whereas Agastya and Devika in their political matters of making political relations with different partiers and persons. Dina Nath Attri had also been meeting them off and on. This had become more significant for marking their existence in the forthcoming assembly elections. Encouraged by their win in the last bi-elections, Agastya, Devika, Dina Nath, and the other party workers had been making their all-out efforts to become one of the leading political parties in the state. In every district, from where they might send their party candidates for contesting elections. They put their prospective candidates in these centers with the instructions to make their presence felt there by their work and publicity. From other districts also, if the district organisation could satisfy the headquarters and some candidate wanted to contest the election on his or her own risks and expenses, headquarters would allow and would only be doing flying visits and election campaign tours. The rest would be managed by the party candidate.

Soon the party started attracting the attention of other prominent party leaders and politicians. Some of the parties had started making pre-election speculations, estimations, and assessments of their own and other parties. Having seen the result of the last bi-election and with the present image of parties, the ruling party had made the election ties and pacts with the parties to form their group and alliance. Because in the present political scenario, no single party appeared strong enough to fight and win majority to form the government. Making alliances had become the need of the time. Under this scenario, an election pact was signed in the party headquarters of the ruling party in Lucknow between the ruling Sarwajan Party and Ra. Ma. Dal, in which top leaders of both the parties were present, including Dina Nath Attri, Devika, Agastya, Priya, Balendu, and Nidhi. It was considered another big achievement of the party after the bi-election win. The yet another big achievement of the party came after the next three days in the form of a letter to Agastya, which said Agastya had been appointed as the rural development minister of the state. And the next day, oath was to be administered. On the day of the oath-taking ceremony, all the party leaders were present in the ceremony. Dina Nath Attri was again on the political peak in the country. He was thinking he was with the right party and the right type of workers.

Agastya and Devika made several visits to Gorakhpur University, the college of Rohan, and got Rohan regularised in his studies after explaining the tragic story of Rohan to the authorities there. Now Rohan was busy preparing for his final exams and his project report. He was perfectly all right. But sometimes he had been feeling how many years back he had gone in life. This was more of a psyche problem. But then he had been consoling himself; even much more he could have suffered. Now he was with family and friends, making up for the losses, which hopefully he would make up. Agastya, Devika, and Priya were determined to see that Rohan was well settled in life.

Agastya and Devika, in consultation with Dina Nath, planned an official state tour of Agastya. Within the next six months he would complete these visits. He would especially visit his district organisation from where his party candidates would contest election and, of course, other areas also. He had decided and instructed his department officers that action-taken reports on various problems and other work records were to be presented to him within the time schedule. He visited his area of Dera, Haati, Bangdu, Kuhar, and Khairi. The people of these areas took him as their own family member. They on their own also had been inviting him, even on their family occasions. Even though he was minister now, still the people had been treating him the same way. He went to Kuhar; Devika and Priya were with him. These two were the elder sisters of all youngsters and daughters for elders. Here, all these three went to see Mukesh and Naina and congratulated them on their marriage and spent time with them at tea at their place. Gauri and Anika had also joined them. Mukesh shared how an old man saved him, his staff, and bank, and also how a saint saved him from dacoits. He further requested him to provide security cover for the bank and staff. Especially when going out with cash.

Agastya, after hearing these incidents, thought deeply and thanked the divine souls, ghostmen, for their benevolence and said, 'You need not worry. Nothing will happen to you. I'll look into the problem.' He called his staff and dictated for making in Kuhar a police station and Haati, Dera, and Bangdu police posts. He also dictated a letter to the head office of the bank to post a full-time guard at the bank. All got so happy on this prompt remedy of the problem. They all got up to move. Naina bent low and touched their feet. They wished her a happy married life. Agastya said, 'We are friends, equals. Otherwise, we wouldn't have come. Next time we all will take lunch together at your place.'

They visited the sites of the new works and discussed progress and target dates of these. He also proposed on the spot a link road from Kishanpur to Haati via Dera, and to Bangdu, with the instructions to submit bimonthly progress reports of the work to him. Wherever he went, he spent time with them and asked about their problems and noted these. These were no longer dormant villages of people having no work. But now these were a changed village with good-looking houses and people busy in their one or other works.

Agastya and Devika tried to convince Priya and Rohan to enter active politics. But both expressed their regrets; however, they assured their full support to them and their full cooperation in party progress work. At this stage, Priya was engaged in many social works, besides her college responsibilities and project for PhD degree. Rohan had also planned on the same lines. He had prepared a good project and had been working hard to get good percentage and college career line. Though Priya was in the field of botany (life sciences) and Rohan was in sociology (social sciences), he had been preparing and working on the guidance of Priya. She had a good reputation in the college and had introduced him to the sociology department professors and other staff and also to the librarian. He was authorised to get books issued on the card of Priya. He had been living in Lucknow in close contact with Priya. Only for appearing in exams, he had planned to go to his college. Both Priya and Rohan were interested in academic and social works.

Agastya's becoming minister had become an added advantage for the party and of course for the alliance–ruling party too.

In all the political works, mostly Devika had been with Agastya, be it going to Allahabad or Lucknow or touring to some other place in the state, Delhi, or other parts of the country. Only on tours to Dera side, maybe Kuhar, Haati, etc., Priya had been with them. In this small friends' circle too, two sectors were formed, one pursuing academic interests—Priya and Rohan, both based at Lucknow—and the other one political, with Agastya and Devika, based mainly at Balrampur, Gonda, and Lucknow. But all were happy in their work, helping each other.

In this smooth sailing of their lives, Priya had been observing which way the wind of the ambitions of Agastya and Devika might be blowing. What changes might come in thinking, liking, and prioritizing in their lives. Though Agastya had been the student of sociology, a social science, and Priya that of pure science, botany, with no place for emotions and sentiments, by postponing some of her important decisions of life, like marriage, she had adopted the policy of 'wait and watch'. There was nothing in her mind and no change in her thinking and behaviour or expressions for anyone. She was as lively, active, and humorous as before. She met Agastya and Devika the same way. No one could ever notice any change in her. Even Agastya had been living the same old way in this friends' circle.

Rohan had been in the scene when Agastya was not there. When Agastya made entry, Rohan had passed in the background. Now that he had again reappeared on the scene, but reappeared as a result of the efforts of Agastya, Priya, and Joshi (now Joshi had gone behind the scene), Rohan might like a career equivalent to a political career of Devika, but he had preferred to go for a career in the closeness of Priya and away from Devika. But none of these had dislike for the other's work

The family members of all these friends were happy and satisfied with the achievements of their children. The parents of Priya were happy their daughter had been throughout first class and she had become assistant professor. She was popular in Gonda, the villages around Dera, and even in a big city like Lucknow. She had good connections. She was a dependable, helpful person for all, and a good social worker. Her marriage was fixed with a nice boy of her choice, who was a very popular, nice human being, a popular leader, even a minister now. What more can be expected of a daughter?

The parents of Devika were happy. Their daughter had been a serious case of depression, for over a year completely bedridden. One fine day, Priya and Agastya met her. Her good time had come, or was it a sudden charisma of God that she saw life in friends and suddenly, without any medicines, got all right? She had become a very successful, popular leader of the area and the state. She was vice president of her party. She was a well-sought-after social worker. Her boyfriend, Rohan, with whom she had once decided to marry, was also a good boy of scholarly taste.

The parents of Agastya were happy. Their son had become a popular, successful, and highly sought-after young man, social worker, and leader. In about a period of two years only, he had become minister of a big state like UP by winning an election through a party of his own.

The parents of Rohan were happy. They got their son back, whom they had accepted as gone forever. His joining back into the family was no less than a miracle. It was a sudden, happy surprise to all the family members when all of a sudden they saw Rohan standing in front of them. And besides this, with their son they got his very high-profile friends' circle and possibly his high-level-leader prospective bride, Devika. If nothing more, at least they got their son back, who had good academic achievements and prospects.

In every respect, these friends had a wide field of action in front of them in which they were so busy that they had no time to sit and think about their personal matters. They had only to go ahead and ahead, aiming at where the sky was the limit.

All these four friends had made their pairs. But as luck would have it, the pairs they made initially for their lives were not coinciding with the pairs that chance had made—the professional working together. But their commitments and hearts still stood firm for their pairs for lives. So much so that what Devika once decided still stood firm for that. She would marry only Rohan or she would not marry at all. Similarly, Priya at one time even had gone very close to Agastya but now did not look so keen. But they were close friends, with all decency in their friendship.

Even their parents had accepted these pairs of their sons and daughters, which had reached their final stage of marriages at one time. But what had happened later, that neither one was thinking about that issue, nor was anyone talking of what had made them all so silent on that issue. Even these boys and girls, though living together with all freedom, were not giving any place to such things in their thoughts and actions.

As first reaction, what could be said about their personal life? Only this—that at that time, all these four were comparatively less mature, fresh entrants in the youth age, with no aim or goal of life before them in the offing. As rightly said, empty mind's the devil's workshop. At that time, they were aimlessly busy in their studies. In such a stage of their lives, students and the unemployed take small favours on their requests, like agreeing to a girl for company at a coffee table or later for dating, and start taking these as their achievements, and these unchecked small favours go further and further, reaching sometimes to their complete destruction. Mostly non-achievers or those who think about what more they can get, not perceiving the completely destructive outcome under-instinctive, short-sighted, false heroics effect, plunge into irreversible acts to the point of no return—matters like sex and other unlawful acts. They indulge in sex matters and other undesirable activities. Nothing of such could happen with these four, because these went on gaining heights of achievements by their mindset for choice of right actions at the right time. Also, youth in good company, having their high goals set and action plans in hand, working with their strategies, think things like love affairs etc. too small and futile, not worthy to think about. They think such things destructive for their mission and aims.

WORRIED MOMS

Priya came to her home in Dera during her leave for about seven days. One day, her mother, sitting by her side, initiated talks, asking her, 'Where is Agastya these days?'

'Must be in Lucknow. He may go anywhere, a politician and a minister,' replied Priya.

'He is good boy, very respectful for all. Considers this area as his own.'

'He is political person. For good behaviour and good work, people vote him and his party. And this is his area. He won his seat from here. If he would not consider this area as his area, the area too would not accept him. His position depends on this area and its people.'

'Why giving so short, unsatisfactory answers about him? He is your close friend. Hope you are still on speaking terms with him.'

'Yes, he was my fast friend, he is still my friend and hope this friendship would continue. Should I dance for him?

He and Devika keep on roaming here and there. Whenever they meet, we talk. If I can do something for them, I do. But they are big men now. Minister. They can get their things done just by asking for. So many are there to work for them,' said Priya.

'What about your marriage? We think now it must be done. You have completed your education. You got good service of your choice in a good place. What more we should wait for?' her mom asked.

'You need not worry. Leave for God's wish. He must have fixed time, place, and person. Things get going in destined ways. Why are you worried about things not in your control? It's not going to make much difference, even if I don't get married. There are so many girls, very well placed in their lives, but they prefer to remain single. I would be happy if could be one of them,' said Priya, and she smiled, looking at her mom.

'Don't tell all this, dear daughter. You have worked so hard. Have made so good a career. You are so good looking. Why should you remain single? Your papa is there. He will arrange your good marriage. God has given us enough, why should our daughter remain unmarried? Tell me if you have changed your mind and now don't want to marry him. Let him be any big man, a minister. If you want to marry someone else, we will see and arrange for it accordingly. You just tell us. Explain your mind to us. Don't keep anything in mind,' said her mom.

'Oh, Mom, there's nothing as such. Why are you so much worried for nothing? I'm still very friendly to him. Anytime, I can get him here. He is still so considerate for us. You may ask him whenever he comes this side,' said Priya.

'Thank God. I got so much worried, thinking there might have developed some misunderstanding between you two. Because there was a time, about two years back, you were so interested in him that marriage could be done that time. And now so silent. What happened?' asked her mom.

'That was different time. We were simply students knowing nothing about future. There was also no pressure in mind of any responsibility. So got drifted away with the flow of time. Now Agastya keep on running every time— party meetings, MLA's meetings, ministerial meetings, calls from CM, public demands, fear of coming election, who would win, who would lose, how many seats may came to party, and all that. Where is the time for him to think of a thing like marriage? Where's place of marriage among all these things? Even people would start saying, if number of votes fall downward, "Minister has gone to get married". Even the newly married wife would weep, sitting in home, doing nothing. Going for shopping with the domestic helps. Thank God I'm not that type. I've created more works for me than the minister. I can't get bored. I'm not meant for all these only. Even then, I'm not saying no to my marriage. Let the time come,' said Priya.

The same was the scene at the house of Devika. Her mother asked, 'Devika, now that with God's grace Rohan has come and he's all right—he had done his final exams— why don't you find out his mind? We should initiate the matter seriously. Your papa would go and meet Rohan's parents. You tell us your mind. We are from girl's side. We must take an initiative.'

'What's there if you are from girl's side? Why should you feel small? Let Rohan take initiative. His parents may also ask for. If they aren't keen, why should you run about? Moreover, I can't spare time for all this for some more time. I've to see the life and future of so many people, my party workers, and party. The fast-approaching election is on our head. I can't spoil the whole show at such a crucial time by enjoying parties, marriages, honeymooning, etc. It's not important in life. There are many much more important things to do in my life than becoming a bridal decoration piece,' said Devika.

'Dear, there is an age for this at which it looks good. On becoming overage, there appear many problems. People will start talking about us as if we haven't done this essential thing for our daughter. Or we are more interested in saving money than in the life of our daughter.'

'Mom, why are you bothered about the talking of the people when I'm not keen? I don't want it, especially at this time. Let people see what I would do for them. I consider myself not only a child of my parents but of whole village, this area, the country. Let me be able to do something useful, some good for people. People have sacrificed their lives. Can't I sacrifice a small thing like marriage, which is so insignificant that many a people go without it and live happily?'

'Doubtfully, have you changed your mind for some other boy? If it's so, tell us. We'll see the other possibilities. Don't hesitate telling us your free mind. You are educated, have become a popular leader. You have a good recognition in the area and state. We won't doubt your choice. We would accept it and would work accordingly. After all it, is the question of your life. You would have to spend your whole life with the man. It should be of your choice. I'll tell your dad accordingly.'

'How has this thing come to your mind? Have I ever given you any such hint to think so? For God's sake, please never think so. Once I had made up my mind for Rohan, made up. That's my final. If I would ever marry, would marry him only or I wouldn't marry at all, even if I become a minister or even chief minister and he remains a jobless. This is our character. There are so many, so highly placed men having married to simpleton, very less educated village women, living only as housewives. Lately this trend of serving ladies has started. Why can't a lady have a lower-placed man? And when both husband and wife serve in different capacities, it may go up for some and bit slow for other. High and low rises in services are matter of chances. That way, every now and then husbands and wives must keep on changing with the ups and downs in their social status? And then even after marriage, a husband may suffer loss in business, loss of service, some ailment, some accident, should he be left then? The same has happened with Rohan, it could have happened after marriage also. At this time, he needs my support. Why would I leave him for this reason? He would be further demoralised and depressed. What sort of love it would be? And it's also not that I would be marrying him out of mercy or feeling pity on him to save him form depression and demoralisation. But it would be for my love and for my words, my mind for him. Either it would be he or none. But not now, at such a crucial time.'

'And if he is married to someone else by his parents? They may not be knowing such a determined girl is sitting only for him.'

'Doesn't matter for me. I'll shine more brightly in the sky heights. Because then I'll have no one else to serve except my dear mama, papa, brothers, sisters, and my countrymen. My achievements will surpass all others. But be sure I'm not going to fall ill or bedridden for any Rohan from now on.' She further said, 'After long time, I could come to spend time with my mama. To eat food cooked by you, rest in your lap in the courtyard of my home, to recharge my physical energy to resume work with full zeal. Whatever I've said today may be got written in big, big letters. And may be read to all who want to know my mind on this issue. So that I don't have to empty my mind again and again to tell others.'

'No need, Didi. No need to write. I had switched on the voice recorder purchased by Papa only last week, a good Japanese piece. I have recorded my dear Didi's voice. Otherwise, also voices of big leader like you are to be recorded,' said her younger brother.

'I'll see you, naughty boy. Good you told me. Now I have to remain cautious even in my own house.'

'Rightly said, Didi, at times opponents have prepared video cassettes of big leaders for use in elections against them. And these were shot very much in their personal rooms,' said the brother.

'Good you alerted me. Now go and play on this to Papa. Otherwise, he too may come to make his dear daughter a decorative bridal piece.'

Thus Devika could avoid this everyday talk of her home. Sometimes her daddy used to get angry at her mother, saying that she being a lady and mother might talk more closely and freely with her. He had shown his inability to talk to Devika on this issue. But the mother too couldn't convince her. And after Devika left for Gonda and further to Lucknow, the mother gave a detailed account of her talk with Devika and her philosophical thoughts on her marriage to her husband.

Thus, both the girls were avoiding their marriages for interest of the other one, to wait for who would take the lead. But who would catch the male members, Agastya and Rohan, who had been home very rarely, that were too in state of running? Parents now get no time to talk to them on such issues. One day, Agastya was caught by the media in a press conference. A media person floated a question to him. 'Sir, you have wonderfully come up on the political horizon of the state. Just in two years of your start of your political life, have become minster of a big state, what is your future plan for personal life?'

'After entering into political public life—WWE arena—no personal life is left. I'll be getting boxes or punches, thrashings from all-sides. What personal is left for me?' answered Agastya.

The clever media person, not getting the answer of his choice, again surrounded him and tried to catch him, asking, 'It is said that behind every successful man, there's a woman. May we know who is the lucky woman behind your success?'

'Yes, this is true in my case too. In my case there are three.'.

'Three?'

'Yes, three.'

'May the public know who these three women are?'

'First one is my mother, who brought me in this world and made me so capable that I'm in this position today. Second and third are two ghostgirls, I mean, girls. The second one became my close friend and took me and introduced to the third one, who was really fierce dormant volcano of energy at that time. This dormant volcano got active and, starting from her long bedridden condition, within five to six months, had become better positioned than me.'

'Should we take that, you two being so close and you being so impressed by her, she may come in your personal life?'

'She would always remain a part of my life—but as my friend, philosopher, and guide. I adore her, respect her as my real sister. We live so close. Wish, and I would do my best to see she enters her personal life.'

'We got who she is. Your vice president. Kindly give us the idea about the second one, in between respected Mummy and your VP.'

'She has changed my life. She has been the source of my energy. She had given me lesson of hard work with honesty and sincerity and public service, serving the needy. Which she herself is doing in much better way than me, a politico. And she's shining in the world of scholars. It depends on her now, which way she takes me further. We are very close friends but not talking on this issue. There was a time when we had made up mind of living together. Now I would respect whatever path she chooses for herself and for me. But we would ever remain same way, close friends with mutual respect for each other's feeling and freedom.'

'We got who she is. There has been so much pathos in your expression. We honour it. With this, getting her has not been difficult. We got her. Hope and wish her path comes your way. And you both walk together on the same path. Wish you and your party all success. Thank you very much, sir.'

As soon as the press conference was over, Priya rang up and congratulated him on his successful conference, saying, 'Hi, Agastya, and congrats. I'm happy. Have become successful politician, anyone may take any meaning of the answers. Played safe and buttered the ghostgirls very well. They must be very pleased and would be helping you. I'm also happy, you would continue to keep me as your friend.'

Devika also rang up and conveyed her satisfaction on the conduct of the conference. 'But you have spoken too high about me. You have come up to this level because of your abilities and hard work. You deserved it. In fact I am because of you.'

Time went on passing swiftly. Everyone remained busy in the routine, usual work. Agastya had made several visits of his constituency area. And due care was taken for each and every constituency in all districts of the state, with extra care for the areas from where the election was to be fought. But none of the four friends was thinking of personal life, about marriages etc. This had worried their parents more. They were thinking their children, especially girls, were fast crossing their marriageable age. During this time, Rohan had cleared his MA exams with good percentage. He had become a social worker and a journalist. He has also joined part-time journalism classes in Lucknow.

———————•—————

GRAND SUCCESS IN
STATE ELECTION

Elections had come very close. Every party started finalising the lists of their candidates with their constituency. The ruling party could hardly finalise the names of 120 clean-chit candidates of good public image. Finding no other way, they offered the remaining constituencies to other allied parties. The Ra. Ma. Dal now got 90 seats, against the 40 allotted earlier. This had made the work of Dina Nath, Devika, and Agastya very difficult in the last moment. They invited all their members, including Priya and Rohan, to the meeting. They had already selected 50 candidates. Here was the problem of selecting another 40. They asked all those willing to contest the election with their preferential constituency. This way seeing, their past record, 30 more were approved. Now 10 more were needed. Rohan and Priya were asked with lots of pursuance. But they both were not ready to join politics.

Flatly saying no, Priya expressed her inability to join politics. She said this was the life where she could pursue her interest and chase her dreams to come true. She would work for her dreams rather than joining a new field under compelling situations. 'Only in the area of interest can one achieve excellence. And that's where there can be the real contribution of an individual to his society and to the world. Only excellence makes the people special, giving them recognition.'

Rohan also said something similar as Priya, adding that he too would like to live and work for his interest. However, both assured their full support in the election and thereafter. Priya had gone even to the extent that should any candidate be registered from the party from Lucknow, she would make him or her a sure win for the party. Ultimately, somehow they could have 10 more candidates. Thus, finally they prepared the final list with their constituency against each one. A lady, Prabha De, was nominated from Lucknow. And the responsibility of Lucknow was given to Priya, as the Lucknow constituency was considered most tough, the most prestigious seat for all. Each and every candidate was instructed to take intensive measures and prepare specific strategies for each area, taking into account the specific advantages and disadvantages of each and every area. In every concerned district's nomination, papers were submitted with religious ceremonies, bands, and slogans. All the nominations were found correct, in order, and eligible. Now was the time for canvassing. All the time, during canvassing, their areas remained full of activities. The college students, staff, children, their parents, other people—everyone was feeling it was more than sufficient

In other constituencies of the Ra. Ma. Dal also, there was almost the same scene. There, everyone for whom she had worked was working as per instructions of Priya. With very little involvement of money, ample manpower was working.

Finally the election dates arrived. A good number of observers from the party, on their own, took their responsibilities on every polling booth. They kept their sharp eyes on every step of the election work. On vote-counting date, the scene was sort of panicky. There was perfect peace all around. On the forehead of most of the people was a stretch or big dot of vermilion or sandalwood paste. All were remembering their gods and goddesses. Suddenly people were seen running in a direction. Some shouted to get an ambulance, to hurry up. They came to know that a candidate got a heart attack. The ambulance arrived, and timely he was evacuated. This was the scene in Lucknow before the start of counting at 9.00 a.m..

It struck 09.00; counting started. Candidates and party reps started concentrating on the counting site, and the figures started coming up on the board. The figures and positions were changing very fast on the board. When their figures were up, they used to get relief, and on the rise of others' figures, tension used to grip their mind. Such things continued for the individual candidates till they reached the safe-zone margin or their result was finalised. But the party leaders were seeing the figures in totality. They were seeing the possibilities and equations with every rise and fall. First came the result of Lucknow candidate Prabha

De, winning with record margin. People reached there with bands, crackers, and sweets. Priya and her college students, staff, fellows, and others arrived to greet their winning candidate, Prabha De, and took her around in the form of a procession so that she could thank the public. She was not keen to go at this stage when her other colleagues were staggering through. Moreover, she was interested in more results, especially that of Devika, Agastya, Balendu, Nidhi, and several more. Though every seat was a matter of interest from alliance parties, she found herself helpless, and then Devika—and Agastya also—told her to avail of the opportunity. The iron was hot; all would feel delighted at their victory. And the atmosphere would build up. Her party and the ruling party leaders were happy to get the prestigious Lucknow seat. So both Prabha and Priya were taken in a grand procession by their friends and supporters through main roads. The public was greeting them. All were congratulating Priya and Prabha. Soon more results followed. As per latest positions of the election, one by one most of their candidates were coming through as victorious. By evening all, results were declared.

Out of the total 90 candidates of the party of Ra. Ma. Dal, 84 registered their glorious victories. Agastya, Devika, Balendu, and Nidhi made glorious victories. Dina Nath Attri was in a jubilant mood. Those who could not win were also happy and were celebrating the party victory and its prospects. But the ruling party was at a loss: out its 120 candidates, only 72 could win. The other two alliance parties got 44 and 36 seats. In total, this group of four parties got clear absolute majority of 236 seats out of 380.

All the group members were celebrating their victory. At the same time, everybody was astonished by the glorious rise and victory of Ra. Ma. Dal, a hardly four-year-old party of young leaders of boys and girls, with Dina Nath Attri as their political adviser-cum-president.

Dina Nath, Devika, Agastya, Prabha, and Keshav Nath Mishra, ex-chief minister, went to the governor with their claim for forming the government and the list of all their winning candidates—MLAs elect. The governor went through the papers; his adviser and technical officer also discussed the issue. By the time they could finish tea and discussions with the governor, the adviser and technical officer, having gone through the submitted papers, the relevant records, and their validity, established the claim as in order and acceptable. The governor accepted the claim, and an invitation to form the government was issued by the governor's office. All the team members thanked the governor, his adviser, and the technical officer, and left for the present Ruling Party Headquarters. There, the outgoing CM offered the chance to the party with the maximum number of MLAs, the Ra. Ma. Dal, to form the government and that the other three parties were with them. All the four parties held their separate meetings in their privacies, taking their own time. And then all parties had their collective common meeting under the chairmanship of Dina Nath Attri.

Keshav Nath Mishra requested the chairman to proceed further. The chairman said, 'I welcome you all to this first meeting of the group of newly elected assembly members who are going to form the government. First of all, we will select the new chief minister. He will be invited to occupy the chair and do the needful. We go ahead with the selection of the CM.'

Devika stood up and spoke, 'For the post of chief minister, I propose the name Mr Keshav Nath Mishra.' Everyone was surprised, except members of Ra. Ma. Dal. Even Keshav Nath didn't believe it. He thought how it could be. *They are in majority. Even then, giving the chance to me to be CM may be a slip.* His party and other party members also thought the same. Soon Agastya stood up and seconded it. Keshav Nath was not understanding how to thank them. After that, for some time, there prevailed silence, waiting for another proposal. Keshav Nath was thinking himself in doldrums. But the second name never came.

Dina Nath spoke, 'Any proposal for second name?' A pause of time . . . no second name. 'I declare Mr Keshav Nath Mishra to be the new chief minister. Three cheers for Mr Mishra! Hip-hip hurray! Hip-hip hurray! Hip-hip hurray! I welcome Keshav Nath Mishra as our new chief minister.'

Keshav Nath, leaving his seat from the gallery, walked to the central main seat. He expressed his gratitude to Dina Nath Attri for his nice leadership, to Devika for her nice gesture to propose his name, and to Agastya for seconding the name and wished him too the very best of luck. And then to all the other members of the party and to his own party members. He expressed his sincere thanks to all and occupied the chair offered to him by Dina Nath.

Dina Nath Attri stood up to address the house. 'Honourable chief minister, all other guests, media persons, and newly elected members of the assembly. Today I'm very happy to be with you and addressing the state assembly's government-forming members. You must have felt it strange why we selected chief minister from other party and not from our own party. Was there not a single capable member for this responsibility? Well, our members and their capabilities are before you, you have been seeing all yourself. But we kept the interest of the state and its people in the forefront. Mr Keshav Nath Mishra had been chief minister. He is an experienced person. He has vision for the state for the welfare of the people of the state. To achieve his set goals and targets, he must have diverted available resources, must have implemented his ideas and policies. Had we put another chief minster in his place simply because we had the power to do so, it would have affected all the incomplete works. The time, money, energy, and resources spend on these must have gone to waste. And in this process of the changes of government and the state head, the ultimate loser must have been the public.

'We have seen the interest of the public and the state and, of course, thereby of the country. It's this that we preferred to continue with earlier existing chief minister and expect a government of perfect transparency and honesty from him. The public and the country is above us all, their welfare must be above us all. The other thing we expect is the impartiality. Now, all MLAs of alliances and oppositions must be given their dues, treating them all at par. For running the government, we must all be together.

'Hope my ideas are clear to all in the same spirit, I actually meant these. The purpose of the media must also have been solved. With the best wishes to the chief minister and you all, I conclude. Thanks. Jai Hind.'

Then the chief minister elect addressed the meeting. 'Mr Dina Nath Attri, guests, media person, and MLAs elect, I'm thankful to Mr Dina Nath and his party members and other MLAs for electing me as their head. Particularly I would like to thank Mr Dina Nath and his party for having vested so much of faith in me. I assure you, sir, I'll do my best to keep up to your expectations. All that you have thought for the ongoing works and schemes in the benefit of the state and its people will continue undisrupted. The government will be run by us all jointly, and there will be no partiality for anyone. All will be treated at par with due respects and regards. So far I had been hearing of the greatness and foresightedness of Dina Nath-ji, but today with me you all have also seen his broad-mindedness. He has given to the state so much, an undisrupted, continuous government and welfare of all. But in bargain, he asked for nothing for his party and party worker. Whatever he demanded was equality, impartiality, and transparency for all party members, which would benefit me too.

'I'm sure, with the cooperation of you all and with the guidance of Pandit Dina Nath, we will be able to give an ideal, highly efficient government and a leading not only uttam pradesh but sarvottam pradesh [best province]—Uttar Pradesh (UP State). Thanks. Jai Hind.' He further desired and said, 'This meeting is over here. Now five members from each party, including president, vice president, and three more from each party, with the list of their MLAs elect, may please come with me to my chamber, others are free to move.'

In another fifteen minutes' time, another meeting started in the chamber of the CM elect, and he said, 'Friends, we are here to form the setup of the government, i.e., ministers. We will finalise the list of ministers and also their departments. You please go through the list of your MLAs and give me list of fifteen to twenty names. Initially we may start functioning with thirty-five to thirty-six ministers. Proportionately we will take this number from each party. Later if need be, we will take from these lists. Hope you agree. If there's any suggestions, please put up. Here is the list of departments.' He passed one list each to the four party presidents. 'This we will consider under second agenda item.'

Thus, there came a list of thirty-four ministers in the first phase, according to party strengths 10, 9, 8, and 7. Agastya, Devika, Balendu, Prabha De and six more MLAs of the party were in the list of ministers.

Under the second agenda point, various departments were allotted to these ministers.

Agastya was in charge of Rural Development and Road Transport.

Prabha De was in Tribal and Minority Sections' Development and Small-Scale Industries.

Balendu was appointed to Electric Power Development and Distribution and Non-Conventional Energy.

The CM prepared the list of ministers and their departments; eight departments were still with the CM. This was done with the mutual consent of all party leaders. At the close of the meeting, he thanked the meeting members and wished to see them soon. He told them that now he was going to the governor to discuss their list and fix the date of the oath-taking ceremony, which would be tomorrow or the day after tomorrow. Thus the meetings ended. They called it a day, and the CM left to call upon the governor. There, the list of ministers was handed over to the governor. And the third day was fixed for the ceremony. The programme with day, date, time, venue, and all was communicated to all MLAs, secretaries, senior officers concerned, and guests. Ministers Agastya, Prabha, Balendu, and Devika especially invited their parents, Priya, and her parents, and the college principal, the DIG, his missus, and the DSP, Alok, with his missus were also invited. The ceremony was held in a graceful way.

It became a great day for them, their parents, and their friends. After taking their oath, all MLAs reported to the assembly secretariat and obtained the essential literature, instructions, and annual schedule. Everyone, especially the newly elected members, first termers, started preparing for the first assembly meeting. But now after having gone through such a pressure of election, followed by busy meetings schedule, many of them had gone on some days' leave.

VICTORY CELEBRATION
IN DERA

Agastya and the others knew the role of divine souls (ghostmen) in their success and in making them reach these positions. They all decided to offer their prayers and thanks to them by visiting their place. They all, including Balendu and Nidhi, went to Dera. The parents of Priya, Devika, Agastya, and Rohan also joined them. It was appearing as if all these MLAs—three of them ministers and others, Nidhi, Priya, and Rohan, being in high position, also as good as ministers—were from one family. Even every parent was taking them as being all alike. And each one of these was also treating every member of every family with no difference. At lunch, all were together at Dera. On the dining table, the father of Priya was inviting the attention of Surya Dev, father of Devika, and looking at the parents of Agastya and Rohan, said, 'How lucky I consider myself, all these'—he touched wood—'so highly positioned, ministers and others. All so successful are our sons and daughters. May God bless them all.'

'Uncle, in fact we are lucky, we all are you children,' said Devika.

Pointing to Rohan, Jagannath again spoke, 'My son, Rohan, why don't you talk so freely? You look some reserve and quiet.'

Devika looked at Rohan, his parents, and at Jagannath and felt how close knit they all were. So concerned about each other. The parents of Rohan also felt the same. 'It's for this closeness and affection of all these for our son that we got him back and he could rise so high, which was otherwise impossible for us. Our daughter's marriage also could go so well because of these.'

Then Rohan said, 'Uncle, I lost my two years in these forests. I'm thinking of them.'

'Why don't you take this the other way? That it's for being lost in these forest that you are so much recognised today,' said Agastya.

'It's by chance for you all that I and the other three could get life again. Otherwise, I could have gone into oblivion for life, like many others.'

'Why troubling your head and spoiling your life for fear of a thing which hasn't happened? Enjoy whatever's with you,' advised Jagannath.

Rohan had no answer and in a way nodded.

'If still you think so, I think you are searching for a thing which is no longer there. It has come back to you in several times, multiples of it. It is for you that this big international gang is busted. The Rapti Bridge, these roads, this progress, this banyan tree, Joshi hollow. Where are the roots of all this? It's all because of you. Even then, if you think you have lost your two years here and you are searching for those, then search for the equal number of years of Devika too, who remained completely bedridden for you. You went missing for your reasons. It could be with anyone. There were three more with you. But Devika, why she suffered? She suffered for you. And it was our good luck that she could recover. Otherwise, she was gone forever. At least you could come. Dear son, all's well that ends well. Forget that, and make your perfect pair with Devika. It's up to you both who take the first step. Now give us your good laugh. Have a fresh good start,' said Jagannath.

'Uncle, you have taken a very sharp turn. From bringing Rohan out of his state of remaining lost reached to me. You were praising me and my love or preparing for my send-off. Rohan, you can't surpass my philosopher uncle,' said Devika.

'You are correct, he is highly thoughtful, and we are very small for him,' said Rohan, addressing Devika. And addressing Jagannath, he said, 'Can I laugh alone? I would look joker.'

'What would be strange, one would look as one is,' said Devika as a passing remark. There occurred a sudden burst of laughter, including Rohan. Quietly Priya stood up to leave the place, but Devika noticed and asked her, 'Why? Leaving us here, you started going?'

'Dad has come in his philosophical mood, better I go to kitchen. I may be his next target.'

'Oh, Super Queen, now you are going, after making me target. Come on, sit in your chair. Have your lunch with us. We won't say anything, take as much as you want. Must have thought of going and taking lion's share there. Would turn fat,' said Devika.

'Keeps eyes on my eating also. What sort of Di Di you are. You should ensure I had taken full, like all elders do for youngsters.'

'I don't want my beautiful sister turning into fatty gunny bag. But no restriction for today.'

DEVIKA AND PRIYA
GET MARRIED

In the meantime Devika's younger brother joined the family gathering with a tape recorder and was saying, 'All, attention please. Please listen the real philosopher, my Di Di. Some time back, she desired her nice thoughts be made audible to family members. And no more bothering her on her marriage issue. Here I think, this would ease the work of everyone.'

Devika went to stop him from doing so, but he went on trying. Devika ran after him, but then Priya ran faster and caught hold of Devika. Helpless, she could only express her anger. 'Won't spare you, silly boy. You are gone today. And you too, my well-wisher, my sister.' But the player was started. It went on and on starting from, 'What's there if you are from girl's side?' The more it was going on, reproducing Devika's recorded voice, the more serious and motionless the listeners were becoming. By the time the record player came to a stop there, everyone was a dumbfounded, motionless onlooker on Devika, who too was sitting motionless, lowering her face into her hands in the arms of Priya. For some time, there was pin-drop silence, then a sudden burst of clapping with the words 'Wow, Devika! Wonderful!' Priya tightened her grip on her.

Then, after calm for some time, all looks turned on Rohan, who said, 'Oh my god. Devika, you're really great. You eased my problem. But no way.' He was looking to Devika. 'I didn't know your mind over our closeness before. Hearing this, I consider my self blessed . I propose from my heart to you for marriage.'

Devika couldn't say anything. She was giving a smile and looked at Rohan and then onto her mom.

'My worry's over. Long live Rohan, my son . You did wonderful.' She looked to her husband. 'Listen, Devika's daddy. Now happy? I have done my duty. Now it's your job. I say, we all are here, solemnise simple marriage right here under the banyan tree within this week. And give big party or whatever you want there anytime,' said the mom of Devika. All started congratulating Surya Dev, his wife, and mummy and papa of Rohan and the two young hearts.

'Di Di, any more recording? But recording proved very useful,' said the brother of Devika. Not able to say anything, Devika could only look up and give an arc line of a smile.

Priya's mother also started whispering to Jagannath, 'See how good things happen all of a sudden? I say you too perform your responsibility with this only.'

Overhearing her, Priya, leaving Devika, said, 'You too started, Mama. Turned extra fast.'

'What's wrong in it? Have to do someday. Would be better together,' said the mother of Priya.

'Quite a good idea though. Let me discuss with Bro Surya Dev. And do away with lunch first,' said Jagannath.

'No lunch. First must be sweets for finalising two, two marriages,' the mother of Priya said.

'Mama, distribute sweets and all but for Devika,' Priya said.

'Now it's up to us. We'll do it our way,' said the mom of Priya.

Devika just gave a brief smile to Priya and whispered, 'Look. Surely you too are gone now.' And only after two days, in an auspicious time suggested by a priest, the parents of Priya and Devika solemnised the marriages of their daughters with their earmarked grooms under the banyan tree in a very simple way. Keeping it completely a family function, they kept it only up to families, close relations, and friends. From outside, only Monika and her husband, the principal of Priya, the principal, and Professor Soram from Balrampur College, the DIG, the DSP, Camp Commandant, the BSF, and Rupesh could join. Later combined big receptions were arranged in Balrampur, Gonda, and Lucknow. And now Agastya and Priya, and Rohan and Devika were happy couples.

The first five years' period of the party ruling went very well, with good achievements and public satisfaction. In the next state general election, Ra. Ma. Dal did still better, and even Keshav Nath, the former CM, proposed the name of Agastya for state CM. But he preferred to remain deputy. Things had been going on very well—Agastya and Devika in politics and Priya as assistant professor and social worker. Rohan had been a successful columnist and press reporter. And Rupesh, the favourite boy of Agastya made financially independent by a ghostman, chasing his dream and clearing the State Service Selection Board, joined as SDM in Pilibhit. He had very often been meeting Agastya and Priya. After joining his post of SDM, he specially came to Agastya and the other three and expressed his desire to visit the banyan tree. Priya told him to definitely go with his parents and that there he would stay at her house or she'll be angry.

TIME CHANGES VERY FAST

Rupesh, with his parents, went to the Dera banyan tree by taxi and offered his prayers. And after relaxing under the tree, he opened their packed lunch, which they had brought in surplus. Before taking his lunch, Rupesh looked around if there could be some needy. He saw an old man sitting at a distance. With due regard, he asked if he could join them for some eatable. The old man looked up towards him and, giving a pleasing look, said, 'Good offers should never be denied. Would be happy to get some.' Rupesh, serving him sumptuous service on a leafy plate, took his lunch with his parents. Finishing his food, the old man expressed satisfaction to them and asked Rupesh several things about him and his family and left the place. They were still taking their meal leisurely when they heard someone saying, 'Had been happy to meet and eat with you. I'm happy that you realised your dreams. I have kept up my promise. Remember? Told you, "I may see you some time on your realising your dream".'

Rupesh stopping eating. 'Baba, did you hear some voice?'

'Yes, something, something like realising dream . . .'

'Yes, Baba, very much. The one ate with us wasn't some man. He was the ghostman. The one who helped us, giving his wealth.' Bowing to the food and begging his excuse, they stood up and looked around and wished if they could see him. But they could see none. They heard a feeble voice.

'No use. Purpose's served. My blessings. Enjoy life.'

When they couldn't do anything more, Rupesh and his parents, coming to their places, restarted their meal.

After the meal, as desired by Priya, they went to her house and met her parents and other family members and left for Balrampur. After this, he purposely went to Agastya and Priya to narrate this awesome incident and expressed his sadness of not seeing him to satisfaction and could not expressing thanks to him. But Agastya could only say, 'Life is a chain of such pleasing, unpleasing events. No use repeating these in memories and feeling sorry. Otherwise, nothing would be left in life but sadness. On happy things, we would be sad because these are no longer with us. And on unhappy, because these are there to make us sad. Time of happiness appears passing away very fast. After passing away of happy time, we get double pain. One of missing happy moments and the other one of facing hard time. Happy time ends in difficult time. Opposite to this, the time of sadness appears as if stopped, not passing away. But after it passes away, it too looks sweet. It gives us a feel of success, we have faced and overcome problems. And then we get into happiness after that. Happy time, keep in mind, is short lived. Use it as time for preparation for facing tough time. And take tough time as a testing time, a time of learning, getting confidence, and going higher and higher. Go on, look forward, thanking him, the nature.'

Meeting them, Rupesh returned to his place.

Both the happy couples had been sailing on smooth seas with favourable trades. But the trades end up in stormy westerlies. Not necessary that only happy time would prevail for all times. In the fourth year of the next assembly period, Rohan, the journalist, got some clues of some misappropriation of public funds in one of the state departments. He silently went into investigating its details, and with undoubted proofs, successfully established it—a big scam. A departmental enquiry was set up. In the findings, one officer and three subordinates were found guilty. And the case had gone to the State High Court. The deparment was under Minister Devika. Taking the responsibility on herself, on moral ground she resigned and quit even politics. She was much persuaded by Agastya, the CM, Keshav Nath, and several others that there was no necessity of taking that extreme step and that such things are part of political life. But she felt very much demoralised for the wrongdoings of others. And praising the decision of Priya in keeping away from politics, she finally decided to work only as social worker and help the party in its work.

Now she was closer to Priya in social activities. She somehow got the impression that due to some overdoing of Rohan to gain popularity, the situation had come up in such a big form due to the media that she had to resign. And one day in their personal time in the family, in the presence of all these, with all seriousness, she had spoken to Rohan, even to the extent that she said, 'Would have been better had you remained in forests.'

But Rohan, understanding every bit of it, to save the family atmosphere from being tense, passed a light remark. 'One was that Devika who risked her life to find her love, a true loving Devika. And now's this Devika, ready to send him back to dark world, a professional, a politician Devika. What a change in the same person over time by profession.'

But soon she realised and felt sorry, saying, 'I didn't mean that. I'm sorry.' And the family situation was saved.

Now for Agastya with Priya, Devika with Rohan, and all friends together, life though more or less uneventful was going smoothly. All were having recognition in their respective fields. Tired and exhausted from working for months in the crowded, noisy, and polluted city life, to refresh and recharge their body cells with fresh oxygen and fresh air, they, the two families were spending time in wet monsoon in Dera. Sitting together in their balcony, enjoying hot tea and pakoras, they were seeing green-bathed forests with the sound of falling rain showers in perfect closed calm. Agastya, looking at them and out in the open, could only murmur this:

Oh, rejuvenator of life, monsoons, you came
but when every thing has met its end in the
forest here. In the last blazing summer, in

the devastating wildfire the old banyan tree
with Joshi hollow has also met its end.

End is painful, but not always, there's life and
progress beyond it.

All things meet their end, and that marks a new
beginning.

Maybe sky's the limit, but contented, I would
keep on going ahead, not bothering what may
comes my way.

And he got lost in the thought of ghostmen, his heart
transmitting thus:

Thanks a lot, o ghostmen, keep on visiting
us for ever.

Missing you, in parting pain, hope you
would say 'no', never.

धन्यवाद हे   देवदूतों,   इस   बगिया   में   आते   रहना ।
गला रुँधा है आँखें छलकी, विदा कभी तुम ना कहना ।।*

---

*   Dhanyawaad hey Devdooton, is bugiya mein aate rahnaa;

Galaa rundhaa hai aankhen chhalki, 'VIDA' kabhi tum naa kahnaa.

466

The End, no!

Beginning of Some New Story . . .

ABOUT THE AUTHOR

Destiny perhaps governed the life of the author, Dr P. C. Sharma, on the principle of 'Rolling stones gather no moss, but shine'. This could be the reason that a boy from a remote village, unable to go for formal education up to ten years of age, finally made a career in the field of academia, earning a master's in geography from Gorakhpur University, master's in education from Shimla, and PhD from Meerut University.

Having lost his father only as an infant, he charted his own course in life. His career as a teacher and an administrator spans over three decades, in various parts of India. Having started as a teacher in various reputed schools, he has also rendered service in the Rashtriya Indian Military College (RIMC), Dehradun, and Rashtriya Military School (RMS), Chail (Himachal Pradesh). After serving as principal of two Kendriya Vidyalayas at Sambalpur and Pachmarhi for nearly twelve years, he retired from the post of education officer at KVS Headquarters, New Delhi. In his post-retirement phase, he had been administrative officer at Bharat Scouts and Guides National Headquarters and country coordinator of HAPI (Healthy Adolescent Project in India), a sex education project of the Family Health International (USA), implemented by the World Association of Girl Guides and Girl Scouts (London), through B S&G NHQ (New Delhi) in ten districts, mainly suburbs and tribes of West Bengal, including Darjeeling.

With this rich experience and passion for geography, literature, philosophy, metaphysics—natural and super-naturals—the author took to writing with the intentions to share interesting experiences gathered from the people, with the people of global society.

He is settled in Greater Noida with his family.

Printed in the United States
By Bookmasters